gren

Translated from the Swedish by Judith Kiros

Arctis

W1-Media Inc.
Arctis Books USA
Stamford, CT, USA

Visit our website at www.arctis-books.com

1 3 5 7 9 8 6 4 2

Library of Congress Control Number: 2022907545

ISBN 978-1-64690-030-5
eBook ISBN 978-1-64690-611-6

Printed in China

A NOTE ON THE SWEDISH SCHOOL SYSTEM

In Sweden, grades 1–9 comprise primary school, and secondary school (high school) lasts for three years, the equivalent of grades 10–12 in the United States.

Förskola (ages 1-1/2–5): Kindergarten

Lågstadiet (ages 6–9): Elementary school

Mellanstadiet (ages 10–12): Middle school

Högstadiet (ages 13–15): Junior high

Gymnasiet (ages 16–18; most people graduate the year they turn 19): High school

Man was made for Joy & Woe,
And when this we rightly know,
Thro' the World we safely go.

Joy & Woe are woven fine,
A Clothing for the Soul divine;
Under every grief & pine
Runs a joy with silken twine.
—William Blake

Forever wandering
These dark halls of despair
I am the madness that devours
—Dark Cruelty

INTRO

At first, I couldn't write at all.

The blank white page blinded me. The cursor blinked. I wrote one paragraph and was disgusted. The text felt false and fake, every word dripping with fear.

There was so much to be afraid of.

And then the entire world turned upside down.

I was supposed to have worked at Gröna Lund again, but ended up in limbo. The day for the planned premiere came and went. I couldn't pay my rent with only student loans; it had been a while since I stopped talking to my roommates, but I still resented moving back in with my parents, into my old room. Like crawling back into a shell that had become too small.

I took down all my posters, my pictures.

You could tell exactly where they'd once been on those sun-bleached walls. Mom carried rolls of wallpaper up from the basement. She'd obviously planned for the moment when I'd finally clear away my teenage angst. Instead: flowers and birds in bright colors.

Every day was the same.

Dad taught his students from home. Mom came home

exhausted, her face marked by her face shield. I sat on the floor of my room, trying to do research for my dissertation. We were three caged animals, our house a zoo. At the dinner table, we spoke about the same things as the rest of the Swedish population did. Later in the evening: each of us in our own silence.

I applied for jobs I didn't receive. Got stuck in front of makeup tutorials and film reviews. Returned to games I hadn't played in years. Reread books from my childhood. The world was on fire; I retreated. Back into my shell. Too small, but safe.

Except at night.

The hairline cracks in the ceiling remained the same; I stared at them and they stared back at me. I kept waking up covered in sweat. Instead of going back to sleep, I'd put my headphones on. Listened to a podcast or some harmless YouTuber. One video followed another, according to the mysterious workings of the algorithms.

And then: a haunting.

Even though I'd cleared my history, started anew, it was there. The video I'd seen so many times in this particular room, during my waking nights.

I was half-asleep when the familiar sound reached me. Tinny, uneven, damaged. I opened my eyes, turned the screen toward me.

A shitty VHS recording from the end of the eighties.

Dark Cruelty's final performance.

The empty scene at the youth center. The tiny,

expectant audience. And then the band enters: the final lineup.

Tony "Berserker" Lehtonen shuffles toward the drums. He raises his arms and twirls the sticks; his long fall of hair gleams like gold. You can't make out the band name stamped on his shirt, but I know it's Master. I've seen it in the pictures in Håkan's photo album. The same Håkan "Maimer" Nordin who's shouldering his bass guitar and tuning it. He's in blue jeans, even though they agreed to wear all black, and I know Malte, who glances in his direction, is annoyed. Malte Lundell, who called himself "Iago" at the time. His own T-shirt, sleeves cut off at the shoulders, is plain; his arms look childishly soft against that harsh aesthetic, the spiked bracelets and bullet belt. An inverted pentagram in a chain on his breast. The necklace swings when he bends over the guitar, looks up again, tosses his blond hair. Looks sideways. Here he comes: the one who's going to be dead in just a few weeks.

Grim.

The poor quality of the recording makes it look as though his face is melting. Greasy black hair hangs heavy in front of his pale face and eyes marked with black paint as he tunes the guitar. His mouth gapes open when he grips the microphone. Then his voice through the cracked audio, the goose bumps on my arms when he hisses:

Through death . . . I rise . . .

The opening riff of "Nocturnal Allegiance."

PAUSE.

Grim's face, upturned as if in ecstasy. The left arm raised, the fingers crooked like claws. A pose that's since become standard, "squeezing the invisible orange," and so on. But this predates the clichés.

Why did this particular video find me?

It felt like a sign.

The next evening, I asked to borrow my parents' car.

The streets were empty. I was tense, driving unevenly into the city's heart, then out toward Djurgården. I left the car in the run-down parking lot, looked toward Gröna Lund. A crane raised itself out of the Main Area. The towers, the arcs of roller coasters, stood out against a pastel sky. The neon stripes on The Free Fall glowed. The sun on top of Icarus revolved.

Grönan, as people in Stockholm call it.

At that time of day, the sounds from the rides, the music, and the shouts should have been traveling across Djurgården, annoying the neighbors. Instead, the air was thick with silence, and I ached as I walked toward the theme park.

Everything had gone wrong.

What more could I have done?

What could I do now?

Blackbirds sang from the eaves. Benches were stacked on top of each other in the alley called Lilla Allmänna Gränd. Workers should have been moving here, ambling between the Main and Minor areas. Gossip in the smokers' tent, what happened at Skeppsbar last week, who did what with whom.

My steps echoed beneath the covered bridge. Dandelions grew in the gutter. A tour bus should have been parked here. Bass notes from the stage, the roar of the audience. I caught a glimpse of my pallid face in the tall mirror at the stage entrance. Threw another look at the windows of that box in the upper floor of The House of Demons. A memory of myself and Kasper at the whiteboard that first summer: Who's doing makeup? Who's doing masks?

Longing and concern erupted in my chest.

I sat down at the wooden dock, letting my boots dangle over the muddy water. The sky was bright and endless, the boats tugging against their constraints. On the other side of Saltsjön, Södermalm luxuriated in the evening sun, with windows like rows of gold teeth. At my right, the Octopus rested on its barge with its arms lowered; at my left, the gulls cried over the island of Beckholmen's heights.

We stood there on his nineteenth birthday, Kasper and I, one of the dry docks beneath us, the theme park where we worked before us. Maybe if I'd acted in some other way that night, things would have turned out differently. Or: it wouldn't have changed anything.

Perhaps I'm blaming myself for no reason at all. And yet I can't stop myself from doing just that.

The city was so quiet.

Like the silence in The House when the looped sound effects and music got turned off. The silence after Grim's final whisper in the hidden outro.

I suddenly knew how to begin.

Kasper had always adored Gröna Lund.

For his sake, I have to write about what happened.

But I have to turn it into a story, write it as if to a stranger.

I've tried to find out as much as possible. Sometimes, though, it's hard to know who's telling the truth, whose memory is correct. And I obviously don't know how they thought and felt at every moment. But I can try to imagine it. I can try to understand.

I will be leaving out some details.

The truth I seek is of a different kind.

To reach it, I will need both light and shadow.

Appendix 1. Excerpts from an ad for Dark Cruelty's EP *Ancient Bloodlust*.

Dark Cruelty
Ancient Bloodlust

Label: Necrodamned Records
Format: Vinyl, 12*, EP, Limited Edition, Numbered
Country: Sweden
Released: June 198■

Tracklist

A1 A Foul Mist Obscures the Sun (Intro)
A2 Ancient Bloodlust
A3 Nocturnal Allegiance
B1 Unholy Shadows Reign
B2 Curse of the Lost
B3 Untitled (Hidden Outro)

Credits

Bass: Maimer
Drums: Berserker
Guitar: Morbid Eradicator
Guitar: Iago
Vocals: Grim

Notes

Self-released on the band's own label in an edition of 666 copies.
Hand-numbered by Grim or Maimer. No 452.
With insert. Stamped dust sleeve.

Condition

Media: Near Mint (NM or M-)
Sleeve: Very Good Plus (VG+)

Comment

Signed by the legendary Grim!

KASPER

Kasper had always adored Gröna Lund.

There was something eternal about the theme park. It didn't matter that the rides changed throughout the years. After one season, the old ones were forgotten and the new ones felt as though they'd always been there—no one really missed Disco Jet or Extreme. The thing that made Grönan wasn't in the capsules whirling through the air, the smell of fried food and popcorn, the tinny tunes of the carousels, or the hit songs performed on the main stage.

It was in the laughter. It was in the screams.

The rules that governed the everyday ceased at Gröna Lund. People flocked to this place to experience something beyond the drudge of ordinary life, beyond the routine. At Grönan, you could taste danger without actually being in danger. Hurl toward the asphalt for a few seconds, before the powerful brakes intervened. That knife's edge of horrified amusement: maybe this time the chains will break. Maybe this time we'll slam into the ground. Screams turning into laughter and into screams again.

Kasper understood that Gröna Lund, like any theme park, dealt in illusions. People lined up for an hour for a ride that took seventy-five seconds and told themselves it was worth it. Cotton candy left buyers with cavities and sticky fingers. And still they came back. The brightly colored scenery beckoned, still full of promises. Maybe this time the laws of gravity would be undone: the cotton candy would be as soft as it looked, the trick would turn out to be actual magic. Reality was nothing like fantasy, but we could pretend it would be.

The scenery was so obviously scenery. Still, Kasper thought it shimmered.

And nothing shimmered as beautifully as The House.

THE HOUSE

Welcome to The House of Demons! Ever been here before? No, you'll have to pay for a separate ticket, the wristband isn't valid here. Let's start off with a few rules. You cannot touch the performers and they cannot touch you. Flashlights, filming, and photographs are forbidden. Whatever happens, keep moving. Please enter through the turnstile!

You're standing in front of The House now, the building practically plucked from the set of the Addams Family or Scooby-Doo, designed by the American company Scream Corporation. The doors are tall, and a stone demon—not actually made of stone—grins down at you. The mist in the garden hisses out of a hidden hose. The ride called the Broom whizzes through the air behind you, while the seagulls—famished for hot dogs—screech, and the sun beats down. You are as far away from a desolate moor or a ghostly forest as possible. Still, you can't help but feel a vague sting of concern when the doors creak open. How frightening could it be?

You're waiting in a pitch-black space between two double doors. A man's recorded voice tells you a story about Doctor Dreamcraft, a scientist and occultist who opened a portal into another world, a world peopled by demons that manifested as your deepest fears. Since then, the voice claims, no one has seen Doctor Dreamcraft, and no one has dared enter The House.

The doors before you open. The first thing you see is a black wall decorated with made-up symbols. They're meant to be reminiscent of symbols from satanic rituals, like upside-down crosses and pentagrams, but without offending possibly religious visitors.

When you walk toward the stairs leading down into the basement, you can hear thunder, organ music, and distant shrieks. You're not sure which ones are recorded and which ones come from other guests.

In the basement, bars in a grid pattern extend along both sides of the corridor. Behind them, bones litter the floor. Coffins are haphazardly arranged along the walls. Some of them are open; inside them are bodies wrapped in filthy shrouds. Whimpers and loud knocks can be heard from the closed ones. Buried alive. A fear originating from the nineteenth century, when it was difficult to distinguish the intoxicating sleep of morphine from the eternal one. You're about to leave the Tombs when one of the corpses rips off its shroud and throws itself against the bars with a crash that makes you jerk. A very much alive twenty-year-old with patchily applied white paint glares at you, hissing: "You'll never get out of here alive."

You act like that idiot in a horror movie.

You keep walking into The House.

The next room has a high ceiling. The organ music rumbles through it. A broad staircase leads to the next floor. Every eleven seconds, thunder explodes and light flashes through the colorful mosaic windows on the floor above. Surrounding you is Doctor Dreamcraft's laboratory, kept behind a tall iron fence. Huge test tubes filled with glowing liquids, a stack of grimoires, more symbols painted on the floor. A cauldron with an arm in it tilts above the plastic flames in the fireplace. It remains unclear whether the good doctor is a scientist, a magician, or a cannibal.

Perhaps he's a so-called triple threat.

You step onto the staircase, and a cloaked figure detaches from the shadows by the fireplace, dragging a stick across the fence. But she showed up too late. You're already on your way up, toward the horrors of the second floor. Black cables dangle from the doorway you now enter. A mechanical anaconda snakes toward you, hissing. There are plastic reptiles everywhere. The next room features webs in which massive spiders are nesting. A male doll, wrapped in a web, moans faintly. His head twitches from side to side. The demons—the name for the workers in The House—call him Frodo. You turn the corner and trigger the sound of chopping axes and screams. Bloodstained menus have been taped to the walls. In front of you, daylight filters through the gaps of a closed door. You don't consider the bars to the right of the door or the draperies behind those bars.

The timing of the next scare is perfect. Just as you open the door and are blinded by the light, the Chef, clad in an apron and an executioner's hood, tears aside the draperies and swings a roaring chain saw toward you. You scream and laugh as you stumble onto the balcony. When the door shuts behind you, the Chef murmurs into her two-way radio that a single guest has just passed and is on their way to the Doll. "Do your worst," the Chef says to the Doll, but you obviously can't know this as you're catching your breath on the balcony. Perhaps you glance at the emergency stairs leading into the garden. This is where the guests who want to end the tour can depart.

"The Doctor will see you now," a voice to your right announces.

A janitor holding a broom is standing at the other end of the balcony. He holds up a door, and when he shuts it behind you, the screams from the theme park fade again. A narrow corridor, lined by vaguely Egyptian-looking sarcophagi, extends before you. When you pass a sensor, one of the lids turns transparent, revealing a monstrous creature within. A growl can be heard. Tensing, you pass a black door with a hatch at face level, but nothing happens. The Chef is busy scaring other guests.

At the farthest end of the corridor is a row of bars; behind it is Mats the Mummy, as he's been named by the demons. Bandages dangle from his limbs, his head is a grinning skull, and when you approach, he tilts forward awkwardly. The jaws open and close. You gaze at the mummy with some disdain, but then the Doll leaps forward in its onesie and roars: "I WANT TO PLAY!" You jump and then laugh out of surprise. The Doll copies you. You turn another corner and jump once more when a hatch opens in the wall. The Doll's rosy-cheeked mask peeks out through the plexiglass and cackles insanely. You can't help but feel a little stupid.

The corridor you're in begins tipping sideways with a subtle groan once you enter the Nursery. A melody from a music box and the eerie laughter of children; every toy is monstrous. There are two mirrors on the walls, one on each side of you. The Doll pops up in one of them, but you were prepared for it. Most of the demons feel that the mirror is a difficult bit to pull off. "COME BACK AND PLAY SOON!" the Doll shouts. You walk down a narrow staircase, toward voices chanting in faux Latin. There are more symbols on the walls, painted in white. A statue of a devil rears up behind an iron fence. Then: a body draped across an altar suddenly contorts.

"Help me!" the Possessed yells. "They're in me! They're taking over!"

She starts to spasm, the screams turning guttural. You have to hand it to her—she's working hard. Still, you're not afraid.

In the next room, one wall is covered in mirrors, and you see yourself reflected several times over. There are three doors on the opposite side. When you open the one to the left, you're faced with your own reflection. When you open the one in the middle, the Possessed throws herself at the fence, laughing. The right door leads out of the house. The final scene is rarely manned by personnel, and is simply referred to by its number.

And there, to your left, is the turnstile.

As you exit, you can't help but think that it all went by quickly. The Broom sails overhead. Children and seagulls cry out. The gates creak loudly when those behind you pass through them. Somebody says: "I almost shit my pants."

And somebody says: "Was that it?"

KASPER

It was a summer without rain.

The heat came in May, and by June the grass had yellowed, the ground cracking and turning hard. It was Kasper's first day at Gröna Lund and it had begun badly.

He had applied to The House of Demons but had been accepted by the Magic Carpet Ride, the final stop at the Fun House. When the guests came whooshing down the slides, his task was to fold the carpet they'd traveled on and toss it into a hole. A conveyor belt transported said carpet back up again. This was the only position in Rides you could work without being taught, or broken in, as the workers at Grönan called it. He'd been dropped off by a stressed-out team leader, alongside another newbie called Dennis.

"Today's a little bit chaotic," the team leader said, demonstrating how to fold the carpets as effectively as possible. Kasper immediately forgot what she'd done and how. "Someone will be by and sort it out." Her smile was bright and white. "You've got this, guys. Go for it! Drink plenty of water!"

That had been two hours ago.

"Do you think they've forgotten about us?" Dennis said.

According to his badge, he was from the suburb Älta. Two tiny flags informed the guests that they could speak with him in English and German. There was only a Union Jack on Kasper's own badge.

"My friend's on his second season and he told me they sometimes dump people in the Magic Carpet Ride for an entire day," Dennis went on. "My arms are starting to cramp up."

"Mmm," Kasper said, stretching. His back had started to ache about an hour ago.

"I hope they haven't messed it up," Dennis said. "I was promised The Broom."

It was the third time he'd said that. Apart from that, he talked incessantly about the different parties he'd attended, one of which was the big launch at the start of the season at Grönan. Kasper had missed it because he had ended up as a second choice, not having been offered a job until May. He'd stared at the e-mail then, at once happy and disappointed.

"But where are you really supposed to be?" Dennis asked suddenly.

"The Octopus and the Flying Carpet," Kasper said.

"Ah, the Octo-route," Dennis said, pulling a face that Kasper couldn't interpret. "Was Rides your first choice, then?"

"I actually wanted House of Demons," Kasper told him.

"Probably for the best that you didn't get it. Must suck to stand around inside a dark house all summer."

It's pretty dark inside the Broom, too, Kasper thought but didn't say out loud. He was trying to cope with his bitterness. He'd heard that there were 10,000 applicants for 1,200 jobs each year, only half of which went to new employees. He'd been lucky; it was just hard to feel lucky at the moment.

"My friend says the people in House are pretty weird. Stick to themselves," Dennis went on, taking a drink from his water bottle. "Wait, sorry. You applied there."

He laughed. It wasn't a mean laugh. Kasper could easily have added something self-consciously ironic about his own weirdness; it was the perfect setup, a way to own any behaviors Dennis might consider strange. Better to laugh at himself before someone else could do it. But he hesitated, and Dennis spoke about recognizing the workers in House because of their black clothes, that he couldn't stand haunted houses, that he was so easily scared that he'd almost been awarded "the School Chicken" at his graduation party.

"But I got the school's 'Solid as a Rock' award instead," Dennis said humbly. "Did you graduate this year?"

Kasper folded the carpet the latest guests had left behind, grateful that his hair hung in front of his face, hiding his expression from view.

"Just finished second year," he responded.

He'd hoped the questions would stop after that.

"Where?" Dennis said. "I mean, which school do you go to?"

"Fredrika Bremer."

"Huddinge, right?"

"Haninge. Handen."

"But you are eighteen? You have to be eighteen to work the Rides, right?"

He might as well have it over with.

"I turned nineteen in September," Kasper said. "I had to retake a year because I switched programs. From Tech to Art."

It was the truth. No one had to know the reason behind it, after all.

"That's cool, man," Dennis said. "I mean, figuring out that you want to do something else and then just going for it."

"Where did you go?" Kasper asked, hoping to end this cross-examination.

"Nacka High School. Social Science," Dennis said. He bobbed his head to a song that carried over from the Pop Express. "Sometimes I think I should have gone for Natural Science, so I might take a year to do those courses, too. My parents are engineers, so . . . What do your parents do?"

There was no simple answer to that question. His dad and mom had had more jobs than Kasper could recall: nurse's aide, mover, personal assistant, postal worker, gardener, cleaner, substitute teacher, care worker, shop assistant . . .

"My mom's a photographer," Kasper said. "And my dad's a musician."

"A famous one?"

There was no simple answer to that question, either. In some circles, Kasper's father, Håkan Nordin, was a legend. Two things earned him that particular status: In the beginning of the '90s, when Swedish death metal became an actual commercial success, he was the bassist in one of the scene's biggest bands, Exenterate, and played with them for almost fifteen years. And before that, he'd founded Dark Cruelty, a band that had earned cult status.

"People who are into death metal tend to know who he is."

"Death metal!"

Dennis stretched out his index finger, little finger, and thumb in what he probably thought was the sign of the horns, but which actually meant "I love you" in sign language. Kasper did not correct him.

"I never got the difference, to be honest," Dennis said. "Is death metal the one where they scream?"

Kasper took a deep breath. It always hurt a bit to simplify a subject he was so passionate about, but when people asked him this question, they were rarely interested in a lecture about subgenres in extreme metal and various screaming and growling techniques.

"Yeah, they scream," he said.

A high-pitched shriek as two teenage girls came flying down Kasper's slide, all short shorts and long legs. When the carpet came to a stop, they burst into hysterical giggles. Then they looked at Kasper and giggled even harder. He averted his eyes and paid attention to the carpet. The girls began roaring with laughter as they stumbled toward the exit. Kasper didn't actually think they were laughing at him, but he still couldn't help but worry. *Do I look like some kind of pervert, standing around and ogling the guests' legs? Like an antisocial freak who's had to retake an entire year of school? Are there patches of sweat on my shirt? Is my zipper open?* The rough carpet fibers scraped against his fingertips.

They're just thoughts, his psychologist had told him while he was still seeing her. Other people don't notice us as much as we think they do; they're busy with their own things. Like Dennis, who carelessly continued to talk about what his friends had said about the rides in the Main Area.

"Anything beats the Minor Area and all the families. The children aren't the worst of it, though—it's the parents. They come here, too, obviously, but they're literally everywhere in Minor. The most boring thing in the Main Area is the Hall of Mirrors. Unless you're hungover, in which case it's awesome. But the Octo-route . . ."

He fell silent, as if catching up with himself.

"What?" Kasper was beginning to get slightly sick of Dennis.

"All right, I'll be honest with you," Dennis said seriously. "The Flying Carpet is shit and the Octopus is on a barge."

He raised his eyebrows meaningfully at Kasper, as if this conveyed something. It didn't, so Dennis went on: "The barge sways and you're stuck on it, watching the Octopus spin around and around for hours. Tons of people get seasick. And tons of kids puke."

As if on cue, a white-haired little boy stepped off a carpet and vomited. Kasper scattered the lemon-scented absorbent powder on top of it, according to the directions he'd been given.

"Sorry, but I'm, like, emetophobic," Dennis said. He was balancing on his toes, as if to get farther away from the pile of sick. "My friend says people sometimes pour water on top of that powder. Big mistake."

"What happens?" Kasper said, sweeping up the vomit that had turned grainy, while holding his breath.

"It makes a sort of *foam*," Dennis said.

Appendix 2. Excerpt from Kasper Hansson Nordin's final project for the Art Program: Illustration and Design, Fredrika Bremer High School. Tutor: Ms. Gunhild Berg.

There are several genres of extreme metal. Death metal is one of them. Some of the characteristics of death metal are heavily distorted and down-tuned instruments, deep growling and/or screaming, aggressive drumming, and major shifts in key and tempo.

The lyrics usually concern exaggerated violence, inspired by horror movies, but also occultism, religion, mysticism, death, and evil in general.

It can be argued that death metal evolved out of thrash metal, with some inspiration from hardcore, and emerged in the United States in the 1980s. However, the genre was also shaped by and in the U.K. and Sweden.

Metal, and especially foreign acts such as Kiss and Iron Maiden, was very popular in Sweden in the 1980s. In the '90s, several Swedish death metal bands became big both in Sweden and abroad.
But at the end of the '80s, the Swedish death metal scene was still small, consisting of less than a hundred active people. Almost all of them were teenagers. My father was one of them. His band was called Dark Cruelty. And the singer was called Grim.

KASPER

At long last, Kasper and Dennis were relieved and could go for lunch. A few drops of water fell from the sky; you couldn't even call it rain. Dark pinpricks dotted the asphalt as Kasper crossed the Main Area. Dennis had gone to meet the friend who had returned for his second season and was probably telling him all about the freak he'd been forced to work with. Then again, Kasper probably wasn't interesting enough to make fun of. It was more likely that Dennis regaled his friend with a story about the child who puked.

It hadn't always been like this.

Once upon a time, the adults around Kasper had called him a beam of light. He's so easy to deal with, they'd said. He lightens the mood in the classroom, at soccer practice, at summer camp. If someone falls over and hurts themselves, he's always there with a word of comfort. He has a group of friends, but gets along with all his classmates. A real ray of sunshine.

Kasper couldn't remember when, exactly, he stopped feeling the smile on the inside and it became just something he wore on the outside; or when he discovered that the quick, easy solution was pretending that everything was fine, instead of talking about the things that hurt him. The distance between what he showed and what he felt kept growing. The mask became more and more difficult to remove. Until the day when everything collapsed. It had been two years since then. Everyone seemed to think that Kasper had recovered wonderfully, that he was back to his old self again. It was as though Kasper was the only one who wasn't sure about who that old self was.

A boy came running with a slushie in his hand and tripped. Small knees and ice hit the pavement, a piercing scream joining in with the shrieks from the rides. The boy's mother rushed toward him, throwing an accusatory glance Kasper's way, as if it had somehow been his doing. He looked away. Maybe he should walk up to them, tell them where they could find the nurse. Instead, he quickened his steps. At Grönan, you were supposed to face the visitors with a smile and exude warmth and positivity. So far, he'd failed on every front.

He tilted his head back as he walked, allowing heavy drops of lukewarm rain to hit his forehead. The back of his neck was hot and sweaty, but he didn't like the way his face looked when he wore his long hair up. Much like he didn't like the way his skinny legs looked in shorts. When he'd chosen his uniform, he'd settled for the pants, and he regretted it now. His entire body was sticky with sweat.

Was he going to be able to do this? The raucous voices, the rattling and roaring coming from the rides tired him out, and this was a relatively calm moment in the Main Area. The weekend would be worse. Had he made a massive mistake?

Tor had suggested that Kasper apply to Grönan. Tor, who was five years older and Kasper's stepbrother, had worked at the theme park for several seasons, and was rapidly promoted from Rides to UC, unit chief, and on to TL, team leader. Currently, he was working as a diving instructor in Australia while in college, but he still spoke warmly about Grönan.

"It's like the world's best summer camp," he'd said at the home of his dad Atle and Kasper's mom Anja this Christmas. "Everyone has a great time. It's a bit cultish, but in a good way. A bunch of us already became friends at the launch party."

Naturally, Kasper thought as he walked toward the door labeled STAFF, to one side of the Main Stage. Everyone loved Tor. Kasper understood why. Tor was the charming salesman type, but he also had a genuinely caring side. Kasper was almost sure Tor had put in a good word for him.

Was that why he'd taken the job? To not disappoint Tor? Or had he thought Grönan would somehow transform him into Tor? Attractive and relaxed. What a joke.

Kasper passed through the staff door and stepped into the alley, which split the theme park in two. He passed the smokers' corner and opened the door to the Minor Area. He crossed between parents and their overheated offspring, high on sugar. A final, sad scattering of water fell from the sky. The asphalt stuck to his shoes as he aimed for the main entrance. The staff cafeteria, called the green room, was on the right. That was how they spoke at Grönan: instead of "job interview," you said "audition." You got your uniform from the CS, costume storage. The employees were, naturally, "cast members."

"Artists," his dad had said with a laugh. "I guess you can tell by the pay."

Kasper stopped outside the green room, unsure which of the two entrances to choose. Through the window, he saw his colleagues seated at the tables, eating together. It looked as if everyone already knew each other. He was tempted to go to the changing rooms and eat the bag of chips he had with him. But he'd promised himself he'd at least make an effort.

He opened the left door and caught a glimpse of his pale face in a mirror. *The show starts here!* was written in green text at the very top of the glass. The message was obviously meant for the departing cast members, reminding them that they were walking on stage the moment they stepped into the theme park again. But a different show was happening in the green room: the social game behind the scenes.

Tor had said that the green room was like a school cafeteria and Kasper immediately understood what he meant. It wasn't just the smell; the majority of the workers at Grönan were young. Like Kasper, some of them were still in high school. According to Tor, it was as cliquey as school, too. The different departments rarely mixed. The Restaurant people hung out with other Restaurant people, Rides with Rides, Games with Games, and so on. "Rides has the best people," Tor had said, as if stating an objective fact.

When Kasper had applied to Grönan, he had applied to The House of Demons, which was its own unit under Rides. He'd wanted a second choice, though, and had thought that manning the roller coaster was better than selling burgers or cleaning. Working with the extroverts in Games and standing next to a wheel of fortune was a personal nightmare. Still, he'd had his hopes up for The House of Demons—and ended up in Rides with people like Tor: sociable, confident, and about to become best friends with one another.

Kasper paid for his fried fish with his employee card and looked around. He thought he recognized some people from Rides but wasn't quite sure. He ran the scenario through his head: walking up to them and asking if a seat was free and then being stared at as if he were an intruder. No. Not today. Tomorrow he'd hopefully get to know some people from the Octo-route. Kasper sat down at a table, empty except for a girl in black clothes, her hair dyed a deep, dark red.

At first, he didn't consider where in Grönan she might be stationed. Or maybe he'd known and that had been the reason he'd joined her in the first place. Afterward, he couldn't tell for sure. But Dennis had mentioned that the employees in The House wore black rather than the standard uniform, with its shades of green. They had to be able to blend in to the haunted house's dark corridors.

Kasper sipped his apple juice and the girl reached across the table for the salt. That's when he saw it—the tattoo on her inner forearm.

Dark Cruelty's logo.

Was he mistaken? He couldn't be. It was the ornate, indecipherable logo he knew, designed to exude evil and mystery.

Kasper stuck a piece of fried fish in his mouth but could hardly taste it. From the corner of his eye, he saw the girl tuck a lock of hair behind her ear.

It was deeply ironic. Here was someone he definitely shared interests with—a horror fan, or she wouldn't be working in The House, and clearly into metal. She would definitely be into talking to Kasper Hansson Nordin, son of Håkan "Maimer" Nordin, the founder of the band whose logo was etched into her skin.

Which was why talking to her was completely out of the question.

Nice tattoo. Do you know who my dad is?

The mere idea made Kasper cringe inwardly.

Besides which, the tattoo could be a warning sign. Some fans of Dark Cruelty were, in his dad's words, "intense." A girl who wore every band member's name in lockets around her neck had been writing to his dad for years, demanding he send her a lock of his hair, and preferably Grim's, too, as if his dad had a stash of his dead friend's hair lying around and ready to mail.

Kasper threw a quick glance at the girl's badge. *Iris. Unit Chief.* So she was an actual *manager* in The House. Two small flags on the badge signaled that she spoke English and Finnish. His eyes were drawn to the tattoo again.

"So are you a fan, or what?"

Kasper looked up. Iris was pointing at the tattoo.

"Or are you just trying to see what it says?" she continued, her smile crooked.

"No, I know what it says," Kasper said, feeling his cheeks heat up. "You were staring."

"I was just surprised."

It slipped out. Iris raised her eyebrows.

"Why?"

Kasper could see the suspicion in her eyes. Female metalheads were often quizzed and challenged, forced to prove that they were "true" over and over again. Both Kasper's mom and his dad's ex, Leah, who played and sang in a metal band, had talked about it.

"Because I was just talking to someone else about Dark Cruelty," Kasper hastened to explain. "So it was a weird coincidence."

"Oh," Iris said, relaxing slightly. "May I ask why?"

"It just came up," Kasper said.

"So the other person was a fan?"

He couldn't be bothered to talk around it anymore. Letting go felt nice, somehow. At least it would make something happen.

"Håkan is my dad."

Iris blinked.

"Håkan," she said. "You're . . . You're kidding me. You're *Maimer's* kid? You're kidding me. You are!"

"No," Kasper said.

"And I was like, 'Are you trying to see what it says?'"

Iris hid her face in her hands and groaned.

"Sorry," Kasper offered.

Iris looked up again, her expression faintly outraged.

"Why are you apologizing? This is embarrassing for *me*. I can't handle this, I'm sorry . . . That band has meant so much to me. Well, clearly. Holy fuck, you look just like him, I see it now. Jesus, I am embarrassing myself so *hard*."

She started to laugh. She laughed so hard she teared up. Kasper couldn't help but smile.

"I ruined your lunch," he said.

"No, I ruined *your* lunch," Iris said and snorted. "Being an insane fan, and all. Sorry, my name is Iris, and you are . . ."

Her eyes caught on his badge and Kasper awaited her reaction. Because he was named after Kasper "Grim" Johansson, the singer in Dark Cruelty.

"Fuck me," she said quietly. "Of course, they were best friends. That's so fucking beautiful and so, so sad. Ah, Iris, shut your mouth."

She hid her face in her hands again. Kasper could hear her taking deep, sniffling breaths.

"Are you okay?" he asked.

"Yes," Iris said. "But no. Sorry. These kinds of things must be so annoying for you."

They could be. Despite the pride Kasper felt for his dad, other people's reactions could be a little much.

"I don't think you're annoying," he told her honestly.

It almost sounded flirtatious. He blushed again, but when Iris looked up, she was several shades pinker. Her brown eyes gleamed wetly.

"You sure?"

"I'm sure," Kasper said. "You're funny."

It sounded so dumb that he laughed. Iris joined in.

"So my suffering is just entertainment to you?"

"Absolutely," Kasper said.

"Well, I'm glad I can pay you back in some way, after having ruined your lunch."

"You didn't—"

"Is this your first season?" she interrupted.

"Yeah. I'm in the Magic Carpet Ride at the moment."

"Fuck," Iris said.

Another black-clad girl approached them, placing her tray opposite Iris. A small gem glittered in one nostril.

"Sorry, but your lunch is over," she told Iris. "Duty calls."

"I'm on my way, but this is Kasper." Iris gestured at him. "Kasper, this is Selam. She and I are the UCs in The House."

"Hi, Kasper," Selam, who was apparently from Gothenburg, said. She turned to Iris again. "Have you been crying?"

"Laughing and crying," Iris said. "Or, well, I don't know. It's a long story." She looked at Kasper. "We can*not* abandon you at the Magic Carpet Ride."

"You're in the Magic Carpets?" Selam said. "Shoot me."

Kasper was about to explain that it was only temporary, but Iris got there first.

"Do you want to work in The House?"

Kasper was about to respond, but Iris interrupted him again:

"I'm not asking because I'm a crazy stalker. Because I am not a crazy stalker, I swear. I just have your dad's band tattooed on my arm, but that's fine, I am an idiot, that's all, folks."

She threw her head back and mimed screaming at the sky.

"We've lost some people, so we need to replace them," Selam told Kasper between bites. "But we need to talk to the TL first."

"Yeah, of course," Kasper, who couldn't believe this was happening, managed.

"Or maybe you don't like The House," Iris said.

"I actually applied for it."

"Ha!" Iris exclaimed. "I knew it. The House is the best."

"The Haunted House in Liseberg is better," Selam said.

Iris hissed, "Blasphemer."

"I simply speak the truth." Selam turned back to Kasper. "It's not everyone's thing, standing around in a dark house all summer."

"And we make little children cry. If you can't handle that, you can't work there," Iris added.

"I can handle it," Kasper said.

"Kasper, the Not So Friendly Ghost," Selam said with a smirk.

On his way out of the green room, Kasper saw himself in the mirror again. There was something in his gaze that he hadn't seen for a very long time. As if he'd been infected by Grönan's shimmer.

Appendix 3. Excerpt from a forum.

Anyone in here sitting on facts about Kasper "Grim" Johansson? Brother-in-law claims young Johansson was some kind of self-proclaimed warlock and that the other members of Dark Cruelty ritually murdered him in a subway tunnel. Am aware that some bizarre shit went down in the metal scene in the '90s, but this was a bit earlier than that, and I think a satanic subway homicide would have ended up in the press in the '80s? Looking for details. Cause of death, f x?

Edit | Delete | Reply

Wasn't much to write about in the papers as the police wrapped up the preliminary investigation in no time. Check the thread and you'll find links to the few articles that exist. That said: your brother-in-law is full of it. I'd estimate about 90% of what people say about Grim is crap. I know some people who were in the scene at the time. G. moved down to Stockholm from Hudiksvall or some other backwater northern town to sing in D.C. A weirdo. Screw loose. Interested in occultism, but most of his bandmates didn't share that interest. Yeah, some mentals think they murdered him to get attention for the EP that was released the same year. But if so, why did they break up the band when he died? Which they did. A rumor on par with that one in pure idiocy is that Grim was slain by a demon while conducting a magic ritual. He was just a broken person valorized by other broken people. Decent vocalist, though.

Edit | Delete | Reply

I've been listening to extreme metal for over thirty years. We definitely used to think bands like Dark Cruelty were real misanthropic madmen holed up together in a cave somewhere. i.e., before the Internet ruined the mystery. That rumor about the demon is one of many spread by Dark Cruelty's guitarist, Malte Lundell (called himself Iago until the parrot in the Aladdin flick showed up . . .). Went around talking shit about the surviving band members in fanzines in the '90s. Sent them death threats, the way people did in the evil old days. A genuine psychopath. But his music is insanely good and he loves the motherland so I'm willing to forgive him hehe. As for Grim, I thought we all knew he died of something congenital?

Edit | Delete | Reply

Read up on the case. A killer is loose. At least one.

Edit | Delete | Reply

KASPER

The very same day that Kasper met Iris and Selam in the green room, it was confirmed: he would be "broken in" in The House the following day.

He practically floated up the escalator from Handen's train. Emerging from it, he cast a look at the building on the left, where the child and adolescent psychiatry office was housed two floors up. The times he'd spent in that clinic, with its green doors, felt further away than ever.

He entered the tunnel called Cave of the Naiads and walked past the closed-off staircases that had once led to the bus station. It had been moved, replaced with apartment buildings. Not that the bus station had been a particularly charming place, far from it, but Kasper didn't know what to make of the changes of the past few years. A part of him wanted things to stay the way they'd always been.

Handen, meaning *the hand*: a strange name for a very ordinary place. There were municipality buildings, a shopping mall and green spaces, a bunch of nondescript apartment buildings surrounded by industrial parks, fancy residential areas, and low-rent apartments with bad reputations. A place in-between or a center, depending on who you asked.

When Kasper had been a child, his dad told him the story of how Handen got its name. A road once ran through the town, carrying those doomed to die at the executioner's spot called Galgstenen.

The carts the prisoners were transported in shook so violently, and the prisoners were so tightly chained, that body parts occasionally flew out of the carts. A hand fell off and landed in the middle of the road. "And a few miles from here, you'll find places named after the arm and the shoulder," his dad lied. Kasper wanted to hear that story over and over again. Then he'd been taught in school that it was probably derived from some local inn, or possibly the Hanveden forest. As the teacher seemed unsure, however, Kasper chose to believe his father's version. Dead man's hand.

Handen had always been the center of Kasper's world. His dad had also grown up there and his grandma had been within walking distance when Kasper was little. His friends were, too. Rudan Lake. The soccer field. And the Cultural Center, a white cube by Poseidon's Square, between Haninge Center and the new apartment buildings. The library inside it had tall windows that made it feel like you were reading among the trees that grew on the other side of the glass. Kasper had spent hours in that library as a child, fascinated by stories and myths. There were traces of them all over Handen. Odenvägen, Odin's Road. Streets named after Odin's eight-legged steed, Sleipner, and Idun, the goddess of youth. The Cave of the Naiads, the water nymphs, led to the god of the sea, Poseidon's Square.

When Kasper reached the square, he checked the outdoor seats but didn't see anyone he recognized. The fountain was shut down, probably because the municipality had to save water. The heat was overwhelming despite the lateness of the hour. Windows and balcony doors gaped open, voices and sounds from television shows filtering out. The sky was pale. Kasper turned to the right of the Cultural Center and continued in among three-story houses.

He'd already written to his mom about the new job, but not to his dad. He wanted to personally tell him that it was thanks to Dark Cruelty that he'd gotten it.

His heart skipped a beat.

A familiar figure exited a door and continued straight toward Kasper.

Marco.

No. It wasn't him, just a guy with a similar hairstyle and build. When Kasper got closer, he couldn't understand how he could have confused the two of them. Still, he hurried home.

The guitars echoed into the stairwell. Early Judas Priest. The door was unlocked and Kasper was greeted by a pair of gigantic Converse that had been abandoned on the hallway carpet. They definitely didn't belong to his dad. But he could hear his dad's voice coming from the kitchen, in the middle of one of his long rants. Kasper could only catch the occasional word, but he sounded animated.

"I've always . . . Ernesto, on the other hand . . . ah, who the fuck knows. . ."

The voice fell quiet and someone's steps receded. Kasper entered the kitchen. The windows were open wide. The table was cluttered with beer cans and two empty pizza boxes—and there was Tony, sitting at the table, bent over his phone. A Sodom tee stretched over his broad chest. There was no sign of his dad.

"Hey there, old man!" Kasper said. Tony looked up.

"You rude little shit!" he roared.

A second later, Tony threw himself forward, embracing Kasper and pounding his back in a way that made his inner organs jiggle.

Tony Lehtonen was a giant, long and muscular with curly blond hair that flowed down his back. It wasn't frizzy, in the manner of many older metalheads. Tony had always taken care of his hair, even when unwashed and straggly was trendy. Besides, he was married to a hairdresser now. Tony's eyes were bright blue, his nose smashed after slipping on the ice during a hockey game.

He looked like the archetypal Viking. The stage name Berserker, which he'd used as the drummer in Dark Cruelty, suited him almost too well.

"Your dad's having a cigarette," Tony said, nodding at the living room, where the door to the balcony was ajar. "So I'm staying away."

"New Year's resolution still going strong, yeah?" Kasper said.

"Even on the road," Tony said with some pride.

He'd recently returned after touring with Malodor, one of Stockholm's older death metal bands that had made it in the nineties. Tony started playing with them after Dark Cruelty split up, and they'd been active intermittently since then.

"Almost lost my shit when I ran out of snuff in Rotterdam, though," Tony said, shoving some of said snuff under his upper lip. "Good thing Stasse always has something stashed away."

He sank back down on the chair. As usual, it looked slightly too small for him. Kasper leaned back against the sink.

"Håkan said you're at Grönan this summer," Tony said.

"Yeah," Kasper said. "First day today."

He pulled at his T-shirt, which stuck to his body.

"That's a real dream job, huh?" Tony said. "Remember when we went to see Alice Cooper?"

"Of course."

The two of them had been to countless gigs together. When Kasper was a child, Tony used to carry him on his shoulders. Then he'd perch up there, earmuffs firmly on, his view far better than his mom's and dad's. While they were still married, the entire family would spend a lot of time with Tony. But then there was the divorce, and Tony met Emira, his current wife, and had a kid. Kasper didn't see Tony as frequently anymore, but he was still like a close relative. The uncle Kasper had never had.

"Grönan, eh?" Tony said. "Manning the roller coasters or frying up food?"

"I actually got to switch to The House of Demons today. The haunted house."

Tony exploded into laughter.

"Awesome! You're getting paid to scare the shit out of people on a daily basis?"

"Exactly," Kasper said, smiling.

"Awesome!" Tony repeated, bringing a beer can to his lips, taking a sip, and shaking the rest into his mouth. "This goddamn weather. Everything's piss warm in one second."

"I'll get you a cold one," Kasper said.

"Thanks," Tony said as he grimaced and flexed his wrists.

A couple of years ago, he got an inflammation in the joints. Kasper's dad said he'd never seen Tony that scared before. Since then, he had dutifully done his physical therapy exercises; not being able to play was his worst nightmare. Kasper could relate. Some of the illustrators he followed would post about pains and aches in their hands and wrists. Kasper felt a surge of worry just thinking about it.

"How's your mom and sisters?" Tony asked.

"Fine," Kasper said, taking a beer and soda out of the fridge.

"And the Norwegian terror?"

Tony actually liked Atle, but he couldn't help himself.

"Training for an Ironman," Kasper said, handing Tony the beer.

"Maniac," Tony said, clearly impressed. The can hissed when he popped it open.

Kasper had a sip of his soda and immediately remembered that it wouldn't actually lessen thirst, but increase it—one of the numerous health tips that his stepfather, Atle, shared with him. Kasper remembered all of his advice but rarely followed it.

"Your dad says you've been doing well this term," Tony said. "In school and everything."

He almost looked shy when he said it. Kasper obviously knew

what he meant by "and everything": that Kasper had stopped taking his antidepressants but still managed to go to school and act like a normal high school student. He had a regular sleeping schedule, he did his homework, he'd even gone bowling and to the movies with his classmates.

"Yeah, definitely," Kasper said. "But I'm happy about vacation."

"Yeah, thank fuck for vacations," Tony said with a laugh.

He seemed relieved that Kasper hadn't delved too deeply into the subject of his mental health, but Kasper didn't take it personally. Tony didn't really talk about feelings, but he'd come running if Kasper ever needed his help. He'd proved it.

"Are you heading out tonight?" Kasper said just as his dad returned to the kitchen.

Håkan Nordin was a head taller than his son, wiry and weather-beaten. Tattoos covered his arms, peeking up from beneath the collar of his Autopsy T-shirt. His ex, Leah, had done many of them—as she was a tattooist as well as a musician. His long salt-and-pepper hair came down below his shoulders, and his beard and mustache were perfectly trimmed. He was wearing the glasses he only ever wore at home.

"Your son's asking if we're going on a bender tonight," Tony said.

"Nah, we're staying in for a good old talk," his dad said. "Watching a film."

"Maybe something Italian," Tony said. *"Giallo Italiano!"*

"Nice," said Kasper. "I might join you."

His dad peered at him through the glasses.

"You seem to be in a good mood," he said, smiling. "Was it a good first day at work?"

Kasper began to grin as he told them about the encounter with Iris. His dad and Tony listened attentively, exclaiming, "No, really?" and "I'll be damned!" and laughed in all the right places.

"What are the odds, though?" his dad said. "That she has a DC tattoo and then you show up, out of everyone . . . Crazy."

"Who'd have thought your old dad would turn out to be useful, after all." Tony grinned. "Couldn't have seen that one coming."

"He's not *that* old," Kasper said.

"The lack of respect, from the pair of you," his dad said, clearly moved. He squeezed Kasper's shoulder. "I'm glad you got what you wanted. Ghost House."

"The House of Demons," Kasper corrected him.

"*Demons!*" Tony exclaimed. "Haven't seen that one in ages."

"I've got it on Blu-ray," his dad said.

A few hours later, Kasper was in bed and on YouTube, watching secretly filmed videos taken inside The House.

It had been a nice evening.

His dad had rushed out and bought them ice cream to celebrate Kasper's new job in style. Then they'd watched the Italian '80s film *Demons*, or *Dèmoni*, about a bunch of idiots being attacked by zombies in a movie theater. After that, it was time for Tony to head home.

"We'll talk to Ernesto tomorrow," Tony told his dad, both of them standing in the hallway. Then he turned to Kasper. "You just go for it, all right? Show no mercy."

His dad shut the door behind him.

"What are you talking to Ernesto about?" Kasper asked.

Ernesto Moberg had also played in Dark Cruelty, under the pseudonym Morbid Eradicator. He was the only member of the band, and one of the few metal musicians in Sweden, who made a living off his music. His heavy metal band Vile Prophets was big in the United States and South America. Kasper's dad had been a guest musician on a few of their albums, and both he and Tony had gone along on tours when the ordinary members had had to call off for one reason or another. With that in mind, them talking to Ernesto wasn't strange in and of itself. There was, however, something strange in the air. Kasper recalled his dad's animated voice: *I've always . . . Ernesto, on the other hand . . . ah, who the fuck knows. . .*

"It's just something we're discussing," his dad said, heading into the kitchen. He emptied the last of the beer in the sink and put the cans in a plastic bag.

"What?" Kasper asked, shaking the final drops of lukewarm soda into his mouth before tossing the can to his dad.

"Aren't you curious?" his dad said, amused, dropping the soda can into the bag. "It's a bit of a mess, to be honest. A lot to think about. I'll tell you later, all right?"

Kasper nodded reluctantly. His dad wasn't usually a particularly secretive man.

"Your new job sounds amazing," his dad said, opening the dishwasher and passing clean mugs to Kasper. "This'll be your summer."

Kasper laughed, putting the mugs back in their designated cupboard.

"What, can you predict the future?"

It sounded unnecessarily bitter, and he immediately regretted it.

"No, but I've got great instincts," his dad said, stacking the clean plates. "And so do you. Trust your instincts."

But Kasper was in bed now, asking himself how one recognized a truly valid instinct. Was it the euphoria he'd felt walking up the escalator at the train station? Or the feeling that unfolded inside him while watching clips from The House? Then there was the feeling that he'd ruin everything, disappoint everyone. He hadn't even gotten the job on his own merits, and if not for Tor, he'd never been employed at Grönan to begin with. If it hadn't been for his dad and Dark Cruelty, he and Iris never would have spoken.

He put his phone away and turned to face the wall. Traced the pattern on the wallpaper with his finger, the way he'd done countless times before. Thought of how he'd reacted when he saw the guy he'd mistaken for Marco. Ghosts. His dad was wrong: Kasper couldn't trust his instincts. If he did, he'd hardly leave the apartment.

There was the soft sound of a sliding door opening in the next room, and then his dad was digging through the closet, where he kept his vast collection of band T-shirts. A short while later, he shut the door behind him again. His dad moved almost soundlessly. He used to say he'd been raised not to stomp around and disturb the neighbors. "They had to put up with my music instead," he used to add with a laugh. His dad laughed a lot, and at first, that's what Kasper thought he was doing in there. That he'd seen some funny clip on his phone and chuckled with a hand pressed to his mouth, so as not to wake Kasper.

But his dad was crying.

Kasper lay unmoving, listening. The sobs sounded painful, as if they were hurting his dad. They hurt Kasper, too. He'd seen his dad cry at funerals, and when that horse sank into the swamp in *The NeverEnding Story*, but he'd never sounded like this before, so helpless and abandoned. Should Kasper go to him? Comfort him? Or did his dad want to be alone?

The sobs stopped as abruptly as they'd started. The bedroom went quiet. Then Kasper heard his dad go into the living room and turn on the television. While Kasper considered joining him, sleep finally claimed him.

That night, he dreamed about Grim for the first time.

Appendix 4. Excerpt from an interview with Håkan Nordin, made in conjunction with the Dark Cruelty EP *Ancient Bloodlust*'s twenty-year anniversary.

So I was a bit young at the end of the '8os, but that era brings out some real nostalgia in people from "the scene." Why do you think that is?
First of all, we were thick as thieves, all of us. We were this little group bent on finding a rawer, faster, more brutal sound. We weren't dreaming of being famous or anything, underground recognition was all that mattered, other bands naming you as an inspiration alongside Morbid Angel and Repulsion in some fanzine. In those days, none of us in Exenterate could have imagined that we'd get to travel the world and meet our heroes; that wasn't even part of it at the time.

We lived and breathed music, basically. All you did was go to school or work, write letters, trade and listen to new demos. People who listened to other kinds of metal didn't get us at all. Most of them thought we were a bunch of brats who couldn't play properly, and that was true, in a way. Most of us were in junior high when we started. There was punk spirit in what we did. DIY. We helped each other out, supported each other's bands. No one wanted to be a rock star.

We weren't all the same, but it didn't matter if someone was a model student and the other cut school all the time. We only talked about music, anyway. Some people were oddballs, but it was fine in the scene, you know. You could just be yourself.

Something we had in common, though, is that we didn't think things through. Maybe that's typical of all or most sixteen-year-old boys, but we took that to an extreme, too. There was this feeling of now, now, this moment being everything. As if we knew we were living in the exact right time, that we just had to discover new shit, do all that new shit. I think that's why there are so many powerful memories and strong bonds between those of us who were there while death metal was still underground. Even though it was such a short period of time, a few years.

The best days of your life?

In a way. I can't be wholehearted about it, because of what happened with Grim. And later in life I became a dad. I actually like getting older. There's not as much prestige and bullshit in the bands you play with, fights about setlists and stuff. You get better at handling conflicts, too.

Grim was heavily mythologized after his death. How would you describe him?

Talented as fuck, tricky as fuck. We had a great time together. He was my friend. I still miss him. I do.

KASPER

Kasper was at a Dark Cruelty gig, worlds away from the local youth centers they'd usually played at. The band was standing on the stage of a vast theater. The silence was deafening. One solitary blue spotlight cut through the darkness on the stage. The musicians were shadowy silhouettes, Tony hardly discernible behind the drums. Håkan, Ernesto, and Malte stood unmoving, their backs turned, as if waiting for some signal. Kasper thought he should be able to recognize his own dad, but he couldn't tell the three of them apart. Only Grim could be picked out in that blue light. His long black hair fell across his face. The microphone hung from his loose fist. Blood seemed to trickle down his hand, dripping onto the stage. He was also waiting.

And then Kasper was wide awake.

He reached for his phone, turning off the alarm just as it began to sound, sat up, and crawled over to the foot of the bed where his bag lay on the floor. He took out his sketchbook and a pencil and stumbled over to the desk, leafing through killer clowns and the ghosts of children before finding a blank page. He began drawing Grim, with the shadowy band in the background.

Sometimes the urge to draw felt almost physical, as real as hunger or thirst. He could feel it in his hand and eye, the desire to take ahold of the pen, to watch the image grow. It was that thing, both difficult to describe and clear as glass, called inspiration. He had heard about artists being inspired by their dreams, but he'd never experienced it before. Like a direct link to something absolute and indisputable.

Time and space disappeared as he worked. All that was left was the scritch of the pencil against the paper, the picture expanding. And then it was done. Kasper looked at the drawing, his heart pounding hard, as if he'd been running.

In looking at the results of his efforts, Kasper usually felt some level of frustration. Whatever he'd produced rarely matched up to his imagination. But this was different. Yes, the drawing was rough, but in a good way. The essence of it was there.

There was a knock on the door.

"You up?" His dad sounded stressed.

"Yes!" Kasper called, checking his phone.

He'd been drawing for forty-five minutes. Just like that, he was in a hurry. He couldn't be late for his first day in The House. Still, he couldn't help but take another look at the picture.

Grim. The singer in Dark Cruelty, his dad's best friend, who'd been dead for almost thirty years now. Kasper had never dreamed of him before.

This must have been brought on by Iris and the tattoo, he thought.

His dad was in the hallway, stepping into his shoes. He moved aside so Kasper could sidle into the bathroom.

"Eric called," his dad said. "Someone's broken into the rehearsal space."

"Shit," Kasper said, squeezing toothpaste onto the brush.

Eric was lead guitarist in Blood Libation, the sludge metal band his dad had been playing in for the past nine years. They were housed in a rehearsal space complex in Midsommarkransen.

"Hopefully they didn't steal anything off of us," his dad said. "Though I obviously don't wish it on anyone . . . I have to go and find out how bad it is."

"Fingers crossed," Kasper said, mouth full of minty foam.

"Break a leg in the haunted house!"

His dad smiled at Kasper and pulled the door shut behind him. Kasper heard his steps disappear down the staircase. The sound of him weeping, alone and abandoned, felt so far away that Kasper wondered whether he'd really heard it. Had it been a part of the dream?

Iris was the one who was coaching Kasper. She'd suggested they meet at twelve, half an hour before the morning meeting, so they'd get The House to themselves for a bit.

Kasper was nervous. Not just for the job, but also about what it would be like to spend more time with Iris. Whenever he bumped into his dad's fans, he worried about being compared to his father. At Kasper's tender age, Håkan had already founded and then ended Dark Cruelty, recorded Exenterate's pioneering debut, which was still counted as one of the world's best death metal albums, and toured Europe. His dad had shaped an entire genre of music; Kasper had accomplished nothing of value.

But that nervousness disappeared relatively quickly. Iris was all business, bent on teaching Kasper the basics. He changed into his new black uniform and was given a thorough tour of The House. It looked different when the fluorescent lights were on. Kasper had never before noticed the hidden passageways Iris pointed out, used by the demons when they wanted to move rapidly through The House.

"One of the most difficult things is finding your way around," Iris said, showing Kasper a secret passage from the Lab in the great hall to the Possessed. "Don't panic if you get confused, and don't hesitate to ask Selam or me for help. Or anyone really. Almost everyone's on their second season or more, so they know their way around. And everyone's got a radio on them. Speaking of which . . ."

She pulled a small, round box from her pocket and handed it to Kasper. He removed the lid, uncovering a mushroom-shaped piece in soft plastic, somewhat reminiscent of an earplug.

"Attach it to the two-way radio you use," Iris explained, leaning against the fence that normally surrounded the Possessed. "We've all got our own. Hygiene, you know. Do not lose it. Also, get regular earplugs, too. Earpiece in one ear, plug in the other. Especially when you're in the Lab."

"Right," Kasper said, contemplating the peeling devil statue on the other side of the fence.

"We'll get you a flashlight as well. Having worked here a while, though, I bet you'll find your way in complete darkness. You can try it tonight, when I've got the final round," Iris said. "After closing, the UC has to do a final check, just to make sure everything looks all right and no one's, like, hidden themselves away in some corner."

"Has that ever happened?" Kasper asked.

"No," Iris replied, but she didn't seem entirely confident. "Anyway. On the way back, I tend to do a walk-through with the lights out. Do you want to tag along?"

"Yeah, okay," Kasper said. "Totally."

Somehow, he felt calmer. No one seemed to expect him to know everything at once.

After the meeting with the team leaders and setting the day's schedule, Iris took Kasper into The House again and had the other demons scare them. It was important that he saw real examples of what they did, she said, and that he understand the importance of variation. "It'll be boring as fuck for the visitor if every scene is exactly the same," Iris said. Kasper worried a bit about getting too worked up and humiliating himself in front of the others, but Iris was clearly more frightened than he was, startling at every new scene. It was clear that the demons were making an effort for their UC, and maybe also for the newcomer.

"The funny thing is that I'm extremely easy to scare," Iris told Kasper when they stepped out into the heat of the balcony. "A lot of demons are, actually. Maybe that's why we love scaring other people. I love horror movies, for example, but I end up terrified every time. Where do you find yourself on the spectrum?"

"I'm inured to it," Kasper said with a laugh.

He'd loved horror and ghost stories his entire life. If anything, he found them comforting.

Iris explained the fire-safety measures and ran through the different scenes with Kasper. Each of them had their own challenges and possibilities. She showed him where to hide, how to pound his fists or kick the doors without hurting himself, gave him a stick to rattle against the fence in the Lab. She told him that the bars were there to protect the demons, pointed at the alarm buttons in every scene, told him what they did. One button lit up the ceiling. Another one summoned security. A third kicked off an emergency signal in which a recording told everyone to evacuate the house in an orderly manner.

"You can use the radio to get a guard in, too," Iris said. "Don't hesitate. Better safe than sorry, right?"

Kasper nodded, wondering just how bad it could get.

When there weren't any guests, they talked. Or Iris talked. Kasper found out that she was twenty-one and an Aquarius. She was trying to learn the meaning of every individual tarot card by heart and her Finnish was "tragically, grammatically incorrect." She rented a room in Örnsberg and couldn't stand her roommates, as they were "pretentious assholes who never cleaned up after themselves." The only one of them she liked was the cat, Caligari, which was also the background of her phone, a black cat with delicate white socks. Iris had named him, so "he's mostly mine." She did film studies in college, "which guarantees that I'll be 200 percent unemployed."

But she never mentioned Dark Cruelty. It was as though she was actively avoiding the subject, determined not to repeat yesterday's collapse into utter fangirl behavior. She didn't even react when Kasper got a message from his dad, telling him they'd been spared by the people who'd broken into the studio. It wasn't until late in the evening, after closing up and the day's concluding meeting, that Dark Cruelty came up again.

Kasper came along when Iris walked the final round through the empty house. He couldn't help looking for unwelcome guests, but they only found a lost earring in the Hall of Mirrors.

"You ready for the darkness?" Iris asked, stopping at a dashboard.

"Dunno," Kasper said. "But go for it."

Iris turned off the lights, launching them into a darkness that was as black as pitch.

"Follow my voice," she said. "Touch a hand to the wall and turn the flashlight on if it's too much."

Kasper reached out a hand. The wall was closer than he'd thought. He could hear Iris starting to walk away.

"I know this is a lame question," she said, "but what's your sign?"

"Virgo," Kasper responded.

He didn't understand the point of astrology. Things might have been different if he'd had a slightly more evocative sign, but the only thing people seemed to say about Virgos was that they were neurotic perfectionists.

"Oh," Iris said, and then she fell silent in a way that struck Kasper as uncharacteristic. He could guess why.

"Grim was a Virgo, too, wasn't he?" he said, into the darkness surrounding them.

Grim died on the fifteenth of September, and the seventeenth was his birthday. Kasper had been born between those dates.

"Yes, that's correct," was Iris's response. "And unfortunately, I also know your dad's sign. That's how much of a creep I am!"

Kasper laughed. Suddenly, the wall disappeared, and he was fumbling through empty space. He stopped, listened, but couldn't hear Iris's steps, only a mechanical whirring.

"Hang on a sec."

He sounded more desperate than he'd intended to.

"I'm right here," Iris said, and a flashlight switched on a few steps away from him. She lit her face from below, the way Kasper and his dad used to do when he was a child and they told each other ghost stories. "You all right?"

"I'm fine." Kasper found his way back to the wall. "You can turn it off."

A click and the darkness swallowed Iris's face. Kasper couldn't imagine knowing these passageways by heart, not even with the lights on, but he was suddenly determined to succeed.

"So when is your birthday, exactly?" Iris asked him.

He tried to aim for her voice, dragged his hand over what had to be a door.

"The sixteenth of September. That's why I'm named after him, I guess."

Kasper's parents had been planning on visiting the grave in Timrå that year, but his mom had been so far gone that they decided to stay in Stockholm and hold an informal ceremony of remembrance with Tony. He'd ended up driving them to the hospital.

"Here are the stairs to the Nursery, so watch out," Iris said.

"You can talk to me about Dark Cruelty," Kasper assured her, taking one step at a time.

"Do *not* tempt me." Iris's voice, from up ahead.

"Can I ask you something?" Kasper said. "Why did you get that tattoo? You don't have to answer if it's too private, obviously."

He bit his lip. Why was he rambling?

"It's a long story," Iris replied, "but it was a gift to myself, on my eighteenth birthday. I'd decided to come out as trans and I . . . I needed something that had empowered me on my body, that still empowered me. God, that's lame."

Kasper said, "I don't think so."

Iris fell silent, and he wondered if he'd embarrassed her. Maybe he shouldn't have asked her about it; maybe it was too private. He felt as though he should tell her something, too, as an exchange. Anything, really. Something about the dream, perhaps. About how he'd felt when he'd woken up, that overwhelming feeling of inspiration. But talking about your dreams was possibly the dullest thing you could do.

"We're here," Iris proclaimed.

She opened a door and Kasper squinted against the light, knowing the moment was gone. Some things were easier to talk about in the dark.

It would be a long while before they spoke about Dark Cruelty again.

Appendix 5. Typed version of Kasper "Grim" Johansson's first letter to Håkan "Maimer" Nordin. Original version handwritten in black ink on lined notebook paper.

198███████*Timraw*

Hail Maimer!

I send word from the very center of Sweden. I recently visited the capital and had the fortune to purchase Dark Cruelty's first demo, "Sadistic Abomination." Upon my return, I shoved the cassette into my tape deck and HOLY FUCK!!!!!! The killer riffs slamming through my headphones destroyed my skull! The stains on this letter are, in other words, brain matter, and I'm writing to you from the other side with something of a proposal:

I'm the editor of Sweden's most evil metal fanzine, HEADED FOR DEATH, and would like to interview you. Should you be interested, write to the address below (you know the drill, return the stamps!!). If not, you can go to hell. Ha! I'm joking. Because I am in hell and we reject all POSERS!

Through Death I Rise!

Grim

P.S. If you want to trade tapes, consider me intrigued!!
P.S. 2. "Ancient Bloodlust" is without a doubt the best track you've made, but I suspect you already know that!

Headed for Death
c/o K. Johansson
Assway (Ashway)███
███████Sörberge

KASPER

The forests burned that summer. And that summer, The House became Kasper's world. He found a home in its dark corridors.

Dennis from the Magic Carpet Ride had been right: those who worked in The House kept to themselves. Each demon had their personal locker in one of the changing rooms, but most of them got changed at home or in one of The House's bathrooms. By half past twelve, there was a small gathering in the alley called Lilla Allmänna Gränd outside the office opposite the stage entrance. Most of the workers in Rides met earlier in the day, but The House didn't open until one. "One of the many benefits of working here," as Iris expressed it. "We open later and close up earlier. It's mostly toddlers before one o'clock, and too many bodily fluids after nine."

The office was in a wooden building, with a tall staircase leading up to it. Standing on the stairs were a couple of TLs who were in charge of the meeting. Kasper thought the team leaders looked unnaturally alert and vigorous in their crisp white shirts. It made sense that his stepbrother Tor had ended up among them; the moment they'd laid their eyes on him, they must have thought "one of us."

Every day began with a presentation of the previous day's numbers, and then a prediction of how many visitors were expected that day. Then the TL spoke loosely about the week's main company values, such as "Impossible doesn't live here" and how to apply that to your work. The black-clad demons lingered in the shade, listening patiently to earnest reminders about drinking enough water. Then they walked as one to The House and squeezed into the upper dressing room, which the demons used to get ready and run through the day's schedule. Between the two entrances was a long table supplied with sinks, makeup, and illuminated mirrors. At the very end of the room, outside of the bathroom, was a whiteboard. On it, the UCs had written the names of the twenty or so demons that worked The House for the season. The ones who quit or switched to some other job at Grönan were marked by a tiny cross or an RIP next to their names. Every day, Iris and Selam separated the present demons' names into two columns: makeup and mask. Makeup included scenes such as the Tombs and the Lab. Mask included the Chef and the Doll, as well as the register. The demons could mostly choose which route they wanted to be on, but variation was encouraged.

In the evening after closing down, everyone gathered in the great hall, Doctor Dreamcraft's laboratory. The demons sprawled across the staircase or leaned against the iron fence while Iris or Selam summarized the day with a TL present. Finally, the UC would ask if anyone had a funny guest story to share; most of the time, one or more of them had reacted in a hilarious or bizarre way. The most outrageous reactions were written down on a piece of paper that was posted on the wall in the upper-level dressing room. However, the guests' reactions weren't always funny. Demons were quite often forced to call security. On Kasper's third day at The House, it had been Santiago's turn to do so. A tall and skinny young man who, when he painted his face and shaved his head, could do a great imitation of Nosferatu in the old films. He'd worked in The House for six seasons.

"I timed it perfectly with this tiny little guy when I was the Possessed," Santiago said yawning, removing a bit of makeup that had stuck to his eyebrow. "And this fucking leprechaun lost it.

Started screaming and banging on the fence. So I ran and hid until he left."

"Did security get him?" Cornelia asked. She'd just returned from an acting course in England. She was working her first season in The House, as well as applying for jobs in television and movies, Kasper had heard her say.

"Unfortunately, the small rats are the quickest," Santiago concluded.

"You okay, though?" Selam asked.

"Another day at the office," Santiago sighed.

Iris had told Kasper that the bars and fences were there to protect the demons from the guests, not the other way around. Still, it wasn't until then that he'd really grasped what she meant.

"I saw a mom use her child as a human shield," Cornelia said. "That was . . . something else."

The demons' laughter was somewhat reserved. They were used to every kind of human behavior.

"For the record, can I just say that I miss the blood in the make-up," Santiago said.

A few demons murmured in agreement.

"You used to have blood?" Cornelia asked.

"We tried it last year," Selam admitted. "But a few of us got a bit too excited, didn't we?" She frowned at Santiago, who rolled his eyes. "The House isn't splatter."

"You can get your fill of blood during Halloween," Iris told Santiago.

Kasper felt a small tingle of excitement at the word. Most demons also worked during Halloween, and he'd heard some of them talking about how amazing it was, much wilder and more exciting than the summer season.

"The balcony was a fucking nightmare today." This came from Krille, the oldest of them all, now in his early thirties. No one knew what he did when he wasn't at Grönan, but most of them assumed that it was something suspicious. "We can't stand there when it's this hot," he went on. "Not even at night."

"All right," Selam said. "We'll let the Groundskeeper stay in the Lab for now."

"What happened to the new fans?" asked Jennifer, who was on her second season in The House.

"On their way," Iris said.

"That's what you said last week," Krille pointed out.

"I know," Iris said. "But this time I believe it's actually happening. Right, Elliot?"

Team leader Elliot, tall and freckled, looked up from his phone. Like all other TLs, he was glued to it.

"Huh?" he said.

"The fans?" Iris said.

"The fans!" Elliot's smile was slightly astonished, as if life had given him another lovely surprise he didn't quite know what to do with. "They are on their way! Yes! But please drink a lot of water, everyone."

A weary murmur of assent. The demons were tired and wanted to clock out.

Kasper felt dazed at the end of every shift, but when he changed back into his regular clothes, he'd be weirdly energized again. That's when the night really began. Iris and Selam had already brought together a loose gang consisting of Santiago, Cornelia, and Elliot. Sometimes they tried out some rides before heading to some open-air bar. Every Sunday, however, they'd follow Grönan's tradition, going to Skeppsbar to sweat along to ancient hits in the cellar. Sometimes they sang karaoke together. Most of the time, they'd end up at Cornelia's, since she lived in central Stockholm, close to St. John's Church, and her parents were "in the country" during the summer.

Kasper was the youngest member of the group, the others between twenty-one and twenty-five. Sometimes he wondered why he was included in it as he was still in high school. What did he have to add? Did Iris feel responsible for him after recruiting him to The House? Did she pity him? He tried to push those thoughts aside.

Every night before he fell asleep, the soundtrack from Doctor Dreamcraft's laboratory played over and over in his head. Lights flashed before his eyes. And the next day, it all began again. He sailed through it, high on endorphins and adrenaline. He could howl and roar, pound and kick on the doors. If he held back, he was doing a poor job. Not managing a scare could be embarrassing, but the high he got from pulling it off beat it. And he could share it all with the demons, the hits and the misses. But despite all their differences, they had a shared goal of scaring the shit out of people.

"Kasper!"

The high voice of a child cut through the sounds of the theme park and the ominous music from The House. Kasper peeked out from behind the cash register, which was in a small booth, and saw Leia and his mom coming toward him. They passed the witch's tree, which was a part of the Broom and spat fire whenever the ride passed by. His mom waved at Kasper, who waved back; he'd recommended they come when The House opened, because apart from there being fewer people, he could make sure he'd be at the register. He'd given them some of the tickets and wristbands he'd been rewarded after working his tenth shift.

"Kasper, did you know," Leia said as she wiggled through the fence, "once we get in, *I* am going to scare the ghosts."

She went up on her tiptoes by the desk, eyes shining behind the glasses she mostly refused to wear.

"All right, just don't scare them too much. They're my friends," Kasper said.

Leia laughed triumphantly. His mom, meanwhile, leaned in and gave him a hug. She smelled like sunscreen.

"You sure it's not too scary for them?" she whispered.

The age limit in The House was thirteen, but seven if accompanied by an adult.

"I'll tell them to be careful," Kasper whispered back, and his mom kissed his cheek, let him go.

She was wearing aviators and an old Girlschool tee with its sleeves cut off, which had accompanied her throughout Kasper's childhood.

"God*damn*, it's hot," she said, looking around. "Where did Diana and Atle get off to?"

"You sweared," Leia said.

"Moms are allowed to swear."

"Can I swear when I'm ten?" Leia asked.

Kasper caught sight of Diana, who was holding Atle by the hand until she reached the gate. Then she let go, carefully moving through the turns in the fence without making contact with it.

"Hey, Diana," Kasper said when she reached the register.

"Boo!" Leia shouted at Diana, who blinked.

Diana was eight years old and a year or so older than Leia, but Leia was taller. When Kasper visited the apartment, Leia would play with him until she grew tired, at which point Diana would take over. She shared Kasper's obsession with stories and myths. They would curl up together, making up and drawing new kinds of monsters.

"Kasper! What's up?" Atle called in his distinctive mix of Swedish and Norwegian.

When Atle and his mom first started seeing each other, Kasper had had some difficulty understanding him. Atle used to joke that he spoke "Sworwegian."

"Why aren't you in a zombie suit?" he went on.

"We've got to look 'normal' when we're at the register," Kasper told him.

Atle nodded, stroking a hand over his beard. Kasper had seen pictures of him as a teen, his huge spiked bracelets loose on his skinny arms. Nowadays he looked more like the antique statues Kasper had seen when he'd studied art history: a mature Hercules. Atle often tried to get Kasper to work out with him, but Kasper almost always turned him down. His body couldn't quite tell the difference between the increased pulse that came from working out and that which exploded into panic attacks. He'd often tried to go running, only to end up as a shivering heap on some park bench. Besides, and though he meant well, training with Atle was a blow against anyone's confidence.

"Kasper, is Icarus fun?" As usual, Leia was the most intrigued by the rides she was too little to go on.

"Yeah, it's probably my favorite next to The House."

Leia looked longingly at the tower, crowned by a sun. A group of guests shot up into the sky and hung there, suspended, for a moment. Then down again. Leia laughed.

"Icarus got a pair of wings from his dad," Diana informed Kasper. "But when he flew toward the sun, the wings melted and he crashed to earth and died."

"Exactly," Kasper said. Out of the corner of his eye, he saw his mom smile.

"Hello! I want to go in! Now!" Leia demanded, showing Kasper her wristband.

"Wristbands don't work in The House of Demons," Diana said, pulling at Leia's arm.

"Not like that," Atle told Diana calmly.

"Sorry," Diana said automatically, but she looked a little confused.

"You were right about the wristbands, Diana," his mom said,

placing the tickets Kasper had given her on the desk. "But Leia probably didn't know."

Diana bit her lip.

"All right," Kasper said. "I have to tell you about the rules now, so listen carefully."

Diana and Leia turned their faces toward him while he updated them about the rules in The House. Kasper's mom pushed Diana's bangs out of her eyes. They were both ginger haired, while Leia was dark blond, like Atle.

"Are you ready?" Kasper said, once he'd finished.

"Yes!" Leia shrieked, and Diana nodded determinedly, plugging her fingers in her ears in preparation. She was sensitive to loud noises.

"Welcome to The House," Kasper said as he opened the turnstile, watching his family approach the doors. "Kasper at the register here," he said into the two-way radio. "My little sisters are on their way, so take it easy, will you?"

"I read you," Santiago, lurking in the Tombs, replied.

"Loud and clear," Cornelia added from the Lab.

"No one gets to make Kasper's sisters cry," Iris said. "Be nice, all."

Thanks to the security cameras, Kasper could follow his family's tour through The House from his seat at the desk. It really did look as if Leia was trying to scare the demons. Diana walked as close to his mom as possible.

A man and a woman in their thirties approached the register. The woman was holding a huge soda. Kasper knew he had to tell her that drinks weren't allowed in The House. Most visitors didn't mind, but others seemed to be looking for an excuse to get upset. He smiled as politely as he could.

"I'm sorry, but you're going to have to leave that behind," he said, indicating her drink.

"Seriously?" the woman, who was clearly the other kind of visitor, snapped. "So what you're saying is I should throw it away? Throw my own money away?"

The man who was with her shifted uncomfortably.

"You can put it here," Kasper said, pointing at the ledge behind her.

"And you'll make sure no one spits in it, will you?" the woman said.

Kasper wondered what she did when she saw an abandoned soda.

"I can't be in charge of the things people leave here, but it's usually fine," he assured her.

The woman put aside her drink and rolled her eyes while the man paid. Kasper told them the rules and let them through the turnstile.

"Two on their way," he said quietly into the radio, and added, since it was their job: "Scare the shit out of them."

"That wasn't scary at all." It was Leia's voice.

The four of them came up to Kasper again. Diana looked thoughtful. She was probably mulling over questions to ask Kasper the next time they saw each other. His mom raised her phone to Kasper. He sighed, but he was used to it, having grown up with a photographer as a parent.

"I get why you like this job," his mom said, lowering her phone with a grin.

"Yeah, I really like it," Kasper said.

"And your friends are so sweet," she said. "They were so careful. I can tell they care about you."

Kasper felt himself smile.

He wanted nothing more than for her to be right.

There had been a time when Kasper had trusted easily. He'd had friends and taken them for granted in the way you should be allowed to do, counting on them to be there, assuming you were giving as much as you were given. Not every second, of course, but in the long run.

Kasper and Marco became friends in kindergarten, and in middle school they'd started hanging out with Oliver and Ali. They grew up together. Rode a snow racer down the steep slopes of the old gravel pit turned park, ran to the corner shop for a chocolate bar during recess despite the school's ban on sugar. Went to the mall and checked the games shop, back when it was still around. They went swimming in Child's Lake, scaring each other with stories about it being named after the drowned children that littered its depths.

In junior high they started talking about applying to Fredrika Bremer, so they could go to high school together. By their final year, though, Marco began mentioning prestigious schools in central Stockholm. He sat next to Kasper during classes, but disappeared with his girlfriend and her friends during lunch. He began to answer Kasper's messages sporadically, then rarely. It hurt, but Kasper still had Oliver and Ali. Everything would have been fine, if not for that feeling: always off rhythm, a bit too early, a little bit too late. Kasper was always the one waiting for Oliver and Ali. Either that, or the two of them were already there when he showed up. The two of them, and him. He still applied to the Tech program at Fredrika Bremer, because they'd all said they would. They were still his friends. And everything felt normal between them when they were playing League of Legends together. It's just that there had been a time when he hadn't thought of it as "normal." It just was.

The feeling didn't disappear. It only got worse. A dull ache, a heavy weight in his gut. During the summer between junior high and high school, they only got in touch when they were gaming.

And then one day in the beginning of freshman year, Marco wrote that they wanted to quit playing League. Oliver and Ali agreed. Kasper didn't understand what was going on; they'd played together for years, Kasper, Marco, Oliver, Ali, and Oliver's brother. Kasper hadn't noticed that they were getting sick of it. Something was definitely wrong, but Kasper tried not to think about it.

A week passed. Then another. When Kasper joined Oliver and Ali in the cafeteria, they'd fall silent or switch subjects. One evening he sat in his room and tried to make himself draw something, but what was the point? Everything he made was useless. The screen on his phone lit up; it was a message from Oliver in their old group chat. *Still on for nine?* Heart racing, Kasper took a screenshot. He immediately suspected that Oliver had made a mistake, sent a message in the wrong chat. When Oliver removed it, he knew he'd been right. They'd started playing without him. Probably replaced him with Carl from Marco's class in his fancy new school.

The pain was so sharp it left him breathless. He gasped, trying to force air back into his lungs. They had lied to him. Then the pain turned into anger. He sent the screenshot to the chat and added a message he instantly regretted. But it was too late. They'd seen how much he cared, how much of a child he was. They didn't even deny it, just wrote: *We thought you were the one who was over it. You've been so quiet. You've been so awkward. It felt like* you *didn't want to hang out with* us. They repeated it until Kasper went along with it. Blaming himself was easier than admitting his friends had let him down. Because that was the worst of it: he still wanted to stay friends with them.

How can you trust yourself to walk again when the ground's disappeared beneath your feet? You could just as well stay exactly where you were. It wasn't until he'd started working at Grönan that Kasper realized he hadn't moved from the same spot in years. The people he sometimes hung out with in school weren't really his friends. He'd never let them come close enough. Had never dared to find out if they were compatible as friends. He'd been holding back.

But he didn't want to hold back anymore.

He was trying to walk again, take one uncertain step after another.

His gaze fixed on the horizon.

Not looking down.

And it mostly turned out all right.

He was sitting in Cornelia's parents' living room with the others, listening in, adding a comment here and there. He even managed to make someone laugh, even though he felt off in this room, in this apartment, which was huge and probably cost a fortune. The ceiling was high, the decor a mix of antique and modern. Oil paintings framed in gold and abstract art hung on the walls. Everything looked expensive; he felt as if he was dirtying the armchair he was ensconced in.

An American rapper Kasper didn't know was playing on the stereo. Elliot, the team leader, was in the kitchen on the phone with his girlfriend. She was working in Gotland over the summer. Santiago dozed on the sofa with his legs across Selam's lap, while she texted frenetically. Cornelia and Iris lay on the thick carpets, comparing tattoos. As usual, Kasper was completely sober. Still, the general intoxication in the room infected him, somehow. He felt comfortably sluggish.

"Kasper." Cornelia looked up at him, her eyes big and blue. "Do you have any tattoos?"

"Jesus, Cornelia, he's a child," Selam said.

"He is not," Cornelia shot back. "He's of age. He's a young man."

She smiled at him, and Kasper felt himself flush. Was she making fun of him?

"No, but I've thought about it," he said. "And my dad's ex is a tattoo artist, so I'd like her to do it."

Kasper had spent a lot of time in Leah's studio when she and his dad were together. On Kasper's eighteenth birthday, she'd given him a voucher he could cash in whenever he felt ready. When he was a child, he'd been obsessed with drawing on his own skin, on his parents'. But when the chance to finally get a real tattoo came, he felt paralyzed with anxiety. He'd made countless drafts but couldn't settle on one.

"But you do art in school!" Cornelia said. "Maybe you could design my next one?"

Kasper doubted she was being serious.

"What would you like to have?" he asked, trying to make it sound like a neutral, theoretical question, and not like he'd gotten his hopes up over a joke.

"Another one of these," Cornelia said, pointing at the mermaid on her right bicep. "But a guy. Could you draw a really built mer . . . What do you call it?"

"A mer . . . guy?" Iris suggested, promptly collapsing with laughter.

"It isn't exactly my specialty . . ." Kasper trailed off.

"Huh?" Cornelia said, looking at him with some confusion.

Whenever she got drunk, she peppered people with questions and then immediately forgot she'd ever asked them.

"Mermen," Kasper clarified.

Cornelia didn't seem to take in what he was saying, tenderly stroking Iris's Dark Cruelty tattoo.

"Why make a logo no one can read? Because you want to come off as niche?"

"Sort of," Iris said, exchanging an amused look with Kasper. "But this one isn't that complicated."

"Yeah, you should see other logos," Kasper said.

"What was the deal, again? You and that band?" Cornelia turned to Kasper. "Your dad . . . He was the singer, wasn't he?"

"No, he was the bassist," Kasper said. "But it was his band, or whatever. He started it and wrote or cowrote all the songs. But it was a long time ago. In the eighties."

"What were they called?" Cornelia squinted at Iris's arm. "Dark . . ."

"Dark Cruelty," Iris said.

"Isn't that a weird name for a band," Cornelia said, taking a sip of Iris's beer. "How could cruelty be anything other than dark?"

"That's deep, man," Selam said, not looking up from the phone.

His dad claimed he didn't remember how he'd come up with the name, but Tony, who'd been along from the start, said that his dad had wanted something that reminded people of the band Dark Angel, "but meaner."

"He was, like, fifteen when he came up with it," Kasper said.

"Sorry," Santiago said sleepily. They all turned toward him. "Sorry if I've misunderstood or if it's, like, sensitive, but . . . Didn't someone die in that band? Didn't you tell us that, Iris? Last summer? When I asked about your tattoo, I mean."

Iris lowered her gaze and Kasper felt himself go cold. What had she told them? Personally, he'd never gone digging in the rumors surrounding Grim's fate. He'd picked up enough over the years, though, to know that there were some sick theories out there. Like the rest of the band sacrificing Grim to a demon in exchange for success.

"Yeah, the singer died," Kasper said. "Grim."

"Shit, I'm sorry," Cornelia said. "What happened to him?"

Kasper hesitated. When he'd been younger, he'd asked his dad the same question a few times. His dad had answered him, but then got awkward and quiet. He was happy to talk about Grim when he was alive, but he rarely and reluctantly talked about his death.

Kasper hadn't asked him about it for several years now. Why would he? He knew the story. It wasn't a secret. Still, it felt wrong to tell the others. Sensationalistic, in some way.

"No one really knows," he said, noticing Selam put her phone aside. There was something thrilling about being the center of attention, all of them focused on what he had to say. "It started with him disappearing. Which wasn't all that odd; he did that, now and then. Sometimes he'd be gone for days."

Like having a cat in the house, his grandma used to say, with a small, sad smile. She'd often talked about Grim, especially toward the end of her life.

"The thing was, he'd missed work that time. It wasn't like him," Kasper went on. "So my dad and a few others started calling everyone in the scene—"

"Which scene?" Cornelia interrupted.

"The death metal scene in Stockholm," Iris said.

"Did they wear tights and have big hair?" Cornelia asked. "Like Mötley Crüe?"

"Oh my God," Iris groaned. "Is that your only point of reference?"

"Metallica?" Cornelia suggested.

"No, that was thrash," Kasper said. All the little lectures his parents had given him meant he responded automatically: "Dad and his friends listened to that, too. Like Slayer, a bunch of bands from Germany and Brazil. Then death metal came along. It was a tiny scene at first, even globally, I mean."

"It's pretty cool that a group of ordinary Swedish kids helped shape an entire genre of music," Iris said. "And they were so young!"

Kasper smiled. His dad and his friends. Teenagers with long, unwashed hair, worn sneakers, and band T-shirts beneath flannel shirts. Carefully copying logos onto denim vests and jackets, band names written in white pen on the back of a leather jacket. When their guitar strings broke, they could barely afford new ones. They could never have imagined that people would be talking about them thirty years later. Or could they have?

"So, like, what does it sound like?" Cornelia asked.

"Imagine a group of Orcs starting a band," Selam said.

"She's not wrong," Iris conceded.

"Or a group of ringwraiths," Selam said.

"But that's more—" Iris began.

"Okay, not to be like that," Cornelia interrupted. "But I honestly don't understand how you can stand listening to it. It's just noise to me."

Kasper had heard that objection a thousand times. Theoretically, he got it, but he couldn't relate. He'd grown up with death metal. To him, it was just one of many types of music.

"You need to break through 'the wall'!" Iris said excitedly. "I was terrified the first time I heard death metal, but when you start listening intensely, you break through it. And then you hear it all! The riffs! The melodies!"

"Hallelujah," Santiago said.

"I'll make you a pedagogical playlist," Iris said.

"Okay, go on," Cornelia said, turning back to Kasper. "Grim disappeared and your dad and his friends called everyone."

"Yeah," Kasper said. "No one had seen Grim in ages. And then there was a knock on the door at my dad's place—well, Grandma's, he was still living at home at the time. It was the police. They told them they'd found Grim. There are loads of subterranean tunnels beneath Stockholm, service tunnels and things like that. They found him in one of those. Dead."

The music had stopped. The silence was only interrupted by the murmur of traffic, by Elliot mumbling in the kitchen.

"What was he doing in there?" Cornelia pressed. "In the tunnel?"

"Dunno," Kasper said. "He used to go off and explore abandoned buildings and shit. They took their band photos in one of them, for instance."

Both his dad and mom had told the story of that photo session. It had given rise to some of the mythmaking around Grim.

"Why'd he die, though?" Cornelia said with a hiccup.

"Maybe something congenital," Kasper said. "They couldn't find the cause of death. But it wasn't a murder or anything. There are rumors like that, but it's all bullshit."

Kasper snuck a look at Iris. She was inspecting her black nail varnish and seemed to avoid his eyes.

"How old was he?" Selam asked.

"Nineteen," Kasper replied. "It was right before his twentieth birthday."

"That's so fucking sad," Cornelia said.

"Yeah." Kasper nodded. "They broke up the band after that. Didn't feel right to keep going, Dad and Tony said. The drummer, that is."

At that point, Ernesto had already left the band. The other guitarist, Malte "Iago" Lundell, had been the only one who wanted to push on.

"Hang on a sec," Selam said to Iris. "Last summer, you said something about edgelords setting churches on fire and killing people. What's that got to do with this?"

"Not a lot," Iris said, shifting uncomfortably.

"I think I listened to a documentary about this." Santiago yawned.

"That all happened later," Iris said. "It's crazy, really. There was this moral panic about metal in the eighties. Like, right-wing Christian groups from the U.S. and Swedish parents' associations taking everything super literally, claiming that the bands were all homicidal Satanists. So a whole bunch of artists had to basically explain that what they were doing was theater and that they didn't really worship Satan."

"I hate it when you have to make that disclaimer," Selam said.

Santiago snorted with laughter.

"Right?" Iris said. "But in the beginning of the nineties, a group of Scandinavian bands ended up taking it very seriously. They said that, to them, it *wasn't* an image. They actually wanted to be evil. It turned into a competition of sorts, like, who could be the most extreme? They were the ones setting fire to churches and murdering people."

"That's crazy," Santiago said, swallowing another yawn.

Kasper thought of Atle, who'd played the guitar in a band like that in Norway in his teens. The singer and the drummer burned a chapel to the ground. The same crowd was connected to a homicide attempt. Atle had had enough and moved to his aunt's house in Sweden, where he met Tor's future mother. Nowadays, apart from being a health freak and Ironman, he was a creative director, and he only played the guitar for his daughters. Most of the people in his old scene had calmed down with age. But in some parts of the extreme metal scene, evil stayed in style. Malte Lundell started wearing it thirty years ago. He still hadn't changed.

The conversation flowed on. Cornelia told them about an urban legend from her old school, about a teacher who died and a student who vanished during a theater performance. Kasper had difficulty keeping up with the story, though. Something felt wrong, as if he'd skipped an important detail or said too much.

Iris still wouldn't look him in the eye.

He got up, walking over to an open window, leaned out with his hands clutching the windowsill.

Suddenly he understood exactly why Iris couldn't look at him. He was pathetic, trying to make himself interesting by talking about his dad's life, his dad's tragedies. All for a crumb of attention. It was disgusting. *He* was disgusting.

Everyone laughed at something Cornelia said. Kasper stayed by the window, frozen. St. John's Church rose up against the bright night sky. Part of the graveyard was right beneath the window. His dad had said that he and Grim used to hang out there sometimes, when they'd visited a nearby record shop.

What if they'd once sat down there, looking up at this window. And now Kasper was here, returning their gaze.

Two shapes moving between the graves. A moment of vertigo. He blinked and they were gone.

THE VOICE

Were you there when it happened, when Stockholm was a different city?

Maybe you hadn't been born yet.

Maybe you were a child.

Maybe you were in a different city, or a different country.

It doesn't matter, because you're there now: Regeringsgatan in the late eighties, in the beginning of March.

There's Håkan "Maimer" Nordin, sixteen years old. He's used to the chill coming through his worn leather jacket, the flannel shirt and thin T-shirt beneath it. There's a wad of cash in the pocket of his jeans, payday not far behind. The stitching on his right sneaker has come loose; in rain and slush, his sock gets soaked. This day, however, the sun has melted the snow off the pavement, and Håkan has more important things to spend his hard-earned money on than shoes. He walks across the overpass that spans the broad and busy street Kungsgatan. He's got a riff stuck in his head; it's been snaking through his skull since he stepped off the train. It would fit right into "Homicidal Intent," a song he's currently working on. *Chain saws cutting through your flesh . . . Entrails rotting on the floor . . . Your tongue ripped out . . . You scream no more . . . Your life is spent . . . Homicidal intent. . . .* That's all he's got so far.

The record store is in a gray building. It opened in the seventies. Håkan opens the door and hurries down a couple of steps. You follow.

Mekong Delta is playing loudly. Håkan greets the two men behind the desk, which fills most of the room. At this point, he knows both of them well enough. Håkan is one of the teenage metalheads who frequents the small shop, is a part of the group that is always on the lookout for something more extreme. Even when they're young and mostly dead broke, they're decent customers: once they get their hands on some cash, they spend it all on records. They come from all over Stockholm, from all over the country. Strangers meet, become friends, start bands together. The shop happily sells their demos. Something is moving among them, these fresh, young bands in Stockholm. Something is beginning.

Håkan stops at the notice board. A black-haired guy is lingering by the listening station, headphones on. Håkan does not recognize him. He reads whatever's been pinned to the board so far. *Distortion pedal for sale . . . Can you play the drums like Dave Lombardo? GIVE US A CALL.* Håkan stuffs a hand into his jacket pocket and pulls out the crumpled note. He borrows a roll of tape from the front desk, holds the paper up to the board with one hand, uses his other hand for the tape. At the end of the piece of paper are several smaller notes, made to tear away with ease, and they have his phone number on them. He takes a step back and feels a thrill go through him when he reads the text: *Dark Cruelty is looking for a new singer!!*

Ernesto has had enough. He'd been unhappy about singing when he'd joined the band, seeing himself, first and foremost, as a guitarist. Recently he'd been moaning about fucking up his voice. It's all bullshit, Håkan knows, but he also knows that they should look for someone who at the very least *wants* to front the band. And in some secret part of him, he knows that Ernesto's vocals won't be enough for the kind of band Dark Cruelty should be.

Håkan mentally reviews the people who might get in touch with him. He knows or knows of most of the people in the death metal scene. A bunch of them meet up at the central train station every weekend and then head off to some party, or bring the party with them, ride the subway back and forth with the latest demo streaming from a shitty cassette player, downing whatever alcohol they'd gotten their hands on. Håkan could easily have asked someone in that crew. Both Tony and Ernesto felt that putting up an ad was unnecessary, but Håkan had insisted. First of all, free advertising's never a bad thing. Second of all, they might come across someone new. The death metal scene is so small it hardly exists, but it's growing.

"You're Maimer, aren't you?"

The voice barely cuts through the intense guitar riffs. A northern accent. Håkan looks up. It's the guy from the listening station. He's a little taller than Håkan, and his long black hair has a curl to it. Black leather jacket, black jeans, and combat boots. If it hadn't been for the Venom tee—which looks professional, despite it being homemade—Håkan would have taken him for a goth. He's carrying a turquoise sports bag.

"I knew you from the photo," the guy says, stretching out a hand. He still hasn't met Håkan's gaze, but the handshake is firm. "Grim," he adds.

Realization hits him. Håkan beams at the boy.

"Headed for Death!"

This autumn, Håkan was interviewed for the fanzine, which had rapidly become one of the most lauded fanzines in their tiny circle. He and Grim had exchanged letters and cassettes with each other ever since. It's called tape trading, and the network stretches across the globe, from Scandinavia and the rest of Europe to North America and South America. Grim is even in touch with a Japanese guy. Most of the people they trade with have their own bands, fanzines, or both. Demos and rehearsals travel across the world. Håkan usually has four, five letters waiting for him when he gets home, even more after the weekend. He bristles with excitement every time he tears open an envelope, especially when it contains music he's never heard before.

When he started it, his mom had asked how on earth he could afford all those stamps. Håkan had showed her: a thin layer of glue on the stamps and clear instructions in the accompanying letter: *Return the stamps!* When he got them back, he held them over steam or simmering water until the glue came off, and then left them to dry on a towel in his room. After that, you could just re-use them. His mom had looked amazed, as if he was some kind of criminal genius, but they all did it.

"So you're in town, huh," Håkan says to Grim.

He doesn't know much about Grim's life, except that he lives outside of Sundsvall, in Timrå, or Timraw, as he ironically refers to it in his letters. Håkan doesn't even know if his legal name is Grim, but doubts it considering the address is c/o K. Johansson. Is "K" for Karl, Klas, Krister, Kristian, or Kristoffer? Asking him had always felt wrong. He always signs off with: *Through Death I Rise! Grim.*

"Yup. It's the winter holidays," Grim says. "A week later than in Stockholm."

"So you're in high school, then?"

Håkan is unsure of Grim's age, but he's going to find out that Grim is two years older than him and in his final year.

"Yup," Grim responds and blinks. His eyes are dark, almost black. "Not up to much else. Except the zine."

Håkan nods. The only band member who's in high school is Ernesto, and that's mostly for his mom's sake. Tony's still in junior high. As for Håkan, he tried his hand at a vocational program, Electricity, but had his fill after one term. Since Christmas, he's been working for the Postal Service. The sorting center is pretty far away, but it's better than slaving away in the warehouses in Jordbro's industrial area with his old classmates.

"So are you getting anything?" Håkan asked Grim.

"No, I'm broke. I hitchhiked. Thought it would turn out all right. Or I'll just go back again."

"Right."

Håkan is fascinated and confused. It's only several years later that he'll be able to explain what he felt: on one hand, Grim seemed so confident and visionary, especially in his letters. On the other hand, he came off as shy and younger than he was, wouldn't make eye contact. Even thirty years later, Håkan found him difficult to understand. But he obviously wouldn't know that now, as the two of them stand by the notice board.

"What do you think?" Håkan says, nodding at the speakers.

"Pretentious German thrash," Grim scoffs.

They grin at each other.

"I'm having a look around," Håkan says.

Grim nods, following him through the stacks, commenting on different musicians and bands. Håkan recognizes the way he speaks from the letters. He's drawn to extremes, full of worship or scorn, and has a subtle but quirky sense of humor that makes Håkan laugh out loud. Grim is awkward, but they quickly find a rhythm to the conversation, maybe because of the long letters they've exchanged, the music they've shared. Maybe both of them feel as though fate has brought them together.

Eventually, Håkan ends up buying an album by another German band neither Grim nor anyone he knows has. It's the best way to maximize the collection: everyone gets different albums and copies them to cassettes.

"We're rehearsing tonight," Håkan says as they wait by the register. "You coming?"

"All right," Grim says. "Can I stay at your place after?"

"Sure," Håkan says.

His mom is used to friends from out of town sleeping on a mattress on his floor.

"All right," Grim says again.

While they walk toward the entrance, Grim lunges at the notice board and tears down the ad Håkan just put up. Håkan has no time to react until they're on the street, only managing to say:

"What?"

"I'm interested," Grim says, pressing the piece of paper into Håkan's hand.

A few hours later, Håkan opens the door to the rehearsal space and walks in, closely followed by Grim.

Tony and Ernesto have just popped open a soda each. They're sitting in the messy room, where they rehearse three times a week, and blink wonderingly up at Håkan: he's usually never late. Then they spot the stranger behind him—his long black hair and black clothes, the Venom tee. They look back at Håkan with an expression that says: *And who the fuck is this?*

"This is Grim," Håkan says, an answer to that unspoken question. "He does *Headed for Death*."

Ernesto and Tony nod, this time with approval and respect.

"Hi," Ernesto says.

"Hey," Tony says.

"So this is Ernesto and Tony," Håkan says, pointing them out.

Grim nods, his gaze lowered. Picks up a mic and weighs it in his hand. He knows Dark Cruelty's songs by heart, he'd told Håkan; he's listened to their demo and a rehearsal tape several times over.

"He's trying out as singer," Håkan says, plugging in his bass guitar and starting to tune it. "We'll do 'Ancient Bloodlust.'"

Ernesto and Tony hate being told what to do. Even though Håkan writes most of the songs and founded Dark Cruelty, they've agreed to make all the major decisions concerning the band together.

But this feels like a decision they've all made together.

Tony grabs his drumsticks, begins to count off.

The first riff rolls out, slow, repetitive. Drums like a funeral march. Grim closes his eyes, stretches out a hand, crooked like a claw, as if toward an invisible audience.

Decrepit tombstones . . . In the moonlight I awake . . .

That voice isn't human. It belongs to something that's just crawled out of a grave, with dirt in its desiccated throat, a smattering of maggots with every shambling step.

My victim's scream . . . it's the music of the night . . .

Håkan gets goose bumps all over his body, including his face.

For the first time ever, they sound like they're supposed to. The music oozes evil. He doesn't have to look at Ernesto to know that he agrees; he can tell by the way he's playing, can tell by the way Tony plays when the tempo shifts and the song tips into sheer frenzy.

Tear out your throat . . . blood in my mouth . . . Eternal thirst . . . Ancient . . . bloodlust . . . Ancient . . . bloodlust . . .

Most of the time, you only realize what moments like these mean in hindsight. Sometimes, however, you can feel them happen.

The right people, in the right place, at the right time. Fate slamming right into your solar plexus. When the music stops, they're breathless. And then Tony screams.

Grim moves to Stockholm two weeks later.

KASPER

The sun shone mercilessly every single day. Not even the nights were cool. The days became the same, somehow, when morning, afternoon, and evening were all equally as warm. They stuck together. Kasper ran with it. Sometimes he could feel anxiety breathing down his neck, but he ignored it. The routine made it easy to refrain from thinking. One step at a time. Quick breakfast, shower, the train into the city, hanging out with the demons, collapsing at home or on one of Cornelia's couches. Repeat. Even on his days off he spent time with people from work.

But then there was a day during the week right after midsummer, when Selam was going on a date, Elliot was sick, Cornelia was on an island somewhere, and Santiago was eating dinner with his boyfriend's family. At lunch in the green room, Iris said that she was going straight home after work to curl up with Caligari the cat.

"I just want to cuddle a kitty, eat ice cream, and sleep. Sleep is number one."

She did look exhausted.

Kasper realized how much he longed for sleep, too, for just staying in. His dad and he had mismatched schedules, only occasionally exchanging a word in passing. He hadn't seen his mom and his sisters since that day at Grönan. He missed his family, but hadn't really thought about it until everyone else was busy.

Why did he erase himself when he was with people he liked? If they wanted to see him, he wouldn't turn them down, regardless of whether or not he was feeling up for it. His will, his desires, dissolved and disappeared.

That's why they got sick of you.

The thought crashed into him when he stood on the ferry on the way home. He couldn't get away from it.

That's why they got sick of you—Marco, Oliver, and Ali.

The psychologist had told Kasper not to be ashamed that his friends had abandoned him. The moment she'd said it, he'd felt even more ashamed. He got an image in his head of an abandoned, whining puppy who'd been kicked out of the house and wouldn't stop scratching at the door.

You were too passive, too weak, too eager to please. You even chose Tech in high school because Oliver and Ali did. Pathetic. And you haven't changed at all.

He got off at the ferry stop Gamla Stan, the oldest part of the city, and set off past Slussen, which had turned into a huge contruction site. The wind blew but didn't cool him down, and the moment it ceased, the air felt drained of oxygen. Sweat poured off him. The thoughts kept coming on the way to Södra station. They felt more real than anything around him.

You're just a clingy fucking kid. Selam even said it: he's just a child. Every joke contains a grain of truth. Isn't that right? Isn't it?

When he reached the platform, the air was unbelievably suffocating, and the train was late. Of course. He leaned against a pillar, trying to breathe the way the psychologist had taught him. His thoughts and his pulse raced against one another. Why had Selam been so vague about her date? Didn't Iris lower her eyes when she said she was chilling with the cat today? At home with the cat, what an obvious excuse.

Of course they'd rather hang out without you. Iris is twenty-one and Selam is twenty-two, you're not even nineteen. They've only kept you around this long to be nice. Maybe Iris thought you were interesting for a bit, but that was because of your dad. She's seen how sad you are, how pathetic, how disgusting, trying to use him to make yourself seem special. They're sick of you.

The train stopped at the station and he stepped on board. It was slightly cooler inside. A man was eating pizza straight out of the box, the scent of melted cheese making Kasper faintly nauseated. He sat down and scrolled through his phone. Nothing new anywhere. Cold sweat made him shiver. He put his headphones on, chose a relaxing playlist. Closed his eyes. Breathed. Breathed. When he opened his eyes again, he was in Skogås. Almost home.

The hallway felt like a sauna.

"Hello?" Kasper called, pulling the door shut behind him.

Silence.

He was sure his dad had said he'd be in tonight. Had he misunderstood, somehow?

Kasper tossed his bag aside and kicked off his shoes. The bathroom door was open, so he threw his sweaty socks straight into the laundry basket. The T-shirt followed. He caught a glimpse of himself in the hallway mirror, in jeans, shirtless. The dark hair fell lifelessly over his shoulders. A few pimples shone on his pale forehead. The thick makeup that alternated with full-face plastic masks didn't exactly do wonders for his skin. He'd call himself short, too, despite his dad pointing out that he was actually an inch taller than punk legend Iggy Pop. He tried to straighten up, but it was as though his shoulders were stuck in a slouch. He turned his arms over. They were neither as strong as Atle's nor as wiry as his dad's. *A child's arms.*

He turned away, disgusted, and stalked into the kitchen. Took an ice pack out of the freezer, wrapped it in a kitchen towel, and pressed it against his neck and throat. Then he opened windows around the apartment. Not that it helped—it was as suffocatingly hot outdoors as indoors. He had to let the water run for ages before it turned cold and he could fill a tall glass.

His heart didn't beat as painfully hard when he finally entered his room. That storm of emotion had passed, his anxiety muted, a dull ache. He opened the window and looked out over the straight trees growing in the patch of forest between the houses. It wasn't dark yet. A blackbird trilled half-heartedly. Boys could be heard in the distance, one of them hollering, "OW, OW, OW," and then bursting into laughter. Kasper put on *Seventh Son of a Seventh Son*. He was used to having sound and music around. During his childhood, there was always a record on, a recorded live show on the TV screen, his mom talking on the phone with a friend while sewing, or with his dad who sat with a guitar on his knee.

While "Moonchild" played, Kasper reached for the sketchbook next to the computer. Over the spring, he'd drawn almost every day, working out ideas for his final project, which would complete his high school education. He'd settled on drawing places in Handen and add the mythological figures and creatures they were named after. Poseidon in the fountain at Poseidon's Square, Sleipner galloping down Sleipnervägen. Drawing an eight-legged horse that looked somewhat realistic had turned out to be an absolute nightmare.

But he hadn't drawn anything at all since dreaming about Grim.

He tried to tell himself that it didn't mean that the depression had returned. It didn't have to be a sign that he was spiraling. He leafed through his sketchbook. He'd posted some of the more accomplished drawings to a social media account he didn't use anymore. No one but classmates, family, and some bots had followed him, and the scant number of likes only made him feel dejected. Sometimes he felt he ought to go for it, get his stuff out there, try to gain followers. But was he even good enough? Now, assessing the things he'd posted six months ago, he found them all embarrassingly bad. So how could he trust himself to know if the things he drew now were worth showing off? Why couldn't he just *look* at the things he made?

Because your gaze is as underdeveloped as your technique. You should be practicing. You should buy a tablet and learn digital drawing.

Should, should, should. The more he thought that way, the more impossible it became to just do it.

He stopped at the drawing of Grim. He had done so several times before. At first, he always thought, *This is good.* And then, *I'll never be able to do this again.*

A crackling sound could be heard in the brief silence before "Infinite Dreams" began. Kasper turned the music off, listening. A rhythmical *pop, pop.* Like when a vinyl keeps spinning after it's played.

Kasper got up and walked to the living room. Shelves lined the walls, full of films, games, and mostly music. His dad had thousands of records, mostly vinyl. Rock and heavy metal, punk and hardcore, soul, blues, jazz, and some country. But also Bach and Beethoven, old-school hip hop, some electronic stuff and pop. Most of the music was from the last millennium.

Kasper went up to the record player. It was empty. The speakers were on, though, and hissing. He turned them off. It wasn't like his dad to leave tech on. That was another thing his grandma had imprinted in him. *Think about the bills, will you, Håkan?*

Something heavy fell to the floor with a thud.

Kasper felt the hairs at the back of his neck stand up.

The sound had come from his dad's bedroom.

He went up to the door and then stopped. Listened. Silence again.

Kasper remembered all those times his dad had hid and then suddenly jumped out, scaring him and his friends. His dad's patience was legendary. Once, he lay behind the couch for an hour. But that had been a long time ago.

"Dad?"

No response.

He pushed the door open.

A plastic box on the bed had tipped over. A shapeless heap lay on the floor beside it. Kasper turned on the overhead lamp, blinking against the light.

It was a mess of objects. He sat down and picked up a denim vest. His dad's old battle jacket from the eighties; he'd shown it to Kasper before. Death's logo was carefully drawn on the back, above Repulsion's and Necrovore's. "No Posers" on the front, Autopsy's right over the heart. "We couldn't just buy patches with whatever logo on it back then," his dad used to say.

Kasper lifted up a washed-out T-shirt. His dad hadn't been able to bring himself to throw it away, as it was one of the thirty Malodor shirts they had ordered for their first gig. "I probably know the name of every single person who's got one," his dad had said.

Beneath the shirt was a long knife in a taped sheath. It lay on top of an issue of Grim's fanzine, *Headed for Death*. Its pages were photocopied in black and white, folded, and stapled together. The cover bore one of Grim's illustrations: a decapitated head vomiting black gall. Iris would be overjoyed if he brought it to work, or even sent her a picture.

The puppy wants attention.

The shame he felt almost made him heave. But that's when he saw the vinyl.

It was beneath a sweater. Kasper brought it closer and went cold as ice. There were scratches in the black plastic, ugly scars. Somebody had ruined it deliberately, carved into it on both sides. The stickers were discolored, but the title on the B-side was legible.

Ancient Bloodlust.

Hardly any records were released in the Swedish death metal scene at the end of the eighties. Bands exchanged and sold demos and recordings from rehearsals. Dark Cruelty did two demos and a few rehearsals, but their final release was an EP on vinyl, named after their most iconic song. "Ancient Bloodlust." His dad and Grim had numbered the 666 copies by hand. The original pressings were sought after by many record collectors that specialized in metal. The few times his dad handled his own copies, he always washed his hands. This had to be a reissue, one that had been produced around the twenty-year anniversary.

At that moment, Kasper caught sight of the black cover beneath a leather jacket, practically in camouflage. He pulled it out. It was slightly water-damaged and uneven. Still, Dark Cruelty's logo shone in white at the top of the cover. At the bottom: *Ancient Bloodlust*, in the font Old English. In the center was a drawing of a goat's skull on top of an inverted cross, a snake twining through its empty sockets. Grim's work, of course.

Kasper turned the sleeve over. The moment he saw the picture of the band, he realized he was looking at an original pressing. All five of them were in it, photographed in black-and-white.

Five pale faces surrounded by darkness. Only the stage names were written down: Berserker, Morbid Eradicator, Maimer, Grim, and Iago. Malte "Iago" Lundell was missing from the most recent edition of the EP.

Kasper checked the number.

1/666

His dad had number 2, 666, and a few others in his own collection. He'd always said Grim got number 1, and that it had gone missing. Had another number accidentally been erased? Kasper turned the sleeve over in his hands again, but saw no sign that anything had come off or been covered over. This really was the missing record. Number 1.

He laid the cover on the floor in front of him, staring at the photo his mom had taken. The faces were lit from below by a strong light source.

Ernesto "Morbid Eradicator" Moberg had his arms crossed over his chest, his black hair hanging in front of his face. Tony "Berserker" Lehtonen towered in the background. Håkan "Maimer" Nordin looked entranced, eyes wide, and was holding a candelabra with lit black candles in it. He'd painted himself black around the eyes, like Grim, who bent his head backward and stared straight into the camera. His black hair blended into the background, and he was holding a knife that pointed downward. Malte "Iago" Lundell, in makeup, too, glared murderously into the camera, from where he was standing to the right.

The knife.

Kasper felt stupid for not making the connection until now. He'd seen this photo thousands of times. He picked up the knife on top of the fanzine and pulled it out of the sheath. The blade was long, thin, and looked sharp. The wooden handle had cracked slightly, felt dry and rough against Kasper's fingers when he gripped it and pointed it downward, like on the photo. It had to be the same knife.

His dad loved to talk about the scene in the eighties and gladly got out old fanzines and flyers. He leafed through photo albums and told Kasper long, involved anecdotes. That's how Kasper knew that the candelabra on the photo had belonged to Ernesto's mom and now stood in the freshly built studio in his home. But he couldn't recall his dad ever saying anything about this knife. He definitely hadn't shown it to Kasper.

Not that that meant anything in and of itself. Kasper wouldn't have thought about it twice if it hadn't been for the scratched record, the one that was supposed to be missing. But maybe he'd misunderstood, or his dad had discovered it somewhere and not mentioned it.

Kasper suddenly felt ill at ease, rifling through his dad's private things. He grabbed the badly mended sheath and stuck the knife back into it.

A sharp pain in his left hand.

It took a moment before he realized what had happened. The tip had gone through the haphazardly patched-up sheath, slicing across the palm of his hand. Bright crimson blood welled up, dripped onto the cover.

"Fuck," Kasper said.

One leg had gone numb, so he stumbled out of the room and into the kitchen. Using the fingers of his left hand, he pressed a roll of paper towels against his bleeding palm, keeping his hand above his head to stem the flow, then he brought the entire roll with him into his dad's bedroom. The thick, ribbed paper soaked up the blood from the band photo. His dad probably wouldn't see a difference; the cover was in a bad way, anyway.

Kasper got up, keeping his hand cupped so as not to trail blood on the floor. How deep was the cut? Would he need stitches?

He went into the bathroom, turned the light on, saw his grimace in the mirror. Blood dripped onto the white porcelain sink. He threw the paper away and rinsed his hand, inspecting the wound. It was about an inch long and ran from the area between his thumb and forefinger, continuing across the palm. It didn't look too bad, but he was bleeding heavily.

"Fuck," he muttered again.

He rifled through the cabinet and found a roll of adhesive bandage. He tried to hold his hand up while wedging the roll between his elbow and his body, and then cut a crooked piece off with a tiny pair of dull scissors. A thin trickle of blood tickled his wrist. He tore at the roll of toilet paper and wiped it off.

The scratched record flashed before his eyes while he tried to get the bandage to stick to his damp palm. His dad had told him about when he and Grim got the records delivered, the way they'd sat in his room, surrounded by piles of records to number. They had considered writing in blood, his dad had said with a laugh, but they'd agreed it would be too messy.

Well, there was blood on the cover now.

Kasper sniggered, throwing the crumpled bandage into the bin. He washed away more blood, light-headed, and tried again with the roll and scissors.

His dad had told him about how proud he and Grim had been of the vinyl, something solid they'd created together. They'd talked about Interrailing, traveling through Europe and getting record stores to stock the EP, maybe get the band some gigs, too.

But just as everything was about to begin, Grim died.

Grim, who was holding the knife in the photo.

It didn't mean anything in particular that his dad hadn't mentioned owning the knife.

It didn't mean anything, really, that he'd said that number 1 was missing.

Still, Kasper felt the same way he had at Cornelia's, when Iris wouldn't meet his gaze.

Something was off.

He finally got the bandage to stick. He looked at himself in the mirror. He looked pale, sickly. The wound throbbed. Black spots danced in the corner of his vision. Long black hair against the white tiles.

Kasper held on to the sink and threw up.

THE SUMMER

The first summer. The best summer.

Grim has been in Stockholm for a few months now.

The days are long, the nights endless. They are young; they will sleep later. The parks are their living rooms. Ernesto has a girlfriend, Linda, whom he met at a punk gig. They party at her house in Tyresö when her parents are gone. Her fancy home on Fornudden fills up with boys who drink beer and headbang to music they've turned up to the max. If anyone has got their hands on a hotly anticipated album, they play it all night to celebrate. Ernesto and Linda make out all over the place, their hands shoved into the back pockets of each other's jeans. Tony walks around in a Panama hat belonging to Linda's dad, pretending he's Klaus Kinski in *Fitzcarraldo*. At the end of the evening, he's sleeping peacefully in some corner. Grim doesn't like to drink, but he helpfully holds Håkan's hair while he pukes in Linda's mom's spirea bushes.

They've been rehearsing intensely since Grim moved. Because he also plays guitar, they've got two guitarists in the band now. This opens up new horizons. Grim has his own guitar—a shitty copy of a Stratocaster—and a small amp. He and Håkan try out riffs for hours. They've decided to record a demo with new songs this autumn, but have already recorded a rehearsal demo in the studio, with a new version of "Ancient Bloodlust" and a Venom cover. Grim's art for it is inspired by the silent film *Nosferatu*. This is the first time their real names aren't on it.

The stage names hadn't been deadly serious when Håkan started Dark Cruelty; he'd mostly been inspired by Venom and other bands who used them, sometimes completely hiding behind their assumed monikers. Håkan had never gone that far before: on the demo *Sadistic Abomination*, it simply says Håkan *"Maimer" Nordin*. Grim, however, has never published his given name anywhere. Not many people outside the inner circle know what his birth certificate says. He told Håkan it was his plan all along to create a persona, since starting *Headed for Death* and tape trading. Håkan is taken with his foresight. They can build on it together now. From now on, they'll be known as as Grim, Maimer, Berserker, and Morbid Eradicator on everything they release.

"We should make people think that we really are a group of maniacs," Grim says, when he and Håkan sit among the graves at St. John's Church.

They're all working their fingers to the bone for the demo. Tony, who just finished junior high, works at a garage as a mechanic. Ernesto is at Clock this summer, detesting every burger-flipping second of it. Håkan and Grim like working at the sorting center. The two of them sort letters, laugh at the things people wrote on their postcards, and talk about music and visions for the band. When they were exchanging letters, Grim had mentioned that he was skeptical about the music being as brutal as possible, the lyrics so over the top in their violence.

"I like splatter," Grim emphasizes, while he's accompanying Håkan on a smoke break, both of them hiding from the heat of the day in the shade. "And Malodor and Exenterate do it well. But it doesn't actually scare you."

"Exactly, yeah," Håkan says, turning to his mom's friend, Lillemor, who's on her way out of the building. She got him the job. "Can I have a smoke?"

"Of course, sweetie," Lillemor says, her voice raspy, handing

Håkan a cigarette and patting Grim on the cheek. "Good for you for not smoking. People are always complaining about you metal-heads, but I've always said they're nice boys."

Her eyes fill with tears, and she leaves them to be alone for a moment. Lillemor has a son, Kjell-Åke, who is six years older than Håkan and as sweet as his mom. He used to lend his records to Håkan and Tony when they were kids, Kiss and Alice Cooper. Nowadays he's swaying with the other junkies in the depressing square Plattan by the Stockholm Central Station. Håkan has seen him around.

"There are two sides to death metal, if you think about it," Grim continues, apparently unbothered by Lillemor's sad eyes. "On the one hand, *death* is blood and gore and all that. But *death* is also philosophy, the end, if there's anything beyond the material realm. The occult is death metal, too."

Håkan nods. Since they decided that Grim would sing, he's put aside "Homicidal Intent." It must be possible to evoke that raw, evil sensation in other ways than by describing chain saw dissections. He discusses these things with Grim, who's still staying in Håkan's room, paying Håkan's mom a small fee as rent. They're often awake all night, whispering to each other, writing letters and listening to the latest batch of tapes. Sometimes the music has been passed on from person to person, someone making a copy of a tape that is already a copy of a copy of a crappy recording from a rehearsal space. By the time it reaches Håkan and Grim, you can't tell the static from the music. But that makes it even more intriguing. They want that sense of mystery, of discovering someone hidden, forbidden.

"We should hide messages in the lyrics," Grim whispers one night. "Only people who have been initiated like we have will get it."

Their initiation consists of them having devoured two books Grim brought along from home. *Necronomicon*, a worn paper-back that claims, in its introduction, to be the original version of the diabolical book H. P. Lovecraft wrote about in his short stories. Grim has explained to Håkan that it's probably fake, seeing as "a book that dangerous could never end up as a paperback," but there's a grain of truth in it. The other book is a history of magic. The British author treats his subject with a heavy dose of sarcasm, but Grim and Håkan want to believe, especially Grim. The only thing they can't see eye to eye on is numerology, the idea that each letter in the alphabet can be replaced with a number, and that said number reveals your destiny. Grim demonstrates this with a quick calculation: G = 7, R = 9, I = 9, and M = 4. 7+9+9+4 = 29 = 2+9 = 11.

"Eleven is a master number," Grim says, dark eyes shining. "An eleven is a visionary or a prophet, people who can change the world. They don't always succeed, but when I gave myself this name, I also gave myself *potential*. Do you see?"

Håkan does not. He can't imagine anything less magical than math and refuses to engage with it. He prefers talking about their favorite books, such as *Dracula*, *Frankenstein*, *Strange Case of Dr. Jekyll and Mr. Hyde*. They binge old horror comics they buy secondhand, go to the library and rifle through heavy English dictionaries, write down interesting words. Grim borrows poetry, becoming obsessed with some French poet called Charles Baudelaire.

"Fiendishly good," says Grim.

During the summer, Håkan and Grim construct a new vision together. It's a darker vision, combining death metal with the satanic influence of some favorite bands from the early eighties. A sound that conveys pure malevolence, an ice-cold hand in the darkness, squeezing your heart. *An ice-cold hand of doom, . . . Crushing my heart in the dark*, Håkan writes the lyrics for their new song, "Nocturnal Allegiance," and Grim adds, *Flowers of evil entwining their roots, . . . In the rotten soil of my soul. . . . I pledge allegiance, . . . To powers that shatter the world, . . . In the dark of the night, . . . I implore their boon.*

One morning Grim shoves a new logo in Håkan's sleepy face. It's so perfect the hairs stand up on his arms.

"Didn't know we needed a new one," Ernesto says when they all come together in the rehearsal space.

"But it's wicked, though," Tony says.

"*Wicked*," Ernesto repeats in a shrill voice. A drumstick hits him in the forehead. "Fuck's sake, that could have ended up in my eye!"

"Sorry," Tony says, smirking.

Håkan can tell Ernesto's going to be grumpy. When he's in the mood, he could easily end up in *The Guinness Book of World Records* as the Grumpiest Guy Ever.

"This new logo fits with the new direction we're going in," Håkan says. "More mysticism and occultism, but still death metal."

"We can leave the brutality to Malodor and Exenterate," Grim says, hands in his pockets and gaze firmly fixed on the floor. "Less 'Sadistic Abomination,' more 'Ancient Bloodlust.'"

Håkan winces. Grim shouldn't have mentioned "Sadistic Abomination," not now. Håkan and Ernesto wrote that one together.

"Maybe you don't need me in the band anymore," Ernesto scoffs. "Looks like you've got it all figured out."

"Come on, man," Håkan pleads.

Grim blinks. Whenever he's stressed, he starts blinking as if he's got something in his eye.

"Of course we need you," he says.

"You play the guitar, too, though . . ." Ernesto trails off. "I can't be bothered. Shit."

He removes the guitar, putting it back in its case. Tony is staring silently at a cymbal. Grim is still blinking, as if it could help him see a way out. Håkan doesn't know what to do, but supposes the best thing is to let Ernesto walk off and calm down.

"Ernesto!" Grim says.

Håkan freezes.

"What?" Ernesto barks, snapping the case shut.

"First of all, we need two guitarists," Grim says. "Second of all, you're the most skilled guitarist. If I keep practicing, I might end up reaching your level, but you're far better than me."

Ernesto looks up. Stares at Grim. Then he starts laughing. "It is what it is," Grim says.

"Yeah, I know, you fucking weirdo," Ernesto chuckles.

"We're taking new photos, too," Håkan says, trying to get Ernesto back on board now that he's in a better mood. "And we're recording the demo in a different studio this time."

Sadistic Abomination was recorded in a studio belonging to a friend of Tony's parents, who are both members of the punk band Preacher's Perversions. He turned out to hate metal and the recording sounded like shit. Tony's mom yelled at him afterward, and the whole thing was embarrassing enough that none of them wants to go back there, least of all Tony.

"The studio that Exenterate used seems decent enough," Ernesto says.

"And next year we're going to release a record," Grim says. "An EP."

Everyone gawks at him, including Håkan. They've talked about it plenty of times, but never like this, like it would happen.

"Uh . . ." Ernesto raises his eyebrows. "A record deal? That small detail?"

"We'll release it on our own label," Grim counters. "Like Tyrannize."

"Who?" Tony says.

He and Ernesto aren't into tape trading. They're not as informed as Håkan and Grim.

"Thrash band from Uppsala." Håkan turns to Grim. "What, they have an EP coming out?"

"Yup. They've already recorded it. Out in a few months," Grim says. "Veljko wrote and told me how they did it."

Håkan can't hide his surprise. Not only had he not been aware of Tyrannize's upcoming release, he'd also had no idea that Grim was writing letters to the drummer and songwriter, Veljko Marić, who's at least twenty-five.

"Isn't that really expensive, though?" Tony says.

"We're not talking full-length," Ernesto says, but he seems uncertain.

"It's not that bad," Grim says. "We'll earn it. Record in February, March. Get it out in May, June. Gigs during the summer and the fall. Maybe go abroad. I've got some contacts."

The four of them look at each other. That feeling is back again, of everything falling into place. Grim goes on talking about what they're going to do and how, and Håkan's chest swells with joy.

They can do this, he and Grim.

They talk all summer, dream all summer. This summer is made for dreaming, the sky incomparably vast, taut above the treeline. They're side by side, ready for the future. The world is waiting for them, Grim says.

Håkan just wishes he could get used to Grim vanishing. The first time it happened, Grim had only lived in Stockholm for a few weeks. The nights were still chilly. Håkan lay awake, waiting, not daring to wake his mom in case she phoned the police. Maybe they should phone the police, though? But Grim appeared at dawn, nose and cheeks red with cold, his turquoise sports bag dangling from one hand. Then he walked straight into the kitchen to boil himself some water on the stove.

"Where have you been?" Håkan whispered, trying very hard to hide his anger and concern.

"In the forest," Grim replied.

"Are you kidding me?"

Grim shook his head, tossing a bag of Lipton into a mug and pouring himself some tea. He warmed his hands on the hot ceramic. "I have to disappear sometimes. Nothing to worry about."

He looked at Håkan, his gaze dark and even, and Håkan nodded. Really, who was he to ask anything of Grim?

He's gone for days sometimes, showing up unexpectedly with homemade cinnamon rolls. Once, he came in carrying an old typewriter. He is reticent about where he's been. Both Håkan and his mom stop asking him about it. Maybe there's a girl somewhere, one who likes to bake for him, Håkan thinks. It's improbable, but his mind has begun moving in that direction ever since he fell for Anja.

Anja Hansson from Trollbäcken, her thick red hair framing her face. Anja, with her sharp eyeliner, a splash of freckles over her cheekbones and shoulders. Anja, with her eclectic taste in music and the Pentax camera she always brings along. She's one year younger than Håkan, but she's about to begin her junior year studying Art at Fredrika Bremer, the same high school where he'd spent one term languishing. Her jeans are stained with photographic developer. She has a blue parakeet called Lemmy.

Håkan knows all these things about Anja because he's quick to pick up on every detail about her. Every time he gets the chance to talk to her at a party, though, his mouth goes so dry he has to drink, and then he ends up so drunk he can't talk at all.

In his circles, only Ernesto and a few others have a girlfriend. Håkan knows that other people, mainly younger boys, talk about Ernesto behind his back since he started dating Linda. It isn't serious, you can't let a chick get in the way of your music, "no girls, just evil," blah, blah, blah. You don't have to be Einstein to figure out that they're jealous.

Håkan has kissed a girl exactly once. It happened last summer, when he spent his designated week at his dad's. He'd gone to the beach to get away, sat down with a book and a bag of peanuts. Twilight came, and so did a group of girls, their hair blond and big with hair spray. They played music that made Håkan want to puke, Bon Jovi and Swedish pop stars who *whined* their songs instead of singing them. The girls passed around a bottle of fruit liqueur and glanced pointedly in Håkan's direction. They giggled and whispered until he couldn't focus on his book anymore. Still, he stayed. It felt as if something was going to happen. Lingering in that possibility was exciting.

Eventually it got too dark for him to keep up the pretense of reading, and he started getting his things together. At that moment, one of the girls approached him, the tallest one. Her jacket was shiny and pale pink, the same color as her lips. She smelled like hair spray and synthetic raspberry, a scent that was both attractive and a little repulsive. Girls like this had gone to Håkan's school. They had always made him nervous.

"Hi! I'm Sussi," she said. "We thought you were a chick."

Håkan stared at her and she sat down next to him.

"Well, because of your long hair," she explained, as if he were a bit slow.

"What, you've never seen a guy with long hair before?" Håkan scoffed. "You listen to Bon Jovi, for Christ's sake."

Sussi laughed, too loudly. Håkan knew that it was for the sake of the other girls, so they'd hear.

"People from Stockholm sound so funny," she said, and then tried to mimic him.

"You sound like a moron," Håkan told her.

He was starting to get pissed off. As if her Gothenburg accent was any better? What did she want with him?

"You're a sulky one, aren't you?" she said.

The next moment she was pressing her mouth, sticky with lip gloss, against his. A warm tongue flicked out, burning him. A second later, it was done. Sussi rose unsteadily and ran back to her girl-friends, laughing hysterically.

Håkan's face burned when he got up, humiliation and involuntary arousal throbbing inside of him. He wanted to turn back and yell something, an insult, but they'd only laugh harder.

After that, he avoided the beach, didn't mention the kiss to anyone. If it even was a kiss. More like a coerced push of mouth against mouth. Sure, he looks at girls sometimes, but it's as if they exist in a parallel universe. A universe he's unsure he'll ever want to visit.

But there is something about Anja.

He's felt it since the first time he saw her, accompanying Linda to the rehearsal space. Now and then, she'd raise her camera and snap a picture. He didn't play right, got frustrated and then ashamed. Maybe that's when silence began to grow inside of him, thick and dense. There was no one he could talk to. Tony would make fun of him and Ernesto would tell Linda, who would tell Anja. And Grim? Håkan can't imagine talking to Grim about something like that. So he says nothing, his unhappy, unrequited love weighing him down like a stone. He tries to bear it. It will pass eventually, he supposes, like a cold.

One night when July is shifting into August, Håkan and Grim are on their way to Linda's. They lead their bikes along the quiet street and past the villas. Grim's bike is a beast of unknown origin, which he refers to as the Hellion. It squeaks loud enough to drive you mad. They're talking about a band they both hate—sell-outs, posers—almost as if they're competing about who can hate them the most, while Håkan takes swigs from his beer.

Suddenly they see something large and dark on the pavement before them. Håkan stops at once. It's a black bird, lying with its wings spread.

"Shit," Håkan says. "Is that a raven?"

Grim lays aside the Hellion and crouches by the bird.

"Can't have been dead for long," he says.

Click.

Håkan looks up. Anja lowers the camera and looks back at him. She has more freckles now than the last time he saw her, he's sure of it.

"Hey," she says.

"Hi," Håkan croaks, gripping the handlebar tightly.

Anja joins Grim, crouching down next to the bird.

"That's not a raven," she tells them. "It's a rook."

"A rook," Grim repeats. "Never seen one of those before."

"They're not that common around here," Anja says. "They're mostly in the south of Sweden, I think."

Håkan adds "expert on birds" to his list of things about Anja. She raises her camera. He watches her take a series of pictures of the cadaver, her focus absolute, as if he and Grim have ceased to exist. He could watch her taking photos forever.

"Hey," Grim says to Anja.

Anja lowers the camera again.

"Do you want to take our band photos?" Grim says. "Dark Cruelty, that is."

Håkan feels himself freeze up. How can Grim just throw it out like that? What if she says no? What if she doesn't?

"All right," Anja says and gets up. "Guess so."

"It might get gruesome, though. So you're prepared," Grim tells her seriously, getting to his feet.

"How gruesome?"

Håkan can see the gleam in Anja's eyes.

"Fiendishly so," Grim says.

His laugh is so unexpected, so joyful, that Anja also starts to laugh, and then Håkan joins in. There they are, surrounded by fancy houses, and laughing themselves sick beside a dead bird.

And in the next moment, Anja looks straight at Håkan, her

bright eyes full of laughter, and he just stands there, paralyzed, while voices and steps come nearer. Tony, on his way with Stasse and Dimman, the brothers from Malodor. Håkan has to say something, has to say something right now, but then Tony skips toward Anja, singing about Pippi Longstocking.

"Pippi's horse, at your service," he says, bending forward and neighing loudly.

"Dumbass," Anja says fondly.

She leaps onto his back and he gallops away with Stasse running after him, roaring, "And I'm her monkey!"

Anja's wild laughter rises toward the darkening sky. Jealousy pounds through Håkan.

A few hours later, he's bent over the spirea bushes, with Grim holding his hair back from his face.

In little more than a year, one of them will be dead.

KASPER

Grim floated beneath the surface of the water. His body was bent backward, his feet pointing downward into the depths. His eyes were shut, his hair waving like seaweed, his clothes billowing around him. His face was so pale, his veins glowed through his skin.

He has to be dead, Kasper thought. But this wasn't how he died. This wasn't how it happened.

So how did it happen?

Grim's body rose, as if lifted by an invisible power. His head broke through the surface, his black hair was plastered to his face, the water foamed around him.

One ruptured eye looked at Kasper.

Kasper woke up covered in sweat, tangled in the duvet cover, which he kept empty due to the heat. The sun was shoving itself through the open window, the air suffocating. He threw his denim-clad legs over the side of the bed, tore the sheet off himself when it twisted around him. Apparently, he had gone to bed with his clothes on, but he couldn't process that right now. He had to capture the dream before it faded from his memory.

Kasper sat down at the desk, opened his sketchbook, and gripped his pencil. Grim floating. The perspective was tricky, and normally he would have avoided it, but he suddenly knew exactly how to manage it. The pencil scratched against the paper. There was a stale taste in his mouth, and he took a few sips out of the half-empty glass on the table. The water was warm rather than tepid. He went on drawing, hardly noticing the front door opening, the steps going into the kitchen and the tap splashing.

Kasper lowered his pencil and looked at what he'd made. It was done. Perfect in its imperfections. He signed it: *KHN*.

"Aren't you going to work?" his dad said through the door.

Kasper checked the phone on his desk. It was way too late. He must have forgotten to set the alarm before going to bed.

He couldn't actually remember going to bed.

His dad opened the door a crack.

"Hello? Morning?"

He was wearing shorts and a sweaty, sleeveless shirt, clearly home from a run. The look he gave Kasper was questioning.

"Are you sick? Or were you getting drunk last night?"

"What?" Kasper said huskily, then cleared his throat. "No, why?"

"The bathroom smells like puke."

A memory of heaving into the sink returned.

"I ate something bad," Kasper said. "Sorry."

"But you're all right now?"

"Yeah."

"Really?"

"Really."

His dad entered the room, bringing with him a scent of fresh sweat and warm skin.

"You know, I had a box of things in my room—"

"I heard a sound and went in to check," Kasper interrupted. "It had tipped over, everything was on the floor."

"Ah," his dad said.

"What, did you think I did it?"

He knew he sounded brusque. And it wasn't as if his dad had done anything wrong; Kasper was the one who'd gone through his stuff.

"Calm down, will you?" his dad said. "I didn't say that. It was just odd, that's all. I don't understand how it could just tip over."

Kasper was silent. He didn't understand it, either.

"Get a move on," his dad said. "There's coffee, but I got the math wrong, so it's mostly tar. Don't know if you'll like it since you were sick yesterday. I'll jump in the shower."

With that, he disappeared into the bathroom. Kasper turned his left hand over. Through some miracle, the bandage was still on. He carefully removed it. The wound was sticky, but not bleeding.

What had happened yesterday?

The sound of running water came from the bathroom. Kasper went into the kitchen and drank deeply straight from the tap. The door to the Nest, his dad's tiny office combined with recording studio, was open and the computer screen was on. Maybe he'd sat there all night after returning from wherever he'd been yesterday. It wasn't unusual. His dad had placed the Emperor Palpatine mug next to the coffee machine, so Kasper filled it with coffee and milk, took two slices of bread out of the freezer and toasted them. Peanut butter and jelly were already on the counter. Emperor in one hand, a plate of toast in the other, he stepped out into the balcony.

The coffee really was tar and he drank it in small sips while chewing his toast. In the distance, there was the roar of traffic. The air was hazy with heat. The sound of children playing in the U-shaped yard echoed between the three-story apartment buildings.

When they were twelve, Marco had come up with a challenge: who could stay awake the longest. Kasper had won, but he couldn't remember what happened between coming home from Marco's house and being woken up by his dad when dinner was ready. Somehow he'd gone to bed in his sleep.

Something like that must have happened yesterday, he told himself. Lately, things had been pretty intense. It was the strain of it, that was all.

Familiar blues riffs played from the speakers in the living room and his dad came out onto the balcony in just his underwear, his wet hair plastered to his scalp. He leaned out over the side and lit himself a cigarette. Breathed out smoke so it wouldn't get in Kasper's face, tapping along to the music with his heel.

"John Lee Hooker?" Kasper took another bite.

"Well done," his dad said, lifting the cigarette to his mouth again.

"Weren't you quitting?" Kasper said with his mouth full.

"I will," his dad said automatically, stubbing out the cigarette, which he'd barely smoked. Stopped in the middle of a movement. "Fuck, listen to this."

Listen to this. This was a recurring phrase in Kasper's childhood. Listen to this riff . . . this solo . . . What does this remind you of? Music wasn't just music, but a language, a history, voices and traditions communicating with one another. It was worlds you could enter, worlds from which you could draw comfort and power. Sometimes Kasper felt as if music was the religion he'd grown up with.

"Fuck, that's good," Håkan said, sitting down on a chair, as if overwhelmed by Hooker's greatness.

Kasper took another swig of tar, even though it was giving him heart palpitations.

"You know, I looked at a few things in that box," Kasper said, quickly adding, "Hope that was all right."

"Yeah, of course," his dad said, gazing out across the yard. "It's just some nostalgic junk. You've probably seen most of it."

"I don't know. I must have misremembered 'cause I thought you said that number 1 of the first *Ancient Bloodlust* pressing was missing." Kasper said.

"I said that?" His dad's gaze followed a squirrel, which was pretending to be Spider-Man on the facade of the house opposite them. "I probably meant that it was ruined. Because it is."

He went quiet. Kasper waited for him to continue. There was always more; his dad's anecdotes came in several episodes, sometimes in seasons. But he still wasn't speaking.

"What happened to it?" Kasper asked.

"Don't know," his dad said, reaching for the box of snuff on the table, and then catching sight of the bandage on Kasper's hand. "What happened to you?"

"I cut myself," Kasper said, "on the knife in the box."

"Oh, shit," his dad said, stuffing snuff under his upper lip. "I noticed the sheath was broken. Taped it together when I got home. Have you cleaned it properly?"

"I think so," Kasper said. "Is it the knife from the band photo?"

"Yes." His dad suddenly sounded exhausted. "Yes, it is."

Something still felt wrong, but what else could Kasper ask him? Why should he keep asking him things? They sat there quietly, father and son. Kasper forced himself to finish the toast, despite being full.

"This goddamn weather," his dad said suddenly, sounding like his regular self again. "Got those new fans at work yet?"

"No."

His dad peered at him.

"How are you doing? You look tired."

"Oh, thanks."

"You know what I mean."

"I'm fucking exhausted. I don't even remember going to bed yesterday."

He tried to say it lightly, as a joke, but his dad immediately looked concerned.

"What?" he said. "Like a blackout?"

"It's fine," Kasper said. "It's been a lot recently, so . . ."

"Huh," his dad said. "Yeah, that's happened to me, too. After intense touring and all that. Your body just shuts down." But he still looked worried, his fingers drumming against his thigh. "I've thought about it, you barely being around. But it's felt like . . . Well, you've got new friends you want to be with."

Can't believe you have friends at all. If you do, that is.

Kasper drank his coffee.

"Maybe you need to take it easy for a bit," his dad went on.

Kasper, who'd had much the same idea, still felt annoyed hearing it from his dad. Like he was incapable of taking care of himself.

You are, though. You've proved it.

"Yeah, I thought so, too," he said.

"And we've hardly seen each other, you and me," his dad said, evidently encouraged. "Want to do something tonight?"

Kasper almost said yes, but then remembered that it was Sunday. Everyone was going to Skeppsbar. He didn't really feel like going, but staying at home and missing out felt impossible.

Pathetic.

"Or you can tag along and cut some grass tomorrow," his dad said. "You're free, aren't you?"

His dad worked for a garden service. When Kasper was a kid, he'd come along and read a book while his dad worked. When he got older, he got to work extra during the summer holidays. When everything collapsed, it became a rehab, of sorts. He'd shovel snow, clear away leaves, trim perennials, and plant tulips. It was almost cliché, the degree to which it had helped him to be out in nature and see the actual result of his labor. To be with his dad, too.

"Sure," Kasper said.

"Then we'll go swimming," his dad said, getting increasingly excited about the idea. "Grab a pizza and watch a film. Or I'll kick your ass in Mario Kart. It's been too long."

Kasper laughed. Mario Kart had always been their thing.

"Dream on," he told his dad.

Hooker's voice suddenly warped as the record slowed down, stopping in the middle of a song. His dad jumped up as if he'd been burned and rushed into the living room. When Kasper followed with his plate in his hand, his dad was bent over the record player.

"Shit. It's dead. How the hell did that happen?"

His dad pulled out the plug, put it back in again. Nothing happened. He swore loudly. Kasper thought about that crackling sound from the previous night, the speakers still on.

"Where were you last night, by the way?" he asked.

"At Ernesto's," his dad said.

Kasper waited for him to provide details. None came. His dad turned the record player off and then on again. Nothing. Abruptly, Kasper got it.

"It's to do with Dark Cruelty," he said. "Right?"

His dad almost looked shocked, and it irritated Kasper.

"What's the big secret, then?" Kasper said.

His dad sighed, then seemed to come to a decision.

"Nothing's settled yet, but . . . remember Trey and Mizuki? You met them when we were at Roadburn."

Blood Libation had played the cutting-edge Dutch festival a few times, and this spring Kasper had gone along. He vaguely remembered an American couple chatting with his dad for a while.

"They own Retrolash Records," his dad went on. "They want to reissue *Ancient Bloodlust* next year. For the thirty-year anniversary."

"And?"

Kasper didn't understand what the big deal was. They'd reissued the EP when it turned twenty, too. Along with the vinyl, they'd added a small booklet with pictures his mom had taken, and essays by prominent metal musicians and critics who talked about what Dark Cruelty had meant to them.

"We're talking about a reunion," his dad said.

"Shit," Kasper managed.

His dad had always treated Dark Cruelty like something sacred. A reunion had never even been in the cards. In fact, the opposite was true—his dad was the one who'd been standing in the way of one. They'd received offers both Tony and Ernesto had been interested in accepting, but his dad had the final say. And what he said had always begun with an N and ended with an O.

"It's a one-time thing," his dad said. "But it's going to be a fantastic release. I found a rehearsal tape that I thought we'd lost. And Grim left some lyrics behind, too. Maybe something could come out of that."

New songs, too. Kasper felt like Alice in Wonderland. *Curiouser and curiouser.*

"It won't be a long tour," his dad continued. "Besides, the money's better if you only do a few exclusive shows. Mizuki said Virginia Death Fest was interested. It'd be nice to do something in Europe, too, and maybe something smaller in Stockholm. Invite some of the old guard."

His dad's eyes shone. Whenever he got enthusiastic, he looked like an eager little boy. He made Kasper feel old sometimes.

"You make it sound like it's going to happen," Kasper said.

"Nothing's settled yet," his dad repeated. "That's why I didn't want to say anything. We've checked the material and rehearsed a bit at Ernesto's house. Just to get a feel for it."

"So how does it feel?" Kasper said.

"It feels all right," his dad said.

But his overjoyed smile conveyed something else.

There was something in the air at Grönan sometimes.

It was a kind of simmering madness, one that could erupt at any time. Kids howled through mouths sticky with ice cream, furious parents screamed at their terrified children, strangers argued with each other in the lines to the rides. The hosts of the Pop Express had to call for security three times in one hour after visitors who hadn't been allowed to pick songs made death threats.

That was the kind of day Kasper walked into after hearing about Dark Cruelty's reunion. In other words, he wasn't able to devote much time to it once he'd rushed to work. The area was packed with guests, most of them close to a nervous breakdown, and it was is if everyone had decided to seek refuge in The House, in some misguided search for shade. A couple of boorish tourists tried to steal a test tube from the Lab. A teenage girl refused to move, cowering on the floor, petrified with fear. Santiago made a small child wet themselves, and The House closed while Iris mopped the floor.

"Maybe don't scare people who look incontinent?" she told Santiago on the radio, and it didn't sound entirely like a joke.

"Sorry for being good at my job," Santiago snapped back.

The demons were touchy, too.

During his last shift, Kasper was in the Chef scene. He hurried from the register and through the secret passageways, stopped to let through a group of visitors who didn't even notice him. As he entered the Chef scene, Santiago frightened some guests who were heading for the balcony.

"Thank *God* the day is almost over," he said, removing his hood and the bloody apron. His face, once revealed, was sweaty in the red light. "Can't believe I'm lucky enough to wrap up with the Nursery."

He was clearly being sarcastic. As the Doll, you had to pull a onesie made out of synthetic material over your clothes, and wear an apple-cheeked mask with fluffy hair. Additionally, the fan in the small, closet-like space you were tucked away in was hands down the worst in The House.

"At least it's Sunday," Kasper said.

"Oh hooray, I get to sweat in the basement of Skeppsbar instead," Santiago drawled.

Kasper couldn't tell if he was joking or genuinely annoyed, so didn't say anything more. He put on the Chef's apron as a recorded growl was triggered outside the door he'd just entered through. The group Santiago had just scared were on their way from the balcony into the Pyramid. Santiago positioned himself by the door and pounded a fist against it at precisely the right moment. Kasper heard screams from the other side. Santiago waited for a beat, peered through the hatch, and then hurried off to take over for Jennifer in the Nursery.

Kasper surveyed the row of masks in the Chef scene and chose the pig-faced one. He pumped disinfectant onto a piece of paper and wiped its insides, then checked in with Iris to tell her the Chef was manned. The Chef was his favorite scene on the mask route. The narrow space was large enough to get a good scare out of it, and if you were lucky, you could get some air when the guests opened the doors to the balcony. These days, though, they only let in suffocating heat.

There were fewer visitors as they approached closing time. Kasper's thoughts started catching up with him.

Dark Cruelty was getting back together.

His dad had said it wasn't decided yet, but he'd made his mind up. That much was clear. Tony and Ernesto were probably pleased. Tony was always ready with the drumsticks, and Ernesto, with his successful career, probably wanted to pay tribute to his underground roots.

Why had his dad changed his mind?

Because it had been thirty years? Because of the money? It wouldn't make him rich, but it was probably significant enough for it to matter. His dad compulsively joked about how meager his pension would be. But that couldn't be it, Kasper thought.

"Lab." Cornelia's voice in the radio. "Four on their way to the Chef."

"Affirmative," Kasper said. "Over and out."

He lifted the chain saw from the wall, went over to the peephole and waited for the guests who'd have to pass through the snakes and spiders.

For most people, Dark Cruelty's rebirth wouldn't come as a surprise. Bands reunited all the time, even the ones who'd claimed they'd never stand on a stage together again. Sometimes it was a final gig, a final tour, or a new beginning. It made sense for Dark Cruelty to do the same. While they'd never been mainstream, they did have cult status, and the reunion would be talked about in the extreme metal scene. Especially among the people who had been young during Swedish death metal's golden era. A lot of people would want to see them play; some people would think they were desperate old men. Maybe they'd quote what his dad had always said: "Dark Cruelty doesn't exist without Grim." Among some of the most orthodox Grim fanatics, a reunion would create bad blood.

And Malte would react, too.

A sensor triggered the sound of screams and axes chopping through flesh. Kasper looked through the peephole and saw four guys, junior high age, who walked in a line with their hands on each other's shoulders. That they didn't spot Kasper was fascinating. But most visitors stared ahead, focusing on whatever could be lurking behind the next corner. Kasper pulled his mask on and positioned himself behind the curtain. He knew when to act: the moment you think everything is over, and nothing else will happen. He waited until the last boy was on his way to the balcony, then he pulled aside the curtain and roared, the chain saw, sadly broken and silent, raised. The guy screamed and tripped through the door that shut behind him. Kasper could hear him and his friends laughing out on the balcony.

"Duuuude!" one of them hollered, and Kasper took his mask off, smiling.

"Chef here," he said into the two-way radio. "Four guys on the way to the Doll. Go for it."

But not so hard that they wet themselves, he almost said, but bit his tongue.

"Yes," Santiago said. "Over and out."

"Kasper to Iris," he said. "The chain saw's died again."

"Oh, for fuck's sake," Iris huffed. "Over and out."

Kasper hung the chain saw on the wall. The adhesive bandage, which he'd had to change several times over, had slipped out of his hand and onto the floor. He threw it in the garbage, then heard through the radio that a new group was leaving the register. In the red light, the wound looked infected and throbbed uncomfortably. The Pyramid started up when the same group of guys returned from the balcony, but Kasper couldn't be bothered to scare them again. Santiago could deal with them in the Nursery.

What would Malte "Iago" Lundell do when he heard about the reunion?

None of the other band members had been in touch with Malte since Dark Cruelty split up, if you didn't count the times he'd threatened to murder them in the interviews he made in the nineties. No one knew whether it was Malte or his followers who'd drawn swastikas on Ernesto's door and poured stinking butyric acid in his mailbox. Similarly, it wasn't clear who'd sent dead rats and dog shit to his dad and Tony. During the period when the threats had come hard and fast, his dad had kept an eye out, he'd told Kasper.

"I couldn't take Malte seriously at first," he said, "'cause he was such a little shit. But back then, a lot of little shits caused a lot of damage, and sometimes they had real crazy friends, some really messed-up dudes. It was so fucking surreal. We didn't want trouble; we were there for the music."

The threats ceased after a few years, but Malte kept being Malte. At the start of the millennium, he'd been suspected of a brutal murder and left the country shortly thereafter. He dedicated himself to Nox Irredux, a one-man project, and began calling himself "M." When the twenty-year anniversary edition of *Ancient Bloodlust* was released, they'd cut him out of the band photo. "Thank God that little rat was on the very right," his mom had said. In the credits, he'd simply been called "M. L." and was placed as if he was a session musician, not a part of the band. This had resulted in a letter to his dad. Kasper had caught a glimpse of it, the letters printed in black ink. Traditional as ever, Malte wrote his threats by hand. Kasper wasn't supposed to hear his mom insist that his dad report it to the police. "He's actually dangerous," she'd said. "He's killed someone." His dad had argued that there was no point. "There's nothing here, because he won't come out and say it," he said. "He's too cunning for that. Reporting him will only encourage him." After that, Kasper had slept restlessly for a few nights.

"Two on their way from the Lab," Cornelia said through the radio.

"'Kay," Kasper said, lifting a plastic machete off the wall. "Over and out."

Again, he positioned himself at the peephole, waiting.

Kasper had only seen Malte once in real life, when he was eleven, attending a festival with his dad. He remembered being surprised at how small he was, the man who cast such a long shadow across his childhood. Wiry and thin, with lank blond hair and a prominent widow's peak. Malte had let his gaze travel from his dad to Kasper, and Kasper had squeezed his eyes shut when his dad dragged him away. There was something about that gaze, something hard and implacable.

The sounds of meat axes and screams set off again as two young men came toward him. Their expressions were unreadable, at once tense and bored. Kasper pulled down the pig mask and went over to the curtain. Just as one of them was exiting, Kasper leaped out with a cry, machete in hand. The second he saw the man's eyes, he knew he'd made a mistake.

"Motherfucker!" the man yelled, throwing himself at the bars.

The impact made Kasper stumble backward and drop the machete.

"You fucking cunt!" the man screamed, gripping the bars and rattling them so hard the metal sang and the curtain fell.

Kasper was frozen. He knew he ought to do something, but he couldn't move. All he could see were the man's wild, wide eyes, his bared teeth. Could the bars come loose? The man's friend held up the door to the balcony, and Kasper saw him reach for something. He thought, *He's got a gun; he's going to kill me.* But it was a phone. He was filming the man, who was still pounding on the bars.

"You motherfucker!"

The fence squeaked, as if something came loose.

Kasper was finally able to move again. He threw himself at the door that led to the Pyramid.

"Security to the Chef's! Security to the Chef's!" he shouted, while slamming the door shut behind him and running for his life.

Mats the Mummy nibbled half-heartedly as Kasper rushed past. He tore off the pig mask. The way leading to the Nursery creaked and tilted, and in an awful moment, he almost lost his balance. The mask fell out of his hand. Farther off, he heard the junior high boys howling with laughter, and there was the Nursery. The door into the Doll scene opened, and Santiago stretched out a hand, dragged Kasper inside, and locked them in.

"Oh, shit," Kasper panted. "Shit."

"I'll turn the lights on," Santiago said. "That usually scares them off."

He pressed a button, turning on the overhead lights in the Nursery. The sound of the musical box and the eerie laughter of children continued; they were controlled by the main computer.

Through the radio, Kasper was informed that no more guests were allowed in, and that security guards were on their way.

"I can't see them on the camera," Jennifer said from her place at the register.

"They probably heard you call for security and fucked off," Santiago told Kasper. He'd pulled off his Doll mask and held it in one hand. "They must have taken the stairs from the balcony . . ."

Santiago fell silent when the sensor in the Pyramid was triggered, setting off the monstrous growling sound.

"They're in the Pyramid," Jennifer said.

"Shit," Santiago said softly.

Mats the Mummy rattled his chains and snapped at someone. Kasper and Santiago backed away from the mirror, just as they heard heavy steps to the right, and the hallway tipped sideways with a creak.

Kasper's pulse careened. On the other side of the mirror, the man who had attacked him appeared. In one hand, he held the pig mask Kasper had dropped. He glared at the mirror on the other side of the Nursery. Then he spun around, turning the glare to where Kasper and Santiago were hiding.

"Fuck," Santiago whispered, soft as an exhalation.

"Hey," the man's friend said. "Let's go."

The man didn't reply, continuing to stare into the mirror. He took a step forward and Kasper grabbed on to Santiago's arm, felt the synthetic fabric against his fingers. The sad little fan turned toward them, then away. Cold sweat trickled down Kasper's body.

The man pressed his forehead against the mirror, his eyes shadowed, his fist raised. The blow that slammed into the mirror made it rattle. Kasper squeezed his eyes shut, clung to Santiago's arm.

The fear was so strong it felt like a creature in itself, pressing against him, pushing the air out of his lungs. He was afraid in a way he couldn't quite understand. His hand throbbed. A powerful feeling of regret washed over him; he shouldn't have done this, but it was too late, it was all too late. A nauseating, sharp smell, like rotting apples, fresh and rancid blood. A dull, droning sound filled his skull.

I am going to die.

When the music and the sound effects shut off, the silence in The House was brutal.

"They're gone," Santiago said.

"They're heading for the balcony." Jennifer's voice, coming through the radio.

Kasper opened his eyes but couldn't focus on Santiago. His voice sounded far away.

"Shit, man, how are you doing?"

"I'm good," Kasper said, but he was shivering as if with cold.

Through the radio, he heard Iris say that security was pursuing the men across the park.

"Kasper?" Santiago said. "Hello?"

"I'm good," Kasper repeated and sank down onto the floor. "Sorry."

He'd seen violence before. At first, it had been games played in school, all bruises and blood, coins fired at bare knuckles, if you move you get a punch, are you a Viking or what? Then he'd taught himself to be wary in certain situations, when unknown boys would circle him and his friends. They had been chased several times. Once, Kasper and Marco had been hiding in the bushes for an hour before they could make themselves sneak home, terrified that the gang that had hunted them would catch up. Kasper had seen tense situations get out of hand, seen a guy's eyes turn black, seen him become unreachable. Afterward, he'd review the situation in his head, realizing how badly it could have ended. He had been afraid before. But not like this. This had been something else.

"Hey, Kasper. Hello?"

Kasper looked at Santiago, who was crouching in front of him.

"That was one of the worst ones ever, hands down. Most of them make a lot of noise, but that guy really wanted to break in. There was something deeply off about him."

Kasper and Santiago both jumped at the knock on the door.

"It's just me!" Iris called.

Santiago got to his feet and opened the door.

"Holy shit," Iris panted, catching her breath. "Are you all right?"

"That was *so* fucking scary," Santiago said.

Kasper could only nod. Iris gave him a concerned look.

"We've decided to close for the day," she said.

"Good," Santiago said. "This doll needs a drink."

✳

Every Sunday after closing, there was a pilgrimage from Gröna Lund via the ferry over the water and into Gamla Stan. On the opposite side of the road from the ferry's endpoint lay Skeppsbar. Long before Kasper had started working at Grönan, his stepbrother, Tor, had informed him that "everyone" from Rides would go there every Sunday night. "That's where you get off," Tor had said, and punched Kasper in the shoulder, partly joking, partly serious.

Kasper was sitting at a table in Skeppsbar's basement. Everyone was clamoring to be heard, and the air was tropical, the walls almost glistening with moisture. Hits from the aughts blared across the room. The faces on the dance floor shone, makeup melted, patches of sweat grew.

Kasper felt numb.

Before closing up, they'd taken an extra moment at the meeting to talk about what had happened. Unfortunately, the duo had escaped the security guards, but at least they had been caught on camera. Cornelia felt terrible for not warning Kasper, despite getting a bad vibe from the pair.

"I thought I was overreacting," she said. "Classic. I'm so sorry."

"It wasn't your fault," Kasper said, seated a few steps above her in the Lab. "I could also tell something wasn't right, but I ignored it."

The panic had gone and was replaced with shame. Shame at having been so scared. Shame at having stood there, frozen, instead of calling for help. In front of the other demons, he mocked himself, described clinging desperately to Santiago. Some of them probably knew what he was doing, while the others laughed. Krille smiled. It wasn't a kind smile. Iris took Kasper to one side after the meeting.

"Be honest. How are you feeling?" she said. "You looked like you were in shock when I saw you. I mean, like true shock."

"It was the adrenaline, that's all. I'm fine now."

"You know what, let's go and see the nurse."

She pulled at his arm. He didn't move.

"I'm fine," he said, with emphasis. "I promise."

Iris seemed skeptical but let go of his arm.

"Maybe you should go home and rest."

"Thanks for caring about me," Kasper said, forcing a smile. "But I'm good, honestly."

He guessed that this was far from the truth but didn't want to delve too deeply into that feeling. Most of all, he didn't want to be alone with his thoughts. He just wanted everything to go back to normal. Because what had happened in The House did not feel normal. Santiago had insisted that he'd been just as scared, but Kasper knew that wasn't true. Where had that scent come from? Had he been hallucinating? Was he becoming psychotic?

Those thoughts were gone now that he was seated among his partying colleagues. Now he just felt hollow.

The DJ must have realized he'd missed a setting, because suddenly the bass came on, pounding through Kasper's bones. He looked out across the dance floor, where Dennis from the Magic Carpet Ride was hitting on a girl who once worked as UC on

Insane. For some reason, working at Insane was considered more impressive than other Rides. Tor, of course, had been UC at Insane. Kasper had a drink of water. On the other side of the table, Iris and Cornelia were deep into a conversation. Santiago was at the bar with his boyfriend and Selam, who'd just arrived, getting himself a beer. They'd all been so supportive but stopped inquiring once Kasper had made it clear that he was fine.

And he was fine. He couldn't understand why.

That thought made him wonder how long his calm would last. And there it was: the pull, a pull downward, immediate and devastating.

Nothing changes, everything ends, you can't have a normal life, you're going to freak out, this time you'll end up in the psych ward, heavily medicated for the rest of your life, you ruin everything with your thoughts, can't even handle a simple job, they've seen what you are, what a freak, they'll cut you off, just as well, they'll forget you the second you're back at school, they're not your friends, you don't have friends, you don't deserve friends, you don't deserve anything.

He had to get out. He rose to his feet and walked toward the stairs, toward the stream of people coming down them. The stink of perfume, deodorant, cigarette smoke, and sweat made him feel sick when he jostled past the warm, sticky bodies that gathered around the bar on the top floor.

Skin, fat, blood, muscle, bone, look at those smiles, they're hollow, just hollow, there's nothing in it, there's nothing anywhere, everything is false and hollow.

The humid night air gave no relief. Kasper hurried across the street, dodging past a taxi that came hurtling toward him, the driver pounding on his car horn. When he reached the edge of the quay, he stopped, sat down. His skin burned and prickled. The sky was bright. His heart was racing. Water lapped against the edge of the docks. Kasper looked at his shoes, which hung over the water as if they were somehow separate from him. His head full of white noise. Kasper closed his eyes and Grim's black clothes billowed around his body as he floated. Breathe. Breathe. Breathe.

"Kasper."

Iris sounded breathless. He turned his head and saw her standing there, the imposing cranes at the construction site by Slussen towering behind her.

"All right if I join you?" she said.

Kasper swallowed and nodded mutely; he was afraid of what would happen if he started to talk. While he tried to focus on his breathing, Iris sat down next to him. The gulls were screaming. He drank in the scent of briny water. Breathe.

"Did something happen?" Iris asked after a moment.

"No," Kasper said hoarsely. "I just . . ."

He made some vague gesture.

"It got a bit too much?" Iris said.

"Yeah. I should have gone home. I just didn't want to be alone."

"Kasper." A drop of sweat trickled down Iris's temple. She dashed it away. "I would have come with you. If you'd wanted me to."

Kasper felt his eyes sting with tears. Because he hadn't even considered that. He turned his face away.

"I didn't want to ruin your night," he mumbled.

"No, of course, a night at Skeppsbar can't possibly be cut short," Iris said gently. "It has to be experienced in full." She opened her bag and pulled out a plastic bottle. "Some water? It's body temperature."

Kasper took the bottle and drank. The water really was lukewarm, but it quenched the thirst he hadn't even been aware of until now. He was sticky with cold sweat. It dawned on him that this was the first time he was alone with Iris outside of work.

"Look, I know everything's a bit unspoken, what with us mostly hanging out as a group," Iris said, as if she'd read his thoughts. "So maybe feeling that you have a personal connection is a bit difficult, or whatever. But you can count on us. Me, Selam, Santiago, Cornelia, Elliot . . . Anyone in The House, really. Well, maybe not Krille. Personally, I would not count on Krille."

Kasper could only nod. He looked at their feet, dangling side by side. They were quiet for a moment. Kasper finished the water, and Iris handed him a protein bar, which he accepted. Broke it into smaller pieces and ate.

"Was this the first year you applied to Grönan?" Iris asked.

"Yeah . . ." Kasper cleared his throat. "My mom's husband . . . His son used to be a TL. He told me about it."

He felt as if he was speaking in slow motion.

"Who is it?" Iris said.

"Tor." Kasper wiped his sticky fingers on his jeans. "Tor Nielsen Eklund."

"Oh, my God!" Iris exclaimed. "You're Tor's brother?"

Kasper knew she was trying to distract him, and it was working. Talking about something else did feel better.

"We don't really call each other *brother*. I mean, he's nice and all, but we don't know each other that well."

Kasper wondered if she was thinking the same thing he had: that he only had the job because of Tor's intervention.

"Super unexpected that Tor would be your stepbrother," she said. "I liked working with him, obviously, but he's, like, a complete extrovert. And you . . ."

". . . mostly want to lurk in a corner and leap out at people," Kasper finished.

"How's that working out for you?"

Kasper laughed. Suddenly, he could laugh again.

"Honestly . . ." he said. "I love it."

Iris raised her eyebrows.

"You're not repressing what happened today, are you?"

Kasper laughed again.

"No," he said. "But it's like you said . . ."

I've got you and the others. He couldn't say it out loud, because it sounded so goddamn lame. But he caught Iris nodding in the corner of his eye.

"Your first time calling security, right?" she said.

"Yeah," Kasper said. "At first I just froze. I didn't know what to do. I was just standing there."

"That's a common reaction," Iris said.

"I just felt like, shit, I should know this," Kasper told her.

"It's different when it actually happens."

"Yeah," Kasper said. "I suppose it is."

He brushed against the fear that had possessed him when he was with Santiago. The smells, that strange droning sound. The deep regret. That profound fear of death.

"I had this bizarre feeling," he said. "I thought that . . ." He didn't want to say the word *psychosis* out loud. It scared him too deeply. "I mean, I haven't been . . . I went through some stuff a few years back."

And he started to tell her. He told her about Marco, Oliver, and Ali. How they'd pulled away, how they'd lied to him. He told her about the void that replaced them, how it grew and grew.

"I didn't have anything to do anymore," he said. "Or, well, I've always liked doing things by myself, draw and read, but . . . I couldn't concentrate. I just sat around hating myself."

And wondered what the others were doing, looked at their feeds. But he couldn't say that, either.

"Never being happy just became normal," he went on. "I either had terrible anxiety or was, like . . . turned off. Shut down. I didn't tell anyone, because if I didn't, I'd be in control. That was the logic at the time, anyway. I pretended as if everything was fine, and then I couldn't anymore."

He told her what had happened around the autumn holidays in

high school. Oliver and Ali were the only people he knew in his class, and they barely spoke to him. He couldn't focus on his studies and started to fall behind, which made him feel stupid, which then made him despise himself even more. He'd spend the nights awake. Going to school became more and more difficult.

That's when the rhythm guitarist in Vile Prophets broke his arm and Ernesto asked his dad along on a month's tour to the other side of the world. His mom wanted Kasper to live with her, but he refused, insisted that he'd be better off in the apartment. It was within walking distance from the school, and besides, he could eat at her place a few times per week.

"I just wanted to be left alone," Kasper said. "And I really tried, with school, but one day . . . I just couldn't do it anymore. I stood in the hallway and couldn't open the door. So I lied to my mom and said I was sick. That I'd caught the flu. She came by with food and stuff. Then I told her school had become too much. I logged in as my dad and reported that I was sick. At the end, I wasn't even gaming. Like, I could hardly make myself go to the bathroom. And I hated that I couldn't get it together. How fucking difficult can it be, getting out of bed, showering, eating breakfast, and just leaving?"

It wasn't difficult. It was impossible. Time expanded; every minute felt endless. He wanted to sleep just to make them pass. Somehow, the apartment grew and shrank. In the days, the distance would grow; he'd feel like Frodo trying to carry the ring through Mordor. Tempted to give up at every step. Walking from the bedroom to the kitchen was like climbing Mount Doom. During the nights, however, the walls crept closer.

"Didn't your parents notice what was going on?" Iris said.

She sounded upset. Instinctively, Kasper wanted to defend his mom and dad.

"I was lying to them," Kasper said. "That was the only thing I could be bothered to do. I commented on my dad's pictures, answered every text he and Mom sent. I held on to that for so long. Making sure no one noticed. Everything was pretty chaotic, too. My sisters were sick constantly that fall, my mom and Atle worked too much, I think . . . They couldn't see it. I've always been independent. 'Easy.' I don't think they could imagine me ever having serious issues."

It had come as a shock to his parents and they'd never stopped blaming themselves for it.

"But yeah . . ." Kasper said. "It got really fucking dark for a while. If it hadn't been for Tony . . ." He paused. "I just couldn't stand the pain anymore. And that feeling scared me so fucking badly. I wrote to Tony. He came over at once."

Tony had a spare key to the apartment. He turned on the light in the hallway. Lifted Kasper from the bathroom floor. It was the only time Kasper had ever seen him cry.

The ferry came in toward the dock. A few passengers stepped off it, ambled slowly through the turnstiles. Kasper suddenly felt sick of his own voice.

"Anyway," he said. "I got help. A psychologist, antidepressants, melatonin . . . I left high school, started hanging out with my dad at his gardening job. Helped my mom with her photography. Then I went back to school, this time to do art. I've been there for two years now, and it's good."

He fell silent.

"I don't know if it was the same for you as it was for me," Iris said, "but after my depression, I kept being terrified it would return. That I'd fall back into it."

Kasper sighed, relieved. She got it.

"You too?" he said.

"Not in the same way," she replied. "But I felt like shit throughout junior high and stayed at home a lot. Just like you said, I couldn't make myself go, I know that feeling. At the same time, I was realizing I was trans, and had no idea how to deal with it. At all. So I stayed in my room, gaming. No one could see my face or body, I could present myself however I wanted. And I listened to a ton of music. Twenty-four hours a day. That's when I became an annoying Dark Cruelty fan," she said, her smile going crooked.

"Is this your origin story?" Kasper asked.

"It's *so* uninteresting," Iris said. "I was fourteen, I had just realized there were other metal bands than Slipknot, and I started following a bunch of accounts. Someone posted a pic of Grim on his death-day. The one from *Ancient Bloodlust*, you know, when he's holding that knife."

Kasper knew exactly. He curled his left hand into a fist.

"They'd written that he was a legend," she went on, "that he and Dark Cruelty were pioneers. I didn't know much about the scene, really, but I basically disappeared down an Internet rabbit hole and never emerged again."

"But why Dark Cruelty?" Kasper couldn't help but ask.

Iris looked thoughtful, kicking her heels against the side of the dock.

"It was Grim, I suppose. The first song I heard was 'Curse of the Lost' . . . and I just . . . goose bumps, you know? There was something about his voice . . . As if everything he felt, all the despair, all the hatred, was there. He put all of himself into it. Then I started reading about him, and yeah. I suppose I was fascinated."

Kasper nodded. When musicians died young, they tended to turn into legends. Some of them were stars, like Kurt Cobain and Tupac Shakur, but the underground had its saints, too. Grim was one of them.

When he died, the news spread quickly through the small but international death metal scene. Several people had exchanged letters and tapes with him and read *Headed for Death*. Fanzines wrote about him. Rumors started spreading about the *Ancient Bloodlust* EP, that it presaged his death. Soon, other bands started talking about Dark Cruelty in general and Grim in particular as paragons. Malte quickly became a part of it, talking about Grim like he'd been a diabolical genius, labeling the others in Dark Cruelty traitors for playing in more "commercial" death metal bands. That's when the threats started to come.

Grim's worshippers were still devoted. Some of them bought Malte's image of him as a dark prophet. Others saw him as a tragic poet, a broken teenager they could identify with or fantasize about saving. Kasper's dad, Tony, Ernesto, and others who'd known Grim tried to make him more nuanced and human, but you can't stop mythmaking once it's started.

"You're so used to knowing everything about famous people nowadays," Iris continued, "but there was so little material about Grim. It's so easy to become obsessed, it's like unraveling a mystery. You fill in whatever's missing and end up with an image of him that's just yours. I needed an image like that at the time. Grim mattered so much to me. And so did Dark Cruelty. When everything else felt like shit, the music was still there. Dark Cruelty saved my life." She proclaimed this in an overly dramatic tone of voice, then turned serious again. "No, honestly. I actually think they did."

She stroked her thumb across the tattoo. Kasper nodded. He'd never looked up to a celebrity like that, but he knew how vital music could be.

"Dad was over the moon when I told him about you," he said. "He loves hearing about younger fans, how they keep the music alive. You have to meet him at some point."

Iris's eyes went wide.

"I'm sorry, but are you being serious? Were you there when you and I met for the first time? How do you think I'd react to *your* father?"

Kasper laughed.

"Fine, but you weren't prepared. You would be, now—"

"And I'd still implode," Iris interrupted him. "Thank you, good-bye!"

"He's really very normal."

"I don't doubt that for a second," Iris said. "But I am not. I can't behave. At all."

"That makes two of us," Kasper said.

He considered mentioning the reunion—his dad hadn't explicitly told him to keep it quiet—but it felt like the wrong moment for it.

"Hey," Iris said. "You know what I said about depression, that fear of it returning? It doesn't disappear completely. But it's, what do you call it . . . muted. I'm not as worried about it anymore." She was silent for a moment, spinning the empty water bottle in her hands. "Not sure whether that's because the risk of getting depressed again is actually smaller or because I've forgotten at least some of how bad it was . . . But, oh well. You can't walk around being afraid all the time." She glanced at him. "And yes, I do suck at pep talks."

"No, I actually feel ready to take on the world now," Kasper said. "You've cured me."

"Oh, good," Iris said. "Then that's over and done with." She paused. "But my point is that it gets better. And you're not alone. All right?"

"All right."

They sat together in silence. On the other side of the dark water, Gröna Lund shone like a beacon. A translucent crescent moon hung above them. Later, Kasper would say that that's when he realized they were friends.

The summer had only just begun.

THE PHOTOGRAPHER

It's a stifling night in August and Anja Hansson can't sleep.

She's in her narrow bed, listening to the whirring of her mom's sewing machine. The sound isn't what's keeping her up, though. Quite the opposite: it had been Anja's favorite lullaby as long as she can remember.

There's a drawer on the other side of the room with a small palm tree on it. Next to the pot is her camera, the lens cap on. A closed eye.

She's photographing Dark Cruelty tomorrow.

Grim rang her the day after they'd found the dead rook. He'd got her number from Ernesto, who'd got it from Linda. A steady stream of words collided with Anja's ear. Grim had some pictures he wanted to show her straightaway. A few hours later, he came pedaling on his nightmare of a bike, closely followed by Håkan. Anja met them in the quad of her old school, and they sat together on a tiny knoll, shaded by some trees. Grim opened a scrapbook and Anja recognized some of the bands: the long-haired guys made malevolent faces, some of them with dark makeup around their eyes. Leather, bullet belts, and studs. Knives and swords.

"Is this what you're after?" she said. "Studded bracelets and stuff like that?"

"We'll see what we can scrape together," Grim told her.

"Olle from Vomitator has a few things," Håkan, who was eating a Popsicle and staring into space, supplied.

It was as though he was refusing to look at her. Was he annoyed that Grim had asked her to do the shoot?

"The band's all in black," Grim said. "It looks better. The interesting thing is, you use black in rituals meant to summon evil. Black is associated with Saturn, the planet of death. A demon can be summoned by sacrificing a black goat or a black rooster. The ground-up brain of a black cat also works, though."

"No animal cruelty," Anja said. "Or I'm out."

"Of course not. I like animals," Grim said, seemingly confused.

"It's just something from a book we've read," Håkan said, slurping on the Popsicle.

"Black around the eyes, too." Grim indicated a picture of the band Sarcófago. "Not Ernesto, though. He thinks it makes you look like a panda, but that's his problem."

Anja snickered. Out of the corner of her eye, she caught Håkan smiling, too. He still never looked at her properly, though.

Not that she cared. She doesn't even know how she feels about Håkan. She knows she likes Grim, even though he's an oddball. Quirky and complicated. Bossy one second, shy the next. But Anja has never found odd things off-putting. No, when others look away, Anja wants to *see*. Like Grim, bending over the dead rook.

But Håkan.

She hadn't expected anything in particular when she'd tagged along with Linda to Dark Cruelty's rehearsal in the beginning of the summer. It wasn't the first time she'd acted the audience for a group of guys. She'd met Ernesto already. He was all right but tried to act older than he was, which meant he came off as younger.

But Håkan had been there. Ever since, she couldn't stop noticing him.

Håkan with his long, tangled dark hair and light-colored eyes. Defined eyebrows that tilted downward a bit, making him look a little sad even when he was smiling. Håkan, who talks to everyone except for Anja.

And she wonders why she even cares.

Because, unfortunately, she does. She cares so fucking much.

Anja sighs and turns over in bed.

It's Friday night, but Linda and all Anja's friends from school were busy. With boyfriends, younger siblings, moody parents. During the weekends, people from the death metal scene tend to meet up at the large city map inside the Stockholm Central Station, but everyone's at a gig in Norrköping tonight, one Anja couldn't afford to go to. She's all alone with her restlessness.

There's a metallic rustling noise from Lemmy the parakeet's cage when he moves. Anja picks up her Walkman from the floor and re-winds the tape Linda made for her, presses Play. "Nazi Punks Fuck Off."

When Anja got to know Linda in junior high, Linda had been restless, unable to sit still. She always finished her ice cream the fastest, always craved more, always turned up the music to max. "Listen to this!" she said. And Anja listened, listened to everything Linda was into at the moment and had gotten from her older sister: Jimi Hendrix, the Doors, the Runaways, Ramones, AC/DC, Motörhead, Girlschool, X-Ray Spex, Siouxsie and the Banshees, Joy Division, Misfits, Bad Brains, Black Flag.

Music was their shared adventure. Music brought them together, long before they became a part of the death metal crew. When Anja bought her parakeets—there used to be two of them—she and Linda named them Lemmy and Dee Dee.

"Bassists and songwriters in two of the world's best bands," Linda said.

Fucking bassists.

Anja would like to talk to Linda about Håkan. She knows, however, that Linda would blow it out of proportion, loving the idea that she and Anja were dating boys from the same band. She'd probably drag Ernesto into it, ask him to find out how Håkan feels about Anja. Unfortunately, this would immediately result in Anja dying of embarrassment. It's so very obvious that he doesn't like her.

The next song starts playing: the opening chords of "Ever Fallen in Love (with Someone You Shouldn't've)." She's seeing him tomorrow. She smiles to herself in the darkness.

Håkan, setting off across the field, can tell he's getting an ingrown toenail. He's borrowed old combat boots from Malodor's Stasse and they're a bit too small for him.

Flowers brighten the grass, brush against his jeans. He can only name the cornflowers and the poppies. White clouds scud across the sky, and a breeze makes the field shiver, shakes the trees surrounding the abandoned house. Grim found it. It seems to be what he does sometimes, when he vanishes: roots around in abandoned places. Maybe he's looking for imps and trolls. Lately, he has been talking a lot about creatures from Swedish folklore, supernatural beings that farmers used to fear and believe in.

"I'm not saying Näcken is a naked guy playing the violin in a stream," Grim says as he walks next to Håkan, his turquoise bag swinging. "But it could be all that remains of a story about an old god that people sacrificed to by bodies of water. And maybe there are other intelligent creatures around, who've hid themselves away since man became the dominant species. Maybe our names for them are trolls, goblins, and elves. It could be."

"Yeah," Håkan says, a lock of his hair catching in his mouth when the wind turns.

He does find Grim's theory interesting, but all he can think about is that they're about to see Anja.

They approach the red, wooden house. Håkan would never have guessed it was abandoned: the windows are intact and so is the roof.

There's no graffiti. Then again, they're in the sticks. Grim claims something horrible happened in this house, said he felt the vibes the moment he walked in. It's because of those vibes they're doing the shoot here rather than in a basement somewhere. Besides: here, they get to be alone.

Grim sits down on the splintered steps and Håkan joins him, watches while Grim unpacks a thermos of water and Håkan's old paints. Despite all their planning, they only remembered that they needed some form of makeup at the very last minute. So Grim wets the cracked black watercolor and swirls the brush in it until it's matted with paint. He looks at himself in a pocket mirror while applying it around the eyes. Then it's Håkan's turn. The wet brush is cool, but the paint stings when it gets into his eyes.

"Looks good," Grim says, tightening spike bracelets, from Vomitator's Olle, made from scraps of leather and five-inch nails in the arts and crafts room at his local youth center.

Håkan looks at himself in the mirror, too. His skin tightens as the paint dries. It looks good. He just wishes Ernesto hadn't said that thing about pandas.

He checks his watch. Ernesto and Tony were going to meet up with Anja in Handen and take the bus here. Grim had given them a hand-drawn map, and suddenly Håkan worries they got lost. Or what if they'd missed the bus?

"Come on," Grim says.

Håkan walks up the steps to the porch, pulling the door open with some difficulty, as the wood is swollen. A foul smell wafts toward him, as if something dead is rotting inside the house.

"That is gross," he says to Grim, holding the door open. "Smell that?"

Grim doesn't answer him. Håkan follows him into a dim room buzzing with flies. Then Grim puts his bag down and takes out a deer skull he's found in the forest, places it on the rough wooden table that constitutes the only furniture in the room. They start covering up the windows with moth-eaten sheets that they found in the garbage. The wooden floor is covered with dirt and droppings. Maybe some animal has crawled under it and died?

"But can you smell it, though?" Håkan insists.

"Come on," Grim says again, and Håkan follows him.

In the corner of the room is a shapeless pile. At first, Håkan thinks it's moving. Then he realizes it's insects crawling across the decomposing body of a bird. He looks away.

"Is it that fucking rook?" he says.

"In necromancy, you use carcasses to attract the spirits of the dead," Grim tells him. "We've got to set the right mood."

Håkan swallows what he actually wants to say, which is that Grim is out of his mind for bringing the dead bird here. It would be one thing if it was just Ernesto and Tony, but Anja . . .

The band is number one, Håkan thinks. The band is always number one, and regardless of what he feels about Anja, she doesn't care about him. Why would she do that when she's caught Tony's attention? He's better-looking than Håkan. Taller. Stronger. That hair, which girls seem to love. And unlike Håkan, he can actually talk to Anja.

"Wicked," he says, nodding at the bird without looking at it.

"I warned Anja," Grim says.

He is standing by the table now, filling a small bowl with dry leaves.

"What?"

"Maybe you're worried about what she might think of all this, but I told her about our ideas. I said it would get gruesome."

"Why would I care what Anja thinks?"

"All right," Grim says. "Got a light?"

Håkan hands him a lighter and Grim sets fire to the leaves in the bowl, blows gently on the flame so it's reduced to a reddish glow.

Thin smoke snakes upward, its scent not unpleasant. Maybe it will hide the stench of the carcass. Håkan looks at the watch he's put in his pocket, straightens the bullet belt. What if Anja thinks he looks ridiculous. Voices approach from across the field.

The moment she sees the house, she comes alive. It looks like something from a horror movie; it's perfect. She starts to grin as she walks toward it with Tony and Ernesto, the camera a comforting weight around her neck. Granddad's camera. The man who'd taught her everything about birds. The weariness she'd felt after her long, sleepless night is gone.

"What a place." Tony kicks at some piece of agricultural machinery, partly swallowed by the grass. *The Texas Chainsaw Massacre.*

"Mmm," Ernesto says.

He's in a mood and Anja knows why. Ernesto and Linda have been fighting. Linda's knocked up, and they've decided to keep the baby, but Ernesto doesn't want to tell anyone yet. He hasn't even told his mom and his stepdad, which upsets Linda. Hiding her stomach isn't a problem yet, but she doesn't want to lie to his family and friends.

Anja thinks Ernesto's being a dick. It's her job to say things like that, seeing as she's Linda's best friend. But deep down she can't understand either of them. Anja has always thought of babies as part of some vague, faraway future. Why are they in such a rush?

Tony, to one side of her, lets the tape recorder swing from his hand. He tears out a piece of grass and places it between his lips like a cowboy from the movies.

"Howdy, ma'am," he says to Anja.

The sunshine makes his hair gleam: Tony's unbelievable hair. Anja is a little bit obsessed with it. Unlike many of the others in the scene, who only began growing it out a few years ago, he has a long fall of hair. And while the others make a show of not washing their hair particularly often, Tony's golden locks glow. There's a bit of friendly teasing about it in the band, but in a few years, their hair will also be smelling of shampoo when they headbang.

"Wait a sec," Anja says, raising the camera. "Stand like that."

Tony stops and she gets a picture of him with the grass in his mouth. People who don't know Tony will think that, because he's tall and muscular, he's a fighter. On the one hand, it means he doesn't have to deal with too much shit; on the other hand, it's made him a target. Fortunately for Tony, he's also great at ducking blows and a tenacious runner.

"Are you a model now, or what?" Ernesto scoffs. "Move it."

"Are you on the rag, or what?" Tony shoots back.

Ernesto mutters something and storms ahead, but Tony just shakes his head and follows. Anja picks a poppy as she walks and sticks it into the buttonhole of her jacket. It hangs its head pathetically. She wishes she could tell Tony why Ernesto's in such a foul mood, but it isn't her business.

Anja follows the boys into the house.

A scent like incense and something else, something nauseating, strikes her.

"Oh, hell," Tony says, making a disgusted face.

"We're in here," they hear Grim say.

The smell is even worse in the other room, its windows covered. Grim and Håkan remind Anja of the young men in the pictures that Grim showed her. Black clothes, bullet belts, studded wristbands, black circles around their eyes. Anja approaches the smoking bowl on the table, touches the skull next to it.

"What is that stench?" Ernesto, who suddenly looks animated, says. "Is that you, Håkan?"

"Hilarious," Håkan says.

Grim hands Tony the watercolors and a brush while Anja looks on in wonder.

"We were in a bit of a rush," Håkan mumbles. "So we didn't get hold of anything else."

"But if Tony wears paint, too, I'm the only one without it," Ernesto points out.

"You could just put it on," Håkan says.

"You wouldn't catch me dead in it."

"I can go without," Tony says.

"Okay," Grim says, "but you'll have to stand slightly behind us."

"Hair in front of your faces."

Ernesto lets his hair down and roars like a demon.

"All ready," Grim says, and turns to Anja.

Anja tries to breathe through her mouth as she affixes the flash to the camera and checks the light. Tony puts the recorder down and presses Play. Celtic Frost's "Into the Crypts of Rays" thunders through the room. The boys line up, all four of them in black. Tony is the only one whose shirt isn't plain. The Black Sabbath logo is almost completely faded, but Håkan still makes him turn the tee inside out.

Anja provides them with instructions and they make suggestions. In the beginning, she has to tell them not to talk while she's shooting, and that Håkan has to try to keep his eyes open. The mood is both focused and excited, and she even starts getting used to the stench. Every photo is taken with care. Film is expensive, and she wants to save herself extra work in the darkroom later on. She takes portraits, too, of each of them. Håkan poses with the deer skull and passes it to Tony, who looks repulsed. He's a vegetarian. Grim has asked to go last. He moves over to the corner, and when he returns, Anja realizes where the smell is coming from. She assumes it's the rook they found, even though it's barely recognizable. Tony whimpers when he sees it and Ernesto presses a hand against his mouth.

"Thought I'd hold it," Grim says.

"Go ahead," Anja says, lifting the camera to her face.

Grim holds up the carcass, unbothered by the crawling insects. Anja photographs him while fighting back nausea, as if in a trance. Grim takes the rook by the wings and stretches them wide. Anja takes a picture. Then, in the next moment, the dead bird falls apart.

"Oh, shit," she hears Tony say as he races for the door with Ernesto and Håkan close behind.

Anja follows them, breathing deeply in the fresh air. Tony is a bit farther away, puking. Ernesto and Håkan are running across the field, leaping and laughing, shouting with elation.

"Any good, do you think?"

Grim's voice behind her. He's standing in the doorway, watching Anja with a gaze that's suddenly uncertain.

"Awesome," she manages.

He smiles his wide-open smile. She raises her camera, snaps another photo.

Years later, Anja will look at the pictures from that day and see something she couldn't at the time: their youth and their fragility. Ernesto. Tony. Håkan. Grim. They were only kids, but somehow huge, the way you only could be when you were that age. Huge in their passion, in their courage. She thinks that's why she gravitated toward them. She recognized the force that drove them, the conviction that you could do *more*. The urge to burst through every single boundary. That fire burned inside her, too.

Back in school, she develops the images in the darkroom. She can see them emerging: the band Dark Cruelty, what they are and what they could be. And she sees him. Grim, with the dead bird in his hands. His head, tilted slightly backward, that pale face and those dark rings around his eyes. His black hair blending in with the shadows. In that moment, he had known exactly what he was doing, she can see that now—deliberately or instinctively, she doesn't know, and it doesn't matter.

When he pulled at those wings, he'd understood exactly what sort of picture he was creating with her.

He's not just an odd teenager. He's not just a singer in an underground band. He has that thing you can't put your finger on, but that's still so apparent.

A star that shines as clear as ice.

KASPER

After that conversation on the dock, it was as though something eased up inside Kasper. His anxieties didn't disappear, but they retreated, became background noise.

He tried to trust in what Iris had told him: that he could count on the others in The House. It wasn't as if he was close to all of them, but he'd discovered a community where he felt a sense of peace. After late nights out, he could wake up in the morning and line up moments like treasures from a beach. Moments that had been good, when he'd been present, when he hadn't overanalyzed every interaction. Maybe it didn't sound like much, but every second when he didn't hate himself, when he didn't berate himself for every mistake and misstep he'd made, was a rare and beautiful gift. A moment to breathe. The absence of pain was the sweetest possible sensation.

And almost as sweet was his moment of vengeance.

It was the final shift of the day, and Kasper was the Chef. He'd kept working as usual after the incident with the man who'd chased him, but he always felt uneasy at that scene. He didn't make proper use of it. He didn't have a problem scaring most people, but younger men now made him hold back.

A crackle in the radio. Krille said a boy and a girl were on their way to the Chef. Kasper peered through the peephole until he heard the sound of meat axes and screams and the couple appeared.

At first he thought he'd made a mistake, much like he had many times before.

But Kasper wasn't mistaken. Marco was actually walking toward him, his arm around a blond girl Kasper didn't recognize, his expression bored.

Kasper hadn't seen him in months, despite them living in the same neighborhood. Or had he moved? Kasper realized he had no idea what Marco was up to nowadays. Doing a year of military service? He'd talked about wanting to, once.

Kasper pulled down his executioner's hood over his face and gripped the shiny new chain saw firmly. He attempted to steady his hand and took hold of the curtain. This was his chance. He peered out and saw the door open. The girl walked in front of Marco, just like Kasper had hoped; Marco's face was lit by the evening sun. He looked more bored than ever.

That's when the Chef tore the curtain aside, threw himself up against the bars, and roared along with the chain saw.

Marco leaped around, his hands coming up to his face as if protecting himself from a blow. His eyes were round, his mouth open. Kasper and the chain saw kept screaming while Marco stumbled out onto the balcony.

Afterward Kasper couldn't stop smiling, and he told the story several times when they went out that night.

"Here's to people getting what they deserve!" Iris said.

"That's the dream," Selam said, eyes sparkling. "That you get to confront some old bully."

Bully. The word suited Marco, Kasper thought, and he had another drink.

A few days later, though, everything turned upside down.

Selam was at home with a burning fever, in the middle of peak season, and she wasn't getting better. After having spent a few days racing around like a stressed-out lab rat, Kasper asked Iris if he could help her with some basic UC tasks. Iris looked at him gratefully, and after that, Kasper ensured tissues and disinfectant were present at every station, and that the costumes that needed washing were handed in on time. A week later, when Selam still hadn't recovered, Kasper started helping out Iris even more, and one afternoon, she took him to the downstairs dressing room. Unlike the one upstairs, this one didn't have windows; people mostly used the room to wash their hands and get changed. A perfect place for discreet conversations.

"This is officially a crisis," Iris told him. "Selam has glandular fever. Poor thing. It can knock you out for weeks or even months."

"Shit," Kasper said.

"You know The House," Iris said. "You know everyone in it. I've spoken to the TL and you can get quick training in UC work. If you want to."

Unit chief. Kasper couldn't process what she was asking him.

"But I haven't even been here for one season," he managed at last.

"Doesn't matter," Iris said. "You're serious about the job, and you and I work well together. That's the important thing. Also, only you and Santiago have offered to help me out, which matters. A lot."

"What about Santiago?" Kasper objected. "He's been here for ages."

"And he's never wanted to be UC," Iris said. "It's not his thing at all. I actually think this year's Halloween is going to be his final one at Grönan. Been a bit sick of it lately."

Had he? Sure, Santiago complained sometimes, but Kasper had thought he was just venting. Then again, he hadn't met Santiago during other seasons, had nothing to compare his current attitude to. He had just assumed that Santiago basically enjoyed working in The House just as much as Kasper did. It was a small shift in perspective, one that shouldn't feel as distressing as it did. But what else had Kasper not noticed?

"Santiago has agreed to have your back in the beginning, on days when you're the sole UC," Iris continued.

"I don't know if I can do this," Kasper admitted.

"If you don't believe in yourself," Iris said, "then maybe you can believe in me." She took hold of his upper arms and looked him in the eyes. "Kasper Hansson Nordin," she said. "You've got this."

Kasper did. He was even quite good at it. He enjoyed making sure the demons were comfortable at their stations, and even scheduling wasn't a chore, once he'd figured out how it worked. He felt himself become calmer, surer of himself. The other demons seemed to trust him, and soon he was talking to people from the other rides. He felt as though he belonged. He hadn't felt that in years, if ever. Because even though he'd found his friendship with Marco, Oliver, and Ali reliable, it had always been riddled with tension. He could see that now. Pointed comments that turned into fights. Comments that hurt, a hurt he had to hide. He'd never really felt fully accepted. Not that he was best friends with every single demon at work, but there was no sense of competition and prestige in their group. They helped each other out.

And he and Iris really did work well together.

It had been a while since they'd reached the point in their friendship where they could talk about their first impressions of each other and laugh at how awkward they'd been. Like Iris thinking *DonotmentionDarkCruelty* every day in the beginning. She'd even bumped into Håkan and Tony when they'd visited Grönan to catch a gig, and she managed to act normal while the three of them were chatting. The fact that she had to run into the dressing room and hyperventilate afterward was a different story.

Kasper and Iris had talked about their dreams and fears. Iris had told him all about the writing courses she'd very nearly applied to, only to get cold feet at the last second. Kasper told Iris that he worried he'd never be a good enough illustrator, that his fear held him back, stopped him from practicing. Iris understood him perfectly.

"Imagine just knowing that all my doubts and all my anxieties would lead me to becoming as great as I want to be. I mean, then I'd just go for it," she told him one night as they were closing up The House. "But what if I don't even have the skill? What if it's all in my dumb head?"

Kasper understood what she meant. There were millions of people who wanted to draw, millions of people who were better at it than Kasper. How could he stop thinking about that and just go ahead and do it? It sounded so simple when his dad and his friends talked about starting bands and recording demos. They just plowed ahead. Somehow, despite hardly knowing how to play in the beginning, they had been convinced they'd found their niche. Had it been easier because there had been so few of them? Or because they didn't see wildly successful people on social media every day? Maybe it was because they were in a bubble, maintaining each other's hubris until their skills finally measured up. Or maybe the doubts had been there but were eventually forgotten because it ended in success.

Memory erases, memory rewrites.

Iris had talked about that, too.

"Memories change; there's loads of research to back that up," she said one day, when so many people had called in sick that both UCs had to be demons for a day.

Kasper and Iris were in the dressing room, painting their faces white and adding black circles around their eyes. The looped soundtrack—organ music and thunder—could be heard from the Lab, occasionally accompanied by the screams of startled guests.

"The risk is especially high when you're retelling a story in the same way, over and over again," Iris continued, "since the anecdote becomes more real to you than what actually happened. Crazy, isn't it? It's not that you can't trust your memories at all, obviously, but they can deceive you. Sometimes we rewrite our own history."

Kasper found it hard to imagine. His own memories were often painfully clear. Except for the depression, that is, which was full of holes, of times blending together. Maybe his memories were slipperier than he knew, though. And how much would he forget in the future?

When Selam came back in August, Kasper was happy for her sake, while still reluctant to hand back the reins. His final days at work were approaching; school was about to begin again. He tried to comfort himself with the knowledge that he could cover for people on weekends, that Halloween was coming.

A few days before Kasper's last shift, Iris and Selam asked Kasper to stay behind after the team meeting in the Lab. They sat down in the upper dressing room and Selam got straight to the point: "I won't be returning as UC next year."

"Oh. Okay," Kasper said.

He'd had the impression that Selam loved her job as much as he and Iris did. Then again, he'd been wrong about Santiago.

"Oh, my God, just say it," Iris said, throwing a plastic cap at Selam, who caught it one-handed.

"I'm applying for TL," she said. "You know I tried it on for a day and have been talking to Nadja." Nadja was in charge of Rides. "They can't promise me anything, but—"

"But they basically did," Iris interrupted.

"Fine—they highly recommended I apply for it." Selam grinned. "Do you see what this means, Kasper, the Not So Friendly Ghost?"

Kasper stared at Selam and then at Iris. If Selam was becoming team leader, there was a spot as UC that needed filling in The House. But they couldn't mean that *he* should apply for it?

"Let me just say this," Iris said. "I've already talked to a couple of TLs and Nadja, and they think you've done a great job. The way has been . . . you know. Paved. So mention it during your final talk with the TL. Oh, and tell them you'd like to be UC during Halloween."

"It's not official yet, but I'll be UC in the Funeral House," Selam said.

"But what about you?" Kasper asked Iris, remembering that there was only one designated UC per ride during Halloween.

"The Castle." Iris's smile was broad.

Every year, Grönan constructed an entirely new, particularly unpleasant Halloween surprise. This year it was called the Castle, and everything about it was shrouded in mystery.

"Shit," Kasper said. "Congratulations."

"But next summer," Iris went on, "it's you and me in The House!"

"And I'll be in charge of both of you," Selam said.

Kasper returned to school feeling like he was just a visitor. The TL hadn't promised him the position as UC during Halloween or next summer, but Kasper understood that they were both basically his if he applied for them. Not that it mattered, really. He'd be happy coming back as anything, even as a regular demon. His life was finally revolving around a fixed point. School was spent waiting, waiting and longing. It was the first time in a very long time he looked forward to anything.

And then September came.

*

Deathdays and birthdays.

They cast long shadows across mourners.

Maybe that was why Kasper's parents named him after Grim. They'd never be able to forget the fact that their son was born on the day between their friend's death and his birth. Better to acknowledge it then, to honor or appease the power that had bound them together, the dead boy and the living one.

Every year on the fifteenth of September, they placed a candle and a photograph of Grim by the record player. As long as Kasper could remember, his birthday had been celebrated under the other Kasper's gaze. He had opened presents while the forever nineteen-year-old had looked on, watching him grow older. It felt natural to Kasper. He'd never found the dead boy threatening; he was just one of those people who weren't around anymore, who Kasper's parents still talked about sometimes, like his grandma.

In the photograph, Grim was looking straight into the camera and smiling. His face was bright, his dark eyes sparkling.

"Who took the picture?" Kasper used to ask when he was little, just to hear his mom say: "I did, sweetie."

During those days, Kasper had a lot of questions about Grim. In kindergarten, Marco would sometimes mention his dead cousin, and Kasper wondered if Grim was his cousin. He wasn't, his dad said.

Once, Kasper asked: "Was the other Kasper nice?"

"Yeah, he was," his dad replied. "Almost always."

"Was he mean sometimes?"

"No one's good all the time."

On Kasper's sixth birthday, he asked his dad: "If Grim hadn't died, would I have been born?"

His dad had stared at him, searching for words. Håkan, who was normally so talkative, went silent.

"Why do you ask?" he managed at last.

This time, Kasper struggled to respond. It felt like there should have been a connection, as if the other Kasper had to die for him to live.

"He died ten years before you were born," his dad told him. "It had nothing to do with you."

As Kasper got older, the steady stream of questions dried up. He didn't think much about Grim at all. But that was about to change.

Grim sat at the opposite end of a table covered in black cloth. The room was dark. Black candles burned in silver candelabras reminiscent of the one Håkan held in the photo on the back of *Ancient Bloodlust*. There were other people around the table, too, but they were unimportant. Kasper only saw Grim, who'd smeared black makeup under his eyes.

So no one can tell he's dead, Kasper thought. *But I know he is. Isn't he?*

Grim's hands were on the table, his palms turned upward. A small snake slithered across them.

He's trying to show me something, Kasper thought, looking up.

Hair fell over Grim's face, but Kasper believed he was smiling. Using both hands, Grim lifted a cup from the table and held it out.

I really shouldn't take it, Kasper thought as his hands closed around the cup. It was as heavy as lead. Grim's fingers were dry and cold. Someone next to Kasper whispered, *Drink.*

He woke up tasting metal. Stumbled out of bed, stiff-legged, and sat down at his desk. His sketchbook and pencil were out. The dream shimmered inside him while he drew. Had it been like this last time? This pure and wonderful? He felt free. Breathlessly, he put aside his pencil, looked at the drawing as if it were something holy.

This was the first time Kasper had drawn something that wasn't a part of his school assignments, since his dad had told him about the reunion. He had tried, again and again, but he'd always ended up gazing at the images of Grim on the stage and in the water. What was the point of trying?

Kasper stared at this new drawing as if he were afraid it would vanish. His alarm rang abruptly, and he turned it off. That's when he realized what day it was.

His dad wasn't home. He'd gone up to Sundsvall with Tony to

visit the grave in Timrå and talk to Grim's sister about the details surrounding the reunion. She was the only close relative of Grim's who was still alive, and she had already given Håkan her permission to use some of Grim's unpublished lyrics.

No one had asked Kasper to take out the photo of Grim, but it felt like the right thing to do. It was in a box, wrapped in a shawl his mom had left behind when she moved out. The photograph gave off a whiff of incense when Kasper uncovered it. He placed the black frame next to the record player, then he moved a candle from the living room table and placed it next to the picture. Flicked on one of his dad's lighters. In the bright morning, the flame was almost invisible as he brought it to the wick.

The twenty-year anniversary reissue of *Ancient Bloodlust* was, like so many of his dad's vinyl records, kept in a plastic wallet, the paper sleeve with the record tucked behind the cover, so as to avoid a mark. Kasper put the cover next to the record player, too, looking at the snake that squirmed out of the skull's sockets. Placed the EP with the B-side up, setting the needle on the second track. Closed his eyes.

The production was raw but rich and fully formed. Drums as heavy as lead, the guitars' sticky and thick riffs twisting around each other above the deep, malevolent pulse of the bass. Grim's cry like a voice from the abyss.

Out of darkness I was born . . . The path of darkness I shall follow . . . On my eternal search . . . For the secrets of the ancients . . . Shrouded in abysmal hate . . . Descending stairs I tread . . . Fallen angel . . . Lucifer . . . As I was . . . As I will be . . . Lost . . . Forever lost . . .

Kasper opened his eyes and examined the photograph. Grim looked perfectly normal, nothing like he'd appeared in Kasper's dreams. There was something faintly childlike about him, as if he was younger than nineteen.

I'll be his age tomorrow, Kasper thought. *And on my next birthday, I'll be older than he ever was.*

When Kasper had been at his worst and tried to look ahead, somehow he'd always stopped at twenty. Adult life, the future, felt like threats. He couldn't understand how he'd get by alone, ever. What was he going to do with his life? When would he have to decide?

This summer he'd seen life after twenty up close. Iris, with her dreams of becoming a writer; Selam, unsure about whether to move back to Gothenburg. Cornelia, always hunting roles in films and television. Santiago, who'd just finished reading up on Natural Science and his ensuing panic when he realized that it left him with no clear answers as to what he wanted to do. Elliot, who seemed to think that things would turn out all right, but would then talk about "not having done anything with his life" whenever he'd had a few beers. People over twenty seemed as confused and muddled as Kasper was. There was some comfort in that.

The song ended, transitioning to the outro that had been a hidden track when the EP came out. Layers of atmospheric sound, Grim hissing the names of demons. Kasper suddenly recalled the release of the reissue, when his dad and Tony were signing at the record shop Raw Power in Gamla Stan. Kasper was on a stool next to his dad, wholly absorbed in his drawing. Maybe he looked up because the man who was approaching moved strangely, his steps small and careful, the record held in both hands as though he was carrying a precious gift. The man stopped in front of Kasper's dad with an odd little smile. Kasper could smell him: sharp sweat.

"Hey," his dad had said.

"I hope I'm not putting my foot in it, but I read an old interview with Malte Lundell," the man said, smiling sheepishly. Kasper's dad and Tony looked wary. "He claimed that only he and Grim were in the studio during the recording of the outro, and that some form of blood sacrifice took place. 'An invocation that the demons may cast their dark blessing over the work,' I believe he said."

Kasper wondered why the man was smiling when he didn't seem happy at all.

"Well, one can't help but be a tad curious. Is it true?"

Tony snorted, shaking his head.

"Malte has his version of the truth," his dad said. "But no, what he's saying isn't right. Want me to sign?"

The man gingerly laid the record in front of his dad, who quickly signed it before passing it to Tony.

"One can't help but hope," the man said, choking back laughter, and then he left.

"Goddamn lunatic," Tony had muttered.

His dad had turned to Kasper: "Don't believe everything people say about Grim. Remember that for me."

Kasper remembered. His palm ached, and he drew a finger over the thin scar that had formed after the cut. The final whisper issued from the speakers and Grim's voice fell silent.

Time for school. He had to hand in work today.

Fredrika Bremer was one of the largest schools in the Stockholm area. Two thousand students attended it, which Kasper often had reminded himself of when he worried about running into Oliver and Ali. But they'd graduated. The school was his now.

The entrance opened onto a spacious hall with a long staircase leading up to the abode of the art students and their spacious, bright classroom slash studio. Kasper would never forget what entering it had felt like that first time. He could breathe easier. And that effect stayed with him; just walking into the room could calm him down. But not today. Something felt deeply wrong. He was sitting at a desk with his presentation before him, the one on his final project: "Mythological Creatures in Handen." He'd turned the paper over so he didn't have to look at the text he'd forced himself to write yesterday. He was about to show it to Ms. Gunhild, the class teacher, who was in the adjacent room.

Right now, Lo was in there. They had worked all summer on an acrylic painting, inspired by the nightmarish, medieval chaos in the works of Hieronymus Bosch, showing animals turning against humans to create a new paradise on earth. Several of Kasper's classmates had applied to the Art program's Illustration and Design orientation because they enjoyed drawing and creating, but Lo had ambition. So did Lydia, who was seated next to Kasper. A garden full of heavy, dewy roses and merry bumblebees flourished beneath her brush. In first year, she'd told everyone that her goal was to apply to Sweden's most prestigious education institute for children's books illustrators. Her final project was, naturally, a picture book. Raman, who sat in front of Kasper, dreamed about working for Marvel, so he was creating a comic. He was by far the best at anatomy, since he practiced drawing by watching videos of live models on a daily basis. The three of them were the real stars. Kasper was among those just beneath them, and then came the rest of the class, according to their level of genuine interest, ending with those who'd applied to Art because it seemed chill. Kasper *wanted* as much as Lo, Lydia, and Raman, but he didn't have their direction. It often made him envious. Like the project: All three of them had chosen something that suited their portfolio, but what was Kasper's plan? He didn't even know what to do once he'd graduated.

He poked at the paper in front of him, nudging it so that it lay exactly parallel with the edge of the desk. He'd worked out five possible ideas to sketch and described why he wanted to do them. The problem was that he wasn't excited about these ideas anymore, not really. What had seemed interesting to him last summer seemed meaningless now. Kasper looked sideways at his sketchbook, which was also on the desk. His phone buzzed in his pocket. Santiago had written about the Star Gala, the party that wrapped up the summer season at Grönan, which was taking place in a week. The theme this year was "the 00s," and Kasper and Iris had decided to dress up as two characters from the *Saw* movies: Billy the Puppet and one of Jigsaw's victims.

"Are you doing anything for your birthday?" Lydia asked him out of the blue.

She dipped her brush in a jar of water and a red cloud billowed around it. Kasper hadn't mentioned his birthday, but it was typical of Lydia to remember. It was largely thanks to Lydia that the class had such a sense of community. She'd personally taken on the challenge to make everyone feel seen, to ensure no one fell between the cracks. And her memory was eerily good. The first day in art school together, she'd reminded Kasper that they had made necklaces for each other in kindergarten, with as much confidence as if it happened yesterday. Since then, they often sat next to each other. They didn't have much in common, but Lydia was a genuinely nice person. Kasper appreciated her company, despite it so obviously being some type of charity.

"I'm having dinner with my family and then meeting up with some people from Grönan," he replied.

When school had started again, he'd had to hold back. Everything reminded him of Grönan, The House, and the people who worked there. He called to mind how dull he'd found Oliver's stories about sailing camp and took that as a warning. Still, maybe he'd gone on about Grönan too much? Lydia looked a little tense when she nodded and said, "Sounds nice."

She tucked her short black hair behind her ear.

"I really meant to go to Grönan this summer," she said, swirling her brush in the red paint. "I wanted to see you as a ghost."

"Come for Halloween," Kasper told her.

"Oh, God. I'll be scared to death," Lydia said with a smile. "But I'll make Lo and Raman come with me."

"Go for it," Kasper said, picking up his phone again when he got a notification.

His dad had added a picture of Grim's grave to his private feed. Cigarettes and a box of snuff were lined up against the pale gray headstone, despite Grim not having partaken in either. A couple of plectrums. A few white and red roses. Kasper had come along once, when they'd been in the area. There were foreign coins on the stone then. His dad had said that some fans left them behind to honor a fallen comrade. Kasper, however, had thought about the myth of Charon, the ferryman who had to be paid to row the dead over the underground river Styx.

But Grim had already been underground when they found him, Kasper thought abruptly, when he looked at his dad's picture of the headstone. Where was the tunnel they'd found him in? How long had he been in there? Were there really no clues at all as to how he'd ended up there?

Kasper had never thought about Grim's death in this way before. It was like admitting to himself that his parents hadn't told him everything. Not that there's anything strange about that, considering he was a child the last time he asked them about it.

He wasn't a child anymore.

The door opened and Lo returned. She pointed at Kasper. "Your turn."

The first time Kasper saw Ms. Gunhild, he thought she looked like a stereotypically dull teacher. Her hair, skin, and eyes were somehow faded, and she dressed almost exclusively in beiges and browns. But he soon discovered how wrong he'd been, because Ms. Gunhild had a fire inside of her. It burned still and it burned steady. She had a natural authority and only had to look at the class for them to sit up straighter and pay attention. Moreover, she had an almost uncanny ability to make everything she taught interesting. She was, hands down, the best teacher Kasper had ever had, and the one that instilled the most respect in him. So it pained him to sit in front of her in the small room with its red sofas, delivering a presentation he didn't believe in. At all.

"I told you about it last summer," he said.

"A good project," Ms. Gunhild said. "Very good, actually."

She was bent over the piece of paper. The wall behind her was covered with pictures of famous works of art. A photo of an ancient goddess figurine holding a snake in each hand caught Kasper's eye.

"I'm not sure, though," he blurted out.

Ms. Gunhild's look was one of mild surprise.

"I know today is the deadline," he went on quickly. "But—I don't know if this is right for me. For my portfolio."

Kasper wondered if this was the expression Ms. Gunhild wore when she was having a serious talk with her children. If she even had children; Kasper had no idea. Picturing Ms. Gunhild outside of school was almost impossible.

"So this is what I'm thinking," she said. "This project is important, sure. But there's also a tendency to exaggerate its importance." With a warm smile, she added, "This won't determine your future, you know."

But what if it does.

"I've been working on something this summer," he said. "Well, I've made some sketches. I don't really know what it is."

He laughed, an abrupt, helpless sound.

"Did you bring anything with you?" Ms. Gunhild asked.

Kasper's mouth went dry. He hadn't shown anyone his drawings yet. Maybe doing so would rid them of some of their magic. It had happened to him before, when he had shown off a picture he'd been pleased with, only to have it fade the moment someone else's eyes landed on it. He opened the sketchbook and handed it to Ms. Gunhild.

"The three most recent ones," he said.

Ms. Gunhild accepted the book and inspected the first drawing; it was of Grim on stage. She looked at it for a long time. Then she turned the page. Looked. Turned the page. Looked. Went back again. It felt as though minutes passed.

"What is this?" she asked him, finally.

"They're from dreams I've been having," Kasper replied.

Ms. Gunhild turned to him, fascinated.

"Is it a self-portrait?"

"No. It's my dad's friend," Kasper said. "He died today."

Ms. Gunhild's eyes went wide with shock.

"I mean, he died on this day," Kasper added quickly. "But it was almost thirty years ago."

Ms. Gunhild went back to the drawings. At once, Kasper felt self-conscious. Had he just revealed something dark and sick about himself, something he was unable to see? He felt exposed.

"I dunno," he said. "Maybe it's nothing."

"Oh, this is something," Ms. Gunhild emphasized, pointing at Grim with the cup and the snake. "You've found something interesting in these pieces. The line, the expression, the composition. It's special. It feels personal, Kasper. The question is what you want to do with it."

He didn't have an answer. Not yet.

"Can I have some more time?" he said. "Just until Monday?"

Ms. Gunhild nodded absently, returning to the sketchbook to look at the drawing of Grim floating in the water.

"What on earth happened to this poor boy?"

"I actually don't know," Kasper said. He was surprised by his own words when he went on: "I'll try to find out."

THE CRY

They record the demo in August; the studio, they've heard, is supposed to be good. The rumor holds up. The owner, Hasse, is into prog rock and used to play in a band called Alla Skogens Djur (All the Woodland Animals) in the seventies. He doesn't know the first thing about death metal, but somehow gets what they're after and guides them through the process.

It's the first time they're working with an enthusiastic engineer, and suddenly, they become aware of things not coming out right. The flaws are more apparent with Hasse present. But he cheers them on, tells them when they really have to re-record and when they're getting hung up on a minor detail.

"Fight on, comrades," Hasse says. "You've got this."

Håkan can tell how frustrated Grim is with his own limitations as a guitarist. He swears, striking himself in the forehead several times. Finally, Hasse grabs his hand, kindly but firmly, and says, "Relax, man. You're good enough."

Håkan looks at Hasse and Grim, wondering how Grim is going to react. But Grim just blinks and nods. Then charges on.

They end up at a greasy lunch spot nearby and share a pizza. All their money has gone to the recording.

"I'm going to be a dad," Ernesto says suddenly. "In February."

Håkan gawks at him. He's got to be joking. But if he were, he probably wouldn't have said "in February."

"You think I'm joking?" Ernesto barks.

Grim lets fat drip from his slice onto the plate between them.

"I was just surprised," Håkan says. "Congratulations, man."

"Yeah, congratulations," Tony says, throwing an arm around Ernesto's shoulders.

"Thanks," Ernesto mumbles.

He looks happy and terrified. No wonder. Håkan can't even take it in. Ernesto is just six months older than him, had turned seventeen in July. Why would he want to be a dad? Then again, maybe he knows something about life that Håkan doesn't. He has Linda, is dating someone he's in love with. Maybe that changes everything, even though Håkan has a hard time imagining it. If he and Anja were to get together, unlikely though it is, he wouldn't want kids at once. Or would he? What does he know, really?

"We need a new guitarist," Grim announces, breaking his silence.

Ernesto is shocked, so shocked he doesn't even get upset. Håkan does, though.

"What the fuck are you talking about?"

Grim's look is one of bewilderment.

"I'm a shitty guitarist," he says. "We need someone else on rhythm guitar. I'm only singing on the EP."

Ernesto's grin is huge.

"Good morning," he says. "Did you even hear what I said?"

"Yes," Grim says, taking another bite of the pizza and talking with his mouth full. "You're having a baby. Crazy. Congratulations."

Ernesto howls with laughter, Håkan and Tony joining in. Grim smiles, but Håkan wonders if he actually understands what they find so funny. But it's nice to let loose and laugh, letting go of their worries for a bit. Because during this recording session, Håkan has started to worry. If the demo isn't good enough, there's no point aiming for an EP.

But the next day they record the vocals, and Grim is so disgustingly good that Håkan's doubts all but disappear. Hasse patiently listens to their suggestions during the mixing, and then, finally, the time has come for them to listen to what they're taking home on tape. Håkan and Grim lie down on the floor in the live room and Hasse turns off the lights.

Håkan closes his eyes. He listens. Just like that, all of his worries melt away.

If anything, the minor flaws and imperfections only make it sound more acute. The passion and desperation they've poured into every precious minute of the session is all there. They can't be the only ones who will hear it.

They're not.

The *Nocturnal Allegiance* demo changes everything.

It becomes obvious that Dark Cruelty with Grim is something else altogether.

It isn't just the new songs, "Nocturnal Allegiance" and "Carrion Summoning." It's also the cover with the new logo above Grim's drawing of a dead bird nailed to an inverted cross. The Aleister Crowley quote in the liner notes: *Ordinary morality is only for ordinary people.* Then the photo of Grim, which they send to the fanzines, the one where he's holding the carcass. When the image spreads in its photocopied, grainy version, it becomes more mesmerizing than ever. The sense of mystery surrounding the band only grows.

"We really shouldn't do any interviews," Grim tells Håkan, when the number of inquiries from fanzines starts to multiply.

Håkan understands what he means. His imagination had also been egged on by musicians who never spoke in public or appeared in photos, who hide behind cryptic lyrics and symbolism. But when they finally revealed themselves, the disappointment was usually overwhelming. Better to stay somewhere in the middle, he thinks.

"That might have worked if we'd been a new band," Håkan says, "but a bunch of people already know us."

Grim is their spokesperson in the interviews, but they respond to the questions together. During the days, they tap away on Grim's gray typewriter, with the D-key that sticks. During the nights, they write their answers by hand, so as not to wake Håkan's mom. They're each in their own bed, in a room that has become both office space and workshop. The typewriter is enthroned on the table, surrounded by pens, scissors, spools of thread, rulers, tape, glue, and Letraset sheets with transferable letters. The floor is littered with Grim's amp and their instruments, the stereo, and the crates full of records. On the walls, they've stuck horror movie posters from *Fangoria*, more posters from gigs, flyers, and Grim's drawings, of course—depictions of murder and mayhem, saturated in Grim's sense of humor, which is black as night.

"This is going to be fiendishly good," Grim whispers from his folding bed, where he's lying on his stomach and writing, using a book of Greek mythology as a makeshift desk. "Look."

He hands the letter to Håkan.

Q: Your lyrics are really dark and cool! In my opinion, there is more depth to them than many other death metal songs.

A: Maimer and I were getting sick and tired of the "gore trend." It's all well and good for those who are into that, but we are treading a different path, the left-hand path. We have included some of our esoteric knowledge in the lyrics, but it's not obvious to outsiders. Where most will only hear an evil death metal song, those with the right mindset will discern the hidden pattern. Magick has been a part of music since the dawn of mankind.

"Wicked," Håkan whispers, handing it back.

"Imagine if we could put, like, real magic in the songs," Grim mumbles, like he's done before. "We need to find a grimoire."

Before Håkan read Grim's book on magic, he hadn't known that a grimoire was an ancient book full of spells. Unfortunately, they're lacking in the library at Handen.

Grim stuffs the letter into an envelope, together with the picture of himself and one with all four of them. Most bands they know let a friend finish an entire roll, develop it, throw away the shittiest pictures, and send off the rest until they're all gone. Anja pointed out that they should let her make copies of the best pictures instead. Håkan felt a bit dumb not to have thought of it before. "That's why you should work with professionals," Grim had remarked.

Now, he licks the envelope and seals it.

"What's that animal called, the one from up north?" Håkan whispers. "Like a mean badger, big claws."

"Wolverine," Grim responds.

Håkan finishes, then hands Grim the note.

Q: Where did you find your inspiration?

A: I grew up in an isolated part of northern Sweden, surrounded by endless forests where wolves and bears still roam and the Northern Lights flash across the sky. Once I met a wolverine and it started following me around. It used to bring me half-devoured smaller animals. I used the bones for magic rites, and we will probably use them in shows, too. We may use some real blood as well, so wimps better beware.

Grim's smile is pleased.

"Perfect," he says quietly. "Like that better than 'I grew up by the fart-smelling fumes of the pulp mill.' But do you know what they said in Timrå? 'Smells like money.'"

Håkan chokes out a laugh into his pillow.

"I like that thing about the bones," Grim whispers, pointing at the letter. "And we should use real blood in our gig. I think you can buy it at the butchers."

They're about to play live for the first time with Grim in the band. He had insisted on waiting until the demo had been released.

They're playing with Exenterate and Malodor at a youth center, and Håkan has a vague feeling that they won't take well to blood.

"They probably won't let us play if we do," he says.

"Probably not," Grim replies. "And mopping it up won't be fun for whoever has to do it. If we cover the floor with a gallon of blood, could be difficult to get out. We'd probably need to pay."

Grim adds to Håkan's reply.

"They'll see that the handwriting is different," Håkan reminds him.

"Multiple personalities," Grim shoots back, and after a moment, he returns the letter to Håkan.

Growing up, I had no neighbors, I had no friends. I hardly spoke before I started school because I saw no need to communicate. I've never really cared for other people and I like to isolate myself. Apart from being in a band, I like to live in solitude. As a child I used to venture into the forest for days and live off whatever I could find. In the realms of blind and brutal nature, I learned to listen to the dark echoes of the past. That's where I found inspiration for my music. I recognize those same echoes in the music of great bands. We're tapping into something profoundly primordial and evil. And if you maniacs want to bang your heads to our tracks, that's fine. But to those who dare listen, there's a deeper meaning, a true, dark essence.

Grim whispers, "It's better if you build it around a grain of truth." Then he signs the letter in his usual way: *Through Death I Rise.* "And the rest is what you wished were true."

In hindsight, Håkan would wonder how much Grim revealed about himself when he said that, and how aware of it he had been.

They continue to distribute copies of *Nocturnal Allegiance*, but their focus is on the future. The EP is going to be called *Ancient Bloodlust*, after the only pre-Grim Dark Cruelty song they're including on it. The song that was his way into the band.

While they dream and plan for the next recording session and the gig, copies of copies of copies of Dark Cruelty's latest demo begin to circulate. So do the interviews, ending up in the hands of devoted death metal fanatics around the world. People who don't know Grim and the band read about them. Some do it literally, only perceiving the solemnity, not catching on to the playfulness, the theatrical exaggeration.

They've cried out to the world.

They will receive an answer.

KASPER

Kasper balanced two steaming mugs of tea and a plate of sliced apples on his tray. Carefully, he carried it into his mom's work space. As always, the desk at which she was seated was a mess.

"Where do I put it?" he said.

"The floor," his mom told him.

She kept typing an e-mail about a gig she was shooting. Her T-shirt depicted four black cats coming together to form the Black Flag logo. Beneath it was printed *Cat Flag*. Kasper would like to borrow it sometime and never return it. He put the tray on the floor. His mom shifted a pile of papers next to the keyboard, and he gingerly placed the cup on the minimal surface available. Then he sat down in the chair next to hers, carefully balancing his own mug on the armrest and the plate of apples on his lap.

"Apple?" Kasper said, holding up a slice.

His mom took it with her teeth and chewed. It had been a record year for apples all around, including in his mom and Atle's garden. The drought meant the fruits were smaller than usual, but they were juicy and sweet. When Kasper had come home from school after the conversation with Ms. Gunhild, he'd picked apples with his mom and Diana while Leia showed off on the trampoline and Atle cooked dinner.

"We'll be eating applesauce all winter," his mom said between bites. "And there we go," she said, sending the e-mail and opening the folder containing her pictures instead. "All right, let's see."

Kasper's mom had spent years digitizing old photographs, her ultimate goal being a book of pictures with primarily Dark Cruelty, Malodor, and Exenterate before they got big. Stasse from Malodor, a freelance journalist as well as a musician, was going to do some interviews for it and write a few essays. Atle was going to design it. Now, with the reunion, the project had started up again. Some friends from back in the day who had a publishing house—mainly dedicated to tabletop RPGs and books about geek culture—were going to launch a Kickstarter campaign once the reunion became official in a month. His mom had been happy to oblige when Kasper asked if he could look at the selection of photos she was making.

"Obviously, they won't be in this order in the book," she said. "But these are some of my favorites."

On the screen, there was a black-and-white photograph of Stasse and his brother Dimman, or Anastasios and Dimitris, as they were really called. Stasse had his arm around Dimman's neck in a way that made it difficult to tell if he was hugging him or trying to wrestle him. Dimman's mouth was open and laughing.

"That's nice," Kasper said.

"Yeah," his mom agreed. "Poor Dimman. Poor Stasse. Fuck."

Dimman had died of cancer when Kasper was little. That was part of the reason Stasse was so passionate about making this book: in his brother's memory.

"Another dead one," his mom said sadly.

In another photo, three boys were walking across a lawn like zombies: Tony, Ernesto, and a third guy holding a beach ball.

"Who is that?" Kasper asked.

"Olle. The guitarist in Vomitator," his mom said. "He left the scene, went on to play in that indie band, shit, what were they called? They were pretty big. Killed himself. He was so sweet. A fucking tragedy."

His mom clicked on an image of Linda seated in a striped brown armchair, a can of soda balancing on her round belly.

"Sweet little Linda," his mom said fondly. "Can you believe she and Ernesto were younger than you are when they became parents?"

"That's crazy," Kasper said.

"We were so close," his mom went on. "But I don't know that I was a particularly good friend when Ossian was born. I was around, of course, but our lives were suddenly so different, and then I went abroad . . . Oh, I don't know . . . Maybe we would have ended up like that anyway. Hang on . . ."

She started searching through the pictures. Kasper considered Linda in that chair, heavily pregnant. He didn't know her like he knew Ernesto, since they'd separated when Kasper was born. He hadn't really thought about her as his mom's former best friend. To him, she was just Ossian's mom. Ossian, who, during Kasper's entire childhood, had been the fascinating and terrifying teenager. He was almost thirty now, with a band called Vanbörd.

"Here!" his mom exclaimed. "From when they recorded *Ancient Bloodlust*."

Tony was holding an infant who had to be Ossian. The father, Ernesto, stood next to them, one hand curved around the baby's small head. Håkan leaned in, one tiny hand gripping his finger. Kasper wanted to laugh; it looked like the metal version of Jesus and the biblical Magi. He told that to his mom, who shook with laughter.

"The holy new Dark Cruelty lineup," she said.

Ossian being the sixth member of the band was a standing joke, as he'd been in the studio when the EP was recorded. And now he was actually going to front the reunited band. Kasper had heard about it pretty recently.

"And look at this one," his mom said, clicking on another photo.

A picture of his dad in Dark Cruelty's rehearsal space, tuning his bass.

"First time I met him," his mom said.

"And you thought he hated you," Kasper, who had heard the story many times, filled in.

"He was so fucking lost." His mom smiled. "Then again, so was I." Another click. "It was the first time I met *him*, too."

Grim sat on an amplifier, elbows on his knees, the microphone dangling from its cord. He was looking into the camera with an unreadable expression. It was as if he were looking straight at Kasper.

And then he just blurted it out: "What happened to him?"

"What do you mean?" his mom asked, zooming in on Grim's face.

"Well, when he died," Kasper said. "You and Dad have been really vague about it. And I understand. I was a kid when we talked about it, so I suppose there were things you didn't want me to know."

"You've been digging around online, have you?" his mom said.

I've dreamed about him. Several times.

"No," Kasper sighed. "I'd just like to know."

His mom dragged a hand through her hair. Some strands of it got caught in her silver rings, and she pulled them out, shook them off. On the inside of her forearm was a tattoo with three names: Kasper, Diana, Leia.

"It's complicated," she said.

She was quiet for a moment, then she spun on the chair to face him. Picked up a couple of apple slices and ate them. Suddenly, Kasper was nervous about what he was going to hear.

"Okay," his mom said, swallowing. "When I heard Grim had died, I just wanted to know if it was murder or suicide. It was neither. So I didn't want to know the details. Everything was so awful, anyway. I never read up on it."

Kasper lifted the mug to his mouth, taking a sip of the hot tea.

"Didn't you wonder why he died?" he said.

His mom frowned.

"They didn't know, did they? All they could say was that it wasn't unnatural, or whatever it's called. 'Unexpected death of unknown cause.' That's what Grim's mom told your grandma. She got to talk to the forensic pathologist. Grim's mom, that is. He said it may have been something congenital, maybe some kind of attack. There's been thousands of rumors, though, and you know who's behind many of them."

Malte. Kasper examined Grim's face on the screen. He'd heard his dad say that Grim brought Malte into the band. Or was he misremembering it?

"So you have no idea what he was doing in the tunnels?" Kasper said.

"No one does," his mom said. "Except, you know, he would go exploring in places like that." She was quiet for a moment. "Then again, that he brought all that stuff along was a bit odd."

Kasper startled. "Sorry, what?"

His mom looked away.

"After the preliminary investigation didn't turn up anything, they wanted to return the things he'd had with him," she said. "The clothes he'd been wearing. Other possessions. Grim's mom said she didn't want them, that we could toss out or keep whatever we wanted. I know Håkan took his leather jacket and those things."

She rubbed her eyes.

"What things?" Kasper said.

"String . . ." his mom responded, a little absently. "The rough, brown kind, you know. A spool of it. A piece of jewelry, a pentagram on a chain. And the knife from the band photo."

Kasper felt the scar on his palm tingle.

"And a copy of *Ancient Bloodlust*, too," his mom said. "But scratched up. That was one of those details that . . . I dunno, it made me really uneasy."

Kasper turned to the window. It was dark outside, the glass like mirrors. He finally understood his dad's reaction to his question about the knife from the photo. Grim had it on him when he died.

"Have you talked to your dad about all this?" his mom said.

"No," Kasper told her. "You know how he gets."

His mom nodded. She knew.

"Why is it so important to you to know how he died?" she asked.

"You only named me after him," Kasper muttered.

His mom was quiet again. Then she nodded, as if she got it. But Kasper himself hardly got it, could barely understand the obsession that had gripped him. He felt obsessed with knowing, with turning over everything he'd once let alone.

"Sorry," Kasper said. "It's just . . . I've heard about him my entire life, but I don't know much at all."

"No, I get it," his mom said. "Have a talk with Tony. It isn't as raw to him as it is your dad."

She reached out a hand and stroked his forehead. Kasper suddenly wished he could turn back time, be a child again, back when everything was simpler. His mom sighed. He wondered if she'd had the same thought.

Kasper's room at his mom and Atle's house was on the first floor and larger than the one he had at his dad's. Some of what his mom had brought with her after the divorce was in there: posters from exhibitions with her favorite photographers, some framed pictures she'd taken, mostly family photographs. One *The Empire Strikes Back* poster and a full-length mirror with a gold frame. A wicker chair that creaked when you sat in it, which had once belonged to Kasper's grandma. There were worn paperbacks on the bookshelf, from King and Koontz. The potted palm tree that had been around since his mom's teens sprawled in a corner.

Kasper sat down on the bed, computer perched on a book of photos in his lap. Even though he'd already decided, he hesitated.

He couldn't help but feel that he was doing something forbidden when he wrote in the search bar: *grim dark cruelty death*

The thread he found was long, and he entered it midway somewhere. He read the posts, feeling increasingly sick. He understood why he'd stayed away. Knowing there were people who speculated about his dad and the others participating in Grim's death was one thing. Actually reading the bizarre accusations, the twisted theories, felt different. He knew he shouldn't care, but he was angry. Didn't these people have lives? Didn't they have anything better to do than speculate about complete strangers? Some of the worst posts exuded smug self-confidence, as if the writer had been patting themselves on the shoulder with one hand while composing with the other.

Whether or not these young men believed in magic as such, or simply desired attention from the media, will remain unsaid. It is, however, fairly obvious that they lured KJ to that tunnel to arrange a thrilling scene, one that would cause a bit of a furor. Then, after killing him, they got cold feet. Fantasizing about homicide in one's bedroom is one thing, dealing with the consequences of it is quite another. ML was, most likely, the leader, considering how he came to use KJ's death to prove that he was "true." HN was probably also a part of the plot. My impression is that he was the doormat of the group and relatively easily manipulated, first by KJ and then by ML. Speaking from my own experience, HN has been highly reluctant to discuss the details surrounding KJ's death.

Kasper's pulse hammered through his skull. *HN*. That was his dad. This person made him out to be a killer, controlled by Malte. Kasper was so furious, he found it hard to focus as he scrolled. He found another post:

People speculate about KJ's death being a failed attempt at a magic ritual, presumably in conjunction with drugs that weren't regularly screened for at the time. But not a lot of people ask themselves why he'd perform such a ritual. My theory: we all know that KJ was somewhat obsessed with black magic. He'd probably heard stories about Robert Johnson, renowned blues guitarist, who met the Devil at a crossroads and made a deal. Or he was inspired by the myths surrounding Näcken, known to bless musicians with supernatural skill. Either way, I think that was the ultimate purpose of the ritual. To become a better musician. Frankly, he needed it. He was a decent vocalist, but a mediocre guitarist.

Kasper tried to call to mind something his dad had said: that most of the people who speculate online don't mean anything by it. Many of them couldn't tell reality and fiction apart, especially considering the way real tragedy frequently was marketed as entertainment. To most of these people, this was just an exciting story, one that added color to their dull lives. They didn't think of Grim as a real person, didn't consider that people who'd known him were still alive.

Kasper took a deep breath and tried to calm down. He scrolled through more or less elaborate theories about drugs from a bad batch, cyanide, gas, an arrow doused in ricin biting into Grim's calf. In one post, someone claimed that Grim's wounds suggested he'd had the shit beaten out of him.

How could they know details about his wounds? Could he find information somewhere? Kasper trawled into the thread's past. Someone had linked to two scanned articles from the newspapers. *DEVIL WORSHIPPER FOUND DEAD IN SUBWAY TUNNEL*, one of the headlines proclaimed. The accompanying images were generic, depicting tunnels, and the articles resembled each other. No real details, except traffic on the green line being disturbed by the discovery of the body. They didn't specify which station it had been. Maybe they wanted to avoid thrill-seekers venturing into the tunnels. Both papers had found out, from rescue personnel, that the dead boy was into heavy metal, wearing a pendant with "a Satanic symbol" on it. It had to be the pentagram his mom had told him about. They also mentioned "alarming discoveries" at the scene. Kasper understood that, at the time, journalists would have been frothing at the mouth at the combination of a dead metalhead, a pentagram, a knife, and a record sleeve printed with an inverted cross. "We can't determine that a crime hasn't occurred, and we have decided to open a preliminary investigation in the case of homicide," said a spokesperson for the police.

The following weeks, a couple of brief notices were published. Police announced that the preliminary investigation had ended, as nothing in the autopsy indicated foul play.

A bunch of people in the thread thought this was wildly misguided. They wanted access to said investigation:

Good luck pal. This won't be available to the public for seventy years.

Kasper read the response.

Don't like your tone frankly. I just want the facts. There's a lot of speculation in this thread, but I won't be convinced until I see some real documents ok.

What's wrong with these people?

What's wrong with me, for reading this shit?

Don't have access to that particular file. That said, I worked at the National Board of Forensic Medicine for years and got copies of some pretty interesting autopsies. You're welcome.

The post was dated years ago. There was a link. In the posts that came after it, people thanked the poster for the files, so there probably weren't viruses or whatever was normally attached to sketchy links.

Kasper clicked on it, but it was dead. Document removed.

He slammed the laptop shut. Had he really been intending to read Grim's autopsy report?

Kasper put the laptop on the bedside table, stretched out his neck, which popped uncomfortably. He felt rotten, somehow. He'd opened the door to a world he didn't want to familiarize himself with; he couldn't forget what he'd glimpsed beyond it.

What if there was something in those theories? What if someone had been with Grim in that tunnel? If someone had killed him?

Kasper reached for his phone, then remembered that he didn't have to set an alarm. Tomorrow was Saturday, without work, and his birthday. He turned off the light. The pillow felt lumpy, so he turned it over, lay on his side. He'd forgotten to close the blinds, but couldn't be bothered to get up.

None of the things he'd read could be true.

He pulled the comforter over his shoulders and neck. It had been hot all day, unusually warm for mid-September, but the chill was finally creeping in. Somehow, he could feel it entering the room. Through the mirror opposite the windows, he could see the garden. Mists hung between the apple trees and thickened while he watched. There was a billowing movement in the fog, one that reminded him of water. Kasper wrapped his arms around his knees. The room was icy. The radiators had to be off.

A movement in the corner of his eye.

Kasper looked away from the mirror and toward the windows. At first, when everything went blurry, he thought he had something in his eye. He blinked rapidly. Still, he could see his hand very clearly. By the windows, however, everything had dissolved.

There was mist in the room.

Kasper didn't move.

It was a dream. It felt as real as the dreams he'd had about Grim. The mist was thick around the windows, spreading toward the foot of the bed. Streaks of it stretched toward the door, blocking Kasper's way out. But why would he run? It wasn't real. His heart beat so fast, pounded like a drum. Had he ever felt his pulse beat like this in a dream before? Had he heard his own strained breathing?

The mist was so thick he couldn't see his room anymore. He was surrounded on all sides. He felt it against his skin, damp and raw, the scent of deep rock and deep earth. And something else, too, something sweet and revolting. Rotting apples.

He couldn't see clearly anymore. It was as though the mist had burrowed through his corneas. And then he heard something.

A heavy sigh.

Someone was there.

A shape at the foot of the bed. Kasper could faintly make out long black hair, dark clothes. A whisper slipped out: "Grim?"

The name stuck to his lips, like sugar after a bite of cotton candy. The mist seemed to darken around him. Or was his sight failing? Was he going blind? Kasper brushed a hand across his eyes. They were open wide but could only see darkness.

A soft, barely perceptible weight at the foot of the bed. The mattress shifted, so slightly that it could have been his imagination—or someone sitting down.

Stillness. If someone sat there, they seemed to be waiting.

"What do you want?" Kasper whispered hoarsely. "Just say it."

The crash startled him out of sleep. He must have screamed because he could hear his own voice ringing in his ears. And the first thing he saw was the framed mirror, which had fallen. The lower edge had smashed onto the floor and shards surrounded it.

Hurried steps from Atle's office, and a second later, Atle was knocking on the door. Kasper heard his mom moving about on the floor above.

"Kasper?" Atle said.

"I'm fine!" Kasper replied. "The mirror . . ."

Atle opened the door and turned the lights on. Kasper pointed. Atle released the breath he'd been holding.

"I thought it was a window."

"What's going on?" his mom asked from a distance.

"Seven years of bad luck," Atle responded. "The mirror came off the wall." He looked at Kasper. "Don't touch anything."

He disappeared, and Kasper heard his mom come down the stairs.

"Shit, that was scary," she said, entering the room.

Weakly, Kasper said, "Yeah."

His phone vibrated and he jerked. Midnight. His screen filled up with birthday wishes from Lydia, Iris, and the other demons.

"Kasper, honey," his mom said. "You're bleeding."

Kasper blinked at his left hand. Blood was dripping from it and onto the white sheet.

THE ANSWER

Piles of mail stack up in Håkan's room. Back when he was tape trading on his own, he'd receive several letters a day. When Grim moved in, the amount more than doubled. Since they released the demo, the mail situation had spiraled out of control. There's usually a small mountain of envelopes on the hallway carpet; the two of them have to carry their replies in bags to the local post office.

Grim's stolen, or, as he puts it, "provided himself with," an expensive black fountain pen, wax, and a seal marked with a *G*. Håkan loves the scent of melting sealing wax dripping onto paper. He's impressed by how vast Grim's network of contacts is and how diligently he handles the correspondence. Grim even has a small black book in which he makes notes to remind himself what he's written to the people he trades with on a regular basis. His handwriting is so small and cramped that Håkan couldn't read it without a magnifying glass.

Grim's sense of organization has come out in different ways, too. Since he moved in, Håkan has started helping his mom out more. It got a bit embarrassing not to when it seemed obvious to Grim to make his bed every morning and wash up after every meal. He always wipes his shoes thoroughly before entering, never tracks mud and gravel into the house. The rent Grim pays is a helpful addition to his mom's budget, true, but that's not why she got him a folding bed instead of the mattress. Every year, she knits Håkan wool socks that he never uses, but she's started making them for Grim, too. Grim wears them indoors. Håkan starts to wear them, too.

Grim gives Håkan a new perspective on the things he's taken for granted, including the place where he's grown up. The municipality Haninge is full of ancient monuments and historically interesting spots, and Grim borrows a book about them from the library, wants to visit them with Håkan. They ride their bikes around, Håkan on his trusty old secondhand steed, Grim on the Hellion, which shrieks like the demonic piece of work it is. Grim is especially fond of Galgstenen, the huge, dismal glacial erratic that's said to turn 360 degrees every New Year's Eve. This is where the blood of doomed criminals flowed. When Håkan presses his hands against the stone, it feels unnaturally cold.

One morning, in the liminal space between autumn and winter, when they're both free from work and answering letters, Grim announces that they're going to the Iron Age burial site in Jordbro. Håkan, frankly, is not intrigued by the idea, but the alternative is that Grim heads off on his own, and Håkan might miss out.

It's foggy outdoors, the moisture like a veil across Håkan's face as he hops onto his bike and rides off. The bike is from the Norwegian brand DBS, Den Beste Sykkel, the best bike. Håkan has told Grim that Tony's mom refers to it as Death By Spokes. Since then, the two of them have tried to work out new variations on what DBS stands for, but only when they're alone, as it's a bit childish. When one of them throws out a suggestion, the other one counters it immediately.

"Devil Barfs Sideways!" Grim calls out as they're riding side by side on the gravel path that leads into the forest by the ancient burial ground.

"Dracula Barfs Sideways!"

"Doesn't count. It's too similar," Grim says panting.

"Death's Broken Shinbone," Håkan flings at him.

"Good one."

Grim rests his elbows on the steering wheel and the Hellion screams.

"Do you know what day it is?" he shouts, adding, without waiting for a response. "Halloween. Samhain."

"Nice," Håkan says, pushing on.

Gravel crunches beneath his wheels. The forest opens up. Fog hangs heavy over the burial grounds. Grim slams the brakes and leaps off his mechanical monster, leads it into a thin path surrounded by ferns, and lets it tip over with a crash. Håkan lays his DBS next to it. Then they walk across the burial site. Grass, heather, and blueberry bushes grow between stones and cairns, the formations enigmatic. The people who buried their dead here have been dead for thousands of years.

Grim stops at a large, flat stone and sits down on it. Håkan joins him, feeling the cold and the chill seep through his jeans.

"Close your eyes," Grim says.

Håkan does. He hears Grim take a deep breath and copies him. Strange how autumn smells so fresh even though everything is decomposing.

"Do you hear it?" Grim whispers.

"What?" Håkan whispers back, without understanding why they're whispering.

"Listen."

Håkan listens. His own breaths, the creak of the leather jacket when he shifts. Grim breathing next to him. A rustle in the grass, the wind in the trees. Crows caw, as if offended. A train passes by. The rumbling sound of heavy traffic.

"I can't hear anything," Håkan whispers.

He opens his eyes and sees that Grim's are still closed.

"Me, neither," Grim says and opens his eyes, too. "Thought we could hear them. The people who were here before. I read that mist erases the border between the world of the living and the world of the dead. That border is especially weak during Samhain."

Håkan shivers. How would he have reacted if he'd actually heard something? With fear or curiosity? He wants to believe he'd be curious, but isn't sure.

"I read another thing," Grim says. "That ghosts can be people who've slipped in from some other time. We could see an Iron Age warrior come walking past."

"Would he see us, though?"

"Sometimes they can. But not always."

"Have you ever seen a ghost?" Håkan asks. He tries to sound neutral, not like a kid. Grim is quiet. He's quiet for so long that Håkan isn't sure if he's heard him.

"Yeah," Grim says, finally. "Not seen one, though. Just felt it. That someone was there."

Håkan waits for more. There should be more: if he made a pie chart depicting the things that came out of Grim's mouth, 70 percent would be about Dark Cruelty and music, and 28 percent would be about the strange or supernatural phenomena he thinks about. The final 2 percent are puns on DBS and "pass the milk, will you?"

But Grim remains silent.

"When did it happen?" Håkan asks.

"A few years back."

"Do you know who it was?"

"Yeah," Grim says. "I do."

The silence returns. Håkan hesitates, unsure whether or not to keep pushing. Had it been a relative? Grim's dad? Is Grim's dad dead? It dawns on Håkan that he knows very little about Grim's family, despite the two of them spending so much time together. They don't normally talk about things like that in their group, but Grim is particularly private. Håkan rifles through his memory to find out what he actually knows about Grim and his life in Timraw. He's mentioned his mom and his little sister, in conjunction with the tragic demise of Balthazar the corn snake, which Grim's sister accidentally let loose in the garden. When Håkan tries to picture Grim's life before Stockholm, he only sees the half-truths and lies the two of them have constructed together. Grim with a wolverine by his side, hearkening to the ancient spirits of the forest beneath pulsing Northern Lights.

They sit there quietly for a moment, the mist dissipating around them.

Håkan doesn't know it yet, but this moment will be etched into his memory. He will return to it over and over again, accuse himself, judge himself. He'll regret not asking more questions. Maybe Grim wouldn't have answered him; maybe he wanted to tell someone, but didn't know how. Maybe he needed Håkan's *Who was it?* to be able to share. Would it have helped him? Would it have made it easier for him to turn to Håkan later on, when the maelstrom was dragging him down? Would he still have ended up where he did, underground? Maybe, maybe not. Håkan will never know.

But there and then, the chilly stone makes them cold, and so they stretch and shuffle back to their bikes. Håkan's DBS is slippery with moisture when he picks it up again. Pulling down his shirtsleeve over his hand, he wipes the saddle. Grim crouches down next to the Hellion, takes a plastic bag out of his pocket, and rips out bunches of grass that he tosses over his shoulder.

"What are you doing?" Håkan asks.

Grim doesn't respond, just shoves his fingers into the soil, grabbing fistfuls of dirt that he puts in the bag before tying it up and putting it in his pocket. Then he drags the Hellion out of the grass.

"Dead Broken Souls!" Grim yells and pedals away.

A few days later, Dark Cruelty is doing their first gig since Grim joined the band. It's at a youth center, alongside Exenterate and Malodor. Adde from Exenterate has made the poster and then photocopied it at his dad's job. In the middle, it reads *DEATH METAL*. Dark Cruelty's logo is at the top—*New demo out now!*—then Malodor, then Exenterate at the bottom. You don't want to be some sort of rock star, putting your own band in front of your friends'. The entrance fee a bargain. The poster also designates time, place, and the closest subway stop. *No posers. No mosh. No drugs or alcohol. Sponsored by the Organization for the Promotion of Study.*

There's been some talk about this gig, especially since the *Nocturnal Allegiance* demo started spreading like wildfire. Some of the interviews in the fanzines haven't been published yet, some never will be, because the person running it is quitting, but the ones that have reached out made an impact. Håkan notices that people who don't know Grim very well have started treating him differently. Warily. They're unsure of who he is.

Håkan is sitting in the youth center's kitchen, swigging apple juice. Most of the others were drinking on the way there and hid the liquor outside, but Håkan wants to wait until after the gig. He wants to stay alert. Ernesto is standing around with Linda, whose belly has grown visibly. Håkan tries not to stare. It's surreal that Ernesto's baby is in there. Meanwhile, Anja is taking photos. She shoots Håkan a quick smile. He, of course, responds by just sitting there awkwardly, so she turns around to photograph Stasse and his brother Dimman.

"Dammit," Tony mutters from where he's seated, a few feet from Håkan.

"What?" Håkan says.

Then he sees that Tony is wrapping his hands in surgical tape. He's been practicing extra hard in his parents' rehearsal space and has ended up with blisters.

"Let me help you out," Håkan says, moving his chair closer.

"Thanks," Tony says.

He holds out his hands and Håkan makes a face. He also gets abrasions on his fingers and wrists sometimes, and it's incredibly painful, but it's even worse for drummers. Their sweaty hands result in the blisters filling with fluid, and then bursting, which is pure torture. Worst-case scenario, they get blood blisters. That's how Tony's hands are right now: they look like raw meat.

"We're on in a second, right?" Ernesto says.

The lineup for the evening wasn't obvious. Each band has existed for about as long as the others, but Malodor has been around for slightly longer. Exenterate has released the most demos, but Dark Cruelty has a new one out. In the end, they decided to draw straws, and Dark Cruelty ended up opening. Grim didn't object but Håkan could tell he wasn't satisfied, and he has been quiet throughout the day. Håkan suddenly realizes that it's been a while since he saw Grim.

Håkan can hear voices and music from the room where they are about to perform. The audience is punctual and already waiting for them. Some of them have traveled from other cities. No one wants to miss out on something as rare as a death metal gig.

"Where's Grim?" Håkan asks and gets up.

"He took off," Adde from Exenterate says, taking a bite of his chocolate bar and then pointing at the emergency exit door, which is ajar.

Behind the center, it's dark and desolate, and Håkan shivers in the cold. There's no sign of Grim. For one awful moment, Håkan wonders if he's taken off for the night. Then he spots a familiar figure pacing back and forth beneath the glow of the streetlights.

"Grim!"

No response. Håkan comes closer. Grim has stopped, his back to Håkan, his dark hair moving in the wind.

"We're on in a sec," Håkan says, and Grim finally turns to face him.

"Okay," he says and blinks.

He's in the same clothes and makeup he had on for their shoot. Håkan decided this morning to pass, with Ernesto, Tony, and himself going for the same look they always did: shirt, band tee, and jeans. They haven't talked about it, but they're all clearly thinking the same thing: they know pretty much everyone there and are worried they're going to embarrass themselves.

Håkan realizes that Grim probably assumed they'd all be wearing their outfits from the shoot, had thought that Håkan had brought his stuff from home. He feels like a traitor.

"Can you give me a hand with this?" Grim says, handing Håkan a small glass jar containing gray powder. "It's ashes. On my hair." He closes his eyes and tilts his head back. "Watch out so it doesn't all blow away."

"Come on, for fuck's sake!" Tony yells from inside.

Håkan unscrews the lid, but keeps it in place when the November wind buffets the two of them. He waits until it dies down and then scatters the ashes over Grim's black hair. Some of it sticks to his face.

"It symbolizes death," Grim says, his eyes closed. "But grief as well, and redemption. Imagine I'm doomed for all eternity. That there's no mercy. That feeling."

"Wicked," Håkan says, his teeth chattering with cold. "Let's go."

When they enter, everyone looks at Grim. Some of them have seen him perform at rehearsal, but never on stage. Then it strikes Håkan that *he* hasn't, either. Personally, Håkan has played two gigs with Dark Cruelty before Grim came along, and a few other ones with Tony's old punk band Häxsvett (Witch Sweat) before then. As far as Håkan knows, Grim has never stood on a stage, ever. What if he can't do it? Håkan is so busy being nervous for Grim's sake that he doesn't worry about himself until they're on stage, tuning their instruments. Grim stands with his back to the audience, bent over his guitar, blinking the way he does when he's stressed. Håkan wants to give him a pat on the shoulder, calm him down, somehow, but it would probably just ruin Grim's focus. Suddenly, Håkan is so nervous he could puke.

"Dark Cruelty!" someone in the audience yells. "Dark Cruelty!"

Tony is trying to straighten Exenterate's backdrop, which hangs askew, but then he throws his hands up and takes his seat behind the drums. Ernesto's little brother, Paul, is on a chair by the stage, taping the evening with a camera that's almost as big as he is.

"Hååååkaaan!" Stasse hollers.

The tiny audience is getting restless. Håkan exchanges a look with Ernesto, who nods. Grim does something with his head that could also be a nod. Håkan gives Tony a thumbs-up. Their setlist tonight is "Nocturnal Allegiance," "Carrion Summoning," the Venom cover, and "Ancient Bloodlust." The lights are blinding Håkan. For a moment, everything goes quiet inside his skull. Grim takes hold of the microphone and screeching feedback cuts through the room. Then he hisses, "Through death . . . I rise!"

Tony counts off and the audience explodes.

Many years later, Håkan will watch recordings from the show and be startled by how small the stage was, by how small the crowd was. At the same time, he can still feel it in his body, the way the atmosphere intensifies every time the tempo shifts, how his shirt is sticky with sweat while they're still playing "Nocturnal." The crowd headbanging, stage-diving, long hair flying. Grim's voice, just as it was when Håkan first heard him. It feels like the first time, when everything just fell into place, and the others feel the same. He can hear it in Ernesto's guitar, which sounds better live than it ever has, in the way Tony bangs away at the drums, blood spraying him. No one in the room gives a fuck when Grim messes up a few riffs in "Carrion Summoning"; or when it takes them ages to retune between a couple of songs. They're in the same magic circle, the people on the stage and the ones in the audience, and this is probably the feeling they're going to spend the rest of their lives trying to re-create, either in basement gigs or headlining Wacken. Sometimes they'll come close.

At the end of "Ancient," Grim stuffs his hand into his pocket.

"For you are dust!" he chants, like a diabolical priest, while throwing a handful of dirt from the Iron Age burial ground onto the crowd. "And to dust you shall return!"

Another handful of dirt rains over upturned faces and hands. Afterward, people will claim that the soil came from a desecrated grave, that there were maggots in it, that it had been mixed with Grim's own blood.

No one knows it yet, *he* doesn't know it yet, but one of the people who is going to spread those rumors is at the very back of the room, staring at Grim with big, round eyes.

He'll make his entrance soon.

Håkan is in heaven after the show, but Grim is ill. Not that Håkan knows what's wrong with him—he's just in bed, the shades pulled down over the window. One day it's his head, the other his stomach. They rehearse without him and Håkan rides his bike to work alone. When Grim has been unwell for a few days, Håkan ends up sorting packages with the only colleague he actually detests. Jensa is a crisp brown, thanks to the tanning bed, and only talks about his year of military service and the movie *Top Gun*, which he loves. He reminds Håkan of the boys in elementary school who'd trip him up, make him participate in "games" in which one person put their hand on the desk and the other rapped it as hard as they could over the knuckles. For some reason, Håkan never got to do the hitting. Then he became friends with Tony and got left alone.

When Håkan and Grim work together, they can cope with Jensa's nonsense. Now the first thing he says to Håkan is, "So, where's your boyfriend?"

Håkan doesn't reply, just puts his headphones on and turns the volume up to the max, starts sorting. It's a demo from Hungary he only just received, but despite it being good, he can't flee into the music the way he normally does.

The joy he'd felt after the show has been fading. There's none of it left in him now. In its place, he finds a concern he can't put his finger on. Something is going to happen or has already happened. Distracted, he throws a package marked FRAGILE.

"Love huuurts," Jensa sings.

When Håkan comes home, Grim has rolled up the curtain. He's in bed with his headphones on and a roll of chocolate cookies in one hand. Carefully, Grim twists one of the cookies open so that the filling sticks to the bottom, devours the top part, then scrapes the filling off with his teeth, and finishes the bottom part, too. And then he says, "Listen to this," handing Håkan his Walkman.

Grim's ears have warmed the headphones. It takes a second for Håkan to understand what he's hearing: someone's tried to pick out the rhythm guitar in "Nocturnal Allegiance." It sounds good. Håkan removes the headphones.

"He wants to audition as our guitarist."

"What?"

"Yeah, we're looking for a guitarist."

Again, it takes a second for Håkan to understand.

"You've written to people?" he says.

"Yeah," Grim says and blinks. "I told you after we recorded the demo. I'm not good enough. Need to focus on my singing."

Håkan nods, but feels the ground rock slightly beneath his feet. They hadn't explicitly decided to tell people they were looking. He had assumed he and Grim would make a choice like that together.

What else is he putting in his letters that Håkan doesn't know about?

"Who's this guy, then?" he says.

"Calls himself Iago," Grim replies. "Like in *Othello*."

Håkan pictures the strategy board game Othello and doesn't get it, which he goes on to tell Grim.

"It's a play by Shakespeare," Grim says. "Iago is the villain. The most evil character Shakespeare ever invented. Stabs everyone in the back, and in the end, when they're all dead, he doesn't regret a thing."

"Wicked," Håkan says. "Let's try him out."

KASPER

It was the night of Kasper's nineteenth birthday, and he stood on the small island of Beckholmen and waited. He leaned against the fence that went around the cliff's edge. The rock plunged abruptly down to the shipyard and its dry docks, where they repaired boats. In the distance, Gröna Lund glittered. The visitors' screams and the rattling of the rides echoed across the area. Kasper couldn't understand why the neighbors complained about it year after year. He thought it was the best sound in the world. But it wasn't helping him relax right now.

He'd spent all day pretending things were normal, but he couldn't keep it up much longer.

Kasper had told his mom that he'd inspected the broken mirror, that he must have cut his hand on it. She bought it, of course, and helped him put a bandage on. Then he lay awake, tossing and turning the entire night, too afraid to sleep and dream again. In the morning, he was celebrated in Swedish and Norwegian. Seeing Atle, his mom, and his little sisters perform the Norwegian birthday song, which also included a little dance, genuinely made him forget about everything else for a bit.

Leia had given him a packet of fake blood. Diana had done a series of drawings of Icarus, "because your favorite ride is named after him," she said, in her precocious manner. She snuggled up in bed next to him and leafed through the story. Kasper realized he'd forgotten much of it. He was reminded of Icarus's dad, Daedalus, not only constructing those unfortunate wings, which melted in the sun, but also the labyrinth that imprisoned the fearsome Minotaur. Daedalus had been imprisoned for revealing the secrets of the labyrinth, which was why he built the wings, so he and his son could flee.

"Why did Icarus get too close to the sun?" Diana had asked Kasper. "Why didn't he listen to his dad?"

In Greek myth, things went badly for people who aimed too high. Hubris was punished by the gods. But that was a bit complicated for an eight-year-old.

"Maybe he was so happy he could fly that he forgot to be careful," Kasper suggested.

"I would *not* forget," Diana said. "Would you?"

"I'd mostly be scared about falling."

"But I'd catch you if you did," Diana said in her practical way.

"Thank you," Kasper said, almost brought to tears.

Because he felt as if he were hurtling toward the ground. What had happened the night before had terrified him. And he couldn't let it show in front of his mom or Atle, or his dad, who came over for dinner in the evening and told them how happy Grim's sister was about the reunion. He brought Kasper a present, an iPad Pro from himself, his mom, and Atle. Kasper had to pretend to be overjoyed; it made him feel like an ungrateful liar.

Now, he was watching the glowing octopus turn on its barge. He looked toward the docks, trying to catch sight of Iris. Meeting here had been her suggestion, when he'd told her he needed to talk. The House should be done with the meeting now.

"Kasper!" Iris cried out from behind him.

He turned around and she ran up to him, giving him a warm hug. "Happy birthday!"

"Thanks," Kasper said shakily.

She stepped back and looked at him.

"Shit. What's going on?"

"It's all right," Kasper said because he could tell he was making her worried. "Can we sit down?"

He walked toward the small concrete tower farther up the height. They sat down on the gravelly ground, Iris leaning back against the tower. It was large enough for one person to stand inside, peering through the narrow openings. Once, Iris had said that Beckholmen was hollow, and that the military used to keep torpedoes inside it. Maybe there was a staircase somewhere, one that led straight into the mountain. At the moment, Kasper wanted to climb down it and hide.

He'd always been like this. As soon as something difficult happened to him, his impulse was to keep quiet. When he was a child, weeks would pass before his mom or dad could get him to tell them what was going on. There were some things they never found out. Since going to therapy, he'd become a little better at opening up, but he'd never kept a secret like this before.

How was he supposed to begin? What would Iris think? She'd think he'd gone mad, obviously. And then she'd have to go to the TL and tell them that Kasper couldn't possibly work at The House, seeing as he believed himself to be haunted. That worried him more than actually being crazy, which had to be a bad sign. He snorted with laughter.

"Oh, no," Iris said. "Are you crying?"

"No," Kasper said. He looked at her helplessly. "It's about Grim."

He didn't know what to say next.

"Is it about the reunion?" Iris asked.

Kasper had told her about it a while ago.

"Not really."

Their phones pinged at the same time. Selam wrote that she'd closed up The House and was on her way to where they were celebrating Kasper's birthday. At this rate, he didn't know if he'd be able to make himself go.

"Take your time," Iris said.

Kasper's therapist had said that if talking felt impossible, he could start with describing how he felt about talking.

"I want to tell you all about it—everything," Kasper said. "But I'm really worried about what you'll think. That you'll think I've lost my mind."

"I don't think you've lost your mind," Iris said.

"You don't know how messed up this is."

"All right, you know what?" Iris said. "Even if you have lost it, it's perfectly fine. Been there, done that. You've been through it before and made it to the other side."

Kasper gave a startled laugh.

"Sorry, was that inappropriate?" Iris made a face.

"No," Kasper said. "It actually made me feel better."

"From the top, then," Iris said. "No stress."

From the top. The evening he'd overheard his dad and Tony talking about what he'd later understand to be the reunion. Kasper started there, told her about hearing his dad cry, that he'd dreamed about Grim on stage, about the urge to draw what he had seen. He told her about the box tipping over, the ruined original pressing— which made Iris gasp—the knife he'd cut himself on, what his mom had said about the things Grim had been found with. He told her about the second dream, Grim in the water, and the horror he'd experienced in The House, the smells and that dull, droning sound. Not everything was relevant, and he was probably forgetting some details, but he went on to recount the third dream, the one with the snake and the cup. Then: last night. His mouth went dry when he described the mist and the shape in it, how the darkness had swallowed up everything, including his question: *What do you want?* Then how the mirror crashed to the floor.

He held out his left hand, carefully lifting the bandage. He had searched for information about scars opening up, but he hadn't found anything that was similar to his own case. It shouldn't be possible. And yet the wound was there.

"Shit," Iris managed weakly.

Her face was pale and she was staring at his hand.

"Shit," she repeated.

She produced a cigarette case and a lighter from her bag. The cigarette crackled when she took her first puff.

Kasper felt emptied out. He'd been hoping that everything would come together while he spoke, but he only felt more confused. He could only await Iris's judgment.

"You know in a horror film, when they find a corpse with two holes in its neck," she said, "and you're like, how stupid must they be not to get that a vampire did it? But that's because you know you're watching a horror movie."

Kasper thought he knew what she meant.

"So if this was a horror film . . ." he began.

"What would you think?"

"That I was haunted," Kasper said. "But that's insane."

"Yeah," Iris said. "You know I can be a bit of a hippie, but I actually prefer natural explanations to supernatural ones. Grim's death is a sensitive subject in your family. Then there's everything with the re-union, and you start getting weird dreams, notice things you haven't before. That's not that strange. And a mirror can fall by itself. But that . . ." She indicated his hand. "How the hell do you explain that?"

Kasper had always said that he didn't believe in the supernatural. But he'd also added, like many people do, that he couldn't be sure, that he was open to being challenged and proven wrong. It turned out that some stubborn part of him refused to accept that that was now happening.

He drew a finger across the bridge of his nose. When Kasper was a kid, his mom used to joke that his dad's nose went cold when his brain went into overdrive. Kasper must have inherited it.

"If it's real," he attempted. "There has to be some reason for it. And the most obvious one . . . What if his death wasn't natural? What if someone hurt him?"

Saying it out loud felt both frightening and like a relief.

Iris drew her legs up and rested her chin against her knees. Her nose was probably also cold.

"How much do you actually know?" she said. "About what people say about his death."

Kasper told her briefly what he'd read the night before.

"So the things you said at Cornelia's," Iris said. "That was all you knew? Before yesterday, I mean."

At Cornelia's. The night Iris wouldn't meet his gaze.

"Yes," Kasper said.

"I thought you were just toning things down," she said, shaking her head. "And I was so ashamed for telling Santiago and Selam the previous summer. Like I'd given them the juicy true crime version, when your dad had lost a friend. It all felt so real, coming from you."

"Oh," Kasper said, "because I was sure you were judging me for talking about it."

"Oh God, no," Iris said. "I was busy judging myself. Speaking of which . . . Don't hate me for this, but I've read that autopsy report."

Kasper was surprised to discover that the thought of her reading it disgusted him, even though he'd been about to do the same thing.

"I know it isn't an excuse, but I was fifteen," she went on. "And I felt like shit afterward."

"You sure it was real?"

"No one's disproved it," Iris said. "It looked legit. Ten pages of a protocol with a bunch of detailed descriptions in doctor-speak, then a few pages consisting of a verdict."

"So how did he die?" Kasper asked her, heart pounding.

Iris took a drag of her cigarette, tried to exhale away from Kasper, but the wind blew it back into his face.

"Well, the forensic pathologist couldn't find any evidence of a crime," she said. "And he couldn't determine the exact cause of death."

"But?" Kasper said.

"But," Iris went on, "there are a few details that people tend to get hung up on. I'll try to sum up the ones that aren't completely wild. The first question has nothing to do with the report; it's the question of who sent for help."

Kasper had glimpsed some of that debate yesterday. *Occam's razor: the simplest solution is usually the correct one. Who usually frequents those tunnels? Addicts and hobos. One of them probably tripped over the corpse.*

"A homeless person, right?" Kasper said.

"That's one theory," Iris said. "But there's a more specific story out there. Some commentor claimed to know the woman who'd worked in the ticket booth that night. She said a young man came up to her and told her about a person in the tunnel. She had thought he was drunk because he was acting strange. And he was a metalhead."

Kasper looked at her.

"I know," she said, finally stubbing out the cigarette. "It doesn't mean anything and doesn't have to be true. But it's out there. And another thing . . . He wasn't dead when the paramedics arrived."

Not dead.

"But he was unconscious. They thought he'd been unconscious for one, maybe two days. You could tell because—sorry, do you even want the details?"

Kasper nodded, but wasn't sure he did.

"You could tell from the body. There were the beginnings of pressure sores and the muscles . . ." Iris stopped. "You know what, no, I won't give you the details, because I honestly want to forget them myself. But you could tell from his kidneys and lungs, too. That he'd been unmoving for a long time."

One to two days. Alone in the dark.

"I read something about his injuries."

"Yeah," Iris said. "Some people make a big thing out of it, claim he'd been physically assaulted or something. But other people say it happened when someone else moved him. Little scrapes and things."

"Moved him?" Kasper said. "Like, the paramedics?"

"Nope, they would have had a stretcher," Iris said. She paused, then: "Someone could have dragged him while he was unconscious."

Kasper started feeling slightly sick, but Iris didn't look as if she'd finished.

"Go on," he said.

Iris huffed out a breath. She looked as if she was preparing mentally for something.

"He had a cut," she said, finally. "Here."

She drew her finger in the air above Kasper's left palm.

"You sure about that?" Kasper said quietly.

Iris said: "It's in the report."

Their phones pinged again, but they didn't touch them.

"Never heard of him having a copy of *Ancient Bloodlust* on him, though," Iris said. "Nothing about a pentagram or a knife, either. It must have remained in the inner circle. If Grim had been famous when he died, people would have talked, and it would have spread. But back then . . ."

Back then, he was just some kid in a band that played at youth centers.

"What about the string?" Kasper said.

"Never heard about it, either." Iris frowned. "But it feels vaguely familiar, somehow."

"I know what you mean," Kasper said, because, oddly enough, he did.

They were quiet for a moment. The air grew cold. Kasper looked at his hand, wishing he could think properly.

"Those drawings you made," Iris said. "Did you bring them?"

Kasper took his sketchbook out of the bag, skipped to the first dream, and handed the book to Iris. She looked at it, then turned to the next one, lingered at the final one. Her expression reminded him of Ms. Gunhild's.

"Whoa," she said. "I'm not an expert, but . . . They're incredible. Beautiful. And so fucking creepy. Sad, too, in some way."

She closed the book and handed it back to Kasper. He held it between his hands, ran his thumbs over the smooth cover.

Tomorrow Ernesto was hosting a gathering at his place. Everyone was coming. An idea started to take shape in his head.

He got to his feet and walked over to the fence. Iris came over and stood next to him. Below them, boats were lined up in the dry docks. The rides at Grönan had gone quiet. They kept glowing in the stillness.

"I think I need to find out what happened to him," Kasper said.

Iris was silent for a bit.

"That's a big thing to take on," she said at last. "Are you sure you want to do this?"

"I have to."

That's how it felt, but he thought about instincts again. Could he really trust himself?

"But will you tell me?" he said, immediately wondering if he was asking too much. "If I get too deep into this?"

"Do you promise to listen if I do?" Iris leaned against the fence.

Kasper looked at her. Her golden eye shadow shimmered in the bright lights illuminating the docks.

"I promise I'll listen," he said.

"All right," Iris said. "Then I will. But you have to be careful."

"I will be," Kasper told her. "I promise."

INTERLUDE

You probably think I seem sensible.

Good thing Kasper had such a sensible friend, a slightly older, slightly wiser friend, someone he could confide in. A friend who asked him to wait and think before acting.

But I wasn't sensible.

Yes, I was worried. I probably sensed the undercurrent that would take hold of him, but didn't understand the extent of the danger. I wanted answers, too. Not just because I had spent so many days in my childhood room staring at Grim's face on the walls.

Secrets have an allure.

It's so easy to think of them as treasures, as rewards rather than burdens.

Maybe those of us who write are especially inclined to think that way. Perhaps we believe we have a right to all the secrets in the world. Or maybe I'm only speaking for myself.

Writing this, I find myself thinking that things might have been worse if I had tried to put him off. Maybe he would have gone ahead, anyway, kept it a secret, even from me. If he had, he would have been all alone.

What I do know is that this was more important to Kasper than I had thought. He was trying to face something that had lurked in the corner of his eye his entire life, something unnameable beyond anecdotes and photographs.

Maybe ghosts are born from secrets.

The soil they take root in is shame and silence. And then they begin their hauntings.

KASPER

Ernesto's house was on a hill. A pair of ornate iron gates opened onto a long, paved driveway, which led to the house, or Casa Moberg, as its owner jokingly referred to it. At the moment, he was in shorts, a sleeveless shirt, and flip-flops, flipping burgers on the grill and greeting the guests as they arrived. His bald head shone in the sun. Kasper had no personal memories of the long black fall of hair he'd seen in photographs of a younger Ernesto.

Kasper pushed his sunglasses farther up the bridge of his nose and leaned back in his chair. He was in the shadow of the sauna. Destruction was playing from the built-in speakers in the patio. A lime-green swim ring floated in the pool. It belonged to Tony's youngest child, three-year-old Scott, who had just been lifted out of the pool, crying and coughing after having gulped down water. Now he was dripping onto his mom's—Emira—lap. Tony was just as soaked, sitting next to them in his black swim shorts. Unlike the majority of those present, he didn't have a single tattoo on his body.

"Hungry, huh?" he asked his sobbing son. "We'll eat soon."

Kasper was hungry, too. More than that, he was exhausted. He'd joined the others last night, despite everything, and it had turned into a magical night. It was as if he'd left all his worry on the island of Beckholmen. They had hung out in a bar and made plans for the Star Gala. Selam had booked a karaoke booth and Kasper had sung "18 and Life." The evening had ended with dancing at Cornelia's. Kasper couldn't remember the last time he'd laughed so much.

And now he was sitting here, nervous about the task that lay before him.

"I have to poop!" Scott proclaimed loudly.

"Should I take him?" Tony said, putting on his sunglasses.

"It's all right," Emira said, getting up with Scott in her arms.

Kasper watched her as she carried Scott toward the stairs leading up to the house. A memory flashed through his head, of his dad one day telling him he was too big to be carried. The rush of panic he'd felt. As if he wasn't allowed to be a child any longer.

"Good thing he didn't poop in the pool," Tony said.

Kasper laughed. This was the perfect moment to ask Tony, but how was he going to put it?

Destruction stepped aside for Voivod. Ernesto had told them the neighbors on the one side would complain about his music, while the ones on the other side found it energizing. This wasn't the most exclusive area in Nacka, but the houses on the heights were fancy enough for Ernesto to take some pride in being an interloper.

Having grown up in the high-rises in Bredäng, he often said that he'd never thought he would end up in a home with a pool. For a year, he's also had a studio behind said home. Kasper's dad was there right now, assessing the latest improvements.

I have to do it before he comes back, Kasper thought.

"Tony," he said.

Tony turned his head.

"Do you want something from the bar?" Kasper said, getting up.

"I'd love some water," was the reply. "Thanks, man."

Kasper cursed his cowardice, zigzagging between guests lingering on the paved patio and the grass, which was as dry as a savanna. Starting maintained fires wasn't forbidden anymore, but Ernesto had the garden hose ready, just in case.

The sun caught and shone in the frame that held a picture of Grim. He was in a doorway, smiling, black makeup around his eyes.

Sometimes the old guard would meet up like this, to commemorate his birthday. Because of the reunion, this year was special. There were more people than usual, around thirty guys and a few women. Some had brought their significant others, others had brought their kids along, and some came alone. Some looked worn and weary, others were in their prime. There were celebrities, and those who'd stayed in the background; people who saw music as their work, and those who saw it as a hobby. There were those who had quit playing completely. They were painters, worked at youth centers and kindergartens. They were builders, electricians, teachers. They were assistant nurses, bus drivers, economists, and carpenters. P-O, one of Vomitator's drummers, was a cardiologist now. Kasper walked over to the provisional bar and wondered who Grim had been to each of them. Friend, acquaintance, competition. How many of them had liked him, how many had admired him, how many hadn't cared about him at all? Had any of them hated him?

Ernesto's wife, Isadora, or Izzy, was serving guests at the bar. Kasper asked her for two waters. Izzy was the regular bassist in Vile Prophets now. She had met Ernesto when he was playing in Chile, where he'd been born. When Ernesto was two years old, his dad had been murdered by the military regime, and his mother fled to Sweden. There, she married Bernt, who adopted Ernesto when his little brother Paul was born. Paul had documented every single Dark Cruelty gig with Bernt's massive VHS camera. He was holding a smaller, more modern version now and interviewing Hasse, the producer and engineer who'd become a legend after having recorded the early Swedish death metal bands. He had retired, but still showed up to do some work in his old apprentice Fredda's studio. Dark Cruelty was going to record there.

Kasper returned, sitting down next to Tony and handing him a glass. He had to do it now.

"I have a question," he said.

"Shoot," Tony said, having a drink of water.

"Well, I'm doing my final project," Kasper said, feeling a surge of nervousness. "And I thought I'd do it about Grim."

"Right!" Tony said. "In what way? What are you doing?"

From the corner of his eye, Kasper saw the photo of Grim. It felt as if he were watching Kasper.

"There are different versions of who he was," he said. "So I wanted to work with those different images. And I wondered if I could talk to you, to find out who he was to you. So I could have something to base the drawings on."

He felt like a liar. Ms. Gunhild hadn't approved of his idea yet, but that wasn't the issue. The problem was that he wasn't telling Tony his real reason for wanting to talk to him.

Kasper still didn't know how to categorize what had happened to him, but he stood by his decision. He was going to find out what had happened to Grim. And if he was going to succeed in that, he had to talk to those who had been around him. Unlike the people speculating online, Kasper had access to many of the people who'd been closest to Grim. He already knew things the general public didn't. There had to be more secrets, more clues.

"Hell yes, you can," Tony said. "Just tell me when you want to talk. Come down to the workshop so we can tinker with a car while we're talking."

He guffawed. Kasper had always been completely uninterested in all motor vehicles, which mystified Tony.

"Seriously," Tony said. "It'll be nice. Tons of memories coming back to me now, what with the reunion."

That's when Dark Cruelty's new singer came sauntering by.

Ossian Holm was twenty-nine and looked like a young Iggy Pop, if Iggy Pop had been six foot two rather than an inch shorter than Kasper. He was pale, muscular, and sinewy, with thick eyebrows and dirty blond hair that fell down his back.

Today he was wearing black jeans and a sleeveless shirt that had once been a Morbid Angel tee. His appearance always had an unwashed, dusty air, as if he'd just been out walking in a sandstorm. His eyes were watchful. He'd had that intensity to him as a child, too, and Kasper couldn't understand where he got it. Neither Ernesto nor Linda had it. It was as though Ossian, at a very young age, had decided to be autonomous.

"Tony," Ossian said.

"Hey, man," Tony said.

A hug and pats on the back were exchanged. Then Ossian turned to Kasper. He immediately started wondering what was expected of him. Should he shake Ossian's hand, or hug him and pat him on the back? It was typical of Ossian not to take the first step. Every time you met him, he'd size you up. Even when he was joking and relaxed, something about him signaled that it was a conscious choice he made, and that he could turn at any moment.

"Hi," Kasper said, raising his hand in a sad little wave.

"Hey," Ossian said.

Small running feet approached rapidly.

"Kasper, look at me!" Leia yelled.

"Don't run by the pool!" Atle, who was standing a bit farther away with Diana, shouted after her. Leia ignored him completely, hurling herself into the pool like a cannonball.

Kasper managed to close his eyes the second before the water hit him. Most of it got on his legs, but he was splashed right in the face. He heard Tony chortle.

"You got wet!" Leia screamed.

"Yep," Kasper said, removing his sunglasses and wiping his face, which stank of chlorine, on his tee.

Leia snorted out water and began to paddle toward the swim ring. Ossian had already left. He was halfway to the bar with his girlfriend, Paola, an Italian silversmith with hundreds of thousands of followers. She was ten years older than Ossian and living in Amsterdam. The bird claw in oxidized silver, which hung around Ossian's neck, was definitely her work.

"Hey!" Ernesto's voice. "Time for a speech!"

Bottles and glasses were passed around. Someone turned the music down. Kasper and Tony got to their feet and walked over to the table on which Grim's photograph sat. His dad joined Kasper, his mom beside him. Kasper saw her take his dad's hand and squeeze it. It made Kasper's heart ache. He would never wish that he didn't have his sisters, but he couldn't help feeling nostalgic for the time when there had only been the three of them. He had never quite understood why it ended. Yes, they argued sometimes, and with increasing frequency before the divorce, but Kasper didn't understand *why* they were fighting. When he asked them, they said it was "grown-up business," suddenly agreeing with each other again. And since the divorce, they had been good friends, spending time with each other, with Atle and Leah, when Leah had still been with his dad.

"Håkan, do you want to say something?" Ernesto prompted.

Kasper looked at his dad, who was holding a low-alcohol beer in one hand.

"Right," he said. "It's huge, us standing here today. Together. Some of us were there when it all happened. Others," he made a sweeping motion, "others came later. Partners. Children." A hand on Kasper's shoulder, a nod at Ossian. "I never thought this day would come, and it's not official yet, but Dark Cruelty exists again."

"Hell yeah!" Ernesto's brother, Paul, shouted, while his husband let out a whoop.

"For a little while," Håkan added quickly, and people laughed. "And we're doing this reunion because we're family. And we're doing it for Grim. To honor his memory, the memory of our brother, our bandmate, our friend." He turned toward the photograph. "Happy birthday."

There was something solemn in the air. The hairs stood up on Kasper's arms. Something was about to happen, something that would affect them all.

"To Grim!" Ossian said loudly, raising his glass.

"For Grim!" Tony said.

When Kasper joined in, he thought he heard a whisper: *For Kasper.*

Dead man's name.

Kasper didn't think about it often, as it was just his name. When people spoke about the other Kasper, they always said Grim. That was how he had introduced himself when he moved to Stockholm.

Occasionally, Grim's fans would refer to him by his birth name, or at least the ones who considered him a lost teenage boy. In this sort of company, however, Kasper had never heard it mentioned before. He couldn't stop thinking about it, sitting by Ernesto's well-lit pool as midnight approached. He wondered who had said it.

The night air was mild. Laughter floated toward him from the table where the others were seated: his dad, Ossian and Paola, Izzy and Ernesto. Kasper hadn't had the chance to ask Ernesto about his final project yet. Well, he had had chances, to be fair, but he wasn't as close to Ernesto as he was to Tony, and Ossian's presence unsettled him. The evening was ending now, all of them gathering to smoke incredibly exclusive cigars, the scent of which made Kasper want to puke. Hence: the pool, sketchbook in his lap.

Beneath the cloud of cigar smoke, it smelled like autumn, and the wind moved through the dark canopies. The light coming from the pool was strong enough to draw by, but the full moon would have been enough. It was so bright, it was almost blinding.

On his phone, he had brought up the photo of Grim holding the dead bird. He was trying to draw it, wanted to show it to Ms. Gunhild as an example of how some of Grim's fans perceived him.

The real question was whether or not he should incorporate the drawings based on his dreams into the project. He should be eager to show them off, but something inside him resisted.

Abruptly, he felt watched. He turned his head.

Ossian was sitting with a cigar in his hand, examining him intensely. Kasper looked back down at his sketchbook, but was painfully aware of the sound of a metal chair scraping across stone, and the sound of steps advancing. Ossian had left the cigar behind, but smelled strongly of smoke when he stopped by Kasper, who tried to shut his book as discreetly as he could.

"Kasper," Ossian said, as if tasting the name. "Long time."

"Yeah," Kasper said. "Yes, I suppose."

He and his dad had seen Vanbörd play at a festival a few years back. The sun had been beating down from a clear blue sky, and the band's long black robes and grayish face paint looked sort of out of place. Afterward, his dad and Kasper had stopped by to say hi to Ossian. Nowadays, though, Vanbörd had reached a particularly sweet spot of underground popularity, and was hyped in the right circles, meaning they could soon cross over into better festival slots and bigger stages. But then they risked being labeled as sellouts. Was Ossian willing to risk it?

"Today is a special day," Ossian said.

"Mmm," Kasper agreed.

He didn't understand why Ossian was talking to him. Ossian was *somebody*, while Kasper was the *son of somebody*. Important enough not to be completely neglected, but not worth much in and of himself. That was how Ossian usually treated him.

He noticed Ossian looking at the sketchbook and realized he'd been holding on to it too hard, as if afraid that Ossian would grab it. That had drawn Ossian's interest.

"Can I see," Ossian said. It wasn't a question.

"All right," Kasper said, handing him the book.

Ossian had that effect on him. When Kasper was a child and they visited Ernesto, the door to Ossian's room was always shut. Kasper would stand outside it sometimes, both wishing it would open and fearing it. A few times, Ossian would let Kasper enter his domain. The reason behind it was always murky back then, and still was. Maybe he was bored. Still, Kasper couldn't resist the attention.

Ossian opened the book onto the latest drawing of Grim, the one with the bird.

"It's just a thing for school," Kasper said, aware of how childish he sounded.

Ossian turned the pages. Then he stopped at one of Kasper's dreams. Kasper caught his breath. He didn't want Ossian to see those drawings but couldn't help but wonder how he'd react to them.

A few crickets sang in the dry grass. Ossian went through the book backward, finding the very first drawing of Kasper's dreams. He stared at it. Turned a page. Stared. Turned another page.

Kasper glanced up at Ossian's face and what he saw startled him. Ossian was looking at the pictures as though they were inconceivable, something he was desperately trying to understand.

Kasper noticed that the table had fallen silent, the others watching him and Ossian.

Gently, carefully, Ossian closed the sketchbook. He held it in both hands. Kasper had the feeling he was either going to throw it into the pool or take it and run. But he gave it back to Kasper and met his gaze. The searching expression was gone, replaced with something cold and crass: there you are, here I am.

"I'll be in touch," Ossian said, and he returned to the table.

Kasper heard his dad say: "Guess I've sobered up enough to drive," and the others laughed.

"What did Ossian want?"

It was the first question out of his dad's mouth when he and Kasper were in the car, Ernesto's house growing smaller behind them.

"Not a clue," Kasper admitted. "He just looked at some of my drawings." He hesitated, then added, "And said he'd be in touch."

One of his dad's hands rested on the steering wheel, the other one's fingers tapping restlessly against his thigh. His expression was difficult to read. They approached a stop sign.

"Now what do I do?" his dad, who was trying to give Kasper driving lessons whenever they were in the car together, asked him.

"You have to stop completely." Kasper sighed.

He didn't even know if he wanted a license. His dad stopped, letting a silvery SUV pass him before driving again.

"Why would he be in touch?" he asked.

"I don't know," Kasper told him. "He hardly spoke. Just looked at the drawings."

What had Ossian seen in them?

"Maybe you shouldn't hang out with Ossian," his dad said.

Kasper laughed. Somehow, it was both adorable and annoying that his dad believed he could.

"Are you serious?" Kasper said.

"I know you're an adult, all right?" his dad said. "It's just a piece of friendly advice."

Kasper only felt annoyed now.

"Why's he in the band, then?"

"He's Ernesto's kid and one of Sweden's best vocalists."

His fingers keep tapping against his thigh. Kasper could tell how badly his dad wanted a smoke.

"But?" Kasper prompted.

"Jesus, all right," his dad said. "Too many drugs, too much of an attitude. To be honest, I think it might become a problem."

Ossian was one of those people who thought the extreme in extreme metal didn't just apply to the music, but also the lifestyle. But his dad and Tony, apart from being musicians, led very ordinary lives with jobs and kids. And Ernesto hadn't had a drink in twenty years.

"Unfortunately, Ossian and I have decided to meet at his place this weekend and share a kilo of cocaine," Kasper said.

"Ha-ha." His dad sighed. "I don't know why I said that. He's not all bad. Besides, he's disciplined. Just look at what he's done with Vanbörd. He's just got so many odd ideas. I respect him as a musician, believe me, but that mumbo-jumbo he's into is too much for me."

When Ossian did interviews, he always emphasized his interest in magical and esoteric traditions. He used to say that music was a kind of magic, a way of communing with something deep and primeval, because rhythm and song existed before language. His dad, on the other hand, was a sceptic, which had irritated Leah, who was more spiritually inclined. She used to point out that his dad and Grim had been fascinated with the supernatural, that it was obvious from their lyrics. His dad would mutter, "Well, sure, it was Satan this and Satan that, but it was mostly to create the right atmosphere." Now, Kasper wondered if that had been the whole truth. Now, he had experienced the unexplainable. And it was difficult not to think of all the films he'd seen, about people getting entangled in black magic and ending up in trouble for it. What if something like that had happened to Grim? What if that was why this was all happening? And in that case, how much did his dad know about it?

"Hey," his dad said. "Take my phone and play the most recent file, okay?"

"What is it?" Kasper said, digging the phone out from between the seats.

"Just something I'm working on."

Kasper pressed Play and music blasted out of the car stereo. His dad had made a drum track and recorded the guitars and the bass. No vocals. It sounded good, really good. Kasper could sometimes feel hesitant, talking to his dad about music, wasn't able to analyze songs like his dad could or describe exactly what it was he enjoyed.

"It sounds great," was all he managed after the song had finished. "What is it?"

"'Tormented Exaltation,'" his dad said. "Grim's final song. He left some half-finished lyrics lying around, but he told me he was happy with this one. There were some riffs on tape, too, so I put them together."

"Cool," Kasper said, and he played the song once more.

The headlights lit up the dark road. While the music was aggressive, it also contained a deep longing, a kind of melancholy. Grim's final song. Had he made the decision that ended with him underground while working on it? Or was it later? If it had been his choice at all.

"Shit!" his dad shouted, slamming the brakes.

Kasper barely caught a glimpse of a boar, its black bristle in the headlights. His belt tightened, and then a thud; he pressed his whole body against the seat.

His dad stopped the car by the roadside, flicking on the hazard lights. The music played on.

"Fuck." He turned scared eyes toward Kasper. "Are you all right?"

"Yeah," Kasper said. "I'm good."

"Fuck," his dad repeated, turning the engine off. The song was cut abruptly short. "Holy fucking shit."

"We're all right," Kasper reminded him.

His dad looked through the rearview mirror and then opened the car door, climbed out. Kasper did the same.

The air was cooler now, humid. Above, the full moon shone like a giant lamp. Kasper had no idea where they were. His dad crouched in front of the car, mumbling something about the fender, and then straightened up. Looked down the road where they'd just been driving.

"Hope that poor pig isn't dying out there."

"Should we check?" Kasper said, but he immediately knew it was a terrible idea.

"Fuck no. Boars can kill you."

A small truck whizzed past and the rush of wind blew Kasper's hair into his face. He brushed it away. His dad took out a packet of cigarettes, empty but for one smoke.

"This is my final one," his dad said, lighting it. "I am done."

"Because you hit a boar?"

"That's one reason," his dad said. He closed his eyes, inhaled the smoke. "Tony said you wanted to talk to him about Grim."

So he'd known but hadn't mentioned it until now.

"I was going to ask you, too. Obviously," Kasper added.

His dad blew out smoke. Kasper couldn't quite see his face where he was standing, turned away from the moon and the flashing car.

"I thought you were sick of my stories by now." His laugh sounded stiff and unnatural. "But sure. You're drawing? They're not going to be published, the interviews?"

"No, they're just for me." It wasn't a lie. "The drawing will be my interpretation of whatever you tell me."

"Yeah, okay," his dad said, taking another drag on the cigarette.

"I thought I'd talk to Ernesto, too," Kasper told him.

"Yeah, great," his dad said. "Go for it. Just . . . Tony and Ernesto both have pretty poor memories."

"And yours is better?"

"Absolutely," his dad said and laughed. "Or—I don't know."

There was a rustling from the bushes.

"Get back into the car," his dad hissed.

Kasper threw himself toward the car, and out of the corner of his eye, he saw his dad doing the same. It reminded him of being little and his dad suddenly whispering: "Zombie attack!" Then the two of them would run as fast as they could toward the car, chased by imaginary zombies and screaming with excitement once they'd shut the doors, "having survived."

"Man, I'm jumpy tonight," his dad laughed, thumping a hand onto the steering wheel. He was just about to start the engine, but stopped himself. "Dammit, I have to report this."

He did just that, and when they finally got home, Kasper was beyond exhausted.

He had just gone to bed when his phone pinged. It was Iris.

don't know if you've seen this

Kasper clicked on the link she'd added. It led him to a thread where people were discussing Dark Cruelty.

>I can't tell you where I got this information, but there's a reunion coming up real soon and they're releasing something on Retrolash. Reliable source.

The post went up an hour ago. Someone had leaked.

Kasper browsed the reactions. A third were wary, a third enthusiastic, and a final third negative. The level of disdain and animosity fans expressed toward bands they ostensibly liked still surprised him.

>fuck I hope you're not right. I always admired these guys cause they knew when to quit. I guess that's gone now too.

>this is why we can't have nice things

>who's on vox? morbid eradicator?! whata fuckin joke, his growl style was the weakest, he's much better suited for clean singing

>From what I heard Ernesto's son Ossian Holm from the band Vanbord is on vocals

>you mean vanbörd, get those umlauts right

>hmm, that's very interesting actually, I've seen vanbord live and he is really good, you can tell that he's inspired by Grim's vocal style

>They're nothing without Kasper.

Kasper stared at his name. Grim's name. He heard the door to his dad's room open. During a long period after Kasper's collapse, his dad would sneak out of bed and stand outside Kasper's door, listening. His dad probably thought he hadn't noticed. Kasper left his bed.

His dad was at the kitchen table with his laptop in front of him. Blue light lit his face in the dark room, was reflected in his glasses.

"I saw what happened." Kasper wiggled his phone.

"Yeah." Håkan sounded tired. "I'm chatting with Mizuki right now."

"Everything all right?"

Håkan turned his head and looked at Kasper.

"It really is," he said. "Go to bed. Sleep well."

Kasper tried.

But he couldn't shake the feeling that this night had been a night marked by strange omens.

Appendix 6. Reactions from comment sections after news about Dark Cruelty's reunion are confirmed.

FUCK YEAH! HAIL DARK CRUELTY!!
- HAIL FROM POLAND
- MExican fan here! Hail Dark Cruelty! Mexico welcomes you! Unleash the hordes! Hornsup!!! \m/

who cares, their desperate old hasbeens
- That's funny since all of them have had careers during the past 30yrs. And the new vocalist is 29
- define career

WORSHIP ANCIENT BLOODLUST!!!!!!!
- I lost my virginity to ancient bloodslut

They seem like decent guys but let's be honest. They're nothing without Grim.
- dark cruelty existed before grim
- They sucked though. They even said so themselves
- grim obv didn't think so. since he joined the band.
- he saw their potential, not the same thing lol
- youre gay
- haha no, that vanbord guy is kinda hot tho

Fuckin money hungry sellouts tryin to cash in on Grim's legacy. HAIL GRIM!
- HAIL IAGO!
- HAIL ALADDIN!
- aaahahaha that guy was so unlucky with his stage names
- Morgov was pretty cool tho
- sounds right about Russian to me

listen to Nox Irredux instead
- I'm sad that Iago's not in the reunited band, but not exactly surprised
- Didn't he kill a guy? I met him once!! Nice guy!!
- Nice if you're a nazi!:)))))))

- fuck off
- It's funny how Malte Lundell and people like him basically have been screaming in your face that they're nazis since the early nineties. But y'all buy his lame ass excuses and refuse to realize that you're being played for fools. It's not one little thing or one little incident. He's used nazi symbols. He named an album after a SS division with Swedish volunteers. He talked about "keeping the vermin out of Sweden." And then all the usual poor excuses: "We're not a political band," "I'm only interested in history," "I hate ALL the humanz," "We have lots of fans in South America," "YOU'RE the problem, you're destroying the scene when you call us nazis." These are age-old propaganda techniques to deflect criticism, look up card stacking, transfer, name calling, etc. Folks like Malte Lundell know exactly what they're doing. We metalheads say we love freedom so fucking much but hey, let's give our hard-earned money to someone who wants to dismantle that said freedom (and yeah, he has had ties to active groups, it's not his private opinion, so many people know this). It's not like nazis are mythological creatures, they exist and we (unfortunately) share the same reality, a reality they want to alter. Wake the fuck up and stop bending over for them!:)))))))) why would he hide his opininos tho if this is true?
- Lol, nazi bands who actually stand for their beliefs don't get to play the big festivals and they don't earn as much money, lying is part of the nazi game, ever heard of Goebbles?
- this is so pc my head hurts, people like you ruin the scene
- and you just proved my point.:)))))

I guess all the hipster posers will be pleased
- whining about posers is the most posery thing to do

lmao, can't wait to see berserker try to keep up at 180 bpm, extreme metal drummers should retire before 50
- Youre so ignorant
- DC songs weren't even that fast & he's not even 50
- Tony is a great drummer, and he hits HARD, not like all those wimps who play superfast but their drums are triggered af

I'm a Brazilian DC fan and I'm freaking out, DARK CRUELTY IS BACK FUCK YEAH! HAIL DARK CRUELTY! HAIL MAIMER! HAIL BERSERKER! HAIL MORBID ERADICATOR!
- this music is not for you
- it's so funny, because these nordic european extreme metal bands basically ripped off south american 80's extreme metal bands and now european racist assholes like you are like "oooo, south american fans are so weird and intense because they're psyched about the music & they shouldn't listen to extreme metal," fuck you, this is OUR legacy!!!!

all these scandinavian extreme metal bands are fucking weak, they were on welfare the whole time
- So they played the system, what's your problem?
- my problem is your weak commie ass
- Try living without sunlight half of the year, let's see who's weak then! HAIL SWEDISH METAL!!1!!!!!!

THE GUITARIST

One Thursday in November, Iago walks into their rehearsal space and introduces himself as Malte Lundell. He looks like a child, Håkan thinks. Thin, with big, round eyes. His pale hair comes down to his shoulders. Some of the spots on his forehead and jawline are inflamed. There: the beginning of a faint mustache. He's only fifteen, goes to a junior high school in central Stockholm. He wears a long black coat over a black sweater and an inverted pentagram in a chain around his neck. The diabolical look is somewhat ruined, however, by the ill-fitting blue jeans and the practical winter boots.

"Where did you get that?" Grim indicates the pendant.

"My aunt is a silversmith," Malte says. "She hates the church, too."

"What, your aunt's a Satanist?" Tony says with a laugh.

"No, an atheist," Malte says, turning red.

The more he talks, the more it becomes clear that he's from an entirely different world, a world in which aunts are atheistic silversmiths, moms are doctors, and dads have gone to fancy universities. A world in which you attend concerts in fancy halls, and everyone knows who Nietzsche is, or at least enough to pretend they know more.

Malte's voice is hoarse, his speech rapid, as if he needs to get all his words out before someone stops him. He is constantly looking around, as if to make sure where in the room they all are. Later,

Håkan wonders if Malte was nervous that day, or just wanted to register the effect of his words.

"Are we playing or are we talking?" Håkan interrupts, once he's had it with Malte's tirade.

Malte shuts his mouth. Literally. Håkan can hear his teeth clack together.

"'Nocturnal Allegiance,' right?" Håkan says, in a kinder voice.

Malte nods without looking at him, taking out his guitar. It's expensive, Håkan notes.

"You can listen first," Grim says.

They start rehearsing the song. Malte leans against the wall, fingering his pentagram. His eyes are fixed on Grim. When it's his turn to play, he does it well; he's got a good sense of timing and rhythm. He'd told them he'd been in a band before, but left it because their taste in music was too lame. They go through the song a few times. When it turns out that Malte's taught himself "Carrion Summoning," too, they give that one a try as well.

"Band meeting," Grim announces at last.

Malte grabs his coat and his guitar.

"Bye," he says hoarsely before closing the door behind him.

"Yeah, bye," Ernesto says.

It's the first thing he's said during the entire rehearsal.

"He's good," Tony says.

"He is," Håkan agrees.

Grim is sitting on the amplifier, turning the microphone over in his hands.

"Talked my ear off," Ernesto says.

"Maybe he was a bit nervous," Tony says. "That's fair, isn't it?"

"We'll take him," Grim says.

A jolt goes through Håkan. Grim shouldn't be saying that, or at least not like that. It sounds like a decision.

"What, 'cause he's your friend?" Ernesto says.

"Not my friend. But I believe in him. He gets what we're going for. A lot of people don't."

"Yeah?" Ernesto says. "Then how come we've sold so many copies of *Nocturnal*?"

"It's one thing to like the music. It's another thing to understand what we're doing," Grim says. "To truly understand."

"Is it?" Tony looks skeptical. "I thought we played death metal."

Ernesto says, "Maybe we don't get it, either."

Tony spins a drumstick, doesn't speak. Grim has hurt his feelings, even though Håkan knows it wasn't his intention. A lot of people can't tell that Tony is sensitive, particularly when it comes to feeling stupid.

"All right," Håkan says. "Let's put it to a vote."

Grim looks disturbed.

"He's taking over for me, so I should get an extra say."

"What, so suddenly you have two votes?" Ernesto crosses his arms over his chest. "One as a guitarist and one as a singer?"

"Why not?" Grim says.

"All right, then give me two votes," Tony says, "'cause I play with my hands *and* feet."

"One vote per person," Håkan tells them. They all turn toward him when he pushes on: "We've decided we're recording in March, and we're rehearsing new songs. We need to be even better prepared this time around, right? Malte has shown us that he catches on quickly."

"Stasse said he'd play with us," Ernesto points out.

"We need someone who'll go for it," Håkan says. "For us. Malodor will always be number one for Stasse. And if it doesn't work out with Malte, we'll kick him out, right?"

Bands in the scene constantly change members. If anything, Dark Cruelty's relative stability is rare.

"Who's voting for Malte?" Håkan says.

Grim raises his hand. Håkan doesn't hesitate, either. He didn't get a particularly good impression of Malte, but a five-man line-up feels right. They can bring in some other guitarist after the recording session if it doesn't work out. It's not like finding another drummer. Tony sighs, raising a fist to join their hands.

Ernesto's arms are still crossed over his chest.

"I don't like him. He's off," he says, and adds, with a look at Grim, "*Truly* off."

"I said we'd kick him out if it doesn't work out." Håkan sighs. "Won't we, Grim?"

Grim nods, his gaze distant.

It's too late to phone Malte when they get home, but Grim gives him a call the next day. Håkan eats yogurt in front of the TV, occasionally checking his watch. Five minutes, ten minutes, fifteen minutes pass.

Finally, Grim exits their room. He's still holding on to the phone, the extension cord trailing behind him. He looks exhilarated.

"We're going to Malte's tomorrow," he says. "He wants to show us something."

They take the train to the Stockholm Central Station, where they will take the subway to Karlaplan. But as they run to catch it, they accidentally get on the wrong train, ending up at Stadion instead. They roam around until Håkan asks a lady for directions. They walk past buildings made out of stone, past facades decorated with columns and statues. Grim peers through an entrance.

"It looks like a castle in there," he says. "Marble and shit. Are there only dukes and barons living here?"

"Nah, Vomitator's new drummer's from around here," Håkan says. "But Östermalm is boring."

He doesn't actually know too much about it, as he's rarely in this part of the city. He came close this summer, when he, Tony, and

Grim took the ferry to Grönan. It turned out that Grim, who had never been to a theme park before, suffered from motion sickness. After one ride in the relatively tame Hully Gully, he threw up in a trash can. He made another attempt with the Viking Ship—"it only swings back and forth and doesn't spin"—but he ended up on a bench with his head between his knees. But it had been a good day. Grim rode the ghost train five times and won a big, round metal box full of chocolates. They finished half of them on the way home, then gave the rest to Håkan's mom.

They pass the staircase that leads up to Östra Real's schoolyard. It's a huge building, made of dark bricks, and Håkan finds himself wondering how old it is. Definitely older than any school he's ever attended.

"Bet this school is haunted," Grim says.

He still hasn't told Håkan what Malte is going to show them. Håkan wonders if Grim knows, or if Malte has lured him in with hints.

They reach Karlaplan, a large roundabout with a dry fountain in its center, surrounded by lofty elm trees with yellow leaves. On the other side is Fältöversten, a bright red slice of pie that covers an entire block, a shopping center and public services on the lower floors, apartments up top. Håkan checks his watch and discovers that they're twenty minutes late. Malte is waiting by the entrance to the shopping center. To his right, a couple of blue escalators lead to and from the block of flats.

"Hi," Håkan says.

"We ended up in the wrong station," Grim tells him.

"It's fine," Malte says. "I was waiting indoors."

But his red nose and cheeks belie him. He hadn't wanted to go inside and warm up, worried he'd miss them. It helps Håkan calm down, somehow. Makes him feel as if he has an advantage.

"This way," Malte says, leading them to the escalators.

Only the one going downward works, so they stomp up the other one, Malte in front, Håkan at the back. Then they enter a small courtyard.

"Welcome to Fältöversten," Malte says. "This is where they put all the drunks and welfare cases."

It doesn't sound as if he's talking about his home but a place that he's been unfortunate enough to be stuck in temporarily.

A woman pushing a stroller opens one of the front doors and they enter behind her. The door marked LUNDELL is on the first floor.

Håkan senses them at once: the bad vibes. He's felt them before, when he was small and lingering in the hallway of some friend, the homes in which you never hung out. But Håkan isn't a child anymore, so he removes his shoes and jacket like everyone else.

The apartment is dim, cramped, and far too hot. An overwhelming smell of disinfectant wafts from the bathroom. The living room, meanwhile, is bursting with furniture, as if someone's moved from a far larger apartment to this one without getting rid of a single item. Maybe that's exactly what has happened. Malte doesn't ask them if they want something to eat or drink, instead showing them into his bedroom and ordering Håkan to close the door.

"You can lock it, too."

Did he hear that right? There is a key in the door, which Håkan turns with a click. A faint light trickles through the closed blinds. Malte turns on the desk lamp.

Whoever had cleaned the bathroom has not been granted access into Malte's room. Dust motes whirl through the air, the bed is unmade, and the sheets give off a musty odor. Malte moves piles of clothing from his desk chair and a stool that had once been a chair, tosses it all on his bed. The only organized spaces in the room are the shelves, where the records and cassette tapes are lined up. At least he has taste, Håkan thinks to himself when he inspects Malte's collection. The expensive guitar is on the wall, alongside some film posters. *Hellraiser. Amadeus. The Magnificent Seven.* Grim is lingering by a terrarium in which a hairy tarantula is perched unmoving on a bit of wood.

"His name is Kurt," Malte says.

"What does he eat?" Grim asks him.

"Crickets," Malte says, walking over to the stereo. "There's a pet shop downstairs, so that's handy. I'm thinking of breeding them myself, but they make so much noise."

He drops the needle. Håkan immediately recognizes the windtorn intro.

"What did you want us to see?" he says.

"I'll get it." Malte walks over to the desk.

He sits down, and Grim sinks down on the stool beside him. Håkan remains standing. His legs ache, but he refuses to sit down on Malte's rank bed, surrounded by his dirty laundry. And the floor is dusty and full of crumbs; he can feel them through his socks. He's not usually this fussy, but this place is gross. He reaches out a hand to drag the window open.

"Kurt doesn't like the cold," Malte informs him.

Håkan lowers his hand with a sigh, leans his back against the window. Malte takes out a black folder decorated with an inverted pentagram painted with Wite-Out.

"Here," he says, handing it to Grim.

Håkan watches over Grim's shoulder as he opens the folder. The pages in it have been photocopied from a book.

"It's a list of demons," Malte says. "It tells you what form they usually assume and what you can ask of them. There are also their symbols, their seals."

Håkan skims the list. The book is written in English.

"Where's this from?" he asks.

"Dunno," Malte says, chewing on a pencil.

He is obviously lying. He doesn't want them to get hold of the book, wants them to need him. Håkan could have laughed at it; Malte is such a child. But in this stuffy, disgusting room, it just irritates him.

"Interesting," Grim comments. "There's a lot here I haven't seen."

"We need to go," Håkan says.

Malte's shoulders slump. He'd clearly imagined the three of them sitting there for hours, excitedly discussing demons.

"I'd like to copy this," Grim says.

"Sure," Malte says, a string of saliva dangling from the pencil when he removes it from his mouth. "As long as I get it back."

Grim nods, getting to his feet with the folder underneath his arm.

"There's more," Malte says. "I can get you more."

"Okay," Grim says.

"Bring it to rehearsal," Håkan tells him, because there is simply no way he will ever return to this place.

On the way out, Grim stops at the terrarium, giving Kurt one final look.

"Do you want to feed him?" Malte asks.

"I'm okay," Grim says.

Back in the courtyard, a worn-out woman in an electric wheel-chair drives past them, liquor bottles clinking inside the plastic bag on her lap. She is mumbling to herself. *Drunks and welfare cases.*

"He's full of himself," Håkan says as they walk down the working escalator. "Why'd he drag us all the way over here? He could have just brought it to rehearsal."

"This list is genuine," Grim tells him. "This is the real deal."

"Wicked," Håkan says.

He breathes in the fresh air, tries to forget the stink in Malte's room. They've talked about using the names of demons in some song, maybe in an outro. The list could be useful.

"At least he was cute," Grim says.

Håkan stares at him.

"Kurt!" Grim goes on. "What a great name for a spider!"

Håkan has to agree. He feels bad now. Malte may be annoying, but he's younger than they are, and he probably wants to impress them. Better to feel a bit sorry for him. And whatever happens, it's Grim and Håkan, Håkan and Grim. No one can change that.

KASPER

A car covered in a tarp was parked outside of Tony's house. Kasper removed a yellow leaf from the hood, twirling the stalk between his fingers, water drops spattering. The door to the garage was open, and inside it, Tony was busy disassembling a motorbike. Music issued from a boom box; its surface was stained with paint. There were two cement mixers outside, one of which had been an absolute bargain, Tony had told Kasper. "Almost new and good to have around." Tony's "good to have around" mentality shaped his and Emira's home.

Making time with Tony hadn't been easy. If the kids weren't sick, he had work, rehearsal, or something else. Almost a month had passed since they'd met at Ernesto's. During that time, Kasper had worked on his two portraits of Grim the way fans saw him: a dark Messiah and a broken teenager. He had enjoyed using his new tablet, and it had been easier to learn than he'd assumed, but these new pictures didn't measure up to the ones based on his dreams.

Nothing inexplicable had happened since the mirror fell from the wall, but the scar shone red on his palm, a reminder.

The sound of metal hitting concrete came from inside the garage.

"Fucking hell," Tony said. He was on all fours, looking for something. "Nearly done!" he hollered. "Just going to get my hands on this thing . . ."

"It's fine," Kasper said, even though he was starting to feel deeply stressed.

Tony had started out by showing Kasper the improved sound-proofing in the basement, where he kept his drums. Then he'd wanted Kasper to meet the family's new cat, Bargain. "Because I got him for practically nothing," Tony laughed. Just as they were sitting down, he remembered that he'd forgotten to sort something out in the garage.

Forty minutes had passed since Kasper arrived. In an hour or so, a nine-year-old and a three-year-old would be back in the house, and any attempt at talking in peace and quiet would go out the window.

Kasper's phone pinged. Halloween was approaching, meaning the demons' group chat was becoming active again. Kasper would be the UC in The House. Now Cornelia had written that she was shopping for clothes and asked if anyone wanted to meet up for a coffee. Santiago quickly accepted and so did Iris. Telling them he couldn't join would just be odd, wouldn't it? Was he overthinking it? Since the end-of-season party, he didn't know how to behave around Cornelia.

Kasper had heard about the Star Gala all summer. He'd never attended a party of that size before, and he felt tense beforehand. But his nervousness disappeared when Iris painted him like Billy, the puppet from *Saw*, and herself like a blood-soaked victim. They were a success, and Nadja, the head of Rides, had come up to Kasper to compliment him for his role as a UC in the summer. During the rest of the evening, he had occasionally replayed her praise in his head, just to feel that warmth again. Pride, he supposed, at doing a good job and being noticed for it.

Unsurprisingly, the evening had ended at Cornelia's. Kasper was going to sleep on the couch, the way he had so many times before, and washed his makeup off. But Cornelia didn't want to go to bed, sulking in her early 2000s Britney outfit. A younger girl from her old school had gotten a part Cornelia had auditioned for.

"Do you know who Clea Borglund is?" she demanded.

"No," Kasper said.

Cornelia looked pleased. She started talking about how doing theater in England had been a mistake, since only a certain impossible-to-get-into acting school in Stockholm really mattered here. Not knowing anything about that world, Kasper couldn't keep up. But he became increasingly aware of how plunging Cornelia's neckline was. Suddenly, it was all he could think about. He wanted desperately to be swallowed up by the sofa cushions. Maybe seek shelter among the dust bunnies. But Cornelia laid a hand on his knee.

"You're adorable," she said. "You really are."

"Stop it," Kasper said, his voice shaking.

"You are. You have really nice lips, for instance."

Her little finger brushed against his lower lip.

Kasper laughed, turning his head away, but then immediately regretted it. He wanted her to touch him. He was just worried he wouldn't be able to do whatever was expected of him.

"Sorry," Cornelia said, removing her hand from his knee.

"It's fine."

"What's fine?"

Kasper pressed his sweaty palms against the sofa. She would probably think he was gross if he touched her.

"I'm not drunk," she said, "if that's what you're thinking."

"Okay," Kasper said.

"Oh, sweetie. You're terrified."

"No," Kasper said. "Yes."

He laughed, and so did she. Some of the tension left them.

"You only have to say yes or no, and I promise I won't take it personally." Cornelia smiled. "Can I kiss you?"

"Yes," Kasper mumbled.

Cornelia leaned in. Her face was so close. Her scent was so sweet. And then they kissed.

They made out for a while, and then Cornelia took him into her room. While they removed their clothes, all Kasper could think was: *How the hell do you do this?* Naturally, he got so nervous his body shut down, but it didn't bother Cornelia. They kissed some more, Kasper gradually relaxing. It all felt unreal. The following morning, he wondered if it had actually happened, even though she was sprawled next to him in her underwear and a tank top. He traced the contours of her arm with one finger, an inch or so above her skin. Had he touched her? Had they really had sex? He fell back asleep, and when he woke up again, she was dressed and in a rush. They hugged the way they normally did when they parted.

Since then, he couldn't stop thinking about her. It was as if his brain was stuck in a rut. Was this a crush? He didn't think so. If it was, he should probably say something, do something, but they were only in touch via the group chat. Now and then, he considered asking her out, just the two of them. What if she was just pretending, the way he was pretending? What if she wanted this to be something more?

She would have told me, though, Kasper thought, putting his phone back in his pocket. *That's the difference between us.*

"There we are," Tony said, leaving the garage and closing it behind him. "Time for coffee."

Tony placed two mugs of coffee on the living room table, each on its own porcelain plate, and then sank down in his armchair. Nintendo controllers and a plastic tractor were scattered in front of the television. One of Emira's projects occupied a desk: a half-finished puzzle depicting a sexy elf that was passionately embracing another sexy elf. One of the elves reminded Kasper of Cornelia. Kasper looked away, taking a small sip of his coffee. It was hot and tasted like tannic acid.

"Can I record this?" he said, putting his phone on the table between them.

He had realized that he needed to be able to review the material afterward, check what had actually been said. What Iris had told him about the unreliability of memory bothered him. Tony hesitated.

"This is starting to feel like a proper interview," he said with a laugh. "You know how I feel about those?"

He avoided them like the plague.

"It's just for me," Kasper reassured him. "I'll be deleting it later."

Tony frowned, but nodded. He reached for his mug and took a deep drink, then made a face.

"Tastes like shit," he said. "One sec."

He got to his feet, returned with milk that he poured into each of their mugs, and then got them oatmeal cookies.

"I'm going to the john," he said, and he went off again.

Kasper was starting to despair. Did Tony actually want to do this? Outside, it began to rain. He drew a leg up onto the couch. Bargain snaked around, watching him. Hopefully, Tony wouldn't come back from the bathroom and claim he needed to cover something in the garden with a tarp.

"I had a thought." Tony returned to the room. The leather armchair creaked cheerfully beneath his weight when he sat back down. "Something you don't think about with a reunion . . ."

Kasper pressed Play while Tony spoke.

"We've played together, off and on, for so many years, but the Dark Cruelty songs . . . We haven't played those for thirty years."

"Never?" Kasper said.

"Never," Tony said, stretching his wrists. "Maybe fooling around with a riff now and then, but that's it. Coming back to something you made when you were just a kid is pretty weird. We were so green. I think that's what makes it work, listening to it now."

"What do you mean?" Kasper asked him.

"Well, we had a limited number of retakes, and we couldn't exactly cut and paste in a computer afterward. Nah, you had to play the song from beginning to end, and you'd get it a bit wrong. But that shakiness gives it some life, somehow. Ernesto talked about that, that some riffs sounded better back then, and feel awkward now that he's a pro."

"Oh," Kasper said.

He hadn't thought about it that way.

"Some of those songs are really strange, too," Tony said with a laugh, reaching for a cookie. "A bunch of riffs just thrown together. Makes you scratch your head. There's one song that's just on an old rehearsal tape, and the recording is pretty shitty, so we can't even tell what we were doing on it. Håkan has the best memory out of all of us. He was there and wrote them, too . . . But a lot of it is physical and no one played Grim's riffs. No one has it in here."

Tony waved his fingers around.

"Maybe you'll have to contact Malte," Kasper said darkly.

Malte hadn't said anything officially about the reunion, but his label had announced that Nox Irredux was releasing a new EP in January. Maybe it had been composed in a fit of anger. At least there hadn't been any threats.

"Oh, he'd love that." Tony swallowed a bite of the cookie. "But anyway. A lot has changed. That's why Ernesto isn't singing, he's been doing clean vocals for the past twenty years. He tried and, to be honest, it sounded like shit. So it's a good thing we have junior. Makes it a bit special, seeing as Ernesto was our first singer, and Ossian's voice sounds a lot like his. At the same time, though, he's hugely influenced by Grim's vocal style."

Kasper nodded, thinking back on Ossian by the pool, his ominous *I'll be in touch*. But Kasper hadn't heard from him. He'd checked Vanbörd's social media, and they mostly wrote about their new album. There was also a post in which the band, or rather Ossian himself—Kasper was convinced he was in charge of communication—announced Dark Cruelty's reunion with Ossian "on vox." *I am humble before this task and proud to carry on Grim's legacy.*

"All right," Tony said, wiping his hands on his black jeans. "What do you want to know?"

Appendix 7. From the transcript of Kasper's interview with Tony Lehtonen

K: Maybe we can start with you saying something about the period.

T: Which period is that?

K: When Grim joined the band, I suppose.

T: That period . . . Huh . . . Well, it was . . . great, to be honest, all the time. We were never at home. (*laughter*) Good times all around. Like, when we started going to Fagersta for gigs, you could just walk up to anyone and start talking. If someone wore the right band tee, you were best friends. Just like that. There was a real sense of community. We all helped each other out, you know? Were roadies, drew logos for each other . . . It felt natural. There weren't many of us at the time, so the bond was real. I miss that bond, sometimes. Then people started releasing full-length albums, which changed things. Labels came into it. MTV. (*laughter*) The deals we got were shitty, but we only understood that later. We were so naive. Well, we were kids! (*laughter*) But back when it was all underground. It was fantastic. (*pause*) There were some downsides, too, obviously . . .

K: Like what?

T: Well, like . . . lots of nit-picking, you know, about what you could and couldn't listen to. I've always listened to everything. My parents were young, seventeen, eighteen years old, when they had me, and then they started their band . . .

K: Preacher's Perversions.

T: That's right! One of Sweden's first punk bands! Growing up with musicians was great. First chance I got, I was hammering away at a drum kit. (*laughter*) Mom and Dad were really cool, not like other people's parents. Well, uh, your grandma was great, but . . . My parents were out there, you know? They supported me. Especially my mom. Long hair, no problem, she said. Dad was a bit more conservative. There was the idea that you had to choose between punk and metal, metal and synth, that bullshit, but Mom would play everything. Punk, rock, new wave, prog, jazz, Sabbath and Maiden, partly to piss him off. Dad, I mean. She *hated* rules. And we came along for gigs, Håkan and I, we were little kids.

Mom stuffed our ears with cotton balls so we wouldn't ruin our hearing, but we just pulled it out. We saw Black Flag, for fuck's sake! (*laughter*) God, I'm rambling on . . . Where was I?

K: You said there was nit-picking . . .

T: What you could and couldn't listen to, yeah. Didn't used to be that way, used to be there was joy in any discovery, really. Håkan and I borrowed a bunch of records off Kjell-Åke, Lillemor's son. And then you'd look for something faster, harder. We drank it all down, as long as it was quick and brutal. But then that whole policing business began. (*laughter*) You wore a T-shirt out and it was like . . . (*mimicking*) "Uh, that band sucks. How can you listen to *that*?" (*regular voice*) Everything didn't have to be death metal and hard as all that, but it was more, like, Fields of the Nephilim are okay, but not *that* band. It could vary from one week to the next, though. But it wasn't like the nineties, some poor sod being suspected of being a poser and getting beaten up. If he had short hair, or a tee with the wrong band on it, or the right band, but he couldn't answer a fucking quiz about them. It wasn't like that for us, but there was a lot of griping. Your dad was a lot like that. Grim, too. Especially Grim. (*laughter*) Don't know if you've heard that story, but he cut up one of my band tees, once. I think it was Testament?

K: He cut it up? Grim?

T: Yeah, cuz he thought they sucked! He really hated Testament! (*laughter*) He could be a real pain. Couldn't even blame drugs or drink, that one, he just got so obsessed, a bit crazy with it. In hindsight, I think he might have had some diagnosis. Was on the spectrum, maybe. But you didn't think like that back then. Like my dyslexia, the teachers just thought you were dumb . . . I'm really rattling on, aren't I? Probably ADHD . . . I'm not joking, I mean it. Anyway, it's not like that anymore, which is a relief.

K: What isn't?

T: That policing. You can just listen to whatever the fuck you want now, whatever inspires you. I don't know any musicians who talk about it like that anymore. It's fans, mostly. Conservative. Want everything to be the way it's always been. But you've heard us moan about it your whole life.

K: (*laughter*) Yeah . . .

T: Shit . . .

K: Do you remember meeting him for the first time? Grim, I mean.

T: I don't think I do . . . I remember him trying out as our singer. Was that the first time I met him? I was gobsmacked. Grim . . . You know, I don't go around saying it that often, but I really looked up to him. Yeah, he was three years older, that could be part of it. But someone older than you with no clue, you end up looking down on them, don't you? But he knew *everything*. He could be such a smug bastard about it, too, but he was usually right. (*laughter*) I've always been a perfectionist about my own stuff, with the drums. But he had a vision. A whole concept. It was him and your dad and a few others who were a step ahead of everyone else in the scene. I think we could have gone so fucking far with Dark Cruelty. (*pause*) A lot of people have a pretty skewed image of him. Grim, that is.

K: How do you mean?

T: Him being so extreme . . . Yeah, he was, in a way. Like that shoot, your mom photographing us in that abandoned house, and he was posing with some decomposing raven. And the interviews he and your dad did in the zines. They really went for it. (*laughter*) But it was a bit of a game for them.

K: But don't you think—

T: (*interrupts*) He was extreme, in some ways. I was in it for the music, but he had that whole philosophy going for him. I thought it was cool, yeah, but a bit crazy, too. A bit too much. That was your dad and Grim, it was their thing. Reading about demons. Dark French poetry. Magic and all that shit. There was more where that came from when they started spending time with Malte . . . But one thing people forget to say about Grim is he was really generous and helpful. If someone wanted a new logo, he'd do it. He made T-shirts on demand, too, made me a Master tee after ruining the other one. (*laughter*) He was a good friend. In a fucking . . . In his own way. There was this thing that . . . After we'd recorded the *Nocturnal Allegiance* demo. My grandma died. It was very sudden. Advanced cancer. And everyone was like, "That's sad," and that was it. But I was broken up about it. She wasn't some old lady who'd spent twenty years in her deathbed. She was young, just over fifty. She'd been like an extra mother to me. I didn't know what to do with that feeling, just went around simmering, didn't even know if I was angry or sad. Wished someone would jump me when we were out, just so I could fight. And I drank. One night, some of us had met up at the Central Station and went back and forth on the red line. Your dad wasn't there, but Grim was. It was pretty rare. Usually you'd get them both at once, two for one. Maybe he was sick, your dad, I don't know. Whatever, for some reason we got off at Universitetet. Sat there and blasted music and drank. Grim took me aside and said he wanted to show me something. Then we went over to one of those doors, what's it called . . . the emergency stairs. It was great. A door, and then these long, broad stairs leading up to the ground floor. Water was dripping from the ceiling, I think, like in a mysterious cave. Well, with fluorescent lights in it. Stank of urine, too. (*laughter*) And I said: "How the hell do you know about this when I don't? I've lived in Stockholm my whole life." He thought that was hilarious. Laughed at it. We walked up those stairs, there was moss growing on them, I remember that. And out of nowhere, I got so fucking tired. It came out of nowhere. I had to sit down. Grim asked me if I felt sick, but I was just like . . . "Nah . . ." (*laughter*) I just broke down, crying. And said my grandma was dead. He knew, but it felt like I hadn't said it before, not really. (*silence*) He sat down next to me. He didn't say a word, but I could feel . . . He just radiated this, what do I call it? Compassion. He wanted me to be okay. He didn't know what to do or say, but who the fuck knew at that age, right? Stayed there until I'd finished howling. (*silence*) He was a real friend. I felt it, back there. (*silence*) He could have been one of the greatest. In my eyes, he *is* one of the greatest. Yeah . . . I only knew him for, what, less than two years? But he made such an impression . . . (*silence*) Fuck. Everything just went sideways. We should never have let that bastard join the band.

K: Malte?

T: Exactly. Malte.

KASPER

At midnight Kasper was in bed, listening to the interview for the second time. With Tony's voice in his ears, he let his gaze glide over the room. A few art prints of mythological beings by a Swedish illustrator decorated the walls, together with a framed poster of Link. Apart from books, the shelves held a few collectible figures from games, and a thick folder containing his old Pokémon cards. There was sadness in Tony's voice when he reached the point of Grim's death.

"When I first heard it, I didn't get it . . ."

A heavy sigh followed. Kasper closed his eyes. He could almost hear his own uncertainty in the question that followed: "What actually happened?"

The silence in Kasper's headphones felt oppressive. He became aware of how hard his heart was beating. Seven beats before Tony's voice returned.

"I know Grim's death is sensitive to Håkan, so you can ask me whatever you want. You must have questions. Talking to him about it can't be easy. Took him years before he could talk about it at all."

At this point, Tony had fallen silent again, frowning. Rain trickled down the windows. The bell around Bargain's neck sang when he leaped onto the couch and lay down next to Kasper, who stroked his fur.

"The first years were heavy," Tony said, his gaze on the cat. "I heard from the others in Exenterate that there was no point scheduling a gig in September, 'cause . . . Well, hate to say it, but Håkan's way of handling that 'anniversary' was to go out and get so wasted that he ended up in the drunk tank two years in a row."

Kasper couldn't imagine it. He'd seen his dad slightly tipsy, but he'd never been close to losing control.

"Anja was the one who suggested we should all meet up instead," Tony said. "Remember him together, the way he'd been when he was alive. I think it made those days a bit easier for Håkan." His smile was warm. "And then you came along. Odd timing, but it turned out to be for the best."

Kasper nodded vaguely. Bargain got sick of him and marched across his thighs, leaped over to Tony's armchair, and curled up comfortably in Tony's lap.

"But to answer your question," Tony said. "What happened . . . September had been a weird one for us. The EP came out in June, which was a feat, believe me. Neither Malodor nor Exenterate released anything on vinyl until the following year. And we'd done it all by ourselves. So we should have spent the summer celebrating. But Grim, well, he lost his spark during those months. He was deeply depressed, but we were too dumb to see it." He stopped himself. "Well, you know . . . Something like what you went through."

It wasn't the first time Kasper heard that Grim had most likely been depressed at the time, but he hadn't considered that he and Grim could have had similar experiences.

"Things really went to hell at the end of the summer," Tony went on. "We had a gig and your dad had to go and get Grim, 'cause he just didn't show up. Then he didn't show up for the next rehearsal. You need to remember that the band was *everything* to Grim. *Everything.* So it should have worried us more than it did, yeah, but we didn't get it. And Håkan's way of handling it was to go easy. He said the band would take a break for a few weeks. Didn't want to pressure Grim. I think he worried he'd take off the way Ernesto had. So, that was the backdrop, basically, to what happened. I remember Håkan phoning me at work on the fifteenth. Phoned and said Grim had disappeared. Well, he vanished now and then, but he hadn't showed up for work, which was odd. Håkan and I called everyone, headed out and looked for him. Grim could be in some pretty weird places. My dad and I even went to that house, the one where Anja took our photos. Then Håkan rang again after the cops had come by."

Tony fell silent, something far away in his eyes. A gust of wind made the rain lash against the window so hard Bargain jumped.

"What did the cops say?" Kasper said.

"That they'd found Grim and that he was dead," Tony said. "And then they wanted to know why he had that note on him. That was why they showed up, so to speak."

The note. Kasper didn't know this part.

"What note?"

"Well, with the number," Tony said slowly.

"The number?"

"Yeah. Grim had written your dad's phone number on a note in his pocket."

Kasper shivered. A chill made its way into the room. Why would Grim have his dad's phone number in his pocket? It must have been his number, too, for over a year. He must have known it by heart.

"Ah, shit, you didn't know," Tony said, almost startling awake. "Me and my big mouth."

"No, Dad or Mom have probably told me at some point," Kasper lied quickly, but then felt ashamed. He had never heard his parents talk about this. "But it makes no sense."

"I know," Tony said. "He knew that number, so it can't have been for his sake. I thought of those cards epileptics and diabetics have in their wallets. Well, it's gone now, but they used to. Virre in

Nuclearathon, he had one of them, being a diabetic. If he fainted in public, the paramedics would immediately know what was wrong with him."

Kasper tried to understand what Tony was getting at. Had Grim been worried that something would happen to him in the tunnels?

A thought struck him, as sudden as it was strange. What if Grim hadn't written the note? What if it had been left there by someone else, someone who had been down there with him? But why would someone do that?

"So that's how the police located your dad," Tony said. "He was in shock when he called me. I could hear it in his voice, just completely flat. And I couldn't take it in. That came later, at the funeral. I don't remember exactly when we heard about the cause of death. Could have been from Grim's mom, when she talked to Ulla, your grandma." Tony peered at Kasper. "Have you been reading about this online?"

"A bit," Kasper told him.

Another lie. He had read most of it by now. A bit at a time, or he wouldn't have been able to cope. To make matters worse, the rumors had started attracting more attention due to the reunion.

"The autopsy report . . ." Kasper said. "Have you seen it?"

"Yeah," Tony said. "That's some messed-up shit."

Kasper could only agree. Eventually, he had found a link that worked. Half of it was impenetrable jargon, half of it things he wished he could forget, just like Iris had said.

"Some messed-up shit," Tony repeated. "I didn't know if I wanted to read it. At the same time, I was like, what if they've missed something? So I looked. And then I spoke to P-O from Vomitator. He's a heart surgeon, not a forensic pathologist, but he thought the conclusions made sense. He thinks Grim had some kind of epileptic fit. Or some unusual kind of stroke."

"But didn't someone move him?" Kasper asked.

"P-O thought it was difficult to confirm."

Kasper hugged himself.

"But what was he even doing there?" he said.

"No idea," Tony said. "Like I said, he liked exploring odd places. I'm thinking about those emergency stairs he showed me. He could have been a regular in those tunnels without us knowing it. Maybe he always had your grandma's number in his pocket. It can be dangerous down there. But then you have to ask yourself why he brought all those things. I'm guessing you've heard about them?"

Tony looked hesitantly at Kasper, as if hoping he hadn't said too much again.

"Yes," Kasper reassured him. "Mom told me."

"We're trying to keep the details in the inner circle. You can probably imagine how some people would drool all over them otherwise."

"Yeah," Kasper said, because he really could.

"How long have you been pondering all this, then?" Tony asked.

"Not that long." Kasper cleared his throat. "I've never . . . never wanted to read about it before. But I did, a month back. Well, when I started researching this project."

"Brings up a lot of things in you," Tony said.

Kasper nodded. If Tony only knew.

"Who do you think found him?" Kasper asked.

"There's a lot of trespassers in Stockholm's subway system," Tony said. "I've heard about it from people who work there. A lot of unfortunates, I guess you could call them. But also graffiti artists, there were plenty of those around toward the end of the eighties. I've always thought some kid came upon Grim, called it in, and ran. They don't want anything to do with the cops, for obvious reasons."

"But don't you think that'd get out?" Kasper said. "I mean, what if that person read about Grim later and made the connection?"

"Well, sure, if Grim had been a dead Eurovision star, that is. But I think you forget how unimportant we are." Tony's smile was crooked. "Most people don't know who Grim is, not then, not now. That person could have gone through their whole life without hearing about Grim, Dark Cruelty, or even Exenterate."

Kasper nodded. He knew that, of course.

"And that's all I know," Tony said. "I've read the same rumors you have, and honestly, take them with an entire salt cellar." He took the final cookie from the plate and stuffed it into his mouth.

"You said something before," Kasper said. "About Malte. That you shouldn't have let him into the band." He hesitated. "It sounded like you were connecting him with what happened to Grim."

"I guess I am, in a way," Tony responded. "I don't think he killed him, I'd like to underline that, considering what we've been saying about rumors . . . But yes, I blame him for what happened. I think, no, I *know*, that he got Grim to isolate himself from the rest of us. He wasn't well. And Malte made things worse. Something started when he joined, and after that, well, it all went to hell."

Bargain jumped out of Tony's lap and ran toward the door. A second later, Kasper heard a car pull in, in front of the house. There was the sound of car doors opening and children's voices, and then Scott and Melissa raced in, their hair wet with rain. Emira asked Kasper if he wanted to stay for dinner, and he did.

They didn't talk about Grim again that night.

Later, when Kasper got home, his dad was in the Nest with his headphones on and a guitar on his knee. He and Eric in Blood Libation wrote the band's songs together and would send each other riffs and new ideas.

Or maybe he was working on a Dark Cruelty song.

His dad looked up, removing his headphones.

"Hey there!" he said. "How was everyone? Have you had dinner?"

"Everyone was fine," Kasper said. "Yeah, I ate."

"Good," his dad said. "Sorry, but I've got to . . ."

He put his headphones back on. Kasper stood there for a moment, watching his father disappear into his own world. Or was he just pretending? Was he concerned about what Tony could have told Kasper? Where did those thoughts come from? He went into his room and put his own headphones on.

Now, having listened to the conversation twice, Kasper was happy he'd chosen to record it. Some things only became clear in hindsight. He rewinded again.

"That was your dad and Grim, it was their thing. Reading about demons. Dark French poetry. Magic and all that shit. There was more where that came from when they started spending time with Malte . . ."

PAUSE.

Kasper put the phone aside. During the interview, he hadn't reacted to Tony's wording.

There was more where that came from when they started spending time with Malte . . .

Kasper had always thought that Malte entered the band via Grim and that the two of them hung out some. He tried to recall if his dad had ever mentioned being with Malte and Grim, the three of them together, but had no memory of it. But he usually had some trouble memorizing details from his dad's anecdotes. Probably because it was so easy to ask if he forgot something.

But maybe Tony hadn't put much thought into what he said.

We should never have let that bastard join the band.

Kasper went over to his desk and turned his computer on. He had an English assignment to do, but managed to convince himself that he could do it in the morning. He was suddenly reminded of the way Marco had started getting better grades in junior high, after always going on about how unprepared he was before an exam, how boring the others were if they wanted to study. That changed overnight, and Marco started to talk about studying as if it was a sport, a tough session at the gym, no pain, no gain. He implied, but only as "a joke," that Oliver and Ali were losers for not keeping up with him. They were too far behind and couldn't get ahead as quickly as Marco did. He ended up getting into his first choice, the prestigious school Östra Real in central Stockholm.

Similar memories had started to emerge lately. Nowadays Kasper rarely felt ashamed over being dumped by his so-called friends. Rather, he felt ashamed that he'd ever considered them his friends. Especially Marco. What had Kasper seen in him? And how had he behaved when they'd been together?

He put his fingers on the keyboard and typed:

malte lundell

Malte's young face, a few years after Dark Cruelty had broken up. He was crouching in a snowy forest, staring into the camera with a gloomy expression. He was all in black and wearing some kind of cloak. On his arms, he was wearing broad leather brace-lets with studs, and he was holding a spiked club. Even though he'd been Kasper's age when the photo was taken, his round eyes made him look younger, and he oozed smugness rather than malice. *Morgov*, it said beneath the picture. Where he'd gotten the stage name remained unclear. It was said to be a surname, but in Malte's case, it was rumored to be his character in a tabletop RPG, which had resulted in some ridicule. A lot of people had opinions about Malte. Some idolized him, while others were openly scornful. What they all shared was that they saw him more like a cartoon character than a real person.

Kasper continued to trawl through Malte's history. After Dark Cruelty, he seemed to have focused on tape trading, until he finally joined a band he thought was sufficiently evil. He started doing interviews. Sometimes he'd say he was a Satanist; other times, he worshipped Odin and wanted to burn down churches and murder all Christians. Kasper found a scanned interview, which had been published in a fanzine at the beginning of the nineties.

Q: What do you think of your former bandmates in Dark Cruelty?

A: What do I think? Ha! They disgust me! They are nothing but life-loving posers. They were too scared to carry on Grim's legacy of darkness, death, and evil. Instead they cry like babies! It makes me want to puke when I read about them playing with sellout bands like Exenterate and Malodor! I want them to live in fear like the spineless wimps they are. I've sent them messages personally. But I encourage anyone who wants to keep this scene poser-free to get in touch with them!

Even though Kasper had heard about it, reading Malte's own words was dizzying. Especially since he knew that some people had heeded Malte's call. Later on, some musicians from Malte's former circle had approached his dad to apologize. "We were so young," said the contrite, fully grown men. Most of the time, his dad had accepted that excuse, which Kasper couldn't understand. His dad had also been young back then, but he'd somehow refrained from making death threats against his peers.

Kasper traced Malte's career through the years. It was both complex and depressing. He had played in three more or less famous extreme metal bands in the '90s and 2000s. One had had a more Satanic message, the second one was pagan, and the third band made songs about nihilism and war. What united them was their evil, violently aggressive image, and rumors that a few of the members were Nazis. After Malte left, the bands didn't stick together for long. Everything crumbled in his wake. Death followed him, too.

In the beginning of the 2000s, an old homeless man was found murdered outside the rehearsal space of the band Malte played with at the time. The bassist, who had been with Malte for years, was arrested. The victim's blood was on his clothes. Shortly thereafter, the police came for Malte. Kasper read articles and posts about the murder, feeling nauseated. The old man had been brutally abused, kicked and beaten beyond recognition with sharpened brass knuckles. Then he'd been left to die in agony in a staircase leading down to the rehearsal space. People had passed by just a few feet away, but no one had seen him lying there, bleeding to death.

The bassist had come home covered in blood; his girlfriend had told a friend, whose sister phoned the police. All the signs indicated that the bassist and Malte had been on the premises together, when they discovered the old man who, being drunk, had curled up to sleep on the stairs. At first, the bassist had confirmed that Malte had been present, and then he retracted his statement. Shortly after that, he hanged himself in jail. Malte was released.

Since then, Malte had lived an itinerant life in Europe. France, Poland, Austria. A couple of years after the murder, he released the EP *Ov the Cataclysmic Void*, as the one-man band Nox Irredux. Apparently, this meant something like *night from which one cannot return*. Nowadays he refused to have his picture taken, called himself "M," and only played live masked, alongside hand-picked anonymous musicians. He very rarely did interviews, and only in niche fanzines, where he'd name-drop philosophers and make lengthy, contradictory polemics.

Kasper's attention was caught by a quote:

"I detest organized religion, though I respect some forms of chaotic and misanthropic Paganism and Satanism. But for me, religion is a very private thing. I have no need of preaching to the undeserving. I am not what you would call a Pagan nor am I what you would call a Satanist. Since my youth, I have nurtured a profound interest in magic, and I follow my own path. That is all I will say on the subject."

Magic and all that shit. There was more where that came from when they started spending time with Malte.

Kasper checked his watch. It was nearly half past one. He was just about to turn the computer off when he noticed a detail in one of the pictures: the inverted pentagram on a chain around Malte's neck. Kasper did an image search. Malte was wearing that piece of jewelry in most photos, including pictures from his time in Dark Cruelty. Back then, getting hold of accessories like that had not been easy, Kasper knew. This necklace had been something special. He enlarged it. Was this what the necklace Grim had been found with looked like? Had it been similar to Malte's? Kasper had checked the box in his dad's closet after the talk with his mom, but found no trace of a pentagram. No string, either, for that matter.

He rubbed his stiff neck and went into the bathroom. His dad was still in the Nest. Kasper brushed his teeth, details from what Tony had told him whirling through his head. The phone number, the murder of the homeless man, his dad, Grim, and Malte.

The phone in the back pocket of his jeans pinged. Iris, texting to check if he was awake. She must have seen that he'd just been on-line. She was probably wondering what Tony had said and Kasper had promised to tell her.

KASPER: sorry, I forgot . . . a lot to deal with . . .

IRIS: good or bad?

Kasper hesitated for a moment. Then he wrote:

KASPER: would you like to hear? I recorded everything

He spat out the foam. Yes, he'd told Tony he was recording it for his own sake, but this had to count. He had to talk to someone about what he'd heard, and Iris was a part of this journey, she already knew. He made her promise to keep quiet, and she did. So he sent her the file and went to bed.

The moment he closed his eyes, he pictured Grim.

How could they be sure he'd been unconscious the whole time in the tunnel? Maybe he just couldn't move. Maybe he tried to scream.

Maybe he had been in pain. Kasper thought about the bleeding old man on the staircase, dying, incapable of crying out. Suddenly, it was impossible to sleep. He took out his iPad and started to draw Grim and Tony on the emergency staircase by the Universitetet stop. The moss grew over the steps behind them.

When Kasper finally fell asleep, his dad was still awake.

THE RITUAL

Dark Cruelty enters a new era. Håkan and Grim send out letters, telling everyone about the band's new constellation. Grim has started sketching out the cover for the EP. They record every rehearsal, listen to the recordings afterward, discuss what to try out in the future, what they can improve. Then there are the new songs. Grim has named one "Curse of the Lost." Håkan has one called "Land of Frozen Shadows," which they settle on calling it "Unholy Shadows Reign," even though Tony objects to that name because when you say the name out loud, it sounds like the shadows are raining.

Malte is fine in the band. He isn't an amazing guitarist, but more stable than Grim. His taste in music is good and he has a few interesting ideas. As long as they stick to talking about music, everything's fine, even good. Other topics invite trouble. An ordinary conversation can suddenly go off in the wrong direction. Like when Ernesto tells them about how Stasse managed to dodge military service.

"He pretended to be, like, a total wimp in the fitness test, but it was probably the Napalm Death tee he wore to the shrink that did it. And he asked them if he could shoot real people, as if he really wanted to try."

Håkan and Tony laugh. Grim smirks, too.

"Awesome," Håkan says.

"I'm definitely doing military service," Malte says loudly.

"What?" Tony chuckles. "You want some dick in a uniform yelling in your face all day?"

Malte turns a violent shade of red.

"I want to serve the nation."

"I only serve Satan," Ernesto says, doing the sign of the horns.

"You don't know what you're talking about," Malte mumbles.

"Be honest," Tony says, "you just want to . . ." He mimics shooting a rifle, BANG, BANG, BANG.

"It's hardly a downside, learning how to handle a weapon," Malte says.

"All right, Rambo," Håkan says.

Everyone laughs. Malte clouds over.

"Calm down, pal." Tony pounds him on the back. "We're only kidding. Go into the military if you want to, Malte. You can defend us all when the war comes."

They continue to rehearse after that, but Håkan can tell that Malte hasn't let it go. Malte doesn't mind laughing at others, but if anyone makes him bear the brunt of the joke, his eyes darken perceptibly.

But Malte keeps the promise he made them in his apartment. He does get them more. First, it's just more photocopied pages, until Grim figures out his source. Malte shamefacedly lets him borrow the whole book. Grim lies awake all night, reading, and then it's Håkan's turn. He gives up almost at once. When he's not working, he spends all his time rehearsing and sorting out any practical issues surrounding the EP. He reads and responds to letters, broadens their network. He and Grim talk about Interrailing, going around Europe this summer and convincing record stores to sell it. Maybe even do some gigs. Grim is discussing this possibility with a German and an Italian. Reading books about magic isn't on Håkan's list of priorities at the moment. All those things that had been so fascinating when he and Grim discussed them during the summer have lost some of their shine. Maybe it's because of Malte's involvement. Maybe it's because there is an element to Grim's attraction to the supernatural that escapes Håkan. A dark streak, an intensity in it that unsettles him. Has it always been there or is it new?

One night after rehearsal, Malte has a new book with him. It's a thin pamphlet on astral projection.

"Ought to test this," Grim says.

He's said that as long as Håkan has known him. But something shifts when Malte says, "I'm free on Saturday."

Grim looks at him and nods.

Håkan, who isn't actually interested, says, "We can be in the abandoned house. We'll be alone in there."

That Saturday the three of them shiver in the icy house, trying to escape their physical bodies and travel into other dimensions. The only result is that Håkan gets a cold. Grim, however, gets a taste for it and wants to try again. Again, their souls stay firmly in their bodies. They try telepathy instead, using a deck of cards. One time, Håkan correctly guesses what Grim is holding, and he feels light-headed. What if the impossible is possible? It's unclear what their experiments are supposed to prove, apart from just that: to see if something can get the dull, gray foundations of this world to shake a little.

One night Håkan wakes up to find Grim leafing through Malte's book about demons by flashlight.

"What are you doing?" Håkan whispers.

"We're going to summon a demon," Grim responds.

"Oh, right," Håkan says and falls back asleep, not really thinking about it again until a few days later, when Grim starts talking about making preparations.

The ceremony he's intrigued by was very obviously made for a different time, when finding coffin nails and the blood of executed murderers was a bit simpler. But Grim thinks that, according to the magical principles he's read about, some equivalent objects should work. The important thing is that they're powerful. He buries nails in a nearby graveyard and goes to a butcher for animal blood.

"The idea with blood," Grim says, "is that there is life force in it. You also need to capture the hatred of the person being executed. But animals must hate whoever kills them, too."

Grim says that focus and intention are the alpha and omega of successful magic. He practices at home, sometimes by standing on one leg for ages, sometimes by avoiding a particular word for an entire day. Håkan is exhausted just being in the vicinity of his efforts. One night, when his mom and Lillemor are out dancing, Håkan and Grim are on the floor of the living room, listening to The Cult. Håkan asks him what the point of all those exercises is.

"You need to understand one thing, Håkan," Grim says. "The big things are also in the small things. And the small things are connected to the bigger ones. The universe is inside the magician, and if he can control himself, he can eventually control the forces of the universe. Man has the potential to be a demigod, but only the magician dares to try."

Håkan still doesn't get it, but Grim looks so peaceful when he closes his eyes and listens to "Black Angel" that Håkan leaves it.

One week before the ritual, all three of them meet in Stockholm's city center, get supplies and revise the plan. According to the instructions, they all have to fast and abstain from bodily pleasure for seven days before the ritual.

"Fast for a week?" Håkan says when they walk down Kungsgatan. "We'll starve to death."

"You can eat," Malte says. "It's just that you can't eat certain things. Like meat. I believe."

"And milk." Grim seems more confident. "But I think I'll try to eat as little as possible. To create a bigger effect. And no alcohol."

"No problem," Malte, who doesn't drink either, says.

"And strict celibacy," Grim adds.

Håkan nods, trying to look as if this is something he isn't already practicing.

"Can you . . . ?" Malte is embarrassed. "You know . . ."

"What, jerk off?" Håkan snaps.

Malte's ears glow bright red.

"Probably should avoid it," Grim says.

Then the day comes when they're performing the summoning of the demon Grim has chosen. He is a Duke of Hell and presides over powerful and hidden knowledge. Håkan thinks he should have started out with a slightly less important demon. Not that he believes in demons, of course, but if the Dukes of Hell exist, they probably don't want to be summoned by a group of adolescent amateurs. He recalls the descriptions of what happens when rituals go wrong. They're probably as made up as the descriptions of successful ones, but you never know.

Still, he follows Grim and Malte to the deserted house. He helps them prepare, lays the circle meant to protect them and the triangle where the demon is to manifest.

Grim will perform the summoning with the aid of incantations and the demon's seal, which he will draw on a piece of paper with a brush dipped in animal blood, which is actually supposed to be blood from a condemned killer. Grim has reinterpreted the material in a few ways. Newly washed clothes instead of new clothes, he said, are probably fine, and he doesn't need a new knife, as long as the one Malte lends him is clean. All this is soothing to Håkan. Even if demons are real, this ritual will not work. They've cut too many corners.

To be fair, some of the instructions are also difficult to interpret. The ceremony is to be performed after dark. Is that strictly night-time, or is a dark afternoon in December good enough? They settle on the latter, as the last bus to Handen departs before midnight, and Malte is heading into the city besides.

They've covered the windows and are lighting indigo candles, as they couldn't find any black ones, and Grim begins the ritual when darkness falls. With a great deal of focus, he paints the seal of the Duke of Hell with blood on a piece of paper. Then he begins chanting the incantations, first quietly and then louder. The only things that can be heard are Grim's voice and the wind, howling outside the house and through the chimney. And something else. A buzzing noise, as if from flies. Håkan thinks of the dead rook, its body crawling with insects. For a moment, he thinks he can smell rotting flesh. Grim continues to chant, having abandoned the initial spell for a stronger, more commanding one, since the demon hasn't manifested. A feeling of being completely *present* overwhelms Håkan. The candles flicker in the drafty room and he's suddenly, painfully aware of being there, of being right now, that every second that passes also is his life passing by, and there is no way back. The thought hits him full force. Cold sweat gathers beneath the thick undergarments and heavy wool sweater he's wearing under his jacket. He is alive right *now*. And in every moment, death is a possibility. He could die at any time and that would be it. No more thoughts. No more self. It's worse than imagining Hell and its torments. How had he once walked around unbothered, as if death didn't lurk behind every corner? No, not behind the corner, but here, now, in the light and in the shadows. Håkan looks at Malte and sees his own fear reflected, but times ten. Malte is terrified, his eyes wide, and he's trembling. Grim lifts the paper with one hand and the knife with the other, moving onto the third spell. The one in which he *threatens* the demon to make it show itself, tells him he will pierce its seal and condemn him to eternal suffering. Håkan has always felt that threatening a demon is a bad idea, and it feels like an even worse one when Grim is actually doing it. Håkan hears sniffling next to him and sees fat tears roll down Malte's cheeks. He suddenly remembers what he's read about rituals in which the weakest person in the group ends up possessed. He puts his hand on Malte's shoulder, but touching him feels awkward and wrong. Malte gives him a dazed look.

The sound of Grim stabbing the knife through the seal makes Håkan startle and look around. Nothing happens. The triangle on the floor remains empty. Håkan doesn't know how long they wait.

"It didn't work."

Grim is speaking. His disappointment is palpable. It dawns on Håkan just how much time and energy he's spent on this for the past few weeks, almost as much as he's spent on the music. Maybe more.

Malte has wiped away his tears and is staring at the floor. Håkan feels slightly sick. Maybe because he's been eating nothing but rice and macaroni for a week.

"Let's go," Håkan says, and he starts to leave the circle.

Grim grabs him by his jacket, keeps him there.

"Are you crazy?" he snaps. "The ritual isn't finished yet. Something could have appeared. The gateway to the other world has to be closed."

"Okay, fine!" Håkan says, pulling himself free.

Adrenaline rushes through his system. He glances at the chalk circle to make sure he's still inside it.

"I forgot," he says. "Sorry."

"It's only one of the most fundamental rules in ritual magic," Malte scoffs, clearly mortified that Håkan caught him crying.

"You about to start bawling again?" Håkan mocks.

"Quiet," Grim says. He begins chanting the invocation meant to give whatever has appeared license to depart, to seal all doors that may have opened.

It feels as if he goes on for a quarter of an hour. Meanwhile, Håkan's irritation grows. This is just like when they met at Malte's place; he just wants to leave. Finally, Grim tears the seal in half, and then lights it on fire. It might be all in his head, but Håkan thinks he can smell something strange and stinging when the seal burns.

What would have happened if he had stepped outside the circle?

They pack their things in silence and catch the bus on time, sit in a row at the very back in silence. It isn't until they approach Handen that Malte says, "I know of a real magician. I'll try to arrange a meeting with him."

"All right," Grim says.

He sounds tired. Malte looks away. Not the reaction he'd been hoping for, Håkan thinks gleefully. A real magician, what a bunch of bullshit.

Håkan and Grim empty the fridge and each have a shower. They don't talk about what happened, but when Håkan turns off his bedside lamp, the darkness is as menacing as it had been when he was far younger. He stares into it, hyperaware of every sound. What if something had come to the deserted house? What if whatever it was hadn't been wholly banished? What if it's here?

"Hey," he whispers, and Grim responds with a soft grunt. "Can we stop this now?" Silence. "That house will be too cold for us soon, anyway."

"You're right about that," Grim says.

After that, the three of them don't hang out anymore. Malte is weird and awkward toward Håkan the first few times they rehearse together, but then seems to put it all behind him. Håkan tries not to let Malte bother him. He's just an insecure little jerk, and they need him right now. He isn't a threat, Håkan reminds himself.

He doesn't understand how quickly things change when you're young, how sudden and drastic those changes can be. Friendships come undone, new alliances are formed, an old identity is discarded for a new one. It can happen overnight. And the person you thought you knew can suddenly seem like a stranger.

KASPER

During a couple of weeks around Halloween, Gröna Lund became ground zero for an explosion of spiderwebs and pumpkins. Fog poured out of a giant cauldron in the Minor Area, while the docks housed the Flying Dutchman, an old restaurant slash boat turned ghost ship. The Fun House became The Funeral House, its clowns furiously homicidal. Area Z, a designated zombie zone, was constructed near the water. This year's main attraction, The Castle, in which the vampiric countess Elizabeth Báthory lurked, replaced the Main Stage.

The House remained The House, but with extra everything—The House of Even Darker Demons. More cast members, more scares. Every group of visitors was guided by the Assistant, a cast member who played Doctor Dreamcraft's sniveling lackey. The guests even had the dubious pleasure of encountering the master of The House in two scenes, acted out by the Assistant and the Doctor.

Kasper had heard that Halloween was more intense, but the change in tempo still came as a shock. During the summer, visitors mostly showed up in waves. During particularly slow days, the demons could even turn the lights on in The House and gather in the Lab for a quick chat. This was impossible during Halloween. There was always a long line outside The House. When the visitors came in, they could have been waiting for at least an hour. They were ready for fun, or frustrated, or furious, or expectantly fearful. The feelings were turned up to the max from the very beginning, making the encounter between guests and cast members more tense and unpredictable. Cast members moved more freely than during the summer. They still couldn't touch the guests, but some guests didn't return the courtesy. Some visitors would slap or push a cast member as an instinctive reaction to a scare. Others were looking for a fight. The very first day, a mummy in The House was attacked and fell over. Kasper took her to see the nurse, where she realized that her wrist was broken. Kasper thought of all the stories he'd heard about people hurting themselves on stage without feeling it, being too high on adrenaline.

Apart from aggressive guests, the demons were the biggest challenge for the UC in The House during Halloween. There were twenty of them in the summer. Now, there were closer to forty. There wasn't the same sense of community, but Kasper did his best to remember everyone's names and make sure that they felt seen, that people enjoyed themselves. One good thing about the rapid tempo was that he didn't have the time to be neurotic about whether he was doing a good job. When the evening came and he was closing up, he was too tired to think. He enjoyed that.

It wasn't until Sunday night, when he was walking the final round, that the weekend caught up with him. Comments the demons had made, quick decisions he'd had to make, everything replayed in his head.

And then there was Cornelia.

This was the first time they met again since the day they received training for the Halloween season. She treated him politely, but with distance, more like an acquaintance than somebody she'd spent the summer with, even slept with. He started to wonder if she was angry with him. Should he have contacted her, somehow? During a hasty lunch with Iris one Saturday, he'd asked if Cornelia had mentioned him at all. Turned out she hadn't even told Iris that she and Kasper had had sex; Iris had only heard that from Kasper.

He felt even more pathetic. Cornelia had always been candid about her sex life. She must have thought that he was an unusually embarrassing misstep. Not even worth remembering.

"She's just weird sometimes," Iris reassured him. "Do not overanalyze this."

That was easier said than done, now that he was walking through The House alone and his sad brain had prioritized brooding over Cornelia.

He tried to focus on his surroundings while he wandered through the labyrinth of The House. In the sharp fluorescent light, the spell should be broken, but The House just looked different. Sometimes Kasper thought he preferred The House when it was like this, silent, ready for the next show. When it only belonged to the demons, and to him. He liked seeing its beauty spots: the scuffed paint on the coffins in the Tombs, the battered grimoires in the Lab, where the Doctor made his first appearance during the Halloween tour to administer an electric shock to the Assistant. One of the doctors was played by a guy called Philip. Cornelia, who played an assistant, knew him from before. He had given her shoulders a rub at the meeting this evening. They were probably at Skeppsbar now. Or back at her place, or his. Philip looked like someone who had his own apartment. The thought bothered Kasper in a way that felt extremely predictable. For the first time ever, a girl had chosen him, and now he was watching her choose someone else instead. Not that there was an *instead*; that wasn't how it worked. But it felt like it.

A loud, creaking sound made Kasper stop on the staircase in the Lab.

He went motionless and listened.

There it was again, a sound that seemed to come from inside the structure of the building itself. As if something was being pried free.

Silence returned.

Kasper fingered the flashlight around his neck, looking toward the tilting corridor. There could be something wrong with the mechanism, something that needed oiling, or whatever it was that tilting corridor mechanisms needed. He walked up the stairs and into the Snake Pit, where a guest had left a strong, lingering scent of sweet perfume that made Kasper think of junior high.

In Kasper's old friend group, Ali was who the girls fell in love with, Oliver was the first who lost his virginity, and Marco had a serious relationship by fifteen. Kasper was the one who'd never been kissed, the unfuckable one. Discovering that he wasn't as repulsive as he'd thought had been a relief. Still, that insight had turned everything upside down. It was as though a new direction had suddenly appeared on his compass. It didn't make the road ahead clearer, quite the opposite. Like the thing with Lydia in school. He had always assumed that she spent time with him to be kind, that she wanted to braid his hair because he was like her depressive mascot. Not even in his wildest dreams would he have thought she *liked* him. And maybe she didn't. But did he have to at least consider the possibility, now that she had written him a bunch of messages and was planning to visit Grönan, even though she didn't like Halloween? She'd sent him a heart in her latest message. In the past, he would have sent one back without hesitating. Now he wondered if he was sending the wrong signal.

Spiderwebs fluttered desolately in a sudden draft when Kasper entered the room. Frodo's face was stuck in an eternal, agonized scream. Kasper bent down to pick up an empty pack of gum and put it in his back pocket. Then he checked the Chef, took the shortcut to the Pyramid.

He was probably making too much of it. What had happened between him and Cornelia didn't mean that he was attractive to anyone else. It could be a bizarre coincidence, maybe the first and final time it ever happened to him. He should do what Cornelia had done and forget about it. Other people seemed so good at letting go of each other. They met, had sex, and moved on as if in a dance, never thinking about each other again. At least that's what it seemed like to Kasper. Why did he stick to people like a burr every time someone showed interest?

The space where the Doll normally hid smelled like feet. The fan was on, so Kasper turned it off. In the ensuing silence, he found himself whistling. He'd never been very good at it, but the tune needed to come out. The melody was painfully familiar, but it wasn't until he walked down the stairs to the Possessed that he could place it. A riff from "Curse of the Lost." He abruptly went quiet and passed the empty altar by the devil's statue, continuing into the Hall of Mirrors. Let his gaze slide over the floor. For some reason, people had a tendency to lose their valuables in here. He kept walking, passing through the right door. Checked Number Eight. Everything looked fine. The route was over.

Kasper turned the lights off and headed back again.

It was just like Iris had said in the beginning of the summer: he had learned how to find his way through The House in total darkness. Moreover, he liked walking through the dark corridors. It felt like a sport, or a trick he practiced by himself and took pride in. The darkness in The House had never scared him.

He opened the door to the Hall of Mirrors and walked inside. A light breeze caressed his face. He stopped. There it was again: a chilly draft.

His first thought was that the door from behind—which the Possessed could leap out—was ajar. He hadn't checked it properly.

Then he realized that the draft came from the wrong direction.

It was coming from the wall of mirrors.

Kasper stood unmoving in the absolute darkness.

The draft wasn't constant, but came sporadically. Cold, raw air, the scent of stone and damp. He breathed as quietly as he could.

Listened. A hammering sound. Was it his heart? Why was he just standing there?

His hand was slippery with sweat when he gripped the flashlight and turned it on. Immediately, the sharp beam of light and his own contour were reflected in every surface.

No.

One of the mirrors was completely black.

An opening.

The hair on the back of Kasper's neck rose. That's where the draft was coming from; he could feel it clearly now. Cold air rushed toward him. Even though he pointed the flashlight into it, the light couldn't penetrate the compact darkness. Staring into it hurt his eyes. It was so absolute that it was blinding, a black sun.

That's when he heard the sound: a dull, droning noise, as if from an abyss whose depth was unimaginable. The scar on his left hand prickled and pulled, as if the skin was about to split open. And that sound was familiar. It was horribly familiar.

It was coming closer.

Kasper stopped thinking. He ran toward the Possessed, the flashlight's beam bouncing wildly over the black walls, hitting the devil's statue and the altar, the white symbols. He tripped on the stairs leading to the Nursery but got back on his feet, kept running. A zombified teddy stared at him. He found the door that led him into the corridors to the dressing room. In there, the lights were on. That's where his things were. He snapped them up and rushed toward the exit. Unbelievably enough, he remembered to clock out on the way.

When he was out, he took a few stumbling steps across the alley and sank down by the facade on the opposite side.

Over and over again, he replayed the chain of events in his head, as if that could give him control over the situation. As if it could give him some insight into what had happened.

What *had* happened?

The sound he'd heard was the same sound he'd thought he'd heard when he hid with Santiago, right after being attacked. Back then, he'd thought he was hallucinating. There was still that possibility, of course, but every detail had been so clear. The smells, the wind against his face. The rectangular opening, like a portal. Where did it lead?

And what did it have to do with Grim? Because that was the only thing he was absolutely certain of: it had something to do with Grim.

"Kasper, hi!" came a voice.

Elliot sailed by, the way only a stressed TL could, before Kasper had a chance to respond.

He noticed that he was still holding the flashlight. He should have put it back on its hook, but that could wait until next weekend. He was not going back in there again.

Kasper's stomach was in knots. How could he ever go back in there again?

He took out his phone to write to Iris, then saw that he had a text from an unknown number.

A flyer for a show next week. Two opening acts, with Vanbörd as the main act. A message:

You're on the list. We are going to talk about Grim. /O

Appendix 8. "Beyond Hunger and Torment" ("Bortom hunger och pina"), by Ossian Holm, from Vanbörd's album *Ill Deeds (Odåd)*, Lemegeton Records. Translation and original.

Onto bloodstained cloth, you were born	På blodfläckad lärft är du född
Downward the headsman's blade sweeps	Nu svingar bödeln sin bila
Dank water fills thy mouth	Dävet vatten fyller din mun
After hardship and toil, you will sleep	Efter armod och slit skall du vila
In the gorge of the marsh, veins are emptied	Ådrorna töms i torvmarkens svalg
You depart from the mortal plane	Du lämnar ditt levernes dagar
For beyond hunger and torment	Ty bortom hunger och pina
No man-made laws do reign	Där råder ej människans lagar
In the mire, the dark one awaits	I nattkärret väntar den mörke
His eternal abyss, an embrace	Hans eviga bråddjup dig famnar
The mind ruptures as you approach	Vettet rämnar när kursen sätts
The cold stars of an endless space	Mot iskalla stjärnors hamnar
Ill deeds shall be thy mission	Illdåd skall vara ditt värv
Your wage shall be paid in blood	Blod skall vara din lön
In the gorge of the marsh, veins are emptied	Ådrorna töms i torvmarkens svalg
You depart from the mortal plane	Du lämnar ditt levernes dagar
For beyond hunger and torment	Ty bortom hunger och pina
No man-made laws do reign	Där råder ej människans lagar
Your mission shall be iniquity	Illdåd skall vara ditt värv
Your wage shall be paid in blood	Blod skall vara din lön
In the dread of perpetual night	Bland den ändlösa nattens fasor

THE JOURNEY

Christmas creeps closer and Håkan's mom buys oranges. Håkan and Grim sit at the kitchen table and push cloves through the skin. The scent is wonderful. Håkan glances discreetly at Grim. Ever since the failed ritual, he's been more quiet than usual, as if the disappointment is inhabiting him somehow. His hands move slowly when he works. Håkan finishes his oranges with double the speed. He's removing a bit of clove that's stuck beneath his fingernail when Grim suddenly gets up and leaves the room. Håkan hears the front door shut. He finishes the last of it himself. Afterward, his mom hangs the oranges in the bands of silk she takes out every year for decoration on the kitchen window and in the bedrooms.

Early next morning, Grim returns, packing his turquoise sports bag as if nothing has happened. Håkan's mom gives him a large bag of candy and a pair of knitted socks, and then he leaves for Timrå to celebrate the holidays with his family. Håkan and his mom try to invite Lillemor over for Christmas Eve, but she refuses, as usual. She wants to stay at home in case the prodigal son returns. The Christmas before last, Kjell-Åke was clean when he came to visit, and the year before then, he'd been high and stolen a wad of cash. Last Christmas, he didn't show up at all. But Lillemor can't stand the thought that he'll ring the doorbell on Christmas Eve with no one there to let him in.

Håkan and his mom watch all the Christmas TV shows that they usually watch. He gets a pack of socks, underwear, and a bag of candy as big as Grim's. He gets his birthday present early, too: a used Walkman. The one he has now is getting a bit moody.

This summer, Håkan skipped his week with his dad in Gothenburg for the first time. He had been too busy with Grim and the band. Now it's back to business as usual, with Håkan traveling down on the twenty-seventh. He gets restless on the train, gets up and starts pacing. When he'd been a kid, he'd thought walking between the cars was frightening, because it made you understand how fast the train was moving. You felt its roars and screams in your bones. He enjoys it now, the dizzying sensation and the brutal noise, the cold air blowing in, the smell of railway.

His dad doesn't meet him at the station; he hasn't done that for years. Håkan gets on the bus with his bag next to him. A skinny metalhead with glasses hops on at the very last minute. He's wearing a leather jacket beneath a denim vest, and there's a drawing of Death's logo right above his heart. When he sees Håkan, he startles. Håkan nods in greeting. The guy sits down on the other side of the aisle and introduces himself. His name is Dagge, he's just started high school, and he's been in the city to buy himself records with the money he got for Christmas. He plays the guitar in the death metal band Teratoid, which he recently formed, and he saw Dark Cruelty play with Malodor and Exenterate at the youth center.

"I wanted to stay and talk," he says, "but my dad had driven us there and was transporting us back."

Håkan can't believe his luck. Dagge is getting off first, but Håkan gets his number and writes it down on the back of his hand. The moment he's alone, the restlessness returns. Restlessness and a kind of steady pressure. He gets off in the quiet suburb, shoulders up in the icy wind, and walks until he reaches the yellow house. There he awkwardly says hi to Ann-Mari and his so-called half brothers, two blond boys with narrow faces. His dad's gaze is already blurry, and he's about to fall asleep on the couch. He was the one who'd suggested that Håkan stay a couple of days extra this time, but is, as usual, totally uninterested. "There's roast beef and potato salad in the fridge," Ann-Mari says. She looks at Håkan with a mixture of pity and contempt. She's from one of those tiny fishing villages where a harsh form of Christianity dominates. She's convinced that Håkan worships Satan, which makes him wish he actually did.

Håkan brings a roast beef sandwich into the guest room and sprawls across the uncomfortable bed. A chubby gray telephone is on the bedside table. Its cord is a bird's nest. Håkan picks up the receiver and lets it hang from the cord, spinning it until it has untangled. Then he phones Grim in Timrå, having brought his phone number on a note. He looks forward to his dad or Ann-Mari discovering the bill later. A woman's voice comes through on the staticky line.

"Inger Johansson."

The only thing Håkan knows about Grim's mom is that she works in the kitchen at Grim's old school and that she taught Grim how to play the guitar.

"Hi, is . . ." He almost says "Grim," but stops himself. "Is Kasper around?"

"And who's this?" Inger sounds as if she's smiling.

"Håkan Nordin," Håkan says stiffly.

"Oh, hello, Håkan!" Inger exclaims. "Kasper has talked so much about you. Your mom and me have exchanged a few words, but I'm glad you and me get to have a bit of a talk as well."

Inger goes on about the weather: they've got snow, and the sun is shining. Apparently, she loves to ski. Håkan listens without getting a word in edgewise. Not that he really minds, as conversing politely with grown-ups is the worst thing in the world.

"It's lovely having him back," Inger says. "But you and Ulla are taking good care of him, I've gathered."

"I don't know, he mostly takes care of himself," Håkan says.

She laughs.

"Well, he's always done what he likes. A free spirit. Hang on . . ." Håkan hears her shout to Kasper that he has a call waiting. "Well, it was nice getting to talk to you, Håkan," Inger says. "Here he is."

She hands over the phone before Håkan can respond.

"Hi," Grim says.

Håkan can breathe again.

"Hey," Håkan says. "What are you doing?"

"Working on the zine," Grim says, and he sounds just like he always has, every trace of his deep disappointment gone. "What about you?"

Håkan tells Grim about Dagge and Teratoid, that he's going to watch them rehearse tomorrow at their bassist Bommen's place. Grim, of course, already knows about them, possibly through Malte, Håkan realizes. On the bus, Dagge had told him that he had met Malte in the audience at the Dark Cruelty show and traded a bit with him since then.

"Lucky I met him," Håkan tells Grim, "or I wouldn't have survived being here until New Year's." He glances toward the door, where a narrow face is peeking in. "Get out!" Håkan tells it, and the face disappears.

When they've hung up, he pulls out his new Walkman and puts his headphones on. Then he slides Grim's Christmas present in: a mixtape he's made himself. He shuts his eyes and presses Play.

Håkan's birthday is on the twenty-eighth of December. He's turning seventeen. When he's at his dad's, he usually gets some cash as a combined Christmas slash birthday gift. No celebration, no cake. When he was a child, it would make him sad, but he's used to it now. At least that's what he tells himself. When he joins the others at breakfast, his dad has already gone to work. Ann-Mari is rubbing wax onto the cutting boards, a small silver cross dangling around her neck, as if to make a point. The blond brothers have received a Nintendo for Christmas and are practically glued to it.

"Want to try?" one of them asks Håkan.

Håkan shakes his head. Nintendo is great, but he's only played it a few times and refuses to be humiliated by a child. He wonders if there's something wrong with him for caring more about Tony's siblings and Ernesto's brother than his own little brothers. The phone rings. Ann-Mari picks it up.

"It's your mother," she says, handing him the phone as if it were a sour-smelling old rag.

Håkan takes the phone and turns his back to Ann-Mari. His mom sings "Happy Birthday," and suddenly, he just wants to go home. He mumbles replies to her questions, throat closing up. He feels like a fucking baby.

"Happy birthday," Ann-Mari says when he hangs up.

Her gaze is distant, her eyes a watery blue.

Håkan heads off with Dagge and watches Teratoid rehearse in Bommen's garage. *Imagine having a rehearsal space at home*, Håkan thinks. Teratoid's an inexperienced bunch, but they are focused, and they're really nice. Bommen's mom serves them hot dogs. Håkan doesn't get home until dinner, which is fish pie. His dad doesn't wish him a happy birthday, hasn't given him a card. When Ann-Mari goes to bed, Håkan and his dad stay in front of the TV and watch an old Western. His dad pours himself and Håkan a whiskey each.

"Happy birthday," his dad says, clinking their glasses together.

The whiskey tastes like smoke. Håkan puts the glass back on the table.

"It's probably best that we end this arrangement," his dad says, "considering you'll be of age next year."

Håkan feels numb but his heart beats so hard he thinks it might burst. It shouldn't come as a surprise; he's always known it would end like this. Now he realizes why his dad wanted him to stay for

New Year's. Håkan is given a few extra days' food and shelter, a dad who does his duty. Then: good-bye and good riddance, don't come back.

"Maybe it's time for you to do something with your life," his dad says.

"What?" is the only thing Håkan manages in response.

"Graduating high school is the least you can do." With a bark of laughter, he adds: "In my time, instead of running through the front doors like the rest of the class, you had to sneak out around the back when you flunked the finals. But they let any idiot graduate nowadays."

His dad drains the glass. Håkan gets to his feet and goes to the guest room, then starts rummaging around in every nook and cranny. An icy thirst for vengeance overtakes him. He'll get what he deserves.

Bingo.

A small television is tucked away in the closet, on top of a year-old VHS player. His dad bought the latest model for Christmas, showed it to Håkan in the evening. "You've got to keep up with technology." Håkan finds a few pornos hidden behind the television: *Swedish Sins 4*, *Fifi's French Fantasies*. He looks at the shiny videos with a feeling of revulsion and savage triumph. What would Ann-Mari with the little silver cross say to this? Håkan places the videos in the bookshelf, right behind the encyclopedia, then stuffs the VHS player into his bag and leaves for Dagge's place. Dagge's bedroom is in the basement; Håkan knocks on the window and then crawls inside. Dagge's parents don't care for videos, but he's got his own television. Håkan plugs in the player, which is in working order. Bommen, who is also there, drives his moped to a twenty-four-hour video rental shop and gets some horror and action flicks. They stay up all night to watch them. When Håkan returns the next day, Ann-Mari is annoyed.

"One of your friends has been calling us all morning," she snaps. "'Grim.' What kind of name is that?"

At that moment the phone rings, and Håkan instantly grabs the receiver. It's Grim. He's come to Gothenburg. Håkan can't stop grinning. But he knows there's no point asking his dad if Grim can stay over.

"It's cool," Dagge says when Håkan calls him. "He can stay at Bommen's. His sister's room is empty, she just moved in with her boyfriend."

Soon they're all gathered in Dagge's room, Håkan, Grim, Bommen, and other death metal kids from the idyllic Gothenburg suburb. The others hang on to Grim's every word. Sure, people respect Håkan for playing in Dark Cruelty, but the way they approach Grim is different, something that resembles awe. He wonders if Grim can tell. It feels as if he's choosing his words more carefully, like he's playing a part. Or does Håkan perceive him differently in this space?

Håkan is barely at home during the final days. He and Grim go to the store where everyone who is into extreme and obscure metal gets their records. Grim surprises Håkan when he reveals that he's brought some copies of *Nocturnal Allegiance* so that the store can sell them. They walk past a church and reach a shop where they see some rosaries in the window. Håkan and Grim look at each other, then enter. Sweaty-palmed, they steal a rosary each. The woman at the register screams. They start to run, the two of them, jump onto a train that turns out to be traveling in the wrong direction. Håkan and Grim can't stop laughing. At Dagge's house, they fool around with the rosaries, turn the crosses upside down. Håkan wears his when he comes home, smirking at Ann-Mari's disgusted expression.

Dagge's parents aren't home for New Year's Eve. Fifteen hammered metalheads sit in the living room, listening to music and headbanging with skill and concentration. "Worship the riff!" Bommen shouts, nearly falling into the Christmas tree. At midnight they cheer for the new year. Håkan goes out to have a smoke, shivering in the winter winds blowing in from the sea. Grim stands next to him, seemingly unbothered. It's like he never gets cold. His exhalations mingle with the smoke.

"This year is going to be legendary," he says.

He's glowing with conviction, the way he did this summer.

"As fuck," Håkan agrees.

Afterward he goes into Dagge's room to look for the box of snuff that must have fallen out of his pocket. He's more drunk than he'd thought and accidentally upturns the pile of letters and fanzines on Dagge's desk. He drops to his knees and starts collecting them, but then suddenly spots Grim's name. If Håkan hadn't been so smashed, he wouldn't have read the typewritten letter, or he's using it as an excuse to do something he would have done anyway.

Grim and I performed our very first magic ritual a week ago. Because we have sworn to keep silent about what happened, I can only reveal that the result would have made most people in this scene hide beneath their beds.

The letter is from Malte. He doesn't say a single word about Håkan, not even when he writes about the upcoming EP. Instead, he makes it sound like it's something that Grim is working on by himself, with occasional support from Malte.

Håkan's first impulse is to grab the letter and show it to Grim, but he stops himself. Grim has seemed so animated since he came to Gothenburg, has some of his fire back. Håkan doesn't want to remind him about his failed occult experiment. Besides, it would be embarrassing to admit that he cares about what Malte writes in his letters.

Steps come down the stairs and Håkan looks up. It's Dagge. If he's angry about Håkan going through his stuff, he doesn't show it, and Håkan realizes it's because he's Håkan "Maimer" Nordin of Dark Cruelty. Suddenly, it disgusts him.

"I've got some information for you," he says, and can hear that he's slurring his words slightly. "Malte Lundell is a goddamn liar. Don't trust a single fucking word he writes."

"Shit," Dagge says, pushing his glasses up the bridge of his nose.

Neither one of them knows that the future bassist in the first band Malte plays in after Dark Cruelty is currently sitting in the living room. He will be among those who make threats against Håkan's life. During the coming few years, people will get sick of him bragging about Grim staying at his place for a few days. At that point, he doesn't call himself Bommen anymore. By the time he hangs himself in jail, after having murdered an innocent man, no one has called him Bommen in a long time.

"I was just going to say that I found a bottle of Cointreau," Dagge says, wiggling a brown bottle from side to side temptingly. "Let's go back upstairs, huh?"

Håkan puts the pile of papers back on the desk. His box of snuff stays under Dagge's bed.

Håkan goes back to Stockholm without saying good-bye, departing at dawn. He picks up the VHS player at Dagge's and then takes the bus to the station with Grim. When they come home, Håkan tells his mom that his dad gave it to him as a gift. She frowns worriedly at the inverted cross around his neck.

"You can't wear that when Lillemor's around, she'll get upset. You know she gets so much comfort from the church."

They rent *Top Secret!* and laugh until they cry, all three of them. Håkan's mom gasps for breath. When they've finished it, Grim rewinds to watch his favorite scenes again. He and Håkan can't stop laughing.

It's nearly midnight when the phone rings. Håkan's mom answers it, then hands it over to Håkan, frowning. Håkan's dad demands that Håkan return the VHS player, effective immediately.

"I could do that," Håkan says. "But then I'll tell Ann-Mari about your videos. I've moved them to a safe spot."

Håkan's dad hangs up. The silence that follows that call lasts for several years. During that time, Håkan goes on international tours with Exenterate, his face is in magazines and on television, and he's an important part of establishing Swedish music abroad. But his dad doesn't get in touch. Håkan takes the first step when he has become a father. He tells Anja that he wants to see his dad through adult eyes, find out what kind of man he really is. He has a show in Gothenburg and suggests they go for lunch. At home, he has a three-year-old son that he misses so much it hurts. The age he'd been when his dad had upped and left for another city. Håkan brings a few photographs of Kasper. His dad looks them over, nodding impatiently. His eyes are shiny, turned inward. When Håkan has had one beer, his dad has had three.

His dad drones on about work and Håkan thinks of all the questions he's been wanting to ask. About why his dad didn't want him, why he had preferred Håkan's brothers. Questions about his dad's family, about whom Håkan hardly knows anything except that they are from Uppsala.

But even before he asks them, the questions have a bitter aftertaste. Eventually, when they get to the coffees, he blurts out: "Hey, I was thinking that I don't know much about your side of the family. Who was Granddad? What did he do?"

His dad looks up, and for the first time he meets Håkan's gaze.

"Drank," he says. "That's what your granddad did."

The rebuke in his voice stings, and Håkan is suddenly enraged that this stranger can make him feel like a child. But he doesn't say anything. He should never have made himself so vulnerable.

"Your brothers have moved out, both of them," his dad says as they leave the restaurant. "Only Ann-Mari and I are left."

Håkan looks up at the sky. The gulls form dark Vs against the darkening clouds.

"She found those videos, by the way, in the bookshelf," he hears his dad say. "That got me into trouble. I blamed you, of course, but she wouldn't believe me."

His smile is a stiff grimace. Håkan watches him walk across the large square.

He promises himself never to be like his dad, wonders if his dad ever promised himself the same thing. And he thinks about Kasper, waiting for him back home. He won't know his granddad, either.

KASPER

The days passed and Kasper did not respond to Ossian's message. He didn't know what to write. He didn't want to go to the gig, but at the same time, it was the only thing he wanted. *We have to talk about Grim.* There was an extremely small chance that Ossian would have any information that was useful to Kasper, but he couldn't let go of the possibility. Iris, however, was more hesitant.

"I know you're curious and so am I," she had said when they first discussed the matter. "But what can he actually bring to the table? He never knew Grim."

She had met Kasper on the docks shortly after he escaped the Hall of Mirrors. Practically stuttering, he told her about what had happened to him, and Iris listened, her expression horrified. Finally, he showed her the text from Ossian.

"I actually might have to talk to him."

That was when Iris had expressed some skepticism.

Kasper shared it, to some extent. He also had some difficulty imagining what Ossian might know, but he was getting desperate. What had happened in the Hall of Mirrors had shaken him to the core. It had not been preceded by a dream or an extreme state of emotion; it had just happened. And the feeling he'd had when he got Ossian's message immediately afterward had been so powerful, as if to underline a connection.

"The scene is so small," Kasper told Iris. "Ossian could have heard something."

"Maybe," Iris said. "But I'm just thinking about everything you've ever told me about him. Do you even trust Ossian?"

Kasper did not. The memories he had of being admitted into Ossian's room were all too clear. Once, Ossian had been playing the guitar while simultaneously tricking Kasper into thinking that mosquitoes were spreading Ebola in Sweden, describing each horrific symptom in detail. Another time, Ossian and a friend had been watching videos of real executions. Kasper had had nightmares for weeks, but he told his parents that some older boys at school had shown him the videos. He felt ashamed. And he didn't dare tell on Ossian.

But that was all a long time ago, and Ossian was a grown man now, one who played in the same band as Kasper's dad. There was no valid reason why Kasper shouldn't attend the gig, and yet he spent the entire week stalling.

On Friday, Kasper and Iris sat on the dock for a while before the park opened. They had just over a week's work ahead of them before the end of the Halloween season. Kasper told her he intended to go.

"Will you know anyone there?" Iris asked.

"Not that I'm aware of," Kasper said. "I'm sure he would have invited the rest of DC, but everybody's on the road right now." His dad, for instance, was in the middle of a two-week tour with Blood Libation. "Besides, he said I was *on the list*. If I don't want him to change his mind, I think it has to be on his terms. Meaning I'll go alone."

Iris sighed.

"Just keep in touch during the evening, all right?" she said. "Promise me."

Kasper made the promise and they walked back toward Grönan. Kasper looked uncertainly up at The House. How would it feel to go back there? Most of all, he was afraid of closing up. The first night, he brought Elliot with him, with the excuse that he wanted a TL to listen to the creaking sound coming from the corridor. Naturally, they couldn't hear anything. On Saturday night, Iris suggested that they speak on the phone while walking the final rounds in their separate rides. Nothing happened.

And then Sunday came.

The first band was on their last songs when Kasper entered the room, which was bathed in blue light. Only a fraction of the audience had shown up by then, but the smell of snuff, beer, and sweat was already thick in the air. The volume was so loud that Kasper could feel the vibrations in his jeans when he stood still. Three tall, blond, eerily identical men with dirty gray makeup stood at the front of the stage, legs apart. Their long hair whipped back and forth in perfect rhythm. The small crowd that had gathered was hesitant, with only a few truly giving it their all. The rest of them seemed to be preserving their energy for the next band, and not least Vanbörd.

The House had had to shut down before the official closing time because a guest had thrown up all over the Tombs and everything had to be cleaned. This had meant that Kasper could head to the concert earlier. He even had time to devour a hamburger with fries, and now he felt sleepy and full. He aimed for the corner beyond the sound guy's booth, put his hood up, and leaned against the wall. The song ended.

"Thank you, Stockholm!" the singer cried, with the same enthusiasm as if he'd just played in front of three thousand instead of approximately thirty. "This is our final song. For Satan!"

The wall on which Kasper leaned began to vibrate. Horns went up in the audience, and a few more than just the devoted fans began headbanging to show some support. The stage lights flickered between blue and white. Kasper felt completely disconnected from what was going on up there, instead compulsively checking the pockets of his jeans. The venue made their guests check their coats, and Kasper was, as always, paranoid about accidentally losing his things. But his card and phone were in his right pocket, his keys and his earplugs in the left.

"Thank you, Stockholm!" the singer roared again, receiving a lone scream in response.

The band exited the stage just as a song by a Norwegian artist started playing through the speakers. A few minutes later, they returned, packing up their gear and guzzling water.

The venue was bathed in blue light. Kasper inspected the audience. Most of them were men. Long hair. No hair. Beard. Vests bearing familiar patches in different constellations. T-shirts and long sleeves with bands both old and new. Both his mom and dad had very strict ideas about which band tee was appropriate to wear when you went to a gig. Definitely not one bearing the logo of any of the acts that were actually on stage. His mom held on to this principle, while his dad argued you could make an exception for an extremely rare shirt. You could, of course, go for a modern band in the same genre, or even better, a historically important band, preferably something obscure. Kasper had gone for a safe bet: one of his dad's Celtic Frost shirts, which he'd borrowed a few times before. Tonight his dad was playing at a festival in that band's homeland, Switzerland. Kasper hadn't told him or his mom that he'd be coming here.

His phone vibrated in his pocket. He was expecting a text from Iris, but it was from a number he hadn't saved. Ossian's number.

Backstage afterward.

When Kasper had said his name at the door, he had received a backstage pass, so that was probably how Ossian knew that Kasper had come. Either that, or he just counted on it. It disturbed Kasper, but at the same time, he felt a strange sense of expectation. This entire situation was so odd. He responded with an *OK*. Then he took a screenshot of the conversation and sent it to Iris.

The audience was flowing in now, a steady stream. Kasper had been to countless metal gigs and usually felt perfectly at home. And on the surface, everything seemed familiar. Plastic cups filled with beer were raised, and old friends and acquaintances met, with ensuing hugs and pats on the back. But the atmosphere wasn't as relaxed as usual. Maybe because it was Kasper's first time alone at a show, so he was perceiving it in a different way. Or maybe there was something about this particular evening. Leah used to talk about an atmosphere of "untreated depression, self-medication, and violence as identity" arising at some extreme metal band concerts.

The next band went on and Kasper put in the earplugs he got from his mom. The guys on stage were from the province Värmland and only a couple of years older than Kasper, performing death metal that was heavily influenced by the Stockholm scene. It was also apparent in the band shirts they were wearing: Dark Cruelty's logo shone on the bassist's chest, while the lead guitarist sported a Malodor tee. The singer, who also played the guitar, had the audience in the palm of his hand, even though most were twice his age. A strong envy combined with self-contempt simmered inside Kasper.

You're almost the same age. What have you accomplished?

By the time the band walked off, Kasper's feet and back were aching, despite having leaned against the wall. An older man with a black-and-white Pinhead patch on his back stood in front of Kasper, a plastic cup of beer in each hand. He downed one and placed the full cup inside the empty one. When both were empty, he shoved them into his back pocket.

"D'you want a drink?" a voice next to Kasper said.

He looked up and saw a man with a shaved head, so tall and

skinny that he reminded Kasper of a matchstick. He opened his denim vest slightly, and a liquor bottle peeked out.

"No, thanks," Kasper said. "But thanks."

The Matchstick quickly looked around for guards and then took a sip.

"Got it on the Helsinki ferry!"

Judging by his accent, the man was from Norrköping.

"It's vodka and licorice! Finns love licorice!"

He said this as if he were revealing a great secret, and Kasper hoped he looked suitably respectful and interested. He had a feeling that the Matchstick was the type of person that could switch in an instant.

"So do you play in a band?" the Matchstick asked.

"No," Kasper said.

"Neither do I," the Matchstick said, letting out a burp. "I'm so fucking sick of this . . . hierarchy. Fucking Stockholm. It's not like you can talk to anyone around here. No, you have to be someone, know the right people. Better yet, be in a band. The big bands are at the very top and then it goes down, down. And at the very bottom, you find us, the regular fans. We carry them, but they look down on us. Assholes."

At that point, the Matchstick seemed to grow weary of his own rant and turned toward the scene, where Vanbörd's backdrop was unveiled. Kasper would have liked to move elsewhere, but it was starting to get absolutely packed, and he didn't want to get too close to the stage. Just a few years ago, Ossian had thrown a rotten sheep's head crawling with maggots into the crowd. Another time, he set a pig's head on fire, and the stench of burning meat had made some people in the audience vomit.

A ginger man shoved past Kasper to the man with the beer cups in his pocket. "Is that Svempa? Holy shit!" he bellowed.

The redhead kissed the other man right on his mouth, jokingly tried to slip him the tongue, then cracked up as if it was the funniest thing that had ever happened. Just as they took a selfie, the lights went off and an ominous red glow lit up the stage. Someone yelled out: "Vanbörd!"

"Fuck yeah," the Matchstick said, and then dove into the sea of people.

Portentous layers of prerecorded noise rumbled through the room. The atmosphere felt dense and the crowd was drawn toward the stage. Kasper didn't know how many people fit in the room, but it had to be well over five hundred. It was incredibly hot, with Kasper's T-shirt growing damp in the pits and on the back. Where the Matchstick had stood, two short girls squeezed in, standing with their arms around each other.

They stretched, in the hope of seeing something. Slow, ponderous drums and distorted voices that seemed to speak in tongues rolled heavily through the speakers. Smoke filled the stage, on which the band appeared like dark silhouettes. Kasper knew that these kinds of soundscapes were often used when bands wanted to tune their instruments without losing the crowd. But there were also other reasons. Atmosphere.

"Yees!" someone shrieked.

And in came Ossian. He wore a floor-length black robe with the hood up. He seemed even taller than usual as he walked toward the edge of the stage, moving slowly through the smoke. Then he took hold of the microphone while the drums in the intro to "Dagbräckning, domedag" ("Daybreak, Doomsday") began rumbling, the first riffs rolled out, the light dazzled the crowd, and Ossian screamed.

A roar came from the audience in response and horns rose in the air. Hands shaped like claws. The guitarists and bassist glared aggressively at the crowd.

And that's when Kasper saw him.

A face in the audience. A face that he'd only seen once in reality, but all the more frequently in pictures, though it had been younger then, less ravaged.

Malte Lundell.

He looked right at Kasper.

The next second he disappeared behind a dark-haired giant.

Had it really been Malte? Or was it like when Kasper thought he saw Marco? He took a step forward so that he ended up next to the ginger man and the man with the beers in his pocket, observed the audience. The man who looked like Malte was nowhere to be seen.

Kasper got shoved in the back and took an unsteady step forward. The woman in front of him stepped aside so suddenly that he lost his balance again. He was drifting in the sea of people now, much closer to the stage than he was comfortable with.

Ossian pulled back his hood and the whites of his eyes shone. His face, and the wiry arms protruding from the robe, were covered in mud and blood. He held the mic with both hands, shouting the lyrics with equal parts desperation and power. *Gryningen randas den sista dagen . . . (Dawn emerges on the final day . . .) Spruckna blickar mot stumma skyar . . . (Broken eyes turned to mute skies . . .)* Kasper felt the hair on the back of his neck stand up. How did you become as *clear* as Ossian? On the stage, his presence was turned up to the max. He was far from the only front man in a metal band who spoke about transforming onstage, but others mostly highlighted their aggression. Ossian devoted himself in a different way, not only channelling a dark and evil power but also submitting to it. It was reminiscent of how people had described Grim on stage. Suddenly, Kasper understood how well Ossian would work as a replacement.

The song ended, and the threatening, layered sounds resumed until the introduction to "Svältmark" ("Starved Earth") began. The smell from the smoke machines was palpable. He was pressed between warm bodies and realized that the concert would almost certainly last for at least another hour. He tried to be carried along by the music, but the truth was that he had never liked Vanbörd particularly much, even though he had given it several tries. He began to feel slightly claustrophobic, started looking for the man who might be Malte. The minutes passed. How many Vanbörd songs were there? Ossian drank discreetly from a water bottle and then grabbed the mic again, crying out sonorously, solemnly: "Some of us are born . . . to endless darkness!"

Kasper recognized the first riffs, but couldn't believe his ears. Could it really be "Tormented Exaltation," Grim's song, that his dad had finished? No one but the band and the immediate circle around them had heard it. Had Ossian really gotten their permission to debut it at a Vanbörd concert? Kasper had a hard time imagining that. The audience, of course, had no idea what they were hearing, probably assuming it was an obscure cover or that Ossian had started to write lyrics in English. As Ossian sang, he stared out across the audience, toward some distant place, and Kasper began to listen to lyrics he hadn't heard before. Grim's lyrics. *Into darkness disappear . . . Into darkness soar . . . I was born to endless night . . . I shall be no more . . .*

Ossian tilted his head back. His long hair had gone dark and matted with soil and gore. His mouth was half-open, his eyes closed, his face shining with sweat.

This is the most important thing in his life, Kasper realized.

He had often thought that it must be exhausting for Ossian to maintain his attitude, to always be on guard, choosing whether or not to measure his strength against all the people he met. And it probably was. But on the stage, he was free. Ossian gazed straight in the audience, pointed at someone with two fingers. Perhaps it was Kasper. And then, finally, something shook loose in Kasper. He became part of the crowd, part of the music, part of the here and now.

When Vanbörd finally got off the stage, it was as though Kasper awoke from a dream. He was sweating. Turning around, he noticed that one third of the audience had already left. There was a line at the merch table.

"There's no fucking order anymore," the older man with the Pinhead patch said as he passed Kasper. "No mosh, dammit!"

"There's nothing wrong with a bit of violence," his ginger friend objected.

Kasper followed them to the coat check, picked up his jacket and then turned back, struggling against the current. A woman who had been shooting the gig stopped him.

"You're Anja's son, right?" she said.

"Yeah, that's right," Kasper confirmed.

"Say hi from me," the woman said, disappearing before she'd given Kasper her name.

Backstage, Kasper was left standing in a corridor with dark red walls. Music was playing. Members of the various bands moved between the dressing rooms and the green room, the members of the young band shooting slightly intimidated looks at the older musicians. No one dignified Kasper with a glance, and he was reminded of what the Matchstick had been ranting about: without his dad, mom, Leah, Tony, he was nobody in this place.

He picked up his phone to text Iris when a hand grabbed his neck. Ossian loomed over him, held him in an iron grip. He looked exhausted and exhilarated at the same time. He had washed himself a little, but was still wearing the clothes he'd had on onstage. He smelled of sweat, of blood and dirt cellars, and something sharp, animalistic.

"There you are," Ossian said.

"Hi," Kasper managed.

Ossian let him go, patting him hard on the shoulder.

"Killer show, man," Kasper said.

As if Ossian would care what he thought.

"Dark energy tonight," Ossian said, more to himself than to Kasper. "Madness and violence. A man in the front got an elbow in the face, the blood just spurted out." He laughed, raised his beer can to his lips and took a sip, then gave it to Kasper. "We have a lot to talk about. Wait here."

He disappeared. Discreetly, Kasper put the can aside. He needed to drink some water. The bassist from the young band walked past with two beers, one in each hand. Then he stopped outside the bathroom, which was occupied, and smiled drunkenly at Kasper.

"You look exactly like Håkan Nordin!" he shouted, louder than necessary, touching one beer can against his Dark Cruelty shirt as if to emphasize who he was referring to. "No, wait . . . Are you his kid?"

Kasper said, "Yeah."

The bassist's eyes grew huge.

"Holy shit!" he screamed. "Is he here?"

He looked around, as if Håkan was lurking in a corner somewhere.

"No, he's touring with Blood Libation," Kasper said.

"Holy shit!" the bassist repeated. "This is huge!"

The singer stuck his head out of their dressing room and gave the bassist a look that said *stopbeingsofuckingembarrassing*. The bassist did not understand this message.

"Here, have a beer!" he said, handing one of his drinks to Kasper. "Cheers, son of Håkan!"

Fuck it. Kasper took a small sip of the cool beer. It was light and refreshing, so he drank some more. The metal was so cold it made his fingers ache.

"Generally speaking, reunions are pretty bad," the bassist said philosophically, "but this is something else, something you really look forward to. Ossian on vocals. That's going to be fucking amazing. That new song was fucking killer." So Ossian had told him what song it was. "Who do they have on the rhythm guitar?"

He looked as though it was something he had been pondering for a long time.

"My dad," Kasper said. "In the studio, that is."

He knew they'd been talking to Stasse about him touring, but logistically, it had to fit with his schedule.

"Tell him I'll do it," the bassist said with a hiccup.

The bathroom door opened and one of the blond giants from the first band came out. His eyes looked inward, somehow, and he ignored the younger men.

"Maybe see you at the afterparty!" the bassist told Kasper as he ducked into the bathroom.

Kasper walked a bit farther away and sipped his beer, got his phone out to look at the photos people were posting from the concert, searching for Malte's face in the audience. Looking at pictures of a gig just after it ended was odd. Most of it seemed paltry, which was not at all like it had felt.

He heard Ossian's voice approaching from behind and turned his head. Ossian had changed clothes and was holding his phone to his ear, talking to someone about the concert, about some technical error that Kasper hadn't noticed. He waved at Kasper to follow him and walked toward the exit.

The cold, damp air cooled Kasper's hot face. Ossian ended the phone call and lit a cigarette, smoking with intensity while responding to text messages. Kasper heard the door open. A young woman and a short, bearded man stepped out into the alley.

"Hi," the man said, crushing Kasper's hand in one beefy fist.

"Hi," Kasper said, confused.

A taxi rolled up and the short girl jumped into the back seat, Beefy Fist following behind. Ossian put his hand on Kasper's shoulder, led him toward the other side of the car.

"Where are we going?" Kasper asked.

Ossian didn't respond, instead pushing Kasper into the back seat and slamming the car door shut. The girl made herself comfortable between Beefy Fist and Kasper. A radio channel playing mellow pop music from the eighties was playing. Ossian, who sat in the front seat, raised the volume. Kasper was once again reminded of being a child, standing outside Ossian's door. Now Ossian had, in a way, ripped that door open and pushed Kasper inside. Literally.

Kasper watched the city sweep by the car window. They were going north. He pulled out his phone and gave Iris a report.

At that moment, Ossian turned around and said to Beefy Fist and the girl: "This is Håkan Nordin's kid."

"Oh, shit," said Beefy Fist as he stroked his beard. "Your dad's a legend."

"I think he's aware," the girl told him.

"Shut up, will you. I'm talking," Beefy Fist said, and then he began speaking about Dark Cruelty's importance to extreme metal in the Nordic countries, as if Kasper knew nothing about it. He tried to ignore Beefy Fist's grating voice. There was an undertone of excited admiration in him that could at any time turn into pure belligerence.

Dad would hate this guy, Kasper thought.

He opened the app for maps, saw that they were driving in the direction of Åkersberga. Even from here, it would take him over an hour to get back home on public transportation. But he didn't regret coming along. He was fine; Ossian was hardly going to hurt him. Besides, he was updating Iris about his location. Then he realized what a terrible sign it was that he was thinking like that.

They left the highway, were traveling around an anonymous suburb with rows of identical houses.

"Here, turn here!" the girl shouted, waving her arm around.

The taxi driver turned into a narrow road surrounded by the forest.

"Stop right here!" the girl shouted again.

Ossian leaped out of the car, hardly waiting for it to stop.

"You're paying, right, Håkan Junior?" Beefy Fist said as he left the car, followed closely by the girl.

Kasper looked at the fare. His mouth went dry. Still, he took out his credit card and paid for the journey. The driver gave him a concerned look.

"Those are not nice people," he said.

"I know," Kasper said.

Before leaving the car, he checked his phone, saw the marker for the GPS blink. He sent the coordinates to Iris and wrote: *FYI.* Why did he do that? Just in case. He tried not to think beyond that.

In the dark, the house seemed to lie nestled in a deep, vast forest, but on the map, Kasper had seen that it was a smaller area where people probably walked their dogs and went running. It was a normal house, albeit slightly scuffed. Rapid-fire blast beats and a singer's nihilistic screaming blared through the open windows. Ossian was standing on the porch, waiting. Steam came out of his mouth. The night was colder here.

"Come," he said, and Kasper followed him inside.

The music was deafening. Everyone they met greeted Ossian with respect, even reverence. Some people looked curiously at Kasper, but mostly they ignored him. Ossian grabbed a bottle of liquor and drank, then handed it to Kasper, who pretended to take a sip before giving it back. In one room, there was a giant television that looked newer than anything else in the house. On the screen, Italian movie cannibals tortured their wailing victims. On the wall above the TV, the Swedish, Norwegian, and Finnish flags hung vertically, so that the crosses were inverted. The cushions of one of the couches had been shredded. Three samurai swords hung above it. A couple of Hells Angels stood next to it, smoking dourly.

Kasper didn't perceive more than that before Ossian dragged a girl with facial tattoos off of the shredded couch and put Kasper in her place. Then he sat down next to him. Kasper got the bottle back, and this time, he didn't dare fake it. He took as small a sip as possible. He had never had pure liquor before and it burned his throat, stung all the way down to his stomach. It was gross, but also somehow satisfying.

Ossian leaned in closer to him. His hair smelled dank.

"Do you understand what this is about?" he said.

Kasper made a quick calculation. If he said "yes" and couldn't explain further, Ossian might get angry. Then again, he could get angry if Kasper said "no," too.

"I don't know," he said.

"Between the days that mark his death and birth," Ossian said. "That's when you came into this world. And you carry one of his names. A name is a strong bond. There is a bond between you and him."

Kasper nodded in a way he hoped didn't commit him to anything.

"And I was there," Ossian went on. "I was there when they recorded the EP. Now I'll be his voice. There is a bond between us, too, between him and me. Between me and you and him." He pointed to himself, Kasper, and a vague point next to and outside of them both. "It's about the three of us. Three is a strong number. So's thirty. Three plus zero. Do you understand what I'm saying?"

"I don't know," Kasper said again.

"You don't know?" Ossian shouted, and Kasper jerked backward, shut his eyes as a sheer reflex.

"You're like a jumpy little kid." Ossian chuckled.

"What?" Kasper said faintly.

"I was the one who suggested that I sing. But it wasn't an easy decision. An honor, but also a burden."

Ossian's eyes were distant, as if Kasper was no longer present. He suddenly remembered what his dad had said about Ossian's crew and drugs. He wondered if Ossian was on something, and, if so, how it impacted his judgment. Maybe he had some paranoid idea that Kasper and he belonged together. Maybe he was mentally ill. Maybe he was playacting, because it amused him. Or maybe it was all of those things at once.

"Here," Ossian said, handing him the bottle again. "Drink."

Kasper took it. The booze didn't burn as much this time but it still didn't taste good. Maybe that wasn't the point of it, though. Ossian nodded approvingly and gulped down a mouthful.

"We're brothers, you and me," he said.

Fuck, no, Kasper thought, and then worried he'd said it out loud. The music was so loud; the alcohol simmered in his blood. He felt as if he couldn't trust his senses anymore.

"Wait here," Ossian said. He rose with the bottle in his hand.

Kasper watched him go. It wasn't until now that he realized that he hadn't seen anyone else from Vanbörd or the other bands at this house. Ossian seemed to have taken him to a completely different party than the one that the bassist with the Dark Cruelty tee had been talking about.

One of the Hells Angels glared at him. Kasper began to feel deeply ill at ease. He didn't want to wait for Ossian to return; he didn't want to be there at all. But how could he leave? He tried to think it through. He didn't have enough money to pay for a taxi home; Beefy Fist had seen to that. But he should be able to locate a bus. In a worst-case scenario, he could start walking, and then phone his mother, Atle, or Leah on the way. The important thing was that no one could know that he was there. Ossian was the lead singer in Dark Cruelty now. It would completely ruin the reunion if Håkan found out that Ossian had kidnapped his son. The thought made Kasper want to laugh out loud. The situation was so absurd. How drunk was he, really?

Kasper got to his feet and aimed for the door. In the corner of his eye, he thought he saw Beefy Fist performing a Nazi salute with great enthusiasm. Kasper kept his eyes lowered and tried not to bump into anyone. In this type of crowd, you could usually find easily provoked men longing for a fistfight. Especially when they were at a party in someone's home, where no one would ever think of calling the cops.

I'm fine, Kasper thought. *I'll just follow the road.*

Outside, it was windy, and Kasper felt like he was sobering up a little. He went down the stairs, gravel crunching under his shoes as he walked.

"There you are," a familiar voice said from behind him.

Kasper turned around and saw Ossian walking toward him with the bottle in his hand. His expression was hard to read.

"I thought I'd get some air," Kasper told him.

"Good idea," Ossian said, pushing Kasper toward the edge of the forest. "They're all cunts, anyway. Let's go."

A brittle layer of frost had spread over the fallen leaves. It crunched beneath Kasper's shoes and Ossian's heavy boots as they walked through the woods together. At least Ossian didn't seem angry about Kasper's failed attempt to escape. He paced ahead of Kasper, his hair tossing when he moved. Something about him was lithe, animalistic, reminiscent of a cat. One shrewd eye shone when he threw a glance over his shoulder, as if to ensure that Kasper was keeping up. They crossed a running track and reached a clearing with a picnic table. Ossian settled on it. Frost glittered on the wooden boards. Kasper sat down far enough from Ossian that he was out of reach of those long arms.

"There is no such thing as coincidence," Ossian said, looking up at the sky, as if addressing the stars. "The patterns are everywhere, both hidden and fully visible. It is only a question of noticing them and then using them for one's own purposes."

Kasper tried to keep up, but it was hard. He hoped that Ossian would come to the point.

"Music is also pattern," Ossian said. "Music is powerful. More powerful than most people can grasp. But you can. I saw it tonight. You felt it here."

Lightning fast, he leaned in and pushed Kasper in the chest. Apparently, he'd still been too close.

"Ow," Kasper said. "Stop it."

Ossian smirked, looking like the annoying, slightly threatening teenager from Kasper's childhood.

"Drink again, little brother."

Ossian handed the bottle to Kasper, who took the world's smallest sip, but he could feel it affecting him. Ossian looked encouragingly at Kasper and he drank again, more than he'd intended to. He gave the bottle back to Ossian, who also drank. A wind swept through the clearing, making the tall pines sway.

Ossian's voice was barely audible through the breeze: "Those pictures came out of your dreams."

It took a second before Kasper connected. Did he mean the images in the sketchbook?

"We've had the same dreams, you and I," Ossian said.

Kasper couldn't have heard it correctly, or Ossian meant it symbolically. His gaze had gone remote again.

"In the first dream, he and the band were on a theater stage. A bull was led out and they slaughtered it. Blood ran across the floor."

The theater. Just like in Kasper's dream. There had been blood on Grim's hand, but Kasper hadn't dreamed of a bull.

"In the second dream, I stood by the sea," Ossian continued. "On the North Island in New Zealand, where there are black beaches and deadly currents. I stood in the water and wondered if the moment had arrived, if the time had come for me to walk into the waves. Then the water quieted, and I saw him. He floated there, in front of me. Grim. And the depths beneath him were infinite."

It sounded like he was quoting a text. Maybe he was. This sounded about as lofty as Ossian's lyrics did. Maybe it was material he was working on, and now he wanted Kasper's opinion on it, because the drawings were reminiscent of his own dreams.

I haven't dreamed of black beaches, Kasper thought.

But the theater stage, Grim floating . . . they were too similar. Was Ossian lying, then? But Kasper had seen his face when he saw the pictures, the shock in his eyes.

"In the third dream we sat at a table. A snake circled over the black tablecloth. Grim handed me a cup and I drank," Ossian said, suddenly looking straight at Kasper. "You were there, too."

Kasper couldn't get his mind together. He stared at a drop of clear snot hanging from Ossian's nose.

"So you understand," Ossian said, and the drop fell onto his jeans. "The storm is here and we're in it together."

Goose bumps spread over Kasper's arms. What if there really was a bond between them? Why else would Kasper so willingly have followed Ossian here? What if Ossian actually sat on some answers, could explain why all this was happening? But it felt more as if he were weaving a web around Kasper, to snare him.

The wind stilled and sounds from the party could be heard from a distance. Music, two male voices roaring at each other. They were either swearing eternal brotherhood or ready to murder each other. It was difficult to tell.

"I respect your dad," Ossian said. "But he's never seemed to grasp what Grim was trying to do. Grim left it unfinished, and here we are.

Everything is cyclical. The patterns appear again. The river is rising. He's the flame, and we're the moths. Everything repeats itself."

Ossian grabbed Kasper's left hand and turned it palm up, revealing the shining scar.

"How did you get this?"

His fingers pressed against Kasper's wrist. Even if Kasper had wanted to tell him, he couldn't. The words wouldn't come. It was completely impossible for him to trust Ossian with that. Ossian, he knew, had his own reasons for everything he did. Kasper couldn't trust him at all. He saw it now: he shouldn't have come.

"I've got to go home," he said, yanking his hand away from Ossian's grasp. "A friend is waiting for me."

It wasn't until he uttered the lie that he realized how frightened he was. He rose a little unsteadily.

"Ernesto said you want to interview him about Grim," Ossian said.

Kasper looked at him. He had e-mailed Ernesto, who had responded that he would get in touch soon. He had yet to.

"But if you want answers, there's someone else you should talk to," Ossian went on. "Malte."

Was he serious? It looked as if he was. Did that mean that Malte actually had been at the gig? *Was he here now?*

"When you want to see him," Ossian said, "I can help you."

"I'll never want that," Kasper said, then added: "Have you met him?"

Ossian looked at him. Then he snuffled loudly and jumped off the table, walked around it. Kasper heard Ossian's steps behind his back, heard the alcohol move inside the bottle.

"Drink up, for fuck's sake," Ossian, who was suddenly beside him, said.

Kasper felt Ossian grip his neck, and then the opening of the bottle was pressed to his mouth, the glass slamming against his teeth. He had to swallow to not choke. When Ossian removed the bottle again, Kasper coughed until he had tears in his eyes.

"Little brother," Ossian said, ruffling his hair, putting his arm around his shoulders.

Kasper felt his warm breath against his ear, heard his words whisper through the night wind: ". . . you will be worthy of his name . . ."

Appendix 9. "Tormented Exaltation" by Kasper "Grim" Johansson

For so long have I wandered
Beneath the hateful skies
I am traveling beyond
Beyond the realm of the mind
Into darkness disappear
Into darkness soar
I was born to endless night
I shall be no more

I am on a pilgrim's path
Of thorns and broken glass
My bleeding feet move forward
Toward the beckoning gate
I kneel before the altar
Invoke the abysmal gods
Give me thy darkest blessing
Feast on my starving soul

Tormented exaltation
Tormented exaltation

I renounce my flesh
I renounce my soul
I shall become
I shall transform
Ascend

ANCIENT BLOODLUST

In February, Anja receives a phone call from Grim. He explains that they're recording their EP soon and need some photos with the whole band.

"All five of us," he says.

Malte usually doesn't come to the parties they go to, so Anja has only met him a few times in the rehearsal room with Linda. He reminds her a little of Grim in that it can be difficult to determine if he's smug or shy. There is one significant difference, though. She's always felt as if Grim means well. She's not so sure about Malte.

On the day of the photo shoot, Linda shows her an old stroller in the garage. It's made of brown corduroy, a little crooked.

"Okay, let's take it on a test run," Anja says.

They put Anja's camera and bag in the stroller and take turns lugging it through the snow-covered suburb. On the way back, Anja pushes it up the hill to Linda's house and thinks of one night last summer, when the two of them toiled up this very hill, singing a Death song in falsetto. They had been drunk and happy, necks aching after intense headbanging. Now Linda is panting, struggling up the slope with her big belly, and Anja is suddenly scared. Scared they'll grow up too fast. Scared because what if life is like a train that hurtles toward death, and what if Anja has as dull a life as her mother, who is never, ever happy.

"What are you thinking?" Linda asks when they stop outside her house.

"Nothing," says Anja.

"It's so crazy, really," says Linda, gingerly rocking the stroller. "I never thought my life would turn out like this."

Unlike Anja, Linda had certain expectations for herself. Her parents, economists with years of school behind them, are in some state of shock. Quitting school and getting pregnant with a metal band guitarist's baby when you're seventeen doesn't happen in their world. Still, they've tried to adapt, and they've even received the father of the child in their home. Good thing they get along well with Ernesto.

"One thing I hate, though," Linda says, and her voice suddenly sounds thick with unshed tears, "is that we don't get to graduate together."

They hug each other. Linda's thick jacket whispers against Anja's leather one. There's the familiar scent of Linda's shampoo. Anja knows that she'll choose a different path than Linda's, but they have to stay friends. She can't imagine anything else.

A few hours later, she meets Dark Cruelty in a public bomb shelter in Handen that Håkan and Grim have discovered. Ernesto immediately asks about Linda. He's worried, wants to be as close to a phone as possible since the baby can come any time. The others are the same as usual. And not.

There's something off about the band. Something in their dynamic has shifted. The energy she felt when she was shooting them last summer is still there, but more volatile, fractured. Like something bad is about to happen. She hopes she is wrong.

She notices that Håkan glances at her when he thinks she can't see. Just the other day, Linda said that she thinks Håkan likes Anja but is too shy to say anything.

Anja thinks she's wrong, but it doesn't matter. Since a party last New Year's Eve, she's been dating Stasse. Stasse who is incredibly hot and a great kisser. He likes her, and she likes him. Still, her stomach does something complicated when Håkan meets her gaze.

When Anja says good-bye and leaves for the bus, she can hear running steps behind her. It's Grim, who says he wants to show her something. They go toward the town center, toward the lake, which is right next to the train station. Grim doesn't say much, but Anja isn't bothered by silence.

The snow crunches beneath their boots as they walk along the beach. The ice has settled. Anja is thinking about the accident a few years back, when a train derailed by the lake and its front smashed through the ice. Everyone survived, though. The pictures in the newspapers had frightened and fascinated her, and she still keeps them between the pages of a book.

"There," says Grim, pointing toward the water.

At first, Anja doesn't understand what she's seeing. Then she realizes that it is a fox. It must have gone through the ice. Did it freeze while swimming toward land? That's what it looks like. Only the ears and a piece of the head and body stick out above the lake's surface, while the rest of the fox is visible through the clear ice. Captured.

"Thought you might like to see it," says Grim.

"Thank you," Anja says.

She takes out the camera and puts in a new roll of Kodak Tri-X 400, wondering if there's something wrong with her for immediately wanting to photograph this. Her heart aches for the dead animal and yet her first instinct is to raise the camera. Grim must have known this. She shoots until snow falls from the sky and her fingers start to go numb.

"Poor little thing," Anja says as she puts the cover back on the lens.

"Yeah," says Grim. "It struggled."

He heaves a long sigh. Snowflakes are caught in his long black hair, his dark lashes. Later she will remember that day and wonder what he was actually trying to show her. Maybe he didn't even understand it himself.

In March, Dark Cruelty returns to Hasse's studio, one year after Grim joined the band. Håkan has barely slept, listening to Grim tossing and turning in the next bed.

This is it.

This is what they have planned for, this is what they have saved all their hard-earned money for, this is what they've fantasized about.

Ernesto and Tony also look a bit dazed. Malte's face is perfectly white, as if he hasn't slept for a week. It is his first studio recording and he stinks of performance anxiety. Håkan almost feels sorry for him, but more than that, he gets nervous. They only have three days. Will Malte deliver?

"It went great last time, comrades," Hasse says. "Just keep on trucking."

He lights a cigarette and doesn't look at all concerned, which makes Håkan feel slightly calmer.

Tony lays down the drums first and it goes well. He has practiced extra hard for this, but not so much that he's destroyed his hands. Then it's Håkan's turn. He has no idea how he's doing. Grim throws out various suggestions and Håkan really tries. Then, suddenly, Hasse declares that he's done.

Then it's Malte with the rhythm guitar and it is clear that he has been practicing like crazy. Håkan drags his fingertips over the palm of his other hand, remembers what it was like when he started playing. How the skin on his fingers had gone hard, became insensitive. He had felt proud when it happened. It made him feel grown up, like what he did was real.

Suddenly, Ernesto tells Malte to stop playing, checks the clock on the wall, says that Linda will be there soon.

"What does it matter?" says Håkan, who has completely forgotten that she was coming. "Why can't he keep going until then?"

"I don't want my kid to get a massive shock coming in here," Ernesto tells them. "It could mess up his hearing. And maybe everyone can stub out the cigs, too."

Hasse immediately shoves his into his massive ashtray. Tony takes a last, long drag on his. Malte groans, despite not being a smoker, and Grim starts drawing in his notebook.

"We can't afford to lose time," is all he says.

Fortunately, Linda arrives punctually, and they decide to take a break, anyway. She's got Anja with her, and they both smell like winter. Håkan's heart sinks like a stone when he sees Anja, knowing she's been with Stasse since New Year's. He still doesn't understand how it happened, hadn't seen any signs of it at all. Unfortunately, it hasn't changed his own feelings.

He tries to focus on the child that Linda gets out from beneath a blanket. It's the first time Håkan has seen Ernesto's son. He's so tiny, just a few weeks old. He isn't bald, like Håkan is in all his baby pictures, but has a shock of dark hair. His eyes are pinched shut. Is he asleep?

Linda looks tired and a little confused, as if she hasn't been outdoors since the birth. Maybe she hasn't; it's been very cold. Maybe newborns can't handle the cold. Håkan, frankly, doesn't know much about it. Ernesto kisses Linda on the forehead. He's moved into her parents' house. The idea of it makes Håkan choke, but they look really happy.

"Doesn't he look like Ernesto?" says Linda, smiling.

Håkan nods, really trying to see it, but he can only see a baby. He notices that Malte is struggling not to look at Linda's breasts, which are huge. Full of milk. Håkan pushes the thought away; it's too weird.

"Who's this little guy?" Hasse says.

"Ossian," Linda announces.

They must have just settled on it, because when Håkan talked to Ernesto yesterday, it was just "the baby."

"Ossian Carlos," Ernesto says.

He beams when he says it. Carlos was the name of his biological father.

"Ossian as in *Ossian's songs*?" Grim says.

"That's exactly what I was thinking," Malte says.

No, you weren't, Håkan thinks.

"Don't know, it's my grandfather's name," Linda tells them.

She hands the child over to Ernesto, who takes him so fumblingly that Håkan gets anxious. What if he drops his own son?

"There you are," Ernesto mumbles, as if to calm himself down. "Does anyone want to hold him? You have to prop up the head; they've got, like, really weak necks when they're this small."

"I can't do it," says Håkan.

Tony says, "Hand me that baby."

Tony, who has three younger siblings, holds Ossian expertly.

"The fontanelle, it's far out, really," Ernesto says, his hand cupping Ossian's tiny head. "That the skull hasn't closed up yet."

"Sorry, but I don't want to think about that," Linda says.

Grim looks up from his sketchbook. That, of course, is what interests him. Håkan agrees with Linda, the thought of the soft, pliable head making him shiver.

"Put a finger in his hand," Ernesto tells Håkan, who carefully places his index finger in the baby's wrinkly hand.

The baby grasps it immediately. He hears the sound of Anja's camera going off.

"Grasp reflex," says Ernesto. "It's so cool."

"It's probably because we're related to monkeys," Malte says. "Some more than others."

He grins as if he's said something funny, but it didn't come out that way. Everyone stares at him.

"What the fuck did you just say?" Ernesto says.

"Yeah, what the fuck?" Linda demands.

Malte looks toward Håkan searchingly.

"Apologize," Håkan orders him.

"It was just a joke."

"Didn't sound like one," Tony mutters.

"Sorry."

Malte turns away. Grim is staring at the ground, blinking.

"Right, well, I'm leaving," Linda says.

As if on cue, Ossian begins to cry.

"Linda," Ernesto attempts.

"See you tonight."

She and Anja leave the studio and the child's screams disappear into the distance.

Håkan tries to convince himself that it was all a clumsy joke, nothing more. But he's starting to wonder if Malte isn't just a victim to his bad impulses, that he uses them, too. Håkan has tried not to dwell on the letter he found at Dagge's, not just because he is embarrassed to have read his mail. Malte's blatant lies and obvious disloyalty made him angry, but also frightened him. When Håkan looks at Malte now, he finds himself genuinely wondering what he's capable of.

When the first day of recording is over, everyone is dead tired. Håkan empty, missing the high energy he'd had when he and Grim were only talking about the EP. Now, he doesn't even dare to ask Grim how he thinks it went. He knows that he will get an honest answer and maybe doesn't want to hear it.

That night Håkan sleeps like he's been clubbed over the head. In the dream, he is still in the control room, but Hasse is not there. Instead, Håkan is at the desk, trying to pretend he knows what he's doing even though he has no idea. There's something off about the sound, and suddenly, with icy clarity, he knows why. A wailing from inside an amplifier. The baby is in there.

The second day in the studio, everything goes smoothly until it's time for vocals. Grim nails most of it on the first take, but something goes wrong with the new song, "Curse of the Lost." He's never satisfied, keeps asking for retakes. *Forever wandering . . . these dark halls of despair. . . .* Grim kicks the wall.

"Come on, man," Hasse says calmly. "Don't go doing that. It sounds fantastic."

Håkan and the others agree, but Grim's eyes are dark, introverted. When they're recording the outro, he makes an odd request. He wants everyone to leave except Malte and himself. The request strikes Håkan like a punch to the stomach.

They've planned this, the two of them, without him.

"I'm not going anywhere," Håkan tells them.

It's my band, he doesn't add. But it's in the air.

"But . . ." Malte says, with a nervous look at Grim.

"It's fine," says Håkan with affected calm, then lies: "I know what you're going to do."

"Fine, sacrifice a goat, then, or whatever the hell you're up to," Ernesto says, yawning. "I want a hot dog. Come on, Tony."

Tony sighs and follows Ernesto through the door.

Hasse looks at Grim, scratches his stomach.

"What are you up to, man?"

"I want to get in the mood," says Grim.

He is staring at the floor when he says it, winding a lock of his long black hair around his finger. Malte shifts from one foot to the other.

"Go ahead," Hasse says, and stands up. "But he's the only one allowed near the equipment." He points at Håkan.

Malte looks offended, entering the live room with Grim. Then Hasse shows Håkan how to work the equipment in the control room, Håkan listening and nodding. Today he's spent some time observing Hasse working, trying to understand.

They are left alone in the studio, Håkan on one side of the studio window, Grim and Malte on the other.

Håkan looks at Grim searchingly, but he just opens his turquoise sports bag and starts unpacking. Wrapped in a towel is one of the glazed bowls they usually use for oatmeal and yogurt. Malte lifts a couple of candlesticks out of his backpack, sets them on the floor next to the microphone, and adds candles.

Håkan, wanting Malte to believe that Grim told him what was going on, asks no questions. But the truth is, he has no idea. And it bothers him.

It sizzles when Malte sets fire to a match.

"Turn the lights off," he says, and then lights the candles.

Grim still won't meet Håkan's gaze. Håkan turns the lights off. In the flickering glow of the candles, Grim falls to his knees next to the bowl and rolls up his left sleeve. Malte hands him something, but Håkan can't see what it is. Malte looks at Håkan and nods and Håkan follows Hasse's instructions.

"Rolling," he says into the talk-back mic.

Grim holds out his left arm and metal glimmers in the candle-light. Håkan hears Grim gasp, or was it himself? It takes a second for him to understand that there is blood trickling down the pale arm, dripping into the bowl. Grim puts the knife on the towel and takes a mic from Malte. In the headphones, Håkan hears Grim's voice, his whispers. Just like they've decided, he is chanting the names of the rulers of Hell.

"*Baal . . . Paimon . . . Beleth . . . Belial . . . Eligor . . . Astaroth . . .*"

Håkan listens with increasing horror, catches a glimpse of Malte's face. His eyes are shining with awe as he looks at Grim on his knees, bleeding and chanting the names of Hell's elites. And Håkan understands that it isn't the demons that frighten him. It's Malte. It's Grim. What happens when they're together.

Håkan says nothing to Grim. He doesn't say anything until they're back home, on their separate beds, and then he can't hold it in any longer.

"What the hell was that for?"

He points to the bandage on Grim's arm, which Håkan himself had put together from the dusty first-aid kit in the bathroom. Grim and Malte hadn't even thought of that, hadn't even brought a bandage. Håkan cleaned up the traces, not wanting Hasse and the others to know what happened while they were away.

Now Grim is sitting with a pillow on his lap, sketching in his fucking notebook. The pen moves across the paper in twisting, winding patterns. He doesn't answer Håkan. In the kitchen, the radio is on, and his mom is making chili con carne. Grim is silent.

"Hello?" Håkan says.

"I knew you wouldn't like it," says Grim, blinking rapidly. "That's why I asked you to go."

He says it objectively, as if that was the issue, Håkan's presence in the room.

"But what was the fucking point?" says Håkan.

"Your own blood is the most powerful thing you can sacrifice."

"But why?"

For once, Håkan won't let it go. Grim doesn't respond immediately. The pen moves across the paper. There's a hole in the neckline of his Venom tee. Håkan is staring at it.

"I want people to remember this record," he says, finally.

Håkan's head is spinning. What does Grim mean?

"Was it Malte's idea?"

"No," says Grim. "Mine."

But Malte didn't stop him. He helped, and Håkan can easily imagine how he had egged Grim on. How much time have the two of them actually been spending together during the winter?

Håkan gets a glimpse of what Grim is drawing: a puzzling, abstract pattern, difficult and dizzying. The paper is covered in similar figures.

"You know, Håkan," Grim says, still not looking up. "I strongly suspect that most magic doesn't work. But some things do. I'm trying to discover them."

Håkan thinks about the night when Grim was lying on the floor, talking about the magician having the potential to become more than human. Is he still chasing that idea?

Why are you doing this? Håkan wants to ask.

Please don't do it again, he wants to say.

But it's their final day in the studio tomorrow and he doesn't want to risk having a falling-out with Grim. For the first time, he realizes that it could actually happen.

So he doesn't say anything.

And then it's done. They've recorded what will be referred to as Sweden's first death metal EP. Hasse hands over the original cassette to Håkan and Grim, the only existing copy. Håkan is terrified that they will lose it, or that it will be ruined, somehow. It's a relief when they're allowed to hand it over to the mastering studio. It is a completely different world, a place of big-name artists, the establishment they despise. Still, Håkan has to admit that it feels pretty cool. As if what they're doing is real.

Then there is nothing more they can do. The wax is being sent off to press, then they'll wait for the test pressings to come through. But they should obviously be celebrating now, says Adde from Exenterate, and he throws a party in his parents' house. When the doorbell rings and Dagge and Bommen appear, having come up from Gothenburg as a surprise, everyone is overjoyed. Håkan and Dagge hug each other so tightly that Dagge's glasses end up askew.

For once, Malte joins the party and is soon absolutely hammered, walking around with a cardboard box on his head like a crown, rings from beer cans on his fingers. It's probably the first time Håkan has heard him laugh properly. Håkan finds that he prefers a drunk Malte to the sober one. Ture, the bassist from Exenterate, walks around and films them, interviews Håkan and Grim. Håkan has no idea what he's saying, only knows that this must be the best night of his life. Ernesto is weepy, proclaiming Håkan to be a great friend. Grim seems happy, too. Maybe even a little drunk? Håkan is not sure. The intoxication isn't usually this intense at their parties, and there's something wild in the air, something unhinged. He and Grim climb the roof of Adde's old playhouse, sit there, and holler a song by The Church. Then Håkan has to have a little nap. He crawls into the playhouse. Grim lies down beside him. "Hope we don't freeze to death," says Håkan. He doesn't catch Grim's response. That night he dreams of a huge, roaring fire.

When Håkan wakes up a few hours later, Grim is missing. And he's not there when Håkan comes home. He's gone for days. When he returns, he is quiet and pale, says he's sick. It seems to be the same illness he'd suffered through after the gig last autumn. He's mostly in bed, staring into the wall. His head hurts. His stomach aches. When he moves, it's in slow motion. He's quiet, so quiet, and doesn't seem to listen when Håkan talks. When the test pressings arrive, he barely reacts. Håkan gets hurt and worried. "Maybe you should see a doctor or something," he says, but a few days later, Grim is restored. Or seems to be, anyway. He walks and speaks and plays and sings and everything seems normal. But it's as if some fire in his eyes has gone out.

It will probably come back, Håkan thinks. It has to.

KASPER

A hand.

That was the first thing Kasper saw when he opened his eyes.

It took him a second to realize it was his own.

He was lying on his stomach in a bed. His own bed. He was back home.

What had happened yesterday?

His head buzzed, as if it had been stuffed full of bees. He tried to think.

Little brother . . .

A horrible taste in his mouth.

. . . you will be worthy of his name . . .

There were only fragments, and he couldn't get them to fit together. Panic started to creep in. What had happened? He remembered riding in the car to the party. But how did he get home? He had no idea.

Then he noticed that his left forearm felt strange, itchy and hot. A sharp pain stabbed through him when he tried to lift it. His arm was stuck to the sheet, and there was blood around it.

At once, Kasper was wide awake.

Blood on the white sheet.

He forced air into his lungs, refusing to let the panic overtake him. He had to think logically.

He moved the sheet away from the mattress. Beneath it was a stain, dark red. He struggled to sit upright, noted that the fabric that was stuck to his arm was soaked with blood and ink. He could glimpse the letters printed on his skin. *GRIM*.

One of Leah's stories popped in his head. A customer had had a tattoo done while drunk at a party, and then went to bed with her clothes still on. The next morning the fabric of the sweater was stuck to the fresh tattoo. She didn't notice until she pulled off her shirt and tore off a little piece of skin.

The world went sideways and Kasper had to close his eyes. What the hell happened yesterday? He fumbled after memories, but they dissolved like smoke when he tried to catch them. He looked around for his phone, found it on the floor next to his jeans and his dad's Celtic Frost shirt. Apparently, he had kept his socks and his underwear on. He picked up the phone; it was half past seven. Grönan opened at twelve today. Or possibly eleven. He wasn't sure.

Kasper did a Google search for *fresh tattoo stuck*. The answer came quickly and seemed wholly unanimous. He rose up, gently pulling the entire sheet off the mattress, collected it in his arms. Then he went into the bathroom, turned on the shower and set the temperature to warm, but not too hot. He sat down on the floor and soaked his arm with the water. As the fabric gradually got drenched, he pulled it loose, very gently. It hurt so much his eyes teared up. His first tattoo. This was not how it was supposed to be. Had Ossian forced him to do it? Had he agreed to it voluntarily? Had he come up with the idea himself? He did not know which option was worse.

In the end, he managed to remove the last little bit that was stuck. Blood and ink on the sheet. The tattoo looked like shit, but thankfully, the letters were quite small.

The person who had made it seemed to have been inexperienced, or at least as drunk as Kasper had been. The skin around the tattoo was wounded and swollen, inflamed. An ugly bruise spread around it. The needle had gone in too deep.

"Fuck," Kasper mumbled.

He went over to the bathroom cabinet, took out an old bottle of antiseptic and bathed the tattoo. It cooled the hot skin slightly. He tried not to think about what could be rushing through his bloodstream at that very moment. Then he thought about how careful Leah was with hygiene, how diligently she disinfected and then covered a newly tattooed area with plastic. He recalled the dingy house, the people there. His dad had said there was a lot of drugs around Ossian. What kind of drugs? Had he been infected with hepatitis C? Would he die?

Suddenly, he felt exhausted. He sank onto the toilet seat and wrapped his right arm around himself. How could he have been stupid enough to go along with Ossian?

The shower nozzle was on the floor, the water still pouring into the drain. Fragments of his memory began to return. Ossian's hold on his wrist when he examined the scar.

How did you get this?

What had he answered? How could people talk about blackouts as if they were hilarious? Maybe, though, it was a completely different experience when you went out with friends, blind drunk, than when it happened at a deeply illicit party with a childhood nemesis.

Malte. Then he remembered Malte.

Kasper felt cold.

Something about Malte. Had he been at the party? He thought he'd seen him at the concert. And then—

Steps approached, but his dad wouldn't be home for a whole week. It turned out to be Iris, who appeared in the doorway. Iris? Kasper tried to get a grasp on the situation. She had never been at his place before, but now she was standing there, looking at the bloody sheet in the shower, then at Kasper's arm.

"Oh, shit . . ." she said. "What happened?"

"I can't remember," Kasper said.

His tears caught him off guard. He cried childishly, loudly, but he was too tired to feel ashamed about it. Iris crouched down next to him and put a warm hand on his back, between his shoulder blades.

"Fuck," Kasper said, sniffling.

Iris tore off a piece of toilet paper and handed it to him. Kasper pressed it against his eyes, crying so hard he shook with it. He didn't even remember when he'd last cried like that. He'd never cried during his depression. He had longed for tears, but they wouldn't come. He didn't cry when he discovered that Marco and the others had gone behind his back. He didn't cry when his mom and dad said they were getting divorced, or even when his grandma died. He just went into his room and lay down on the bed.

People used to say it was a relief to cry, and maybe it was, sometimes. But right now, it just hurt like hell.

Eventually, he ran out of tears and felt a dull headache begin.

"Hey," Iris said. "Have a shower, brush your teeth, get dressed, and I'll make you some breakfast."

A while later, Kasper sat at the kitchen table and ate a cheese sandwich very slowly, sipped gently on a mug of tea. At least he didn't feel too hungover. Maybe he had a hidden talent for handling alcohol. He had heard that people who became alcoholics were often the same ones who didn't feel like shit after drinking too much. It didn't seem like such a great talent, now that he thought about it.

Iris came back from the bathroom with a packet of fluid replacement and another one with painkillers.

"I ransacked your bathroom cabinet," she said, tossing an effervescent tablet into his water.

"I feel fine," Kasper said.

"Oh, you are *now*," she said ominously, placing an aspirin in front of him.

He washed it down with the fizzy water. How would he get through the day?

"Painkillers, water, fluid replacement," Iris said as if she had read his thoughts. "And don't forget to eat."

"How did I get home?" he asked. "How did you get here?"

"I picked you up," Iris said, and then she told him the rest of it.

She had been at her parents' house all night. When Kasper's replies to her got increasingly incoherent, she decided to find him. She had the coordinates. And when she got to the party, she wrote to Ossian that she was outside. It took a second before Kasper understood how she could have Ossian's number: the screenshot he'd sent her from the concert.

"He brought you out," Iris said. "I was actually sort of shocked by how nice he was."

She looked puzzled, but Kasper understood exactly what she meant. Ossian had mastered the art of constructing a reputation for danger, which meant that everyone had extremely low expectations when they met him. After that, he only had to make very little effort for people to find him *so* nice and down-to-earth. When he was in the mood, that is.

"You were pretty out of it, to be honest," Iris said, and he realized that was an understatement. "But at least you didn't throw up until we got here. In a bush in the yard."

Kasper groaned.

"Then you said good night and went to bed, but I thought I might as well stay over."

"Shit," he said. "Thank you. Thank you. I will never stop saying thank you."

"You're welcome," Iris said. "Do you feel like talking about what happened? You can start at the beginning and just, like, see what comes up."

Kasper started telling her about the gig, about maybe seeing

Malte, the Dark Cruelty song, the bassist who was a massive fan, Beefy Fist, paying for the taxi. The room with the flags and the samurai swords. Ossian pushing him onto the couch and telling him they had a bond with Grim. Sometimes Kasper had to go back into the story and add something, but it was easier to remember now.

"Then I tried to leave," he said.

"What happened?"

Ossian, walking through the woods. The picnic table. The wind and the trees. Kasper tried to reproduce Ossian's talk about patterns, storms, rivers, and flames, but it was difficult. It sounded like he was talking nonsense. Perhaps that was exactly what Ossian had done, but he had the ability to make nonsense sound concise.

"He said everything repeats itself," Kasper said. "And he asked about my scar. How I got it. But I didn't say anything."

At least that's what he thought. Who knew what he had said afterward. Darkness lurked beyond the illuminated scenes in his memories.

"And then he started talking about his dreams," Kasper said.

A strong sense of unreality came over him when he reported on what Ossian had said. Last night had been dreamlike. Perhaps he would have doubted that it had happened at all if it were not for the four letters that were etched in his skin, itching like anything.

"He may have made all that up." But Iris still looked shaken.

"I thought so, too," Kasper said. "But how the hell could he guess that those particular pictures were inspired by my dreams?"

"All right, fine, very well. Let's say he's telling the truth," Iris said. "That you have the same dreams. The snake and the cup, for example . . . They're highly symbolic in our culture, so of course they can occur in your dreams. And when your brain is looking for patterns that fit, it's easy to ignore what doesn't. Like the black beach."

But she didn't look convinced by her own words.

"This thing about seeing patterns everywhere," Kasper said, "isn't that a sign of madness?"

"Yes," said Iris vaguely. "But that's how our brains work, too. We look for and learn to recognize patterns and get kind of a kick out of it. There are patterns in art, for example. Music, text, and so on. You know, like Ossian said."

"I'm so worried about what I might have told him," Kasper said. "I feel totally paranoid."

"I get it. But honestly, getting anything coherent out of you at that point may have been impossible," Iris said. "At least I had that problem. I had to search for your address to drive you home. You couldn't even tell me where you lived."

Kasper groaned and hid his face in his hands.

"Besides," he heard Iris say. "What difference does it make what you told him? I realize that this is awful for you, but what use can he have with that information? Like you cutting your hand on the knife, for instance."

But it wasn't so much his own secrets as other people's that concerned Kasper. What they tried to keep in the inner circle. The phone number, the items that Grim had taken with him. He tried to explain this to Iris.

"But don't you think Ossian already knows all that?" she said. "He's in the band now, and he's Ernesto's son."

"I don't know," Kasper said. "The thing about the phone number . . . I'm not even sure my mom knows about it. Tony could have been the only one Dad told about it."

But would Tony really have told Kasper, in that case? Iris's phone rang and she checked it, while Kasper searched desperately through his memory. There was something more Ossian had said.

"Shit, I have to get home to my parents," Iris said. "Return the car before work."

Kasper said, "Malte."

326

Iris looked at him.

"Ossian said I should talk to Malte if I want to know more about Grim. He said he could set up a meeting, if I want to."

"But you don't want to, right?" Iris said, looking terrified.

"No, of course not," Kasper said. "But it must mean that he's in touch with Malte. How can he even talk to him after everything he's done?"

"He might not care," Iris said. "He might think it was a long time ago and that Malte is some kind of . . . dunno . . . cult figure. Like when people say, 'I don't give a fuck who the artist is, the music is great.' I definitely think Ossian can make sense of that in his head."

Kasper tried but failed. He could imagine Ossian not giving a fuck about what Malte had done to strangers, but how could he ignore their personal history? Ernesto and Håkan had been affected the most when Malte sent his followers after his former bandmates.

"Are you okay?" Iris said.

Kasper said, "Sorry. You have to go. And thank you again. Seriously."

"I'll call you," Iris said.

And Kasper had to call his dad.

After Iris left, he took out his phone and checked his dad's schedule. He should still be in Switzerland or on his way to Milan. Kasper wrote and asked if they could talk. His dad called him up at once on video. He was in his hotel room, dressed and ready for the day.

"How's it going?" he asked.

Kasper didn't even know how to begin answering that question.

"Has anything happened?" his dad said.

"I'll tell you something, but please don't freak out. Or maybe it isn't even a thing, but I just have to say it."

"All right," his dad said. He sat down on the narrow hotel bed.

It would have been easier if Kasper hadn't had to look at him. He stared at his own face while he told him that Ossian had invited him to the concert and that he had gone to see him.

"He did that new song," Kasper said. "'Tormented Exaltation.' I just wanted to tell you, so you know. But maybe you had agreed on that," he added quickly.

"No," his dad said wearily. "No, we didn't." He rubbed his hand across his face. "Well, that was fucking unnecessary of him. I don't know what . . . It's such an odd fucking thing to do. Disrespectful. What the hell was the point of that?"

"I don't know," Kasper said. "He didn't say it was a Dark Cruelty song, but there was a guy backstage who knew, so he's probably talked about it."

His dad sighed.

"Shit, I have to take this to the others."

"I hope I haven't ruined anything," Kasper said.

"Oh, Kasper," his dad said. "You're not the one who's done anything. It's that little . . . our new singer. What the hell is he up to? Ossian, shit. It's like he has to test our limits, like a fucking adolescent. A grown man, behaving like that." He sighed again. "Ah well, what's done is done. Anyway, I'm glad you told me. Or I would have seen it from somewhere else." His dad's face became pixelated. "So you were backstage too?"

"Yeah, and then there was some afterparty . . ." He might as well tell him. "This happened. Apparently."

He showed off the tattoo.

"Oh, shit, that doesn't look good." His father's face was in sharp focus again. He looked worried. "How did this happen?"

"I don't really know exactly. I was so fucking drunk."

It was a phrase his dad never heard him say before. Kasper remembered his father's words in the car. *Maybe you shouldn't hang out with Ossian.* He had been right about that. And what would he say if he found out the whole truth? That Ossian had forced Kasper to drink, that he had offered to connect him with Malte. His dad was going to absolutely lose it, Kasper realized. Maybe they'd cancel the whole reunion. And it would be Kasper's fault, because if he hadn't gone with Ossian, none of it would have happened.

"But it's fine," he said quickly. "I cleaned it and . . . I'll talk to Leah. I'm sure she can do a cover-up."

"Really, Kasper, how are you? I'm a bit worried," his dad said. "This isn't like you at all. Should I come home?"

He was prepared to do so, Kasper could tell. Even though he had six cities left on the tour.

"It might get a bit tricky with Milan," his father continued, "but we can probably fly down a replacement for the rest of the route."

Kasper said, "No, Dad, stop. I'm just at work all week anyway."

"You're not wearing yourself out, are you? Maybe you can stay with Anja instead—"

"What the hell," Kasper interrupted. "I get drunk one time and it's a massive deal. What the hell did you get up to at my age?"

Regret filled him as soon as he uttered the words. He was thinking about what Tony had told him, that his dad had gotten so hammered on the anniversary of Grim's death that he ended up in a sobering cell. He'd been Kasper's age.

"All right, fine," his dad said. "I just get worried, is all."

Kasper got it. But it was as if the frustration over everything he couldn't say turned into anger.

"Wait a sec," his dad said.

He angled the phone away and talked to someone. Then Leah's face came into the picture.

"Oh, hey, Kasper!" she said, in her familiar Dalarna accent.

He had completely forgotten that her band Black Hyssop would also be playing at the Swiss festival.

"What kind of shitty, homemade tat have you ended up with?" she said.

Kasper laughed. It was nice. In Leah's world, a drunken tattoo was a common problem that could be easily solved. She advised him how to look after it so it healed as well as possible.

"And once it's done, we'll take care of it, okay?"

When he hung up, he wondered if there was anything going on with Leah again. He could not help but hope. His dad had seemed so lonely since they broke up, and Kasper missed Leah.

His dad and Leah had been a couple for four years, and they lived together for two of those years. The end came six months before Kasper's collapse. It had been a friendly but sad separation. His dad had taken it hard when she moved out, which had probably contributed to him missing some signs of Kasper's illness. Leah had tried to keep in touch with Kasper, but by then he was already sinking into the darkness of depression.

After he got better, they tried to meet fairly regularly, go to the movies together or bowl. Both Kasper and Leah loved bowling. She was an important part of Kasper's life, and yet there was no word for their relationship. Could you be a bonus parent when you weren't in the family any longer?

Kasper took care of the tattoo and drank another glass of water. He went into the bedroom and rubbed at the bloodstain on the mattress with cold water, then wrote down everything Ossian had said to him in a document. Then he went back to his sketchbook. The drawings retained their ability to fascinate, and yet he thought something about them had changed. It was as if they had come to him from some other place, a place that suddenly scared him. He pulled out a drawer and dropped the book in, pulled out a completely unused one instead. Only then did he realize how late he was.

Soon, he was racing down the escalators at the train station and through the passage. On his way down to the trains, he saw that water had accumulated in the platform's V-shaped roof. White clouds reflected in the still surface. He saw the train coming in, quickened his pace, hurried through the doors, and threw himself into a seat, panting.

He put his headphones on and picked up his phone to listen to music. But then he got the strange feeling that there was something he should see.

He opened his photo app. He recognized Ossian's arm due to the other tattoos around his fresh Grim tattoo. Naturally, it looked better than Kasper's. The tattoo artist had probably tried to focus, and besides, Ossian was the type that could sport a shitty homemade tat. Kasper felt slightly sick when he saw the picture. Who had taken it? Had he? Had Ossian?

He scrolled backward.

A series of photos of two people in a dim room. The faces were blurry, vague. But Kasper thought he recognized Ossian. Who was the man he was talking to? Kasper could only discern gray hair, pale skin.

Malte?

Cold sweat came pouring out of Kasper. It could be him. Or not. Why had Kasper taken these pictures? A mistake, or an attempt at gathering evidence?

Kasper closed his eyes and felt how the hangover went from bad to horrible. This day, he was sure, would be hell.

THE CHOICE

When something breaks, it can happen all at once: one blow and then a thousand scattered pieces. But sometimes it takes a while before you realize what has happened. The mark fades, but something on the inside has ruptured, is slowly bleeding out. Someone should stem the flow, but who wants to fail at it? In the moment, it's easier to wait and see. Maybe the damage will heal by itself. Sometimes it actually does. Or, one day, you notice that it's already too late.

They are waiting in the rehearsal space.

Grim is lying on the dirty floor, his black hair a fan around his head. Håkan thinks it looks as if he's falling. Håkan is sitting on an old, broken throne someone's left behind. For some reason, the other bands use this room as their dumping ground. Håkan tries to calibrate his position so that the seat of the stool stays straight, but it keeps tilting. Tony is drumming in the air, occasionally brushing against a cymbal. Meanwhile, Malte paces back and forth on the small space not currently occupied by clutter and Grim's prone body. When something blocks him, he turns dramatically, pausing with a frown before starting up again. It looks as if he's practicing an angry little speech in his head. A talking-to. Håkan hopes he's wrong, because that is the last thing they need.

He looks at the plastic clock that hangs askew over the door. It's only been fifteen minutes but feels like much longer. Since they recorded, Ernesto has been late to every single rehearsal. Once, he arrived forty minutes in, and they had to start without him. Ernesto mumbled an excuse and then played like crap for the rest of the rehearsal.

A muted sound of cheesy guitars comes from another band that is rehearsing. Outside, Håkan knows, the sun's out. It's a bright evening in May, the air fresh, the scent of flowers and moist greenery in the air. It's the kind of evening you take to be warmer than it actually is, and you walk around shivering with cold, but it's fine, the light is right there. The days expand. Summer awaits them.

But in this dusty room, the May evening feels far away. Only faint light reaches them through the barred, grimy windows, and they need to rehearse. The record is going to be delivered soon; they're going to sort out more gigs, maybe even abroad. But Grim hasn't been talking about that lately. Håkan has noticed that he doesn't take notes in his little black book anymore, that his letters remain unopened for days. The silence has crept back in. Except when he's talking to Malte on the phone, which he does a few times per week. His words come pouring out; Håkan can hear it through the door, the door Grim has started to shut when he's on the phone. It hurts Håkan more than he cares to admit.

Now he's staring at the clock, feeling his irritation growing with every tick of the second hand. Steps approach in the corridor and the door opens, letting in Ernesto in his denim jacket and home-made Pentagram T-shirt. Since he got himself a moped, he's trailed by the scent of fuel exhaust and two-stroke oil.

"Sorry," he mutters, putting his helmet on the floor and bringing out the guitar. "What are we playing?"

Håkan sighs. He wants to pour all of his frustration onto Ernesto's head, but the mood in the rehearsal room has been off since they recorded. They're balancing on a knife's edge; Håkan can feel it. So he picks up his instrument. Malte follows.

But Grim is still on the floor.

"Are you serious?" Grim says.

"What?" Ernesto says.

"Are you serious about the band?"

"Grim . . ." Håkan begins.

"Who the fuck are you to ask me that?" Ernesto snarls. "I was in the band before you were."

"Hey, calm down," Tony says. "Let's just play some music."

"You're always late," Grim points out without getting up.

"He is," Malte mutters.

Ernesto whirls around.

"You shut your mouth," he hisses. "Got it?"

"Grim, just leave it. Let's go," Håkan says.

"I'm not talking to someone who's lying on the fucking floor," Ernesto says.

Grim sits up slowly, removes a piece of old candy wrapper that's tangled in his hair. He looks at Ernesto. Blinks.

"I moved to Stockholm for Dark Cruelty."

"What has that got to do with anything?"

"You said you were in the band before I was," Grim says, getting to his feet. "Yes, you were, but I'm still more dedicated to it than you are."

He's angry. No, he's furious. Håkan has never seen him like this, has only seen Grim direct his rage toward bands and musicians he despises, against himself when he thinks he's not good enough. Never at another person.

"I'm here even though I have school *and* work *and* take care of my kid!" Ernesto shouts.

"We have to wait for you every single time!" Grim points at Ernesto. "You're not taking this seriously."

"Say that one more time," Ernesto says, ripping his guitar off himself and taking a step toward Grim, who blinks, raises his hands.

"I get it," Håkan says, grabbing hold of Ernesto. "Linda's a nag."

Ernesto spins around, staring at him.

"What the fuck are you talking about? Linda?"

Håkan is bewildered. He's heard Ernesto complain that Linda would prefer it if he stayed at home every night.

"Well, yeah," he mumbles. "She wants you around all the time, doesn't she?"

"Because she's going insane!" Ernesto screams, his voice breaking. "You don't understand what it's like! He's always crying!"

"Isn't that what babies do?" Håkan mutters.

"All the fucking time!" Ernesto shouts, and it's as if someone's pulled out a plug, it all comes pouring out. "He cries for hours! Do you get it? Colic! Do you even know what that is? It's fucking torture! You think he's done and then he starts again, and there's nothing you can do, nothing you can say to comfort him, because he's just a little baby, you have to protect him, and he's in so much pain, and there's absolutely *nothing* you can do."

His breathing is rapid, his hands balled into fists.

"It really sucks," Tony says quietly. "My youngest sister was colicky."

"But you all think I should just ignore it, right?" Ernesto demands, as if he hasn't heard Tony speak. He looks from Håkan to Grim, ignoring Malte. "You feel like I shouldn't take care of my own child? That I should let Linda deal with it?"

Håkan blushes, because he's definitely thought that Linda, who is a full-time mother at the moment, could take care of the kid herself. He'd assumed babies were mostly interested in their mothers, anyway.

"Let's just get started," Tony tries again.

"Or he chooses."

It's Malte. Malte has opened his fucking mouth again and is glaring at Ernesto with something dark in his eyes.

The words Ernesto says to Malte are ones he isn't proud of later. Still, he says them. Then he leaves.

When he slams the door, the clock falls off the wall.

Håkan's heart is pounding so hard his field of vision trembles. He breathes through his nose, tries to suck air into his lungs.

"His choice," he hears Malte say.

Håkan doesn't look at him when he removes the bass and races for the door, tears it open and heads toward the exit. The sound of drums, playing off-rhythm, can be heard from one of the rooms. Why didn't he run at once? What if he doesn't catch up?

He stumbles through the door, sees the sun glint in Ernesto's helmet where he's straddling his moped, trying to kickstart without succeeding.

"Wait!" Håkan shouts, running toward him.

Ernesto slams a hand down on the carburetor and then proceeds to fumble with the shut-off valve.

"Hey," Håkan says breathlessly, stopping beside him. "Come on."

"Come on?" Ernesto repeats, but he puts his foot back on the ground.

"It all went wrong. Let's go back in. Let's forget about it."

"Son of a bitch," Ernesto says, tilting his head back and taking a deep, sniffling breath.

Håkan realizes he's crying and looks away, not wanting to embarrass him. Ernesto sniffles again, pressing the sleeve of his denim jacket to his eyes.

"So you're letting Malte decide now, is that it?" he says, lowering his arm.

"What?" Håkan says. "What are you talking about?"

"He said I had to choose."

Håkan can feel his frustration coming to a boil.

"And you left!" he says. "You were the one who let him decide!"

"You said we'd kick him out if he was a problem," Ernesto reminds him. "You both said it, you and Grim."

"What has that got to do with it?" Håkan asks.

"So you think I'm the problem?"

"You're the one who's always late!"

Ernesto jerks back as if Håkan has hit him. His Adam's apple moves when he swallows rapidly. And Håkan wonders what he's actually said, what actually just happened. All he knows is that he's close to ruining everything and the panic makes it impossible for him to think clearly.

"Please," he says. "Stop it. Come on."

"Come on," Ernesto mimics him. "Come on, come on. Is that all you can say?"

"Well, fuck off, then!" Håkan yells.

Ernesto spits.

"I quit," he says, and he attempts a kickstart again.

This time, the moped roars to life. The moped starts running and Ernesto sets off along the bunker-like building. Håkan shouts for him, but his voice is drowned out by the trimmed engine.

When he gets back to the rehearsal room, everyone turns to him.

"He left," he says.

He can't say that Ernesto has quit, doesn't want to believe it. He thinks he can convince him to come back, to change his mind.

"Good," Malte says.

"Shut up," Håkan tells him.

"You heard what he said to me, didn't you?" Malte's cheeks have gone red. "You heard it? Grim, you heard it."

He loves this, Håkan thinks. He loves the fact that Ernesto lost control. Had it been his plan all along?

"Did he quit?" asks Grim, who is slumped over on the amp.

Håkan says nothing, which is an answer in itself.

"We don't have a lead guitarist," Grim concludes, and Håkan can sense his dejection.

"Yeah, you all handled this one really well," Tony says quietly.

"I can learn Ernesto's parts," Malte says.

"Good luck," Håkan snaps.

He looks at Grim, who doesn't say anything. His eyes are fixed on the floor. And Håkan wonders how the hell they ended up like this.

KASPER

It took time for the tattoo to heal.

The first week, it itched so badly that it was driving Kasper insane. If it hadn't been for the distraction of work, he might have scratched until he drew blood. He didn't show it to anyone at Grönan. Not until the final party, when he got drunk for the second time in his life. He tried to tell Santiago about what had happened as a kind of funny story, but he only got a pitying look. "Be careful, will you?" was the last thing Santiago said, and then gave him a long hug. It was indeed Santiago's final season at Grönan. Kasper realized they might never see each other again and the thought made him sadder than he'd expected.

He wore long sleeves at school, but one day in the cafeteria, he removed his hoodie without thinking. Lydia, Raman, and Lo stared at his arm. Again, he tried to gloss it over. Make it seem like a funny, slightly crazy drinking story. But as he was speaking, he knew he was failing; all he did was paint a tragic picture of a person who had gone through school all prim and proper, suddenly deciding to let loose and party in the final year. Maybe he really was that kind of person. Raman's and Lo's laughter sounded strained, and they mostly seemed a bit shocked. "That's terrible, it almost sounds like an assault," Lydia said, clearly upset. Kasper tensed, told them he had to go to the bathroom. He stood there, heart pounding. *An assault. Lydia overstated it, of course*, he thought. But ever since that night, he'd felt somehow dirty. Infected. As if those nightmarish parasites that live in some insects had entered him, were eating him, one organ at a time.

That's how he felt. Hollow. He longed for the routine of The House, found school so meaningless. Everyone was ahead of him in their final projects. He hadn't even started on the essay, and he was getting nowhere with the pictures of Grim. But that was not the worst of it. He had promised himself that he'd find out what happened to Grim, and he was nowhere near succeeding. He had to push on. Get further inside. But how? He had read everything there was on the Internet, and Ernesto had gone on tour with Vile Prophets.

And then there was his dad.

It felt as though he and Kasper were moving around each other in some kind of complicated dance, his dad trying to dodge the moment Kasper would say: "Can we talk about Grim?" It was so obvious that his father genuinely feared that moment, and it made Kasper shy away from raising the subject.

Even though the weeks passed, the tattoo continued to itch. The ink had spread under the skin, and it looked uglier than ever. His mom had gone white-hot with rage when she saw it for the first time, seemingly ready to murder Ossian with her bare hands. "Who the fuck does he think he is?" she said. "What the hell is he doing?" Kasper almost found himself defending Ossian. He and his mom quickly made up, but Kasper couldn't understand his own behavior.

On Christmas Eve, everyone celebrated at his mom and Atle's, his dad, too. His stepbrother Tor was in New Zealand and phoned from there. "I've heard you've been a huge win for Grönan," he told Kasper, but Kasper didn't want to talk about it. He asked about the black beaches on the North Island, if Tor had seen them. He hadn't, not yet. "It's a great place to surf," he said. "But the currents are very dangerous. They can pull you out to sea."

Often, Kasper lay awake at night, phone on. Zoomed in and out on the pale, blurred photos of the man who talked to Ossian. Though the images stayed unfocused, he returned to them again and again.

✳

One afternoon in January, Kasper was sitting in an armchair inside Lilith Tattoo in Gröndal, watching Leah make her preparations. It was cold outside, nearly five degrees, and even his dad had reluctantly donned the winter jacket he loathed so deeply. The studio's large windows had fogged up. The walls were covered with framed sketches and stylish photos of customers' tattoos. On a long shelf attached to the wall were animal skulls and pieces of art. A statue of the goddess Ishtar. Artemis, the goddess of hunting and the moon, pulled back her bow. Music was playing, specifically Dead Can Dance, one of Leah's and his dad's favorite bands, which she had introduced to Kasper.

Leah had disinfected everything on the station and was covering the table and armrest with plastic. There was something reassuring in seeing her perform the routine; Kasper had practically been raised in tattoo studios. The mild, chemical smell of surface disinfectants made him feel secure. When he was a kid, he used to come along when his dad and mom were getting inked, sitting and browsing the folders with motifs for hours, then drawing his own. When Leah was with his dad, Kasper had occasionally watched her work. Once, he got to hold the machine and tattoo an orange. Now, it was his turn to lie under the needle. He was nervous, but mostly he looked forward to it. He had waited so long. His healing process had been unusually drawn-out, and then Leah had been on the road and in the studio with Black Hyssop.

Kasper had decided to own those four letters, the name on his arm. He was more entitled to it than Ossian. But he wanted it on his terms, in his own version. He had worked out a sketch that he liked and that Leah thought would work, and then he allowed her to make some final improvements. He knew there was a difference between what a picture looked like on paper and what it looked like on skin. And so: it was time.

He knew it would hurt, but for some reason he looked forward to it. He just wanted something to happen, wanted to feel *something*. Lately, he had been walking around with a thick mist in his head. When others talked, he often disappeared into his thoughts. In the black of winter, the days ran together, one looking much like another. During the Christmas holidays, he had stayed a lot at his mom's house. Some nights he had sneaked into her study, looked through her photos from the late eighties. Stared at the pictures of the younger selves of the adults around him, and the one who never got to turn twenty. Kasper had grown up with stories of the time that had been sealed in by his mom's photos: stories characterized by nostalgia, a nostalgia that had infected him, even though he had never experienced that time himself. But what he felt now when he saw the pictures was something else. A kind of desperation, an impossible desire to be able to repeal the laws of nature, stretch through time and space and grab Grim's worn jacket, pull him to safety.

Not a day went by without him thinking about Grim. It was only right that he had this name on his arm.

"Come on over," Leah said.

Kasper got up and went to the station. They were alone in the studio, both of Leah's colleagues being abroad. It felt strange to be subject to the routine that he had seen her perform on so many others. First, she sprayed disinfectant on his left arm and wiped it off. With her glove-covered hands, she took a disposable razor and shaved the inside of his forearm. Nothing could get in the way of the sharp, sensitive needle.

"Are you nervous?" Leah said, smoothing stencil fluid over his arm.

"Yes," Kasper said, then he laughed.

"Thanks for telling me," she said with a smile, carefully pressing the stencil against his skin. "The customers who have fainted are guys who claimed not to be nervous at all." She removed the paper and inspected the results. "Super. This'll look amazing. And no one will notice the old tattoo beneath. Have a look, tell me what you think."

Kasper turned toward the full-figure mirror, then felt a tingle of anticipation run through his body when he saw the contours of the four letters on his arm.

"Looks good," he told her honestly.

"Have a seat then," said Leah.

He did, putting his arm up on the armrest. On the table next to it were small cups filled with black ink, held in place with a dab of Vaseline on the underside.

"I'm getting started now," Leah warned. "If it gets to be too much, just let me know. I'm thinking we'll take a break, have a bite of something."

She started the machine, which buzzed like a combative, robotic wasp. To Kasper, it sounded like home. It turned out that the pain, too, was familiar, a stinging, burning sensation, like that challenge where people rubbed an eraser against their skin.

"Were you in the studio when they were recording?" Leah asked him.

"Yeah, I went by."

It had been a couple of weeks ago, and Kasper had hesitated before going. He had no desire to see Ossian again. But then he found out that Vanbörd had a gig in Copenhagen on the first day of recording, when Tony was tracking the drums. When Kasper came to the studio, the mood was one of excitement. They had just taken a break, and Tony's T-shirt was patchy with sweat, a red mark over his right eyebrow.

"I broke a drumstick and it hit me smack-bang in the face," he laughed, popping open an alcohol-free beer in the lounge. "You should report it as a workplace accident, you know."

Hasse chuckled. Fredda, who owned the studio, stood next to him, smiling.

"You need Lehtonen insurance when you let him inside the studio," Kasper's dad said, and Tony laughed even harder.

"Do you remember when you threw a stick in my face that time?" Ernesto said.

"Yeah, you were so pissed off!" Tony said.

"I was halfway through the door," Ernesto said. "But Grim convinced me to stay. In his own way, of course."

He smiled and shook his head, then looked at Kasper.

"Sorry I haven't responded to your e-mail, by the way. I'll be in touch soon, promise."

Now Kasper sat in the tattoo chair and wondered if it would happen. He had never really understood why Ernesto dropped out of Dark Cruelty, but he knew that an argument with Grim was part of it. Ernesto might not be so keen on talking about it.

"The reunion seems to be good for Håkan," Leah said. Kasper wasn't certain, but it seemed like she and his dad were dating again. They had seen a lot of each other since that festival in Switzerland. Leah laughed a little and went on: "I actually can*not* believe he quit smoking."

Kasper thought about the head-on collision with the wild boar last autumn. Miraculously, his dad had stayed away from cigarettes ever since.

He looked at Leah's hands. Her movements were precise and routine. He watched as she let the needle work, wiped ink off with some paper, smoothed on Vaseline, put the needle to the skin again.

"Why are you doing your project on Grim?" she asked.

Leah had the ability to ask direct questions without it feeling intrusive. Kasper fumbled for an answer.

"Don't know, I . . . there's a lot of questions. And he's almost been like a family member."

"Yeah, and you have his name," Leah said, dipping the needle back into the ink. "A name can be a powerful bond."

Kasper felt his stomach drop. It reminded him of what Ossian had said.

"How do you mean?"

"Our names are important to our identity," said Leah, who was carefully filling in the contours of the letters. "The names we get or choose to assume. There are lots of magic ideas about names, too. I read that in some cultures, you can't name a child after a living relative, 'cause it can kill the older person."

"And in folklore, telling magical creatures your name is dangerous, because it gives them power over you," Kasper added, wincing with pain when the needle burned across the skin.

"Yeah, exactly," said Leah. "But it works the other way, too. You can defeat a creature if you get its true name."

"But why do you think it matters?" said Kasper. "That Grim and I share a name?"

Leah raised the needle and looked up.

"I think it matters to you. So it's no wonder you're interested in finding out more about who he was."

And what happened to him.

She started up again and Kasper bit his lip.

"He seems to have been something else," she said. "I was only ten when he died, but I heard about him in junior high. There was this small group of elitist metalheads, all guys, in my school, and they worshipped Grim. Malte was one of their heroes, too, so I wasn't really excited to listen to Dark Cruelty at first. Bad vibes."

"I get it," Kasper told her.

The idea of people lumping in Malte with the rest of the members of Dark Cruelty was unpleasant, even though Kasper understood why it happened.

"Shit, it was pretty tough, being a metalhead and a girl, then and there," Leah said. "People around you were either wannabe Vikings or really smug bastards. I went to one gig once . . . I was fifteen and had been arguing for them to let me in, even though the minimum was eighteen, 'cause I was reviewing it for the school mag. And I was the only girl there. The first thing that happened was that a guy twice my age quizzed me like the KGB about Angel Witch, because I was wearing an Angel Witch shirt. Then another man came and put his arm around me and said he would 'protect me' . . . I ran and hid with the sound guy. I guess he felt sorry for me and got what was going on, so he let me hang out there. Stood with him at every gig after that. Fimpen, a pearl among swine. But I must have told you . . ."

"Not that thing about Fimpen," Kasper said with a smile.

"Still going strong, actually," Leah said. "He helped out when we played in Borlänge."

Leah often said that things had improved in the scene, both for female musicians and fans, but Kasper had seen for himself how wariness had become a part of her. He saw it when she was in public, heard it in her voice when she was doing interviews. She was careful, guarded, and did not laugh as freely as she did otherwise.

"But anyway, when I met Håkan, I got a much more nuanced picture of Grim," Leah continued. "And he was fucking huge, in what little time he had. Too bad they're replacing him with Ossian."

Kasper broke out in a cold sweat, not knowing whether it was due to the pain or the mention of Ossian.

"Sorry," said Leah. "Got a bit too honest there."

"He's a great singer," Kasper said without inflection.

"Yeah, he's trying to sound like Grim," Leah said with a crooked smile. "Shit, I'm such a bitch. He's great, I just have a hard time liking him." She paused. "Have you met my friend Igor?"

"I don't think so."

"He was a guitarist in Vanbörd for a while," Leah said.

She lifted the needle then, blessedly, and sprayed on a mix of aloe vera and witch hazel to soothe the skin. Then she wiped it off, very gently.

"What was that like?" Kasper made another involuntary face when the needle returned to his arm.

"It's been quite a rotation with the members," Leah told him. "I don't think Ossian wants it that way, think he has some vision of a loyal little gang, but there's always chaos around him somehow. In the beginning, it's just 'brother, my brother,' but as soon as someone contradicts him, they're out. I think it would be better for him if he was honest about it, just said 'my band, my rules.' But fuck it. Dark Cruelty is only doing a few gigs, and it sounded really good, what came out of the studio."

"Mmm," Kasper said, because it really had.

"Oh, and I get that it can be difficult to say no to him," Leah said. "He's a charismatic son of a bitch."

"What do you mean?" said Kasper.

"I just assumed that getting inked at that party was Ossian's idea."

"I don't really remember," Kasper ground out.

He was definitely in pain now, but he made himself consider what she'd said. Apparently, Leah ran in circles that touched Ossian's, and she was interested in religion and the occult. Maybe she could explain what Ossian had been talking about at the party. But how much should Kasper broach the subject with her?

The pain ceased when Leah lifted the needle, sprayed the area and wiped it. Kasper tried to be brave.

"Ossian said a bunch of things that night. He seems to think there's some kind of bond between him and Grim. And between Grim and me. And then he talked about, like, patterns."

"What kind of patterns?" Leah asked.

"He said they're everywhere. You just have to see them and use them. Something like that, I think."

"Pretty standard magic notion," Leah said. "The existence of hidden patterns and connections in our world, that magicians can learn to interpret and exploit. The idea that everything is connected, that the big things are also in the small things. It's a bit like that poem by William Blake. *To see a world in a grain of sand, / and a heaven in a wildflower, / hold infinity in the palm of your hand, / and eternity in an hour.*"

"Nice," Kasper said.

But he wasn't sure he understood what it all meant, which he also told Leah.

"Okay, so it's like this," she said, dipping the needle back into the ink. "Some people think that whatever happens around us reflects larger goings-on in the universe. But they think it works the other way around, too. The powers that exist in the universe are also in the magician. A magician can learn to channel those powers and influence their environment by performing ritual acts, or concentrating their will. So the planet Mars is responsible for violence and destruction, for instance. If the magician wants to destroy an enemy, they could perform a ritual using the colors, plants, and metals that are commonly associated with Mars. But it's the magician's focus and intention that's central and makes the ritual work."

"Does Ossian believe that?" said Kasper.

"I don't know what he believes in, exactly," Leah told him. "But I'm sure he feels a deep connection to Grim. And he's right about the same thing being true for you."

She had no idea how true it was. Kasper felt slightly shaky. He took some deep breaths, glanced at his left hand. The scar had turned white. Should he tell Leah what Ossian had said about the dreams, about what he had experienced?

But she'd just start worrying about his mental health. Burdening her with that felt wrong.

Instead, he asked about Black Hyssop and the album they'd recorded. And Leah asked him about school, but not in that awkward way some grown-ups do when they want to fill a silence. She was actually interested. Kasper started talking about his concerns for the future, told her about Lydia and her picture books, Raman and Marvel, Lo, who would definitely get into art school. But Kasper, he had no solid dreams or plans.

"I would like to draw, of course. But it's so hard to get anywhere by doing that. And I don't even know where I want to go."

"Have you thought about this?" said Leah, and switched to a magnum needle.

"What?" said Kasper. "I mean, thought about what?"

"Well, being a tattoo artist. You've always had an interest." Kasper stared at the needle moving over his skin, feeling a bit stupid that he had never even considered the possibility.

"How do you even go about that?" he got out.

"You start as an apprentice," Leah told him, and started filling in the letters. "There are courses you can apply to, but even if you get in, you need an apprenticeship."

"What does an apprentice do?"

"In the beginning, it's pretty basic stuff. Safety and sanitation. You clean and you draw. Eventually you get to practice on oranges for example. You tried that once, didn't you?"

Kasper's future had always seemed like an impenetrable darkness, but now it was as if Leah had handed him a flashlight that revealed a way forward. If he could bring himself to take it.

"Well, shit," he said. "Can't believe I've never thought about it."

Leah smiled.

"Sometimes we can't see the most obvious things," she said. "It took me ages before I realized I could actually play in bands. I just sat at home, practicing by myself. Anyway . . . the trickiest thing is getting an apprenticeship but you've got a head start."

"How?" said Kasper, unsure of where she was going with that.

Leah laughed and dipped the needle into the ink.

"I'm offering you an apprenticeship, basically," she said. "If you want one. And we can talk more about it later if you want. Or not. No pressure. But my door is always open."

"Thank you," Kasper managed, so overwhelmed he didn't know what else to say. Sometimes it felt like the worst and the best in life appeared out of nowhere. "Really, thank you," he added. "But honestly, do you think I could do it?"

"Yes, for sure," Leah said as she continued to fill in the tattoo. "Your drawings are really cool, and you're calm, sociable."

Had she just said that to be nice, or did she really have that image of him? Personally, he couldn't see it.

"Time for a break, I think. You look a little pale."

She turned off the machine. In the ensuing silence, the music played on. Kasper looked at Leah as she stood up, pulled off her black plastic gloves. He saw the tattoos on her body in a whole new way. Tender points. And possibilities. *Could I do that one day?* The idea was dizzying.

Leah disappeared into the kitchen to get snacks. Kasper lay still, focused on his breathing. He knew you could feel sick after getting a tattoo, but intense euphoria was also common. He felt a hint of it when he looked at the letters that were gradually growing on his arm. It was going to look so damn good. In his head, he'd already started working out the next tattoo.

The phone vibrated in Kasper's pocket. He picked it up and spotted the notification: a new post in a thread concerning Dark Cruelty.

Well it seems like M finally gave his opinion on the reunion. Wouldn't be surprised if we find them all with their throats slit heh

Kasper's pulse went up immediately. He clicked on the link, which led to a niche fanzine in which Malte had been interviewed in connection to the release of Nox Irredux's new EP.

I read that you dedicate the new EP Promethean Sepulcher to your old bandmate Grim. You have an acrimonious relationship with the rest of Dark Cruelty. You even threatened to kill them. How do you feel about your past with the band and the reunion?

I'm disappointed. I actually thought you were a decent interviewer before this question. But it's typical of how media and so-called "fans" reiterate the same concepts, ideas, and events. I admit bragging was part of the scene's problem in the '90s, that was the mistake many made. Too many evil deeds were committed in the open, leaving media and the general public to giggle like little girls with horror and delight at the spectacle. It made it possible for hipster journalists and spineless "metalheads" to dismiss truly unholy feats as the acts of pimple-faced virgins trying to impress their peers. The years have brought me wisdom enough to realize that our nefarious deeds must be executed in secret in order to make the pillars of this pathetic world crumble. Grim was one of those rare people that are put on this earth as a curse to most and a dark blessing to some, to make humanity catch a glimpse of the terrifying vastness of the great beyond. He was a pioneer, an immensely talented vocalist and songwriter who stared unflinchingly into the void and welcomed it. He would be enraged if he saw what the others have done to his legacy. I know this because we saw eye to eye on most things. I'm the only one who understood what he was trying to achieve, and I have stayed true to the abysmal goals that we set many years ago. I have no regrets. The other members of Dark Cruelty were weak. And the weak deserve no mercy.

"Are you okay?" Leah said when she came back.

She was balancing a tray with a glass of juice and a small bowl of nuts. She put it on a table next to Kasper, who handed her the phone and took a sip of juice. Saw the anger light up Leah's eyes as she read.

"That little *shit*," she spat. "Does Håkan know about this?"

"I don't know," Kasper told her. "I only saw it now."

"Don't give it more thought," Leah said, scrolling on. "Malte's full of it. He just wants everyone to know how 'true' he is. Most people laugh at him behind his back. He'd never really do anything."

Kasper didn't understand how she could be so sure. Weirdly, it was as if people didn't take Malte seriously, even when they knew what he was capable of.

Kasper pictured him again, the man from the Vanbörd gig, and felt almost convinced that it had been Malte. Nox Irredux was signed to a label whose parent company released Vanbörd's records. And Kasper had been checking up on the former tours of Vanbörd and Nox Irredux, noticing that their paths had crossed at several festivals. The rumors also said that the current drummer in Vanbörd, wearing the obligatory mask, had played with Nox Irredux a few times.

None of this would have meant anything, were it not for the fact that Ossian had suggested that Kasper should meet with Malte.

You may have already met him.

"You've got an e-mail," Leah said, handing him his phone back.

It was from Ernesto. He wanted to meet up.

THE LAKE

Ernesto is no longer in the band. Håkan finds this difficult to understand. Ernesto's absence is palpable, wrong. And not just because his technical skills made the songs better. It's more than that. Even though he could be moody and suspicious of change, he always did his utmost. He might not always like Håkan's and Grim's ideas, but he believed in Dark Cruelty. His conviction was part of what carried the band, and now it's faltering. Håkan no longer knows how to run the band without connecting with Grim, and Grim feels farther and farther away, despite the two of them sleeping in the same room. He can't lean on Tony because Tony just wants to play. And Malte is driven, but doesn't really care about the band. On the contrary, he's destroying it.

Malte shouldn't be there. Håkan becomes more and more sure of it. He's got to bring it up with Grim, but they also need to talk about all the practicalities of releasing the record. Håkan has tried to talk about it at home, at work, on their way to rehearsal. But Grim only responds with evasion, doesn't join in and build on the ideas like he used to.

On a Sunday night when Tony is babysitting and Malte is at dinner with relatives, Grim and Håkan are alone in the rehearsal space. It's the perfect opportunity for a real talk, but Grim has a new idea for a song. It's the first time in a very long time that he's working on anything new. He has some riffs and a quote from a poem by William Blake.

"Listen," he says, and reads. *"Every night and every morn, / some to misery are born, / every morn and every night, / some are born to sweet delight, / some are born to sweet delight, / some are born to endless night."*

"Awesome," says Håkan. "A little too soft for us, maybe. A bit too The Cure."

"Yeah," Grim says, his smile crooked. "We've got to toughen it up."

When they leave the rehearsal, Grim suddenly announces that he has to take off. Håkan nods, disappointed. Grim takes a few steps forward, but then he turns around.

"Are you coming with?"

It's the first time Grim has taken Håkan on one of his secret wanderings. The first and last, but Håkan doesn't realize that, when the two of them get off at Central Station, after having left their instruments at home. Grim is silent, his gaze fixed on the ground as they walk toward the subway. They pass the map, where they've met up with friends so many times. Now there's only one lonely lady with a suitcase there, and one lonely pigeon pecking at the ground. There are hardly any people around; the nine-to-fivers are at home in bed. They take the escalator down to the green line and barely catch a train, collapsing on the brownish seats. Grim leans his head against the window and Håkan looks at him. Why is it so hard to talk again? In the rehearsal, everything had felt fine.

Håkan gets up when Grim gets up, and they step off the train, Håkan following Grim to the end of the platform. The tracks snap and pop, and Håkan soon feels a rush of wind before another train comes thundering through the tunnel. The brakes squeal and the doors open with a hiss. A few travelers get off. One man wearing a hat has a pipe in his hand that seems too long to light. The doors close and the train rattles on again. Grim watches it go, waiting for the last passengers to leave the platform. Then he hops down onto the track.

Håkan is frozen. He thinks about when Stasse and Dimman ran around on the tracks a few times, lay down under the protruding edge of the platform when a train rolled in. Håkan never dared to try it.

"Come on," says Grim, disappearing into the tunnel.

Håkan quickly looks around and then walks up to the edge, carefully lets himself down onto the track. When his feet hit the ground, he feels himself go light-headed. What if he falls forward and grabs the third rail? One of the few things he remembers from his short time practicing to be an electrician is the teacher who told him that the current in that rail is so strong that your hand will stick to it, and then you fry. "There are those who have survived," the teacher said. "But they have to make do with one hand." Håkan hurries toward Grim, who is a bit farther into the tunnel.

"But the trains," Håkan chokes out.

"I know the schedules," Grim says.

He swings around and walks into the dark. Håkan quickens his steps and ends up right behind Grim. They're heading in the direction of the trains. When the light from the platform no longer reaches them, Grim pulls a flashlight from his jacket pocket and lights their way. The air is warm and completely still. The gravel crunches under their feet as they follow the tracks. It smells like burning train brakes. Håkan has difficulty determining how far they've gone when Grim stops. He steps over the third rail, first with one leg and then the other. Håkan turns his flashlight onto the tracks and follows his example on shaky legs, first with one foot and then the other, but he ends up sideways and slips on the rough gravel, catches himself with a hand against the damp stone wall.

"Shit," Håkan mumbles, heart in his throat.

The beam of light is directed away from him as Grim continues into a side tunnel. It's big enough to hold a train, but there's no rail going into it. The ground is no longer covered by gravel; it feels more like a wet, sandy beach under Håkan's shoes.

"What is this place?" Håkan says.

"I think it was a line they started to build," replies Grim. His voice echoes through the tunnel. "And then they changed their minds."

He directs the flashlight straight ahead and it hits a brick wall covered in graffiti. Håkan thinks it's a dead end before he sees the narrow stairs right next to the wall. Grim is on his way there; Håkan follows.

How did Grim find this place? Has he wandered through the tunnels, discovered it on his own? Or was someone with him? Malte? Håkan can't imagine Malte down here in the tunnels, considering he wept with fear during the ritual.

The stairs are steep and end at a steel door. Someone broke the lock and they can just walk in. There's a room inside the rock holding two gigantic fans, both covered in graffiti. Grim shines the light on the fans, and Håkan sees them move ever so slightly. There must be a shaft where wind gets in, a shaft leading up to the world above ground, where the chestnuts have opened their leaves and pale flowers shine in the bright night. That world feels very remote.

"Why are there fans?" Håkan asks.

"If there's a fire, they empty the tunnels of toxic smoke."

Grim points the light toward another part of the room. Håkan notices a coiled fire hose underneath a table. The only thing that can be heard is the sound of dripping water, but Håkan thinks of the graffiti he's seen, thinks that other people have come here. What if they come across someone else? Someone who wanted to hurt them? He can almost feel the darkness behind him when they start walking again, how it presses against him.

The room narrows and the floor turns into crosshatching beneath Håkan's feet. They're crossing the tracks on a kind of bridge, he realizes, and the next moment the rails below them start to sing with an approaching train. Grim puts a hand on his shoulder.

"Look down," he says, and he turns off the flashlight.

Håkan senses the rush of wind, watches lights cut a path through the darkness with the train rattling behind them. The room fills with a deafening roar when it passes under them. He's expecting the grate beneath them to shake from the force, but it barely moves. The train disappears and the silence takes over, the air going dead. It's pitch-black.

"Grim?" Håkan whispers.

An awful, guttural sound, and the flashlight illuminates Grim's face from below. Håkan and Tony used to do that when they were little and told each other ghost stories. Håkan laughs, thinks Grim trying to scare him is a good sign. Anything but silence is a good sign.

"Fuck you," Håkan says, even though it didn't scare him.

Grim rewards him with a short laugh and turns away, continues across the bridge. Håkan feels a thrill of anticipation. Why had he been so jumpy? This place is fantastic. Something they can tell people about later, like Anja, who would love this place. They can take another band photo in here after Håkan has talked to Grim about Malte. They can kick him out, get Ernesto back in, and then a new guitarist. Håkan has heard that Olle in Vomitator has started getting sick of the other people in the band not taking it as seriously as him.

Håkan just has to find the right time to talk to Grim.

It is only many years later, one night when Håkan's trying to sleep on a tour bus with Exenterate, that he realizes why he didn't bring it up. He was terrified that Grim would feel forced to choose between him and Malte. He was terrified of not being chosen, and he let himself be guided by that fear. Another thing to blame himself for in the night, stuck on the highway, while Adde snored in the bed beneath him. If he'd only made himself ask, Grim might have chosen him. And then the chain of events would have been different, everything could have been different and Grim could still be alive.

But *if* and *if not* are yet to become Håkan "Maimer" Nordin's constant companions. At this moment, he's following Grim into the tunnel that opens up on the other side of the footbridge. Barely wide enough for two of them to go side by side. Grim reaches up a hand and touches the ceiling, continues whistling a riff from "Curse of the Lost." Håkan smiles in the dark. This is their adventure, his and Grim's. Perhaps not everything has changed as much as he feared.

"I'm moving out," Grim tells Håkan.

"What?" says Håkan. "Why?"

It's a stupid question. Grim would obviously want his own apartment, if he could find one. He was turning twenty in a few months. Who wants to stay at a friend's mother's house forever? Besides, if Grim gets his own apartment, Håkan can visit whenever he wants. Maybe even move in, eventually. Then a thought strikes him.

"You're not moving home, are you?"

"Home?" Grim says blankly.

"Yeah, like to Timrå."

"That's not home anymore," Grim says, and then he tells Håkan the rest of his story. Stasse has gotten hold of a pad on Tegnérgatan through his uncle. Two bedrooms. "So I get my own," says Grim.

"Great," says Håkan.

Tegnérgatan. Just down the hill from the graveyard at St. John's, where they sometimes end up after buying records. Right in the middle of the city. With Stasse. Jealousy almost overwhelms Håkan. Stasse takes everything: first Anja, now Grim. Fucking Stasse.

They move deeper into the mountain. The sound of dripping water grows stronger. Håkan reaches out, touching one hand to each wall. It gives him the illusion that he could hold them back if they start coming closer, like the garbage compactor in *Star Wars*. That scene always stresses him out, definitely more than any horror film ever has.

"And I got a job at Raw Power," Grim tells him. "So I'm not going to be sorting mail anymore."

Håkan, who has barely recovered from the first shock, reels. Raw Power. It's a record store in Gamla Stan that sells metal, punk, and hardcore.

"Wicked," says Håkan. "Congratulations."

He should be happy about this, having a friend who works in a record store. It's just that they've shared every day for over a year, and in a few minutes, Grim has devastated it.

"You're not leaving the band, are you?" Håkan says.

"What?" says Grim. "Why would I do that?"

"Just a joke," says Håkan. "I just got a bit . . . It was a bit sudden. So I was a little surprised."

"Maybe I can get you a job, too," Grim suggests.

"Yeah. Cool."

He is blinded by the flashlight when Grim turns around.

"We're here," he says.

The path continues for a bit, but Grim directs the beam of light to the right. A metal staircase leads down a narrow tunnel, from which the dripping sound is coming.

"You first," Grim says.

Håkan swallows. Twice. But he puts his hands on the cold, rusty handrails and begins the journey underground, Grim behind him. The stairs screech and shift beneath their combined weight.

"One step at a time." Grim's voice is calm.

He illuminates the area around Håkan's feet. Håkan tries to see what's down there but only perceives the stairs ending with a rusty platform, made of the same kind of grating as the bridge. A ladder is attached to the platform. A ladder that disappears into the dark.

Håkan reaches the bottom step of the stairs.

"Stop," Grim whispers, and Håkan does.

Grim takes a small stone out of his pocket and throws it. There's a splash. Håkan stares at the rings that spread on the surface of the water just a few inches from his feet. The water is so clear that he didn't even see it.

"The Lake," Grim whispers behind him.

"What?" Hakan whispers back.

"It's what it's called," Grim says softly. "No one knows why they drilled this shaft. Or where it leads."

Håkan feels overcome with dizziness when he looks down at the water, his eyes following the rungs of the ladder down and down. They're covered in some sort of yellowish-brown sediment. Why would you attach a ladder to the platform, right where the stairs end? Why was the staircase even here?

"Wicked." He sounds weak.

Grim moves toward Håkan, who backs up against the railing. They end up face-to-face before Grim continues past him and down.

"What are you doing?" Håkan whispers.

He can't explain why he whispers. There's something about this place, something about the cold that radiates from the rock, the moisture rising from the water. Grim gets onto the platform, which squeals beneath his weight. His leather jacket creaks when he crouches down, shines his flashlight into the clear water.

What if he drops his flashlight? Then they only have Håkan's flashlight to get back through the dark.

A splash when Grim puts his hand into the water. He moves it back and forth beneath the surface, like he's waving at something in the depths. Something that's resting there, waiting, something that can perceive movement and light, the heat from their bodies.

Håkan takes a step backward on the stairs. Grim turns his head and looks at him. There is a strange expression on his face, one that makes Håkan's pulse race. It reminds him of when Stasse and Dimman leaped down on the tracks, though Stasse and Dimman had only played with danger, hadn't wanted to die.

But Grim.

Håkan suddenly pictures Grim throwing himself into the water, sees him sink, the light from the flashlight fading before disappearing completely.

"Let's go, man."

Håkan's voice sounds steady, but his heart beats hard enough to burst through his chest.

"All right," says Grim, and he gets to his feet.

Håkan presses back against the railing, allowing Grim to squeeze past and walk ahead, even though he shudders at having the water at his back.

"Really cool place, man," Håkan says. "Thanks for showing me this."

Grim doesn't respond. Håkan just hears his steps going up the metal staircase.

They never talk about the Lake again.

KASPER

Kasper got off the bus in Ernesto's quiet suburb, removed his headphones. His breath was steaming. The January chill had turned into February chill. Snow creaked beneath his shoes as he walked alongside the road. He was cold. He was also nervous.

He would finally get to talk to Ernesto about Grim, but how much would he actually find out? Kasper had known Ernesto his entire life, but there was a distance between them. When Ernesto spoke to him, the rules were clear: an adult talking to a child. Maybe it was because Ernesto had become a father at such a young age.

Ossian's dad.

Kasper stopped at the gates leading into Ernesto's driveway and rang the buzzer. The eye of a small security camera watched him. Something about the iron gates made him think about a haunted house, which naturally made him think of The House. He'd just found out that the job as a UC at The House was his. He longed for it, but was also worried. What if it had been beginner's luck, being capable last year? Could he deal with the responsibility for an entire season?

A heavy weariness had settled in Kasper's head, refused to let go. Despite that, he slept badly. His thoughts spun around, around, around. He was trying to wake himself up now, be alert.

A brief, buzzing sound, and then the gates opened. Kasper started walking up the driveway.

It was the first time Kasper visited Ernesto's studio; it was in a small, windowless, free-standing, white house. There were instruments, recording equipment, and a coffee table. A television screen shared a wall with posters from tours, gold records, and photos. Kasper recognized some that his mom had taken: one black-and-white from the Dark Cruelty era and a couple of new ones of Vile Prophets. A wedding photo, too, in which Ernesto and Izzy were beaming with joy.

"Pretty neat, huh?" Ernesto looked around proudly.

"Definitely," Kasper said.

He hung his jacket on a hook, wiped his shoes and put them next to Ernesto's boots, on top of a local newspaper. The snow sticking to his soles slowly soaked into it.

"I wouldn't even have dreamed of something like this as a kid," he heard Ernesto say. "A rehearsal space with a fridge, that alone."

He opened the stainless-steel fridge. There was mineral water and a few bottles of soda. Milk for coffee. Grapes, too.

"Back then, you would have just stuffed it full of beers and soda. Nowadays, you have to stay away from everything that was fun back then, don't you? Even soda, it settles right here," Ernesto said, patting himself on the belly. "Enjoy it while you can."

He popped open a soda for Kasper and grabbed a mineral water for himself. The soda hissed when Kasper poured it. He sat down at the table opposite Ernesto.

"Just have to answer this e-mail," Ernesto said, thumbs flying across the phone screen.

Kasper put his own phone on the table between them, next to the candelabra from the *Ancient Bloodlust* photo and a fruit bowl. He considered not recording the conversation just because asking to felt so awkward. What if Ernesto said no? But he forced himself to, once Ernesto put the phone aside.

"It's just for my use," he assured him.

Ernesto looked a little doubtful, but he nodded and said it was fine as long as Kasper kept it to himself and deleted it when he was done with the project. Kasper promised, feeling his conscience sting a little, knowing he would send it to Iris.

He started the recording and removed his hoodie.

"Oh, look at that," Ernesto, who'd just seen his tattoo, said.

Kasper had been nervous when he'd peeled off the transparent, protective film in the shower after the first days. But even then, it looked good. Then he'd dutifully rubbed a reasonable amount of salve onto it. The letters, drawn in his own font, shone blackly against his pale skin. A part of him now.

"Leah's great," Ernesto said, and Kasper wondered if he was thinking about Ossian's tattoo. "Right, I was going to show you something," he added.

Ernesto grabbed the remote and turned on the TV, fiddling with his phone. A paused, blurry image showed up on the huge screen.

"I just got this from Ture, the bassist in Exenterate before your dad took it on. We used to skate a bit and I actually bought his old moped. Lost touch, sadly, when his family moved abroad . . . Whatever. He got in touch about the reunion, started looking through his stuff, found this VHS. It's from the party after we'd recorded *Ancient*."

Ernesto pressed Play. The quality was poor, but Kasper could tell that he was looking at his dad's face. The weariness left Kasper almost at once.

The person who is filming, probably Ture, pretends to be an interviewer. He sounds drunk, but mostly happy. In the background: music, laughter, youthful voices.

"Maimer!" Ture exclaims. "Håkan 'Maimer' Nordin of Dark Cruelty!"

Håkan grins and does the sign of the horns. For a second, Kasper saw his own face in his father's.

"Can you tell me something about Dark Cruelty's new EP?" Ture asks. "Is it any good?"

"It's called *Ancient Bloodlust*," Håkan says, and he takes a swig from a gold-colored beer can.

"Is it good?"

"It's decent," Håkan says, grin broadening.

"It's fucking awesome!" Ture shouts. "Sweden's first death metal record!"

Someone roars approvingly.

"What's your favorite cooler?" Ture says.

"Favorite cooler?" Håkan laughs.

Ture corrects himself: "I meant favorite color, and you can't say black."

"Red," Håkan declares.

"Red like blood!" Ture says. "Best Slayer album?"

"Show No Mercy."

"Reign in Blood!" someone hollers in the background.

"Slayer are posers!" someone, possibly Ernesto, shouts. "Repulsion!"

"Autopsy!" Håkan shouts, pointing into the camera. "Exenterate!"

"What message do you have for young people who are fans of Dark Cruelty's music?" Ture inquires.

"Be good to animals and don't litter," Håkan says, gazing sternly into the camera. The image jumps. "Or tiny forest creatures will come and slice you up with very sharp and tiny sticks of wood."

"Pure terror," Ture says, moving the camera to Grim, who's seated next to Håkan. "Grim, lord of the underground."

Grim looks into the camera and waves slightly.

"Hey," he says.

"Tell me about yourself," Ture says.

"About myself?"

"Yeah, who is Grim? The man behind the mask."

"Well, I'm from Timrå, so . . . That says it all, I guess."

Ture laughs. Someone shouts something inaudible off-camera. Grim looks over, smiles, points a fuck you in their direction.

"What do you want to accomplish within the next five years?"

"I never think that far ahead," Grim says.

"Oh, come on."

Grim gazes straight into the camera.

"World domination or death."

"Thanks for that," Ture says, and the camera moves over to a guy who leans in to burp into it.

Ernesto turned the television off, but Kasper's eyes lingered on the black screen. It was the first time he saw and heard Grim speak. His voice was both gentler and darker than he had imagined. It was as though he could still hear it. He wanted to see the video again. At once.

"I got chills when I saw this for the first time. Shit, I still do," Ernesto said. "There's hardly any recorded material with him. Håkan found some old tapes from the rehearsal, a bit of talk in the background, but it's just fragments. And the gigs, too, with Paul recording them. But that was his stage persona. This could be the only recording of him just being himself. As much yourself as you can be when you're in front of a camera."

Ernesto went quiet, took a sip of his mineral water. Tapped his foot lightly against the floor in a way he seemed unaware of.

"Everyone's filming things today, one post per minute," he continued. "You almost forget what it was like back then."

Kasper nodded. It was so obvious, and yet he'd never thought about it. So many of today's people were preserved, while generations upon generations of dead were erased. Faces and voices, gone forever.

At that moment, the lights went out. The windowless room turned pitch-black.

"What the fuck?" Ernesto muttered in the dark.

They both turned on their phone lights. Ernesto got up.

"Wait a sec," he said, putting his shoes on.

Cold air poured in when he opened the door and disappeared into the darkness.

Kasper waited, worry in his bones. The light from the phone illuminated the candelabra. There was a box of matches in the fruit bowl. It was a bit sticky to the touch, the fruit not being as fresh as it seemed to be. A hiss when Kasper lit one of the matches. He transferred the flame to the black candles, one by one.

Grim's face, Grim's voice. The only things that remained of him.

Kasper looked into the flames. This interview had to mean something, had to somehow bring him closer to the truth of what happened to Grim.

The flames flickered when Ernesto opened the door, kicked snow off his shoes.

"It's the same in the big house," he said. "Izzy is checking it out. Oh, well. Let's do this."

The warm candlelight illuminated Ernesto's face as he sat down facing Kasper.

"This is even better," he said.

His phone started to ring.

"Sorry, I'll just turn this little terror off."

He flicked off the sound and put the phone back on the table, screen facing downward.

"All right," he said, looking at Kasper. "What do you want to know?"

Appendix 10. From the transcript of Kasper's interview with Ernesto Moberg.

K: You can probably start with . . . How did you get into metal?

E: It started with Kiss, I guess, like with a lot of other people. There were those collector cards kids carried around—not me. My mom refused to waste money on things like that. But I was interested. Made a classmate record Kiss *Alive!* on tape for me. Then I started taking lessons at the local community center, but they didn't let you play metal. And I was already being drawn to more . . . I was always on the lookout for albums with really ghoulish covers. The music was hardly ever as scary, though, which was a letdown. But I remember hearing Slayer for the first time and thinking, like: *Shit, this is dangerous!* (*laughs*) I remember getting dizzy, having to lay down. (*laughs*) Well . . . I found some really raw thrash bands I liked. Some South American bands. I was getting into more extreme music and met your dad and Tony at that record signing, but you've probably heard enough of that to last you a lifetime. Your dad had already founded Dark Cruelty. I think they'd had a guitarist for all of two minutes, but he never showed up for rehearsals. So we started talking while in line. (*pause*) They were good years. A deep sense of community. Totally DIY, do it yourself. We were close to punk, in that way. Always fiddling with new projects. Your dad and I dyed our jeans black and sewed them so they'd be skinnier, which is why we did sewing in school instead of wood and metal. (*laughs*) There were lots of rules about what to wear, like, you didn't want to look like you were into technical thrash. Your sneakers couldn't be too clean, for example. (*laughs*) Sorry, this isn't all that interesting.

K: No, I like hearing about—

E: We were pretty . . . We were nerds, in a way. Not really hard. If a group came up to us and wanted to fight, we always ran. Everyone thought Tony was some kind of fighter 'cause he was so big, and yeah, he hit some guy at some point, just to protect himself. But his greatest strength was being so fucking fast. (*laughs*) Never mind. We're talking about Grim.

K: Do you remember meeting him for the first time?

E: It was . . . He'd been to the rehearsal to hang out a few times before he tried out as a singer.

K: Dad has always said that they met at the record store for the first time, and that Grim tried out straight after that.

E: No, I don't think so. I think Håkan's getting it all mixed up, into one event. Grim had been in Stockholm a few times, we knew him a little when he became part of the band. But it was, like . . . We didn't know *that* side of him. I was relieved and broken up about it, you could say. I wanted to quit singing, I'd asked for it, but I got a bit upset that he was *so* good. (*laughs*) But, yeah . . . Håkan had so much energy, founding the band, and when Grim came into it . . . It got turned up to eleven. I was proud to play with Dark Cruelty. Things were happening. I think we could have gone really far. Looking back, it's pretty rare for everyone in a band to be as driven as we were. A lot of the others were . . . Some saw it as a chance to hang out with friends, others did it for attention. But the bands that kept going, that became something later, they had one or two guys who had that drive, you know. And they kept on, carrying the torch, while the others went on to do something else. But we're all still musicians, even Malte, it's pretty incredible. Grim would definitely still be active.

K: What was your relationship with him like?

E: He could really wind me up! (*laughs*) In the beginning, I couldn't tell whether he was shy or an ass, but he turned out to be both! (*laughs*) Honestly, one great thing about our little scene is that a lot of oddballs fit right into it. We only cared about the music, didn't give a shit if someone was "weird," as long as he liked death metal . . . But my general feeling about him was that I respected him, and it was mutual. He could have a one-track mind, but he cared about people. I wasn't into trading, but if he found something obscure he knew I'd like, he always shared it with me. Brought tapes for me to the rehearsals. One reason for the occasional tension, you know, was probably that I was ready to move on. Dark Cruelty's always been your dad's band, and then Grim came into it, and they shared the songwriting and the vision . . . I think I wanted to do my own thing but still held on. Because we'd worked so hard on Dark Cruelty and it felt like things were moving . . . But I don't think I was satisfied, not really. I've thought about it that way in hindsight. That I didn't just leave because of the conflicts. It was the entire situation . . . And I had my own issues . . . That whole thing with Linda and having a baby . . . I was madly in love with her and when she told me she was pregnant, shit, I was over the moon. I was going to be a dad, you know? I felt proud. Grown. But I had no idea what I was doing. I thought I could carry on as usual, but having a kid . . . I wasn't really there, not in the way I should have been. (*sighs*) Well, we're all friends now . . . And I'm sober. Another problem from that time. Not so much from the DC era, but touring with Vile Prophets in the nineties . . . Shit. There was a lot of alcohol. I never drank around Linda and Ossian as a rule, but I'd just be a wreck instead. Restless and moody. So I made up excuses, went off to rehearse, slept at a friend's . . . It wasn't fair to Ossian. Linda and I fell apart, obviously. (*laughs*) Sorry, I'm heading off in the wrong direction again. We're talking about Grim.

K: It's fine . . .

E: Well, it's all over and done, no point moaning about it now. I've done enough of that. But Grim . . . One thing I've thought about is that we had some things in common that we never talked about. We didn't know our biological dads. My dad was killed in Chile, my mom fled, met Bernt . . . He adopted me. "Moberg." I love the old man, but I knew I had another dad. Same thing with Grim. His mom had already had him when she met that guy, what was his name, Lennart? Both Grim and I had half siblings. He didn't know much of anything about his biological dad. I met relatives, had photos. And my mom told me stories, but in Spanish, or Bernt would get a bit jealous. (*laughs*) But yeah, we had something in common in that, Grim and me. Then there was that whole thing about being a "fucking foreigner," people calling you names just 'cause your hair was black . . . Keep Sweden Swedish, all that shit. Skins by Gamla Stan . . . I can imagine Grim had to put up with some of that shit, too. But both of us were busy trying to ignore it, I suppose . . . (*silence*) We mostly talked about music. (*laughs*) Hanging out with us must have been boring as fuck, we were obsessive, just music, music, all the time. We were in our own little world. Yeah, we had some fights, but we were good, we were brothers. Well, everyone except for him.

KASPER

"Malte," Ernesto said, shaking his head.

He poured himself the last of the mineral water and drank it down. Kasper touched the phone lightly, making sure it was still recording. The candlelight flickered.

"I said no to having him in the band at first," Ernesto said.

"Okay," Kasper said.

He wasn't sure he'd heard that before.

Ernesto nodded to himself, disappearing into some memory.

"Tony said my dad hung out with Malte and Grim sometimes," Kasper said. "Just the three of them."

"He did?" Ernesto frowned. "Maybe in the beginning . . . They were some kind of unholy trinity for a while, just the three of them off together. It was that 'occult' interest that Tony and I never shared. Then again, I don't think your dad liked Malte, even back then. I'm not even sure Grim did."

"You don't think he liked Malte?"

"No . . ." Ernesto sounded thoughtful. "Or, I don't think he spent time with Malte because he thought Malte was such a great person. That wasn't it. But when Grim was into something, he got obsessed with it. Music, at the start, then more and more of that esoteric stuff . . . I don't know why, I suppose he was searching for something. Malte shared that. I think he nurtured that side of Grim, pretty consciously."

"But my dad was also interested?"

"Håkan found it exciting, yeah, even before meeting Grim. But when Malte came along . . . I think it became a competition, kind of. Håkan knew that if he didn't hang out with Malte and Grim, they'd just go off without him, and he couldn't stand that. That's what I think, anyway. We haven't really talked about it."

Ernesto fell silent, something remote in his eyes. Suddenly, Kasper saw how alike they were, Ernesto and Ossian.

"Malte was an insecure little shit," Ernesto said. "I've seen that kind many times. First they're fanatic fanboys, a bit younger than everyone else. Then they decide to be scarier and more extreme than the people they used to look up to. Sometimes, I've thought . . . Was it something we did? Could we have treated him better? But no . . . There was something off about him. A wrong one. I don't know, though . . . I acted like a child, leaving the way I did. We all did. Well, we were kids . . ."

Kasper became aware of how chilly the room was, guessed that the heating had cut out along with the lights. He pulled his sweatshirt back on while Ernesto continued speaking.

"It wasn't great between us, not for a while after that. But we were still friends, except Malte and I, we avoided each other. It felt like shit, quitting right before the release, we'd worked ourselves to the bone for it. But all those plans . . . They didn't lead to much. Probably because Grim wasn't well. I don't know much about what happened at the end, but I could tell it wasn't good. He had a sense of humor before, he was sociable around people he knew. But he started to withdraw. Became darker, somehow."

Kasper looked at Ernesto's hand. He was twirling a bottle cap between his fingers, pressing his thumb against the plastic on its inside.

"I was shocked when Håkan phoned to tell me Grim was dead. It hit me hard. Back then I didn't understand my feelings, but . . . I was angry at him, because he had gone into some fucking tunnel . . .

and I was angry at myself. I felt like I had let him down somehow. I think your dad felt the same way. Probably more than me, much more. I regret not going to the funeral, I do . . ."

He sighed deeply. Kasper pulled the hoodie tighter. He wanted to get up and get his jacket, but he didn't want to disturb Ernesto. He was so open, in a way that surprised Kasper.

"I've thought a lot about his death," Ernesto went on. "I know that Håkan avoids everything related to the subject. And Tony's been scouring the entire Internet, that's his way of dealing with it. I guess I've chosen some kind of middle way. I try to keep track of what is being said, but I don't want to dig too deep. But it's enough to keep you awake at night. I do lie awake sometimes."

Kasper shivered, not understanding how Ernesto could be completely unmoved by the cold. His face was turned away. He sat there, quiet, for so long, that Kasper began to wonder if he had fallen asleep.

"One thing I can't stop thinking about," Ernesto finally said. "Ten years ago, it was in connection with the reissue of *Ancient* . . . It was released while I was on the road. We were in the Czech Republic, gone to some festival, and there were some guys backstage . . . A Romanian band, I think they were, but they didn't play at the festival; they were friends of someone who did. One of these men came up to me and said we had to talk. It was as if he had something really important to tell me, something he had to get off his chest. He was probably a little high, but I could tell it was something serious. We walked away from the others. He rambled on about always admiring me as a guitarist, and he threw himself into some kind of confession. Said he'd spent time with bad people when he was younger, done a lot of bad things. I thought, you know, he's about to apologize for sending me a dead rat twenty years ago. But he started talking about Malte. Apparently, he'd hung out with Malte in the nineties for a bit. He said, 'You need to know something about him. He knows more than he says about the death of your friend.'"

Kasper felt suddenly light-headed, as if the air contained too little oxygen.

"I said that Malte talks a lot," Ernesto continued slowly. "Been suggesting for years that Grim was down there trying to do some, like, arcane demonic ritual or something. And then maybe he did, and then he had a seizure down there, all alone. But anyway . . . this guy, he said to me, 'You don't understand. Malte knows *exactly* what Grim did down there.' And so he tried to explain."

"What did he say?" said Kasper, his voice just a whisper.

"There was a lot of hocus-pocus. I wish I remembered more details, but I'm totally uninterested in that shit. It all just goes in one ear and out the other. I remember him saying something about a labyrinth. Or maybe he meant the tunnels . . . his English was kind of odd, great vocabulary, but there was something about the way he put the words together that made it hard to keep up. But one thing he said was very clear."

A sweet, sticky smell was suddenly all around them. It was the smell of rotten fruit.

"'He wasn't alone.' That's what he said. I asked him what he meant, of course, but then he got all scared. He told me he absolutely didn't want anything getting back to Malte. What did he call him? 'A jinx.'"

Kasper thought about all the damage Malte had left in his wake, wherever he went.

"We left after that," Ernesto said. "And then I didn't see him again at the festival. I wanted to talk to him, so I spent some time trying to figure out which band he was playing in, tried to get his contact details via their label. But I didn't get an answer when I wrote. I asked around a bit, but this guy seemed to have decided to just disappear. There are a lot of odd people in that scene, that's for sure."

He fell silent. Kasper thought the smell was stronger now, and he wanted to ask if Ernesto could also smell it, but he was unable to make himself say the words.

"Malte is back in Sweden," Ernesto said slowly. "Ossian told me. Apparently, they met at a party."

He looked right at Kasper. His dark eyes shone in the candlelight. "I'm really sorry about Ossian. I love him, but I don't understand him. And I think that the fault lies with me."

The lights came on. Kasper blinked. It was as if the pressure had dropped, a presence had suddenly vanished. Ernesto looked at Kasper, pale, face glistening with cold sweat.

"Shit, where were we?" He sounded dazed. "I feel completely out of it. I think I need to look at the ventilation in here . . ."

"We're done," Kasper said.

He turned off the recording with his shaking hands and got to his feet. Ernesto wiped sweat from his forehead, visibly confused.

"I think I have to go lie down," he murmured. "Maybe I've got that flu."

On the way home, Kasper listened to the interview. And then he listened again. The young voices of his dad and Grim. Ernesto's mature voice, how it had become increasingly vague, almost dreamy.

When Kasper came into the hallway, he had his headphones on and didn't hear Leah and his dad calling him from the kitchen, where they were having dinner together. Kasper removed his headphones.

"We're off to the movies," his dad said. "But we left food for you."

"Come and sit with us for a bit," Leah added.

Her smile was warm, but the idea of sitting down at the table and talking with her and his dad felt physically impossible right now.

"Sorry, I've got something for school."

He went into his room and closed the door, sent the interview to Iris. Then he sank onto the bed. His head felt stuffed full, like his thoughts couldn't fit into it.

There were so many questions about what Ernesto had told him. But the biggest was this: Why would he tell Kasper all those things?

The cold. The stink of rotten fruit. No. *Rotten apples.* Just like when Kasper hid with Santiago. Just like when he saw the shape that looked like Grim at the foot of his bed, right before the mirror fell.

Kasper stared at the four black letters on his arm.

Had Grim been present in Ernesto's studio? Was it his presence that had made Ernesto talk like that?

And why did Kasper have the feeling that it wasn't the first time it happened?

He put his headphones back on, opened the interview with Tony, and listened. There it was. When Tony started talking about the phone number. He got that absent, vague lilt to his voice. Kasper tried to remember his conversation with his mother last autumn, the day they had picked apples. Had something similar happened then? He had a feeling it might have, but he wasn't sure.

Ossian. Their conversations appeared in a new and even more disturbing light. Had Ossian said all those things about his dreams of his own free will, or had he been influenced by some external force? But Kasper had not felt any presence then. Or had he? Maybe he'd been too drunk to notice.

But the common factor was clear: Kasper had been there to talk about Grim.

There is a bond between you and him.

He heard his dad and Leah putting their coats on in the hall, and when they yelled good-bye, he answered. Shortly afterward, he heard the door close, their steps in the stairwell dying away.

What would happen if he talked to his dad? Did he even dare to do that?

Iris texted to say she had listened to the interview and wondered if they could talk. He called her and saw her familiar face pop up on the screen.

"Did you hear anything special when Ernesto talked?" he asked.

"Yes," Iris said, frowning. "At the bit at the end. He sounded almost . . . like he'd been drugged?"

Kasper described what had happened. It sounded absurd when he said it out loud. He felt light-headed again, like he had been in Ernesto's studio.

"Shit." She looked shaken. "This is *so* fucking scary, Kasper."

"I can't talk to my dad about Grim now," Kasper said.

Now that he understood the effect he had on those he talked to about Grim, he couldn't do it to his dad. Watch his eyes go far away, hear him talk in a way he wouldn't otherwise. It was a terrible thought.

"But what should I do now?" he said. "Should I try to find that Romanian guy? I should be able to find out what festival it was. I know the year, I can try to move on from there."

"I'm sorry to say this," Iris said. "But do you actually have to keep going with this?"

Kasper stared at her. Had he heard her right?

"You said I'd tell you," she reminded him, "if I thought you were too deep into this. If it became too much."

"But it's not *my* choice," Kasper objected. "Things have happened to me. I didn't make them happen. The dreams, the wound, what happened in the Hall of Mirrors—"

"I know," Iris interrupted. "But we may have approached this completely backward."

He knew that she said "we" so he wouldn't feel called out, but she very clearly meant "you."

"What do you mean?" Kasper said warily.

"I've been thinking about what Ossian said . . ." Iris began.

"Ossian," Kasper groaned.

"Let me *finish*," Iris said. "He said that Grim was the flame and you were the moth, or whatever. The flame is there, yes. But maybe you shouldn't fly toward it. Not to be like that, but you know what happens with moths and fire."

Kasper couldn't believe what he was hearing. Iris, of all people, should understand this.

"He talked about the storm and river, too," Iris continued. "But you can seek shelter from the storm, get to a higher point when the river rises. You don't have to stay."

"So you're saying I should just abandon him?"

He was surprised by his own words.

"Kasper," she said quietly. "Grim is dead."

"He was there. He was there today. Or do you think I've lost it?"

His voice cracked. He was being unfair to Iris, he knew that, but he couldn't stop himself.

"You felt *something* was there, yes," Iris said. "You know I believe you. But we actually don't know for sure that it was Grim. We haven't talked about this, I haven't even wanted to think about it, but . . . if there are things that we don't understand, if the supernatural exists . . . there might be something that's trying to trick you. Lure you in. It could be something that wants to hurt you. Or maybe that's not even how it works. Maybe it's just, like, a . . . force. Maybe it doesn't have a will or a goal, maybe it's just *there*. Something left behind. And it seems to be getting stronger. You said this happened to Tony, too, but then it wasn't as obvious. What if this power is growing because you're focusing on it? Like that thing Leah talked about with you, about the magician's focus and intention making the ritual work . . . But no matter what this power is, it's something that can make Ernesto sit and . . . well, reveal his deepest thoughts about his own son. That thing about Ossian . . . it sounded like something he barely could admit to himself. I don't want to scare you, but . . . have you thought about what this force might do to you? How much does it affect you?"

Kasper stared at the screen. He felt hollowed out.

There was logic to what Iris was saying, but he couldn't take it in. She was right, but she was also completely wrong. He knew it.

How do you know? Your instinct, is it? Do you trust it all of a sudden?

"I don't want to shove your face in it," Iris said. She was clearly making an effort to sound calm, her voice trembling with the strain. "But you promised you'd listen if I told you to stop. And I would never ask it if I wasn't really worried." She paused. "This is the hardest thing for me to say, but . . . you actually have to consider that this might be too much for you. I know you want to know what happened, and so do I, but there may not be any answers. And even if there are . . . I really, really think this is too dangerous. You saw what happened today. I'm sorry, but I'm your friend, and I love you, and I have to say this. I think you have to stop."

She sounded as if she was near tears. And it was Kasper's fault.

"You're right," he told her.

"I don't know, I just—" Iris began.

"Yes, but you're right," Kasper interrupted. "I promised you I'd listen."

Iris breathed a sigh of relief. Kasper felt relieved, too, knowing he'd freed her of a burden. He had to carry it himself now, but that was fine. It was just as well.

"I have to eat something," he said. "But I'll talk to you tomorrow."

"Okay," Iris said. "We'll talk later. Bye."

"Bye," Kasper said, and he hung up.

He got up from the bed, went and sat down at his computer. An opened bag of chips was next to the keyboard. He shoved a fistful into his mouth. Then, with greasy fingers, he accessed a forum in which the most devoted Grim fanatics discussed every aspect of the dead man's life. Kasper quickly found the post he was looking for.

Grim spoke of books of magic in many of his interviews and letters. Do any of you know the titles?

Among the answers were references to previous posts with scanned fanzine interviews and letters that people who'd tape-traded with Grim had posted.

Grim was interested in magic. In all likelihood, he'd attempted a ritual before he died.

He wasn't alone.

The Romanian musician had said that Malte had the answers. That is exactly what Ossian had said. Ossian, meanwhile, had told Ernesto that he met Malte at a party, and Kasper was sure he knew which party it had been. Perhaps Iris was right, in that this force wanted to hurt him. Because it felt like it was pulling him toward Malte.

But he wasn't there, not yet. Hopefully, he never would be.

Kasper compiled a list of titles. If he was to understand what happened to Grim, he had to understand what he believed in, what he'd been searching for.

Iris was right.

He was in too deep.

So deep he couldn't turn back.

INTERLUDE

A lot of this has been painful to write about, and the worst is yet to come.

But before I go on, there's something I'd like to say about Kasper. Because I'm afraid I haven't managed to describe him as a friend.

I know how hard he could be on himself. I know because he told me about his thoughts. We had so many conversations, Kasper and I—no, it was just the one, long conversation. We wrote to each other almost every day. We lay awake together, each in our own room. He didn't know everything about me, but almost.

There's so much I want to talk about.

Like that time I had a panic attack on the subway and Kasper came and got me.

Like the time we went to Grönan in January and pressed our faces against the bars just to see what it looked like when it was all covered in snow.

Like when he came with me to the vet when I thought Caligari was dying and waited with me all night.

I'd like to show you the portrait of me he made me for my birthday. He would say it didn't turn out right, but he would be wrong.

I'd like to tell you about the first time I let him read something I'd written and something happened to the text just because I knew he'd read it. All the time he spent reading new versions of it, his criticism always warm and honest.

I'd like to list all of the times he asked me how I was doing, all of the times he wrote me back at once when I told him I needed to talk, all the music he sent me, all the times he laughed at my stupid jokes.

That list would be far too long.

But I want you to know that there was so much more than what you can find in these pages.

THE RECORD

It arrives in June.

A delivery consisting of 666 copies of *Ancient Bloodlust* waits for them at the depot. Håkan's grin turns stupid when he gets the message. He throws himself onto the phone and contacts Grim.

Since Grim moved out, they've only met at rehearsals and once when Håkan went to Raw Power. Håkan talked to one of the owners while Grim worked out back. He only came in for a quick hello, wearing a pentagram just like Malte's. He doesn't show up to parties anymore, either. A couple of times he said he would, but he ended up not coming. *Go to hell*, Håkan had thought. He imagines Grim in Malte's revolting room, feeding Kurt crickets while yammering on about those goddamn demons. The jealousy is worse than what he feels when he sees Stasse kissing Anja.

But the record is going to remind Grim of what's important, Håkan thinks. They've been working so hard to bring it about. They meet up at the depot, and then Tony's dad arrives to drive them and their haul to Håkan's place.

Håkan's mom is thrilled to see Grim, even though he hasn't been gone for long. She even hugs him. Håkan is a bit embarrassed; it isn't like his mom to carry on like that. But Grim allows the embrace, even closes his eyes. He looks so tired. While his mom cooks a casserole, Håkan and Grim carry the records into Håkan's room, stacking them in piles where Grim's bed used to be. Only then do they take a copy each, Håkan and Grim, and look at the record with reverence. Its front. Its back. They pull out the dust sleeve, smell new, shiny vinyl.

"Do you want to . . . ?" Håkan nods at the stereo.

"But what about you?" Grim says.

"It was your idea."

It wouldn't have happened without you, Håkan wants to say.

Solemnly, Grim carries the record to the stereo, and Håkan stands beside him. He watches Grim drop the needle, so excited and terrified he thinks he might burst.

Church bells ringing. The roar of a huge fire. And then a heretic's agonized screams, coming closer as the intro crosses into "Ancient Bloodlust."

Håkan and Grim stand frozen by the stereo, listening to the A-side in complete silence. Then Grim gestures at Håkan—go ahead. Håkan lifts the needle, turns the record over. Drops the needle again. The bass pulses satisfyingly in "Unholy Shadows Reign."

> *I kneel before the altar . . . Drink from the cup of virgin blood . . . Blasphemous legions howl . . . Will tear your soul apart . . . Old ones, hear my incantation . . . Below the winter moon . . . In the temple of the night . . . In the darkness of the tomb . . . They bide their time . . . Unholy . . . Shadows . . . Reign . . .*

Their eyes meet. They grin like lunatics. For one beautiful moment, they're in sync again. This is really happening; they really did it.

They listen until the final invocation of the demonic elite fades away. Håkan thinks he might have held his breath the entire time. That's how it feels.

"Again?" Håkan asks.

Grim turns the record over.

They're up all night, numbering records. A year ago, they had discussed doing it in blood, but they'd quickly realized that it would be too sticky and difficult to read against a black background. Håkan is glad that they decided against it in the end. He has gotten hold of two white markers. Grim starts counting the records and notices that they've been given 685 copies. Either someone entered the wrong number at the pressing plant, Håkan suggests, or they've been given some spares in case of defects. They decide to hand out the extra nineteen copies to the inner circle.

They drink soda while printing numbers on the sleeves, adding the lyric sheets they've photocopied themselves. Grim sounds almost shy when he asks if he can have number 1. If so, Håkan can take number 666 and number 2.

"Take number 3 as well," Håkan tells him. "Number 4 is for Tony and number 5 for Ernesto."

"Six is for Malte," Grim says.

Grim isn't wearing his pentagram today, Håkan notes.

Håkan talks about which record stores they should bestow the honor of selling the EP to. He's continued writing to his international contacts about the release, tried to plan for the EPs to get out to as many countries as possible. But Grim is the one with the larger network. Håkan carefully asks him how it's going, if he has heard anything from the German and the Italian who could help them get gigs.

"Haven't written many letters lately," Grim says.

Håkan remembers the piles of unopened mail he took with him when he moved.

"Okay, but we'll go Interrailing, right?" he says.

"Don't know." Grim lowers his gaze. "I'm broke."

Håkan is stressed, knowing that they have to get the record out now. Stockholm won't be a problem, of course, and when Dagge from Teratoid visits, they'll give him a bunch to bring back with him to Gothenburg. But the world is waiting for them. Grim said so himself.

"I'll talk to the guys at Raw Power," Grim says. "Maybe they can help us distribute it."

"Yeah, that would be awesome," Håkan says.

"I think I wrote the same number twice," Grim says. "But I'll sign one of them to make it up to whoever gets it."

The old Grim is still there. As they number the records, Håkan feels a sense of calm come over him.

KASPER

Thirty years ago, Dark Cruelty walked into the studio to record Sweden's first death metal EP. Now, they were releasing their first single since that time, "Tormented Exaltation." The reactions were mostly positive. From one review:

"This is no effort to turn back time. Håkan Nordin has approached the unfinished song as the mature musician he is today, and that goes for the rest of the band as well. The production is modern, without losing that organic, old school feel. As expected, Ossian Holm's efforts are killer. His voice has just the right combination of youthful desperation, fury, and pain to do the lyrics of Kasper 'Grim' Johansson justice. I wouldn't be surprised if the spirit of the deceased singer was present at the time of the recording."

His dad tackled the band's social media with great enthusiasm. He booked podcasts and other interviews before the release in June. Sweden's biggest metal magazine was publishing a special on it. Leah had been right; the reunion was good for him.

Kasper was happy for his dad's sake, but it was more like the shadow of a feeling. Everything seemed faded to him. He was supposed to hand in his final projects but he usually just stared at his iPad. He still hadn't started his essay. Instead, he went back to the books about magic. He had borrowed some of them from the library, others were online. He didn't know what he was looking for when he worked through the winding, often obscure, texts. He tried to read through Grim's eyes. He went through the writers and poets Grim referred to in his interviews and lyrics. His dad had their books on the shelf, Baudelaire and Blake. He listened to the music Grim praised, listened to his voice over and over again. *Talk to me*, he thought. *Tell me what to do.*

Kasper had taken down the box in his dad's closet a few times. He guessed that the leather jacket in it belonged to Grim, that he'd been wearing it when he was found. He had tried it on a few times, noted that Grim was taller than him. With the jacket on his shoulders, he inspected the knife, thought of the wound in Grim's hand. "Your own blood is the most valuable sacrifice." Kasper had read that somewhere. Had his own blood mixed with Grim's when he accidentally cut himself? *Accidentally.* Ossian had said there was no such thing as coincidence. Kasper held the EP in his hands: *Ancient Bloodlust*, number one of 666. He had studied the sleeve several times, but it wasn't until a night in April, when his dad was at Leah's, that he found it.

As so many times before, he was examining the sleeve, damaged by dampness, running his fingers over it, trying to discover some unevenness. He scrutinized the scratches in the record, tried to see if there was a pattern. There wasn't. The lyrics sheet was missing. He put the record back and then realized where he hadn't looked.

Kasper took the record out again and peered into the sleeve.

Someone had drawn something on the inside.

He took the knife out of its sheath and carefully cut through the glued-on seam. Then he opened it.

On one side, at the very bottom of the corner, someone had drawn a stylized maze. The ink had run a little because of the dampness. In the heart of the labyrinth was a U. Next to it, something had been written in tiny, cramped letters. Kasper had to get out the magnifying glass from the detective kit his grandma had given him when he turned eight.

This I say unto thee: Thou opened the gate when I called and I hereby license thee to depart without doing injury to any living creature. This I say unto thee: Thou art free to go, withdraw in peace under the blessing of the Most High, and seal the door that thou for my sake hath opened. This I say unto thee: Let there be peace between thee and me. Amen.

Kasper lowered the magnifying glass. He could feel the force pulling him in. It was so strong. And he worried that Iris was right, that it didn't mean well. Or that it didn't want anything at all. The flame doesn't want to hurt the moth, the storm and the flood have no desire to destroy what came in their way. They just are.

He took out his phone and photographed the labyrinth, carefully wrote down the words. Then he went and got more glue, sealed the sleeve back together again. He'd been given a thread to follow.

THE SUMMER

The second summer. The worst.

They throw a party at Stasse and Grim's place to celebrate the release of *Ancient Bloodlust*. They party until the neighbors start hammering on the door. Then they go to the record store at Regeringsgatan to look at the EP. Håkan managed to get them a spot in the store window over the weekend. They take pictures of one another with disposable cameras, then go and hang out in the graveyard at St. John's Church, howl at the moon and scare the men furtively leaving the strip joint close by. But Håkan can't quite relax. Earlier that day, he passed by Linda's parents' house to get some records to Ernesto. They talked in the garden a bit, the same place they had partied in so many times the previous summer. Håkan tried to convince Ernesto to come along and celebrate. "I can't," he just said.

Now Håkan is watching Grim, noting how often he and Malte pull away, talk with their heads close together. He's relieved every time he sees Grim talking to anyone else. It doesn't happen frequently enough. Grim walks around by himself or talks to Malte. But Malte has parents who get upset if he's out too late, so he leaves, and Grim is alone. Håkan goes to him. That's when he notices that Grim, who never drinks, is hammered. "I'm so fucking tired," he tells Håkan, and they leave the party together. Håkan gets him home, makes sure he drinks water, and helps him into bed. "The lyrics are done," he slurs before he crashes. "'Tormented Exaltation.'"

Fiendishly good." He falls asleep, and Håkan stands there. Looks at Grim's feet and tries to understand why his socks are covered in dog hair.

THE MYTH OF THE LABYRINTH AT CRETE (one version)

King Minos's wife, Pasiphaë, daughter of Helios, god of the sun, gave birth to a monster. The Minotaur was half bull, half human. King Minos, who was ashamed, asked the inventor Daedalus to build a labyrinth in which to trap the monster.

Daedalus did such a fine job, he himself barely found the way out.

The Minotaur ate human flesh. King Minos forced the enemy state Athens to sacrifice seven young men and seven young women every seven years.

The king of Athens had a son, Theseus, who volunteered, for he wished to defeat the Minotaur. On Crete, King Minos's daughter, Ariadne, met him and fell in love. She was told by <u>Daedalus to give Theseus a ball of string, which he could attach to the opening of the labyrinth, so that he could find his way out again</u>. He defeated the Minotaur, followed the string back to the opening, and escaped.

When King Minos discovered that Daedalus had helped Theseus, he had Daedalus and his son Icarus confined to the labyrinth. There, Daedalus constructed wings with which they could flee.

the labyrinth from without = work of art
the labyrinth from within = hell

KASPER

A gentle spring rain fell over Poseidon's Square on the day that Kasper's class had the private showing for their final exhibition. Most years, the graduating class would exhibit their work at the school, but Lydia had heard that some students had booked the Culture Center a few years back and took that as inspiration. The art students had their works displayed, while some of the music students performed. At the moment, a girl with a guitar sat on a chair and sang about heartbreak. Kasper stood in a corner, answering a text from Iris. She had wanted to come, but there were only two UCs at The House; so if Kasper was here, she had to be at The House.

He put the phone in his pocket and looked around. His mom and Leah were by Lo's magnificent painting, studying the numerous and advanced details. Atle had just left with Diana and Leia for the children's section of the library.

His dad stood in front of Kasper's drawings. He'd been standing in front of them for a while.

Kasper had handed in his project at the appointed time. Three pictures and a short essay in which he described the background to the work. He already knew he'd pass. He also knew Ms. Gunhild was disappointed. She didn't say it out loud, but he felt it. He knew that none of what he had done was nearly as good as the drawings of his dreams. Ms. Gunhild had tried to get him to exhibit them, but his *no* was absolute, and he didn't regret his decision. They showed him something he would never be able to live up to again. He only wished he had had something to exhibit that he could be proud of. Or at least something he could acknowledge, something that didn't fill him with self-disgust and an intense sense of defeat.

The drawing in which Grim was holding the bird was almost okay. The second one, which was supposed to portray him as an ordinary teenager, and which was inspired by the photo they used to take out every year on the anniversary, he never really got the hang of. It didn't look like Grim. His eyes were dead. As for the picture of Tony and Grim on the stairs, he had really tried. The final result, however, was still flat. Two boys sitting on a staircase. Whatever.

Three barely mediocre images were the result of his grand project. It felt both embarrassing and empty.

And now his dad stood there, staring at them.

Suddenly Kasper couldn't bear it anymore. He walked toward the library. He heard the voices of Diana and Leia from the children's section, quickly made for the reading chairs by the tall windows. He sank into one of them. May blossomed outside, pale green. Rain trickled down the glass.

He didn't just dislike the pictures he had made; he was disgusted by them. He was disgusted by himself and his failures. All this had started as a search for the truth and he hadn't come up with anything, just more questions. Wherever he went, he carried those questions with him.

The words written on the inside of the sleeve could be the end of a ritual, when the magician gives the spirit he has summoned license to depart and closes the door to the other realm. Kasper had found examples of similar texts in his research. Perhaps it was the end of the ritual that Grim had tried to perform. But why would he have written it in there? And what did it put an end to?

If there was anything Kasper had learned about magic, it was that intention was everything. An incantation was harmless in itself; it was the will of the person who pronounced the words who made it matter.

For it to have any effect, Kasper had to know *what* to finish. And to know that, he had to know what Grim did in the tunnels. Maybe the labyrinth was a clue. The Romanian musician had mentioned the word to Ernesto. But nothing Kasper had read about mazes had made the picture any clearer.

He wasn't alone.

If only he wasn't so very tired.

Kasper closed his eyes where he sat, huddled in the armchair. It was the time for his graduation, the end of his time in school. He'd doubted he would make it so many times and knew he should be relieved. Should be proud. But maybe he just hadn't grasped it yet, not fully.

Steps approached and Kasper opened his eyes.

Lydia stood in front of him.

Lydia, another reminder of his mistakes and flaws.

"Oh, sorry I woke you," she said.

Kasper said, "It's fine."

Her gaze was uncertain. Kasper knew he should say something, dragged his hand across his face.

"I'm just exhausted," he said. "Hungover."

"Yeah, me, too," Lydia said, with a forced laugh.

She stroked her short black hair behind her ear. She looked so abandoned where she stood, was so obviously waiting for him to say something. Anything. And he just sat there.

Yesterday they had had their graduation party. They had rented a shabby restaurant slash nightclub that smelled like old alcohol and the powder they used at Grönan to dry and remove puke. Hundreds of students must have had their graduation parties there, eaten shrimp brought up from large plastic buckets and served on stale toast, a wilting branch of dill on top. Decades of desperate adolescent emotions were probably trapped inside the walls. Maybe that's why it happened. Or maybe it was because Kasper decided to get drunk. He had ordered an alcohol-free drink with his food, but afterward, Lo suggested a beer and he noticed that the thoughts in his head went quiet. Two beers later, he actually felt present in the moment. It wasn't as if he was drinking straight alcohol. A third couldn't hurt, or a fourth. Then he was on the dance floor with Lydia, who had also been drinking, which wasn't at all like her. In retrospect, he realized that it had been liquid courage. Because then it came: the confession.

"We'll be graduating soon and I just have to say this, because I know I'll regret it otherwise. I kind of like you," she'd said. Then she laughed and rolled her eyes, like she was leaving him the option of treating it as a joke. But it was clear that she meant it. Kasper realized he had to say something, and quick, or he'd upset Lydia. Lydia, who had been so good to him throughout high school. Who had made him a necklace in kindergarten.

"I like you very much, Lydia," he said.

Then he didn't know what else to say. But Lydia's gaze softened and she had to stand on her tiptoes to kiss him. Which she did. And he kissed her back. Someone whistled for them. Lydia laughed and he pulled her close, kissed her again. She tasted like white wine, was so warm and soft. And she liked him. That was crazy. And he liked her, too. Kasper felt dizzy with it. When they went to the bar and ordered more drinks, Lydia started talking about kindergarten.

"Do you remember when you left to begin 'real' school?" Lydia said.

"No?" said Kasper.

They both had to shout to be heard over the music.

"We all said bye, and when I realized you weren't coming back after the summer, I ran off and cried. Because we were such good friends. Well, when Marco didn't want to be with you, of course," she added with a laugh.

Kasper felt his smile go stiff.

"Oh, God, now it sounds like I'm bitter about something that happened when we were children," Lydia said quickly. "I really am *not*. But he pushed you around so much. And you always chose him, anyway."

The worst thing was that she didn't sound bitter, not at all. It was just a dry statement, an observation.

"I hated what he did to you after," Lydia said. "I don't think I've told you, but . . . the same thing happened to me in middle school. We were a group of friends and then, out of the blue, they just dropped me."

"Shit," said Kasper, who had had no idea.

"The worst thing is that you're so ashamed of yourself afterward," Lydia went on.

Kasper nodded.

"How weird is it that we didn't talk about this until now," he said, and he had some difficulty focusing his eyes. "When there are only a few weeks left of school."

"That's why, though, isn't it?" Lydia said.

He received the beer and the glass of white wine from the bartender, handed the wine to Lydia. They danced a little more, which Kasper hadn't done since his birthday party with the demons, and then they kissed some more. When Kasper went to the bathroom, Raman came up to him with a serious expression on his face.

"Look. She's seriously in love with you, so don't mess this up."

Kasper nodded dumbly. And suddenly the thought popped up in his head: *I should go home.* He didn't tell Lydia, just left. When he got off the train, he puked in a trash can on the platform.

Then all of today had gone to preparing for the private showing. And now Lydia stood in front of him.

Lydia, who was in love with him. Lydia, who had been nice to him. Not because she had seen him as a charity project, or as a depressive mascot. She had understood what he had been through because she had experienced something similar. That's probably why she had worked so hard for the class to come together. So she wouldn't get left out again. So no one would.

"I'm sorry I just left yesterday," Kasper said. "I got so incredibly drunk."

"It's okay," Lydia said. "Me, too. I don't even remember what I said."

It was a blatant lie. Her cheeks went bright red. She looked at him as if she still had hope, as if she'd keep hoping. Kasper wished he had had feelings for her, the kind of feelings she'd been talking about. But he didn't. All he felt was self-disgust.

"So I just wanted to say that, uh, if I . . ." Lydia said, then swallowed, "if I said something weird."

"No, you didn't," Kasper said, trying to sound relaxed. "It was a fun night."

Lydia's face shook. It was one of the worst things he could have said to her and now it was too late. He couldn't take it back. He had made it sound as if her feelings were a bit of a joke, something he had taken advantage of in the moment and now didn't care for anymore.

It's probably just as well, Kasper thought when he saw Lydia turn around and walk away, quickly, so he wouldn't see her crying.

It's just as well that she hates me, thought Kasper, sinking deeper into the armchair. *She's a good person. She deserves someone better than me. She thought I was someone else and found out she was wrong.*

Kasper had dinner with his family at the Chinese restaurant by the square. He tried hard to keep up with the conversation, but it was difficult. As soon as he tried to listen to what someone was saying, he was distracted by other, equally loud voices. He had a sinking feeling in his stomach, a feeling of impending doom. Finally, he and his dad went home. The blackbirds were everywhere, scratching beneath the bushes and trilling on the rooftops. The sky was hazy and pale pink. Paper-thin leaves unfolded on the boughs of the trees. Around them, there was the scent of rain-wet asphalt. Kasper used to like this time of year, but now he wanted to shut it down, the entire spring. It felt like the birds were screaming.

It dawned on him that his dad had said nothing about the exhibition. In fact, he didn't say a word all the way home. Kasper was silent, too. Only when they got inside the door did his dad say: "Can we talk a little?"

The feeling of a coming disaster flared up in Kasper. It was how he'd felt when he was a child, knowing he'd done something wrong.

Now Dad will tell you how disappointed he is with you. The exhibition could have been so much more. And who do you really think you are, that took on Grim's story, tattooed his name on your arm? You never even knew him. It's just a pathetic obsession to you, an embarrassing one at that. An attempt to get close to your dad and people who are a lot more interesting than you will ever be.

"Sure," Kasper said.

They sat down together in the living room, his dad taking out an old piece of snuff and replacing it with a new one. The silence was palpable. Neither of them had even made an effort to turn on some music. His father's fingers drummed against his thigh.

"Those were nice pictures you made," his dad said.

"Thank you," Kasper said, convinced it was all bullshit.

His dad's face looked pale in the sheer evening light. The gray strands in his hair and beard had increased the past few years, but he wasn't even fifty yet, Kasper reminded himself. He didn't want to think about his dad getting old.

"We never did that interview, you and me," his dad went on.

"No, we didn't."

He suddenly worried that his father would start talking about Grim. What would happen to him if he did? Would the same thing happen as what happened to Ernesto and Tony?

"I was a bit baffled when you told me about your project," his dad said. "I hadn't really thought you'd be interested in my life that way. And in Grim."

"You've only named me after him."

It came out harsher than Kasper intended. He added: "Of course I'm interested."

"Yeah," his dad said.

He didn't look angry. Instead, he looked strained. As if he was trying to get at precisely the right words.

"I have always been thrilled that you're interested in music and yes, it might be a bit silly, but also that it's metal. It's nice to be able to share it with you. The gigs, the music . . . And yes, I've been a bit of a showoff regarding that, in front of some friends and colleagues whose kids couldn't care less about the scene. It isn't a given, that interest. You could have just not given a shit about music or listened to something I wasn't into. But my point is . . . what I'm trying to say is, that it wouldn't have mattered. I'm, like I said, really happy that we can share this, but I hope you don't . . . well, that you don't feel any pressure. I would have been just as happy if you loved to listen to . . . Europop."

Kasper had to smile at that.

"Yeah right."

"Okay, not *as* happy, but I would have accepted it."

"And asked me to listen with headphones on."

His dad grinned.

"But seriously," he went on. "You understand what I mean, don't you?"

"Yes, of course," Kasper said.

But he felt uneasy. Did his dad think he had no taste of his own, or couldn't make his own decisions and just copied him?

It's because you don't have anything of your own. You're just a pale copy of your dad, and an even paler copy of the first Kasper.

"Anyway, Ernesto and Tony said you had good talks," his dad said. "Was there something in particular that came up? Something you want to ask me about?"

A thousand things, Kasper thought. But would he dare to ask even one of them?

"Ernesto said something," Kasper said, and went for something that felt harmless, but that he actually wanted to know. "You always said that the first time you met Grim was in that record store, that he tried out right after, all on the same day. But Ernesto said that Grim had already been to Stockholm and met you a few times. Before he tried out as a singer, I mean."

"In that case, he's got it wrong," his dad said. Then he frowned, sat quietly for a while. "I think, anyway. I've always told that story like that, in interviews and stuff."

"Ernesto thought that you probably had the events mixed up and turned into one memory," Kasper said.

His dad sighed and shook his head.

"I can't believe I said that Ernesto has a poor memory," he said. "You know, I have no idea. Maybe I'm remembering it wrong. It happens pretty often, which is so difficult to relate to at your age. At least I couldn't do it, not at the time. Even though I didn't go around thinking about the past so much in those days."

Was that really the case?

Kasper had wondered about that many times. When his dad talked about his youth, he often said that he and his friends had lived in the present. How did you live like that? Was it a question of attitude, or did your brains work differently? Kasper always felt like he was haunted by the past, that it could throw itself at him when he least expected it, tear open old wounds. And then there was the future, the uncertain, terrifying future. A place where everything could go wrong, both in his own life and on a global scale.

"Sometimes I envy you," Kasper said.

"What? Why?"

"It just seems like you had so much fun when you were young."

His dad looked at him unhappily and Kasper realized how awful it must be for him to hear what Kasper had just said. Hardly any parent's dream.

"It wasn't always fun," my dad said. "I probably embellish a lot when I tell you about it. Or I choose to tell you about the good things, because that's what I want to pass on to you." He fell silent. "But it's a kind of lie. Because even though I didn't walk around thinking all that much back then, I have done a lot of thinking since then, and I can see that . . . It wasn't always easy. You know that your granddad didn't really keep in touch, for example. But . . . I don't think it overshadowed anything. It *was* a positive time in my life. But the things that you don't deal with at the time, you have to deal with later. I'm trying to do it now." His dad looked a little embarrassed. "I'm seeing a therapist."

A *what* was about to leave Kasper's mouth, but he swallowed it down.

"I've had some insomnia and been under a lot of stress," his dad went on. "Leah suggested it."

Kasper thought of the times his father had spent all night in the Nest or stayed up watching films. He'd always assumed his dad didn't need much sleep, not that something had been preventing him from sleeping.

"How long have you been going?" Kasper asked.

"Almost exactly one year."

"But why didn't you tell me?"

"It's not a big deal," his dad said, even though it clearly was. "Everyone sees a therapist nowadays. And frankly, I didn't want you to worry about it. You've had a little too much worrying."

"But it's a good thing," Kasper said. "Not that I've thought you needed therapy, but I'm glad you're going. Why would I worry about it?"

Håkan laughed. "Shit. I suppose you're right." He shook his head.

"I've always been a little too good at keeping things to myself," Håkan said. "If I have a problem, I think I have to solve it alone, that there's no need to talk about it. Your mom hated that. And that made things difficult with Leah, too. That was a reason why we . . . Well, anyway. You don't make choices out of nowhere; they're obviously connected to the things you've been through in life. But if you're going to figure out *how* it all fits together, you have to dig through all the muck. All the bad choices. I've always found looking back difficult. I mean, I'm very nostalgic, so are all old metalheads. It's just that this rummaging around hasn't been my thing. But if you just run and run . . . You're exhausted in the end."

Kasper sat perfectly still. He saw too much of himself in what his dad was saying.

"And when you refuse to look at some parts of your own history, it's easy to miss other things, too," his dad continued. "Like when I didn't know what was going on with you."

Kasper shook his head. "It wasn't your fault."

"I should've noticed you weren't doing well," his dad maintained. "I should've asked more questions; I should have been watching out for you. I should've noticed that you didn't see your friends anymore, for example."

Kasper looked away. He and his dad were mirrored on the blank, black television screen.

"I don't want you to feel guilty," Kasper told his dad.

"Why?" his dad asked. "You think I can't handle it? Why save me from my guilt when I've actually done something wrong?"

Kasper didn't know how to answer. His dad obviously had an excellent therapist.

"That's just how it is, Kasper, and it's okay. I should have been there for you. I hope I know better now, that I have learned from my mistakes. Like . . ."

Kasper looked at him.

"Don't get angry," his dad said, "but I think you're getting worse again."

Kasper saw his behavior over the past few months in a new light, the way it must have looked from the outside. He had been withdrawn, tired, still not sleeping at night. Mood swings, periods of apathy. And then there was the party with Ossian last autumn, which must have lingered in his dad's mind: Kasper's first trip into the promised land of self-destructive behavior. No wonder his dad had connected those dots, definitely he and his mom, maybe Leah and Atle, too. They all thought Kasper was depressed again, but he wasn't. The problem was that hadn't solved the riddle. If he did, he could put everything behind him and move on. But he could never explain what was going on to his dad.

"Okay," was all he said.

"I've been talking to my therapist," his dad said. "You're over eighteen, so it's adult prices."

Kasper knew that. He felt himself getting restless.

"But I got some recommendations," his dad said. "Anja and I have talked about it, and we can contribute financially if necessary."

"I'm going to work all summer," Kasper told him.

"I know," said his dad. "But still. We want you to know that the option exists. And I can help you book an appointment, if you want."

His worry was obvious from his tone. This was just like when Iris asked him to stop looking for answers. She thought he'd quit, put it behind him, which was for the best. He had to reassure the people around him so he could finish this alone. If that meant that he had to sit and lie to a psychologist, he would. That was the key: to play along. It was best for everyone.

"Okay," Kasper said. "Thank you."

"That's great, Kasper," his dad said so tenderly that it hurt Kasper's heart.

The fact that he could do this to his own father was just further proof of what a disgusting person he was.

"It's going to be okay." His dad smiled a little. "You know, it was actually because of my therapist that I said yes to the whole Dark Cruelty thing."

"How come?" Kasper said.

"I always said I didn't want to do a reunion because it wouldn't feel right doing that to Grim," his dad said. "But really, I was only punishing myself. Because I felt bad." He fell silent for so long that Kasper began to worry. Would his dad begin to confess things now? But he sounded normal when he went on: "After Dark Cruelty . . . I played with Exenterate just when they were at their height. Careerwise, it was really hard to top. But it wasn't my band, my vision. And it's gone on like that. I really like writing with Eric, but it would be fun to have something else. Tony and I have talked about starting something of our own, but I'm always the one who gets cold feet. I do have enough songs for several albums, though . . ."

His smile was almost shy. Kasper had never heard him talk this frankly about his career before.

"It's like I've never allowed myself to have anything of my own after what happened with Dark Cruelty." His dad cleared his throat. "So when the reunion came up, my therapist asked me, 'Do you really think that Grim would have any problem with you being reunited?' And suddenly I realized that that wasn't what had held me back. It was just me."

He scratched his bearded chin. He looked so very vulnerable.

And Kasper knew he had to find out what happened to Grim for his dad's sake, too. For everyone. So that they could move on. Kasper couldn't give up now. The answer must be out there somewhere. He just had to bear it a little while longer.

THE SUMMER

In July, the members of Dark Cruelty take a break from rehearsals. Malte has been forced by his parents to go to Skåne and Tony is in Finland. Håkan has suggested to Grim that they meet, just the two of them, and work out new ideas. Maybe have a look at "Tormented Exaltation." Grim only offers vague excuses. He doesn't even have an opinion on the Norwegian demo Håkan gave him. All he says is that he hasn't listened to it yet. That sentence makes Håkan want to shake him.

Two of Grim's favorite bands are playing in Fagersta with Exenterate as the opening act. If anything, that should wake him up, Håkan thinks. But only Stasse and Anja show up at the bus station. "Grim stayed behind," they tell him. Håkan doesn't understand what's going on. He's furious; he's disappointed. He is afraid, mostly because he's started to get used to Grim staying away, seemingly not caring about anything. Håkan has to force himself to think back on the previous summer, just to remember what they'd been like back then, what Grim had been like back then. He hasn't always been this way, even if that's what it suddenly feels like. Something is really wrong. But what can Håkan do about it?

On the bus, Stasse says that Grim is behaving oddly. He never leaves the apartment, except to go to work. He stays in his room and Stasse has no idea what he's doing in there.

"And he doesn't buy any food, just eats yogurt and cereal."

"I think he's feeling down," Anja says.

"What's he got to feel down about?" Stasse sounds genuinely bewildered. "He's just released a record; he's in Sweden's sickest band, works in the city's best record store."

"I try to check in, now and then," Anja tells Håkan. "But he won't open his door."

"Talks on the phone, though," Stasse says. "I don't know who with, but I guess we'll know by the bill."

But Håkan thinks he already knows.

Must be expensive, all those phone calls to Skåne.

KASPER

It finally happened.

An awful song some of his classmates had picked thundered through the speakers as they ran through a cloud of confetti and into the boiling schoolyard, stopping right before the fence to jump, dance, and embrace. Kasper had a strong sense that everyone in the class had hated him because of what happened with Lydia, but no one seemed to care now. Even Lydia gave him a hug. He was about to apologize, but thought it would just make things worse. He would disappear from her life, and she'd never have to think about him again.

School was out forever.

He had imagined this day so many times, the feeling of freedom that would come with it. He tried to call it up, but everything was so confusing. The crowd on the other side of the fence was cheering, screaming, and honking, waving flags and signs with the graduating students' names and pictures of them as children. *First day with 100% attendance!* it said on the side of a truck that would soon be transporting celebrating students on a victory lap around town. The light stung his eyes and the sky was such a brutal shade of blue, it made him want to hide.

He caught a glimpse of an enlarged picture of himself as a three-year-old, a *Star Wars* logo on his shirt. His dad was holding the sign, and his mom was standing next to him, frenetically snapping photos. Atle and Tony were there, too, Diana on Atle's shoulders and Leia on Tony's. Leah waved both hands. His mom smiled and yelled something Kasper couldn't make out through the din. Maybe it had just been his name. He smiled, straightened his graduation cap, smoothed a finger over its lacquered brim.

Soon, he'd be standing at his mom and Atle's home and everyone would ask him questions about the future. *What are you up to after summer?* But this moment belonged to him. He'd managed something that had once felt impossible. He was on the other side. Something else was waiting for him—maybe life, definitely The House.

He reached for the feeling of expectation, tried to catch it again.

THE SUMMER

In August, they rehearse for a gig with Exenterate and Teratoid, who are coming up from Gothenburg. Grim is back on the guitar, Malte struggling with Ernesto's parts. Grim only perks up when he's at the mic, and even then, something is missing. He is quiet, Malte too, like they're sharing the same silence. It upsets and unsettles Håkan. Stasse is in Greece with his family for a month, and Håkan and Anja regularly go to the apartment on Tegnérgatan. Once, Anja phoned Håkan and said that there was nothing but a moldy tomato in the fridge. She had no money, so he went shopping. When he cracked open the door to Grim's room, he seemed to be sleeping. Håkan is the only one who realizes how bad the situation is, as neither Anja nor Stasse have anything to compare it with. They don't know how tidy Grim was when he lived with Håkan. Since he moved in with Stasse, he stopped making his bed and dirty clothes are piling up on the floor. *It's like quicksand in there*, Håkan thinks. The times he's tried to talk to Grim, he gets the feeling they're both sinking.

Despite that, he isn't prepared for what happens before the gig.

The youth center is north of the city. They're slotted to go on last, but everyone is there early to help out. Grim, however, doesn't show up. Håkan phones the apartment and Raw Power but doesn't get hold of anyone. He takes the subway to Rådmansgatan, throws himself onto the platform as soon as the doors open, and races up the stairs. He hurries along Tegnérgatan, punches in the code

411

at the gate, located between a pet store and Stasse's uncle's restaurant. As usual, the entrance stinks of urine, and Håkan holds his breath when he passes through. Walking up the stairs, he realizes that he forgot to ask Anja for the keys before he left. He reaches the third floor. Some neighbor is frying fish and listening to the radio. Håkan rings the bell on Grim's door. No answer. Håkan opens the mailbox.

"Grim!" he shouts, and he hears his own voice echo up and down the stairwell. "I know you're here!" He hopes he's right about that. "Come on, for fuck's sake. Hello!"

He rings the doorbell, rings it again. A dog starts barking in the neighboring apartment. After a moment, he hears dragging steps approaching. The door is unlocked. And there's Grim.

"Hey," he says, voice flat.

As if he shouldn't be on the very other side of town right now, as if he doesn't have a gig in a moment. His eyes are glassy, almost feverish, and Håkan wonders if he's actually sick.

"We have a gig," Håkan tells him. "Have you forgotten about that?"

"Fuck, no," Grim says, which is difficult to interpret, and then he backs a few steps into the apartment, turns and disappears into his room.

Håkan enters, closing the door behind him. The air in the apartment is stale, as if no one has opened the window in days. In his room, Grim is getting changed.

The dark blue curtain is drawn, but despite the twilight in the room, Håkan can see how bad it is. It stinks of sweat and dirty laundry and something sour that Håkan can't identify. A wasp crawls along the edge of an unwashed bowl. Opened beer cans sit on the amp; records, cassettes, and books are strewn across the floor. A single is collecting dust on the turntable. Håkan looks at the drawings on the wall. They're not his usual motifs, horror and caricatures. These images are more abstract, containing symbols Håkan recognizes from the books on magic. The same motif recurs on several of them. A labyrinth. In its middle is a letter.

"Why does this say U?" Håkan asks.

"It's not a *U.*"

Grim is wearing his clothes for the stage, black jeans, black tee. Two huge studded bracelets. Håkan thinks that Grim won't need makeup tonight, since he's almost black around the eyes.

"They're horns," Grim continues. "It's a Minoan symbol. A civilization on Crete. Two thousand years before Christ. That symbol appears everywhere. There's this theory that it represents the Minotaur."

Håkan dimly recalls a monster from Greek mythology and role-playing games.

"Are they the ones with bodies like horses?" he says.

"No," Grim says. "Those are *centaurs*. In the myths there was only one Minotaur. Half man, half bull, though you don't know which parts were which. He was trapped inside a labyrinth and they let people in there for him to eat. He was, like, the labyrinth's ruler and prisoner. But then a hero came and killed him. A girl helped, too. Gave the hero string, so he could find his way out again."

"Okay," Håkan says. "But what's it all about?"

Grim doesn't respond. His eyes are shining. He looks the way he does on stage or when he's writing, but this is more intense, so intense Håkan is frightened in a way he can't explain.

"I think I've found a way out," Grim tells him, and his voice sounds perfectly calm.

"Out of the labyrinth?"

Grim looks at him.

"I talked to Raw Power. They're going to help us distribute the record. Go get the contract so your mom can sign it. I already have."

"Are you serious?" Håkan says.

It's a massive relief, knowing that Grim has actually gone ahead and done something.

"I don't know a lot about stuff like that," Grim says, "but the important thing is that we get it out there."

"Great."

They won't get a penny for it, but right now, it's as if Grim has kicked a door open. *Ancient Bloodlust* is heading out into the world. Just like they planned.

"You're wearing blue jeans," Grim notes. "We said black tonight."

Håkan is disproportionately pleased that Grim is bothered by a detail like that.

"My mom threw my black jeans in the wash," he says. "Come on, Teratoid will be on soon."

They step out into the hallway and Grim ties his boots, straightens his skinny body.

"Håkan," he says softly. "Thanks for coming to get me."

The hug surprises Håkan. He isn't unused to hugging his friends, but Grim isn't much for physical contact.

"No problem," he mumbles against Grim's sharp shoulder.

Together, they leave the apartment and journey to their final gig.

THE HOUSE

Something is wrong in The House.

As a visitor, you wouldn't be able to feel it, but he does. The one with a dead man's name on his arm.

You can't step into the same river twice. In a steady flow of young people, employed by season, not much is stable. Cornelia is in a Shakespeare play at an outdoor theater all summer. Selam, now a TL, is running around with a phone pressed to her ear. Many of the old demons have returned for another season, but the energy has changed. The sense of community is dissipating. Nasty comments, glares, and whispers. He notices everything.

But maybe The House hasn't changed.

Maybe *he* has.

How odd that you can have exactly the same eyes, but see every-thing so differently from one summer to the next. What he's seeing now feels truer. Last year, he was naive, blinded, tricked by his new, fake self-confidence, imagining that he was doing a good job.

The best days are the ones when he feels completely empty. Those days make it easier to pretend. He knows how to do it, has been an expert for many years, and old habits die hard.

Other days are more difficult. He can't listen properly and for-gets what he was supposed to do. He'll be standing in a corridor, not remembering where he was heading. Sometimes he gets the feel-ing he's swum too far and can't make it back to the shore. Still, he swims.

Both Iris and Selam try to have a serious talk with him. They take him aside, wrapping their criticism in praise. But he understands what's happening. They're about to see him for the fraud he is. During the nights, he lies awake, trying to think of a way to do a better job. He's probably already disappointed everyone, but he can make sure it doesn't get worse, at least. The thoughts won't stop churning. The only time he's really calm is when he walks the closing route alone, wandering through The House in the dark. In the Hall of Mirrors, he always stops, waits. But there are no foreign scents or sounds, and no strange breezes brush over his face.

He finds the opening in his dreams.

Those nights when he can sleep, he enters. He's looking for someone, and sometimes it feels as if he's close, right there, just around the corner. He just has to be patient. Try more, last a bit longer. He's waiting for him.

Leah sends him a link to a vocational course she's talked about, but he can't make himself apply. He's sure he won't get in. He hasn't drawn anything new since this spring, the expensive birthday present lies unused. And he'd never be able to be an apprentice, anyway. Strange that Leah, who's so intelligent, would have such a skewed image of him. It has to be because she's in love with his dad.

Besides, how could he be a tattoo artist when he can hardly take care of the one tattoo he has? Sometimes when he's alone, it starts to itch. When he touches the letters, they burn him like fire.

One day, he works with a new demon and suddenly forgets her name. It makes him realize he can't apply for the position of UC for Halloween. He doesn't even apply as a cast member and knows he's doing everyone a favor. So as not to have to explain it, he says he might have a new job on the way. Everyone seems to believe him, including Iris.

One day, he walks across the Main Area and sees them: Marco, Oliver, Ali. They're there, all three of them, and they're still friends, the way they've been for so long. A thought strikes him.

I don't exist. Maybe I've never existed.

Then one night, when he's closing up The House, he thinks about the black beaches. The ones on New Zealand's northern island. He wonders if Ossian's dream had anything to do with real life, if Ossian had sat on that beach and thought about heading out into the waves, letting the currents claim him. Had Ossian ever really wanted to die? The thought recurs after that, frequently.

In August, he sees Ossian on stage again. The mini festival his dad fantasized about came true, in combination with a release party for his mom's photo book. Dark Cruelty has done their shows abroad, been offered even more. But they've agreed that this is enough. Better to go out on top. And what's better than all the old bands playing together? The ones who kept going and the ones who have quit. Songs from the demo days, old lineups when possible, a small circle of invited peers. Full throttle all night. Nuclearathon and Vomitator. Teratoid, straight from Gothenburg. Malodor and Exenterate. And last of all, Dark Cruelty.

He's in the audience, next to Iris, and their faces are shiny with sweat. Above them are Håkan, Ernesto, Tony. Leah, who came along as rhythm guitarist for the tour. Ossian is at the mic. He looks at Kasper and their eyes meet. The undercurrent tugs at him. There is only one way left to wander. It's time.

THE UNDERGROUND

Håkan has started to detest his job sorting mail. Ever since Grim left, he's been meaning to find something else to do, but now it's September and he's still stuck. Nothing is happening with Dark Cruelty. Grim didn't even come for rehearsals after the gig. When Håkan called, Stasse said that Grim was sick. Håkan decided that they should pause the rehearsals until he gets better. He's seen Grim become inexplicably sick before and guesses this is something similar. He'll be back on his feet soon.

Håkan only wishes that Grim would answer the phone when he calls. It's been almost two weeks without Håkan hearing his voice. He's standing with his headphones on, sorting mail, when Jensa hits him hard on the shoulder.

"Nordin," he says. "You have a call. Think it's your boyfriend."

Håkan ignores his grin and rushes to the phone.

"Hello?" he says breathlessly.

As soon as he hears Stasse's voice, he realizes something is wrong.

"They called from Raw Power. Grim didn't come in today. Not yesterday, either."

Really fucking wrong.

Håkan spots Jensa's mocking grin when he takes his things, lying about a relative who's had to go to the hospital. Håkan doesn't know if he'll get away with it, but right now, he doesn't actually give a shit. He can't stay here. He has to do something.

He bikes home in the drizzle, and once there, he dials Stasse's number. They divide the circle of friends between them, start to call everyone they know. Report back one hour later. No one has seen Grim. At Malte's and some others', they receive no response at all. Tony comes over, goes through the phone book—what's Virre's surname? Is this his dad? The sound when Håkan rotates the disk on the phone makes them hope, allows that hope to live while the signals ring out, dies when the answer comes. Ernesto calls and asks if he can help, but Håkan hears Ossian screaming in the background and tells him that it isn't necessary. Then he calls Malte for the second time. This time there is a click, and a woman answers.

"Lundell, in the middle of dinner."

"Is Malte there?" says Håkan.

"Who am I talking to?"

Her voice is as impersonal as a switchboard operator's.

"Oh, sorry," Håkan says. "This is Håkan Nordin. We play in the same band."

"Oh, hi, Håkan. I'm Malte's mother. He's sick at the moment, unfortunately, and can't take any calls."

Malte's voice is heard in the background.

"One moment," Malte's mom says.

Håkan is practically bouncing up and down, the receiver burning against his ear.

"Hello?" he hears Malte's hoarse voice say.

Håkan explains the situation. Malte coughs.

"Don't know where he is," he says.

"So when was the last time you talked to him?"

"I don't know. Monday maybe." Another bout of harsh coughing. "Call me if you hear anything." With that, Malte hangs up.

Monday. The word rings in Håkan's ears. Grim has ignored Håkan's calls, but he had been talking to Malte just a few days ago.

But it doesn't matter now. Håkan has to put *Monday* out of his mind.

When Stasse calls, Håkan hears the same thing from him. No one in their circle has seen or talked to Grim in weeks. *Except Malte.*

"I don't even know when he was last at home," Stasse says, sounding pained. "He works regular hours and I work late and sometimes we don't see each other for days . . . Fuck."

Håkan tells Stasse it isn't his fault, and besides, they'll find Grim soon. He hangs up. Thinks about the ritual in the deserted house. They agree that Tony should go there with his dad, while Håkan stays at home, keeping guard. When his mom comes home, he tells her what's happened. She insists on calling Grim's mom, and Håkan can't stop her. He can't bear to listen to her talking to Inger, trying to soothe her. There are other places he can look. It's pouring outside, and he pulls on his mother's raincoat over his jacket, takes the DBS and bikes out, heading for some of the places they've visited together, he and Grim. A cold wind blows over the Jordbro burial site as Håkan stomps around in the mud. He stops at the rock they'd sat on once, the rain whipping against his face.

He knows where to go.

An hour later, he gets off at the station Grim took him to one night in early summer. The other passengers leave the platform, and he is left standing there. Anxiously, Håkan stares into the tunnel. Which way was it that he and Grim went? He can't think. Maybe he should talk to someone who works at the station and say . . . what? That his friend might be stuck in the tunnels? Will they believe him? Does he even think so himself? Why would Grim be here, of all places?

For one breathless moment, Håkan wonders if he's only dreamed that they visited the Lake. Can a place like that even exist?

He takes a deep breath and closes his eyes, trying to remember. They went *against* the direction of the trains, but were the trains northbound or southbound? Suddenly, he's sure. He goes to the schedule and checks; the trains still run quite often. He tries to estimate how many minutes it took them to get to the side tunnel, but he lost all notion of time in the dark. Håkan's knees start to tremble so badly he has to sit on a bench. He's gone crazy. He can't do this. But he has to. In his jacket pocket, he has the flashlight he picked up before he raced to the station in the rain.

I shouldn't be doing this alone, Håkan thinks, following along the platform. His wet shoes slap against the ground when he walks, his damp hair sticking to his neck. What if Grim has come home by now? What if, at this very moment, he is trying to call Håkan?

He's waiting for the next train. After that, he has five minutes. If he runs, he should definitely make it. He thinks so, anyway.

The train rushes out of the station and Håkan waits impatiently for the passengers to disappear up the stairs. He tries to look as if he's not doing anything suspicious, standing at the farthest end of the platform, and probably fails at it. Finally, only a solitary figure is left, slumped on a bench. Håkan jumps, landing heavily on the track. He turns on the flashlight and starts running. His pulse beats so loudly he doesn't trust himself to hear the oncoming train when it approaches. The beam of the flashlight jumps, shakes. How far was it to the side tunnel? He thinks he hears that ticking sound in the tracks, the one that means a train is on its way. Sometimes trains that are out of service still travel but aren't visible on the schedule.

But there it is, the side tunnel, and he's forcing himself to slow down, to take a step over the third rail. His pulse is racing. He has a stitch in his side but hurtles on, splashing through puddles of rainwater that have seeped all the way down here. He comes upon the stairs, slips on the first step, and hits his knee but can't feel it. Continues upward, pushing up the steel door. The taste of blood in his mouth as he passes the fans, his shoes thundering over the grate above the tracks, echoing through the space. The beam of light hits the mouth of the narrow tunnel and he thinks about the stairs leading down to the water, the water so clear it's almost invisible.

Inside the mountain, the air feels thick and heavy to breathe, smells dank. A scent of urine and something else, something rotten. Håkan slows down. Horror grips him around the neck like a cold claw as he heads deeper into the tunnel. His heart is pounding after his run and sweat pours off him. He tries to keep the beam steady, but the hand holding the flashlight trembles; his other hand reaches for the rough stone wall to steady himself.

"Grim," he whispers.

He's too afraid to call out. He feels like there's something in here, something watching him. He thinks of the stairs and the ladder under the water, the layers of sediment covering it. The smell grows stronger and Håkan can feel the tears running down his face. He is crying with horror, because something is wrong here, so very wrong.

The beam from the flashlight hits something round on the ground. At first, Håkan thinks it's a rock, but it's an apple, a rotten apple that rats have gnawed on. There's another one, and next to it is a string. A thick, brown thread leading into the tunnel. Håkan accidentally steps on an already smashed piece of fruit and slips. The beam of light goes flying, hitting the upper part of the staircase that goes down into the darkness. Håkan doesn't know how he's supposed to get down. What if he sees Grim lying in the water, or maybe just his jacket, which has floated up to the surface?

He prays silently to a God he doesn't believe in and asks forgiveness for all the inverted crosses and the blasphemies. He tries the only bit of a prayer he knows: *Now I lay me down to sleep, I pray the Lord my soul to keep. Just this once. Please.*

Then he sees Grim.

The string leads to him. A ball of it rests by his left hand. He lies farther away in the tunnel, beyond the shaft leading to the Lake, with his head toward Håkan. His eyes are closed. Dead people have open eyes, don't they? Don't they?

In the narrow tunnel, he falls to his knees by Grim, a rotten apple splitting open under his shin. The sickly sweet scent spreads, mixes with the smell of urine coming from Grim. His head is a little to the side. Around his neck, he is wearing the necklace with the pentagram on it, and Håkan sees that something that looks like salt and ashes have been scattered on the ground. But he doesn't have time to sit around and wonder about that. Grim is breathing rapidly and superficially, his mouth half-open. There is a string of dried saliva in one corner of his mouth. Every once in a while, his breath rattles, like he's got mucus in his windpipe.

"Grim?" Håkan shakes him slightly. Grim's body is completely limp. "I'm here."

No reaction. Grim's lips are chapped and dry. How long has he been down here?

"Grim?" Håkan whispers again.

He puts his hand against Grim's cheek and then jerks it away. The skin is cool and dry, papery, and Håkan suddenly understands that Grim is dying.

What should he do? Should he run and get help? Is he supposed to leave Grim behind in the dark? He can't; it's not possible. Out of the corner of his eye, he sees stairs leading down toward the water. The sound of dripping water comes from below, echoing through the tunnel.

Håkan crouches down behind Grim. He remembers a scene from a film in which a soldier pulls an unconscious comrade backward with his arms hooked under the friend's armpits. But when he tries to lift Grim's upper body, he realizes that he can't do it. Grim is unexpectedly heavy, and he can't get a good grip; it feels like Grim's head could tip forward and break his neck.

"It's okay," Håkan whispers. "I'll get you out."

He steps over Grim so that he stands with one foot on either side of his body, then leans in and hooks his arms under Grim's armpits, drags him close, as if in an embrace. A sigh escapes from between Grim's lips.

"Grim?" Håkan says softly. "Hello?"

No answer. Maybe it was just some air being squeezed out of his lungs. With his arms around Grim, Håkan squirms to get behind him, tries to make sure his head doesn't slam into the rock. He finally manages the soldier's grip. Grim's head hangs heavily on his chest. Håkan begins to pull. It's slow, slower than he could ever have imagined. Grim's body is heavy as lead, and Håkan feels every muscle in his own body strain with tension. A damp wind brushes across his face as he gets nearer the shaft. Goose bumps rise all over his flesh and he struggles to move quicker, to get as far from the stairs as fast as possible. Grim's boots bounce over the uneven ground. The beam of the flashlight is shaking. Håkan is terrified that he'll drop it. He thinks he can see a shadow of something that should not be there. A wet sound can be heard. A thud against the metal from far below. Then another. Then another. A pungent smell of blood and rotting meat. A dull, droning noise. Adrenaline burns through Håkan's body as he drags his friend backward, inch by inch, an apple splitting under his heel. Something rattles, and he sees the string being pulled into the darkness. It must be a rat. Rats are smart. A rat wants the string for its nest. The droning sound is getting stronger. It could be the vibrations of a machine, or several voices united in an impossibly deep tone. Håkan stares wildly in front of him in the leaping shaky beam from the flashlight, prepared for something to appear at any second, and then he feels the grate under his shoes and knows he is on the bridge.

He has to manage it. At least to the room with the fans. Down the stairs will be impossible, he realizes now, but he has to get Grim as far out of the tunnel as he can. The rails sing under him and then

Håkan feels the rush of wind against his wet cheeks as the train plunges past. Screaming, he pulls Grim over the grate, his voice drowned out by the booming and squealing of the train. When the flashlight hits the entrance of the tunnel, he thinks he can see a form—or is it a shadow?—impossibly large, impossibly shaped. Håkan gasps and the flashlight slides out of his sweaty grip.

The darkness comes down like a blade.

Håkan is crying uncontrollably now. The train that passed is safely ensconced at the platform. There, there are people and lights. Here, there's only darkness and death and the shape in the mouth of the tunnel. Is it a step he hears on the bridge, or is it Grim's boots thumping against the grate? Håkan's strength is running out, he can feel it in his back, shoulders, arms, and legs. He's about to break. He wishes he were stronger, he wishes for Jensa's muscles, Tony's height, anything that could give him more energy, just a little more.

And suddenly, he can feel concrete beneath his feet. He sobs loudly as he drags Grim into the room with the fans and gently lays him down, recovery position. What did that look like? He feels across Grim's face and hears the rattling breaths. He whispers that he'll come back soon, he'll get help; he holds him and whispers, "Please wait," and then he gets the lighter out of his pocket, tries to flick it on, but there is only a spark. When he tries again, he drops it, hears it slide away across the floor. He doesn't have time to look for it. With wide, unseeing eyes he crawls across the floor until he finds the wall, rises, reaches out, and all the time he is afraid he'll hear that droning behind him, or discover that he is heading in the wrong direction, *toward* the bridge, *toward* the Lake, *toward* the terror.

Håkan hears a sniffle and realizes it's coming from him. There is the steel door and then the steep stairs. He sits down, the way a child would, makes his way down one step at a time. Fumbles for the wall and finds it. Water flows over his hands, rainwater from above ground. A sharp pain in his shin when he hits a low concrete base. The tunnel feels endless. Like when he was little and woke up in the middle of the night, not daring to go to the bathroom, because it felt like the world had dissolved in the darkness and transformed. He is in that world now.

Then he sees a patch of light, far ahead. It's the platform. He stumbles and falls down on the gravel, knows he could have fallen onto the third rail, but he has no fear left in him. He runs along the side of the track, between the tunnel wall and the rail. Maybe he'll be fine if he presses himself against the wall when the train comes. Maybe not. Gravel crunches beneath his shoes and he starts shouting, his voice echoing through the tunnel. He screams for help, as loudly as he can, and jumps over the third rail, racing down the middle of the track toward the glow of the station. A man in a suede jacket bends down and helps him up.

"What on earth are you doing?" says the man, frightened, and Håkan tears himself loose, runs toward the ticket booth, and hammers against the plexiglass.

The woman in the booth stares at him, a mad, long-haired adolescent, probably under the influence of drugs.

"Please, he's dying," says Håkan. "He's really sick. Please."

The woman just gawks at him. Is she even listening to him?

"He's dying. He's in the tunnel. Please call, you have to call someone."

She's picking up the phone. Håkan repeats it over and over again: "By the fans. He's by the fans."

The woman comes out of the booth. He hears her say something about stopping the traffic, but this had better not be a joke. He hears something about the police, the paramedics, the fire brigade before he starts running ahead of her, coming down onto the platform and pointing. Pointing into the dark.

"He's right there," he says. "By the fans. By the fans."

Alone in there.

"I have to go back," Håkan says.

He tries to get to the edge of the platform, but the man in the suede jacket grips him and is so strong that Håkan gets nowhere. When he tries to slide out of the jacket, that old trick, the man's hands grip even harder.

"You don't get it, I have to go back," Håkan tries to explain. "He is alone."

The light on the platform is so strong. It dazzles him and he sees cops. Or are they firefighters? They're on their way now. Grim will get help.

"Let me go," says Håkan. "Please let go. I won't do anything. They're here now. They're here."

The hands let him go, and he sees that the rescue officer is down on the track, that the tunnel is lit. They'll find Grim soon. They know where to look. And soon, they'll come back with him, take him to the hospital. Because he's alive. He has to live. But Håkan left him there. He smells rotten apples, the stench of rancid blood, and suddenly he has to leave. It's his body running from the platform, up the stairs and out into the September darkness. It's his body racing to the next subway station and boarding the train. Somehow, unbelievably, he makes it home that night.

He comes home to silence. The clock ticks loudly in the living room. His mom is in there, too; she's fallen asleep on the couch with the phone next to her. Håkan enters the bathroom, washes his hands and face. Black stains in the sink. He rubs soap over and into his hands hard, but the smell of damp earth and rot is in his nose, is all over him. He takes off his clothes and drops them on the floor, gets into the shower. The soap stings in the scrapes he up until now didn't even notice.

A gentle knock on the door.

His mother asks Håkan if he wants something to eat, and he hears himself saying, "Yes, please." He gathers the towel around him, goes into his room and puts on clothes. He imagines that Grim is heading to the hospital in a rush, imagines the ambulance's blue lights and the sirens. No, actually, he's probably already there. They'll take care of him. Examine him properly, give him an IV bag and medication, operate on him if necessary. Maybe he'll get a scar he can boast about. Håkan eats the pea soup that his mother has warmed for him and thinks about how he'll visit Grim at the hospital, bring a pile of newly minted comics and put them on the hospital's standard-issue blankets. Grim smiles at him, pale and wan but on the mend, and he asks Håkan to describe once again how he pulled him through the tunnel. Håkan will exaggerate the struggle, of course, say, "You were fucking heavy," and they'll both laugh at it.

His mom talks to him, but he can't hear what she's saying. It can't be important, anyway, because the only thing that's important is that he found Grim, that Grim is in good hands now.

The sharp sound of a doorbell cuts through his thoughts, and his mom gets to her feet, disappears into the hall. He sees her return, followed closely by two cops, coming into the living room after her. They don't notice Håkan where he's sitting; they're focused on his mom. Their expressions are serious. Håkan gets up and walks as if in a trance across the kitchen floor. Hears one of them say: ". . . you have a seventeen-year-old son named Håkan, don't you?"

"Yes?" his mom says.

"Unfortunately, we've found a deceased, unidentified boy about Håkan's age," the cop says. "We found your phone number in his pocket."

His mom says, "No."

And it is only then, when Håkan sees her bringing her hand to her mouth, that he registers the word *deceased*.

"It has to be Grim," his mom says. She looks up, meeting Håkan's gaze.

The cops turn around and look at him, too, look at his mom again while she explains that Håkan's friend has gone missing, that Håkan has been out looking for him all day.

"He's not dead," says Håkan.

All three of them look at him now.

"It's a misunderstanding," Håkan tells them. "I saw him myself. He's alive."

And it is only then, when he hears himself say it, that he begins to understand that Grim is dead.

KASPER

It was late afternoon but black as night when Kasper stepped off the train, eight stations north of Handen.

A fat drop of rain hit him in the eye, temporarily blinding him. He put his hood up and hurried across the platform. Over his sweater, he was wearing one of his dad's old leather jackets.

He hadn't told anyone where he was going.

He could barely admit it to himself.

But he had to turn over every stone. There was only one left.

The rain intensified. Today, it had been thirty years since Grim died. That was the day Ossian, probably for dramatic effect, had suggested they meet when he replied to Kasper's message. His dad had invited Tony and Ernesto for dinner tonight, had been slow-cooking all day. Kasper had lied about meeting up with a friend. And now, here he was.

A strong sense of unreality came over him when he passed people who unfolded their umbrellas or jogged, hunching, through the rain. It felt as if they were moving through one world and Kasper through another. Their world was the real one, and they knew their steps, their lines. But he could barely get from one moment to the next. Every thought was accompanied by a trail of *if, if not, why, why not.* Guilt and shame paralyzed him. How did you learn to just *exist*? He had thought he'd understood it for a little while, but this, like so many other things, had been an illusion. He tried to cling to the things that made his life meaningful.

His family.

Be honest, Kasper. You're a burden to them. Look at your mom, she had to have new children because the first attempt was such a failure.

His friends.

Which ones? Lydia, who you treated like shit? The classmates you never bothered to get to know? The demons? They're sick of you. They can tell how bad you've become at your job. You had Iris, once, but she's also leaving; you're pushing her away just like you've pushed everyone else away. A friendship with you has a best-before date, and then it starts to stink. Just accept it.

His art.

You haven't created anything of value since dreaming about Grim. That was a year ago. You don't even want to draw anymore, so what's left?

Was this what Grim felt like? Kasper wondered. Had he had similar thoughts back then, when his final summer had faded into autumn?

How can you compare yourself to him? Being depressed and a genius is one thing, but you're nobody. You change nothing, you leave no impression, you move like a shadow through this world. If you died today, no one would miss you thirty years later, that much is certain.

The tattoo burned beneath his sweatshirt. This morning, his skin had been red and inflamed. At breakfast, Leah had been sitting right across from him, but he hadn't asked her about it, convinced he had done something wrong.

God, you're boring. Shame and guilt, guilt and shame. What did you expect? You should have removed his name or covered it with something else. You're not worthy of it.

He walked parallel to a heavily trafficked road. It was raining sideways, and he had to shield his eyes with his hand to see. The water pooled, gathering in puddles where he walked. He stepped in one of them and felt his sock soak in water. His jeans stuck to his legs. The entrance to Ossian's apartment was next to a shop that sold clothes for old ladies. Kasper punched in the code he'd been given. The round metal handle was slippery with rainwater when he pushed open the door. He stepped inside, waited until it shut behind him. The stairwell was shadowy. He could hear cars whiz past in the rain outside. He realized that he was freezing, fumbled the phone out of his pocket. Hesitated.

He knew that the sensible thing would be to tell someone where he was. He should at least text Iris. But when he considered it, weighing the decision in his head, at least ten voices countered him. *Don't drag her into this. Every friendship is a balance, and you're always in negative numbers. You may have gained a little for a while, but you're back to where you were. You can't ask more of her, especially after being such a shitty colleague all season. Iris will be relieved not to know; she won't understand why you need to do this, anyway. She'll try to stop you. She'll tell your dad. You don't even know if you can trust her. All your friends have let you down, so why not Iris? It makes sense: you can't even blame her for it. You don't deserve friends. You don't deserve anything.*

The thoughts felt so true, one in particular.

If you've got a problem, you deal with it. Why would you have the right to burden someone else with it?

He shoved his phone back into his hoodie pocket. But first, he turned on the recording app. It was a risk, of course, but he trusted his memory less than ever.

He walked up the stairs and stopped at the door bearing the name Holm, rang the bell. Ossian opened up quicker than he'd expected, giving Kasper a short nod.

The walls in the hallway were painted black. Kasper removed his jacket. Droplets of water hit the linoleum floor. He found an available hook on the coatrack, which was practically full, noted that his hair was damp, his hood so wet he could have squeezed water out of it. He dried his face with his sleeve. The phone weighed heavily in his pocket. When he leaned down to untie his shoes, it nearly fell out.

The apartment was silent. The rain beat against the windows when Kasper entered the living room.

The shelves were stuffed with records and books. On the walls were tour posters and art prints, animal skulls, bones, and a couple of ritual masks. Small statues from all over the world, a few jars in which animals floated in formaldehyde. A vase with dried, dark-red roses in it stood on a side table. They could be Paola's touch, but wouldn't be outside the realm of Ossian's interests. A lot of metal-heads, even the most extreme ones, were really into crafts.

Kasper looked at the vase full of dead roses and the man next to it. His shoulder-length hair was gray, the widow's peak more pronounced than when Kasper had been a child and seen him at the festival. His forehead was heavily lined, the wrinkles around his eyes deep. He looked older than Kasper's dad, despite being two years younger. Black leather vest over a band tee. An inverted pentagram in a chain around his neck. There was no approval in his eyes, no sign of recognition. Kasper almost began to wonder if he'd been wrong, if maybe this wasn't Malte but some other man.

"Does Håkan know you're here?"

Something about the way he said *Håkan* made Kasper go cold. It was as if Malte was cutting off the connection between Kasper and his dad with one blow, making Kasper's treachery apparent. It wasn't until then that he realized what it truly meant, having come here. He would have to keep it secret for the rest of his life, because his dad would never forgive him for it. Neither would his mom. None of their friends. And the question was if Kasper could ever forgive himself. All he'd heard and read about Malte ran through his head, the threats against his dad, the bleeding, dying man on the stairs, and the self-contempt that hit him was so overwhelming it made him dizzy.

But it was too late. He had to do this now.

"No," Kasper said. "No one knows I'm here."

By Malte's reaction, he could tell it was the right thing to say. He didn't smile, but he looked pleased. Leaned back in the couch, his hand holding on to the armrest, muscles tense. He was as far from beefy as he'd always been, but that arm was strong—Kasper didn't doubt it. A *vegvísir* was tattooed on his hand: an Icelandic symbol that helped travelers find their way. Leah had one, too.

Ossian sat down in one of the two leather armchairs. Kasper sat down in the other one. His wet hair and hood stuck to the headrest and his socks had left wet marks on Ossian's floor. He had his back to the hallway and noticed Malte's eyes return to it now and then. Even though he was sitting perfectly still, he still had a somewhat hunted look about him. Kasper could see that now. How would Malte react if he knew that the phone in Kasper's pocket was recording everything? He didn't want to think about it.

Ossian was quiet. Kasper wondered if this was the first time he'd hosted Malte in his living room. Again, he wondered if it was the first time he, Kasper, met Malte, or if they'd seen each other in a house in a forest.

"You look just like him," Malte said with his hoarse, slightly monotonous voice. "Almost eerie. Not much of Anja in you."

"Fifty percent," Kasper said, unable to stop himself.

Malte laughed, a hard, snorting laugh.

"But you haven't inherited the music. You don't play."

"No," Kasper said.

"So Håkan hasn't tried to teach you?"

He had. He had put the guitar in Kasper's lap and showed him what to do. But Kasper had been restless. It wasn't like drawing; there were no immediate results.

"I know a few chords," Kasper said.

"How is Håkan?" Malte asked.

"Fine," Kasper said shortly.

Malte's face was expressionless. Why was he asking these questions? Was he trying to unsettle Kasper, somehow?

"You must have heard a lot about me," Malte said.

"I guess so," Kasper said.

The man on the couch nodded. "I can imagine," he said, taking some snuff. "But I'll tell you what really happened."

Appendix 12. From the transcript of Kasper's recording of Malte Lundell. Ossian Holm also present at the time.

M: I met Grim . . . I had just discovered more extreme metal that autumn, when they released the *Nocturnal Allegiance* demo. We were a few people in my school who were into role-playing games and metal. We had a band, too. But the others stopped somewhere around Metallica and Megadeth. Then it got too much for them. But I got hold of the demo and some copy of *Headed for Death*. Immediately, I felt a sense of connection with Grim. Metalheads aren't very bright most of the time. There aren't that many people in the scene you can have a meaningful conversation with. But Grim was intelligent, well-read, you could tell. So when they played that youth center, their first show with him, I went. It was . . . Exenterate and Malodor played the same evening, but I was there for Dark Cruelty. The rest of the band made no significant impression, but Grim . . . (*silence*) It's a talent in itself, recognizing talent, and I have always had it. I saw his greatness. He was far greater than the others. All bands present included. Grim wanted more. He understood . . . (*clears throat*) I wrote him the very same evening, via *Headed for Death*. (*coughs*) And that was how I found out they were looking for a second guitarist. (*coughs for some time*)
(*Sound of O getting up and going into the kitchen*)
M: Håkan always behaved as though he had some sort of ownership over Grim. And I see why. Dark Cruelty was an insignificant band. Exenterate and Malodor were at the top. Håkan was just trying to catch up. Then he was fortunate enough to meet Grim. You have to give that to Håkan: he was intelligent enough to realize that he had to let Grim set the course if they were going to get anywhere . . .
(*Steps as O returns. Bottles are placed on the table. Bottle caps opened.*)
M: To me, metal was never just about music. When music is truly powerful, it connects us to something bigger and more ancient than what we can grasp. Some of us feel it. Those of us who dare put our ear to the ground and listen to the beats of the beast's dark heart. (*drinks, clears throat*) I had an interest in the occult before meeting Grim. Together, we

went deeper into it. Håkan came along for a bit of it. I can imagine he hasn't told you much about that. (*pause*) Has he?

K: No.

M: We shared some powerful experiences, the three of us. Håkan's problem . . . He was weak. He tried to restrain Grim. He didn't understand what drove him. (*clears throat*) I'm disgusted by the way some people talk and write about Grim these days. Repulsive. As if he was some sort of mentally fragile, I don't know, a delicate fucking flower. He was above all of that. He couldn't relate to other people and knew it for the strength it was. There's a lot of pity going around now, but he was cold. Ice cold. He would have laughed at the way everyone is moaning and complaining nowadays. Pathetic. But geniuses are often misrepresented by the world in which they live, both before and after their deaths. At first you don't take them seriously, then you try to clean them up. And Grim was a genius. Not just in music. His deed was greater than that. He was fearless. Utterly fearless. He knew the risk he was taking and faced death with open eyes, believe me. (*drinks*) You're a quiet boy, Kasper. Not like your dad. (*laughs*) God. Talked my head off . . . Grim knew when to shut up, that was another one of his strengths. (*silence*) We experimented with magic during that time, but . . . We wanted to go beyond the things you found . . . (*inaudible*) . . . the commercialized, that Crowley shit. We wanted to touch the core of it. Something primeval. The source. And I had an interesting contact. This guy in my school, he was part of the role-playing group. His dad's uncle, something like that, the kid claimed this man was a "real magician," that was how he put it. That the old man was in some secret society and had grimoires in his bookshelves. I was pretty skeptical about the truth of what he was saying. This kid was the type who wanted to impress others. Weak. But I thought I should look into it. It took some time, but I found out his name, then wrote him a letter of introduction, but under an assumed name. I wrote that I . . . I flattered his ego, wrote that I had heard he was knowledgeable regarding the esoteric, that I was looking for a tutor in the arts. Something like that. Then I phoned him a week later and asked if he'd received my letter. I could hear that he didn't take me seriously. Not then. Not yet. But he said that I could come over.

So I went with Grim. (*drinks*) At first we were very impressed. It was . . .
He sat on top of a treasure, that old man. I think he was lonely, too. In
need of an audience. He was almost blind, never went out. Had one of
those . . . Cavalier King Charles Spaniel that followed in his heels. You
know that smell of old dog? This dog stank. So did the old man. He had
some maid, a Polish woman, who seemed to take care of most things,
but she can't have helped him shower. But we sat and listened. Young
and hungry for every scrap of true knowledge we could get. He understood that. He fed us as if we were birds. A crumb here, a crumb there.
But we weren't birds, we were wolves. He understood that too late . . .
(*Kasper moves, a rustling in the microphone, audio quality deteriorates.*)
M: (*inaudible*) . . . one day he was drunk, sat there and monologued,
said more than he should when Grim started asking questions. This old
man had spoken a bit about apotheosis. I suppose you're not familiar
with the term.
K: No.
M: The Romans practiced a form of it. Posthumous deification. Great
men becoming gods after their deaths. But it's also the very core of
the magical tradition we were researching. That man has that potential
inside of him. To transcend, become more than human. A demigod, if
you will. If he can only cast aside the shackles of humanity. Whatever
weighs him down. His conscience. The pain. The weakness. Grim was
very interested in that. And he asked the old man of ways of achieving
it. He'd asked several times, but this time, the old man was drunk, started bragging about this ancient ritual, thousands of years old, but written down at the end of the last century. (*inaudible*) . . . Minoan culture in
Crete. The labyrinth and the Minotaur . . . (*inaudible*) . . . myth is really a
story about a ceremony in which a chosen one heads into the maze . . .
(*inaudible*) . . . not a real place, as such, but a different reality one
reaches through labyrinths . . . (*inaudible*) . . . just like Theseus in the
myth, he has to have . . . (*inaudible*) . . . find and master the Minotaur, an
ancient force . . . (*inaudible*) . . . show himself worthy . . . (*inaudible*) . . .
leave body and soul behind (*inaudible*) . . . ascendance. (*silence*) Grim
was obsessed with it. He tried to get the old man to show us the document with the instructions for the ritual. But he refused. Regretted his

intoxicated blabbering. So Grim stole it. (*coughs*) You look shocked. He stole all the time. As I said, he was above all that . . . Ordinary moral . . . (*drinks*) We were a little concerned that the old man would find us, but he didn't know our real names, and then . . . (*inaudible*) . . . accident came at the very right moment, really . . . (*inaudible*) . . . burned down two floors in that building. Probably fell asleep in bed with a lit cigarette. Went up in flames. Stinking old man, stinking old dog. (*silence*) Anyway. It was a particularly advanced ritual. Nothing you can do by yourself. Someone has to be . . . (*inaudible*) . . . Ariadne's thread . . . (*inaudible*) . . . hold on to it, symbolically, but also concretely. Otherwise, the magician performing the ritual can get lost. (*coughs*) I tried to talk to him about it. I told him he should be more experienced, or at least have me there to assist him. But he was determined. When he disappeared, I understood at once that he had gone somewhere to perform the ritual. He often walked alone and through the underworld. (*coughs*) He was . . . (*coughs*) . . . But he never ended it. And that's why we're here today.

KASPER

The rain had subsided while Malte spoke. Only the wind remained, roaring along with the traffic. Malte sat quietly on the couch, his bright eyes fixed on Kasper. His chest moved up and down rapidly, as if he had difficulty getting air back into his lungs after the bouts of coughing.

"So," he said, and Kasper could hear that he was struggling not to sound breathless. "Now you know what happened."

He rose abruptly and Kasper twitched. Malte disappeared into the kitchen. Then the tap started running.

Kasper was freezing in his wet clothes. Tried to understand what he'd just heard: Malte's version of the truth. His hoarse voice, controlled in a way that touched on strained, had painted an alternative reality to the one Kasper knew. He had spoken with such conviction that it was difficult not to be lured in by it. Now Kasper struggled to sort out what he had been told, separating the twisted facts from the blatant lies to uncover a grain of truth.

Kasper had spent so much time trying to understand what Grim had done down in the tunnels and now he might have the answer. He recognized thoughts and ideas from the books on magic Grim had read. The idea that man had the potential to transcend to a higher plane. A vision that appeared in Grim's final lyrics, lyrics that felt different from everything else he had written.

I shall become . . . I shall transform . . . Ascend . . .

Ossian got up, went over to the record player and dropped the needle. Music flowed through the speakers and Kasper recognized the opening tones. Dead Can Dance.

Perhaps Grim had gone into the tunnels to perform an ancient, stolen ritual, a ritual reflected in the myth of the labyrinth and Minotaur, Theseus and Ariadne. The maze was not one physical location, but could be reached through other mazes. The Minotaur was not a monstrous bull-man, but an ancient power, something beyond human understanding. And whoever found it and proved himself worthy, whatever that meant, could leave his humanity behind. The string must have been part of the ceremony, like Ariadne's. But Grim had had no one to hold it. He never finished the ritual. He never uttered the words that were written on the inside of the sleeve. Did that mean he was still trapped, somehow? Is that why he called on Kasper? Or was it as Iris had said, an unconscious force? A stirring coming through a door that had been left ajar?

And why did Malte tell him all this?

Kasper felt more awake than he had in months. His senses felt impossibly sharp. On the surface, everything was calm in the apartment. The elaborate music, the rhythmic pounding of the drums. Ossian got back into his chair while Malte drank water in the kitchen. But the adrenaline rushed through Kasper's body, his brain feverish with activity. At any time, this situation could get out of hand; Kasper felt it. If he was going to get answers, he had to get them soon.

The tap was still running. Malte coughed. Kasper was thinking about what he said about Grim. Ice cold, uncaring, unfeeling. Malte's words left him confused in a way that made him feel ashamed. He thought of how the others had described Grim: his dad, his mom, Tony, Ernesto. What if they were the ones who had rewritten history afterward? What if Malte was right?

No.

The answer was obvious.

The others had described Grim as a complex person, while Malte idealized him. His image of Grim was perhaps not entirely wrong, but it was flat and said more about Malte than it did about Grim.

But that wasn't the most frustrating thing about Malte's story. Something was missing, something fundamental. It made Kasper think about tests, staring down at a question he knew he had studied for, the answer just out of reach.

This time, more than his grades were at stake.

Ossian sniveled loudly. He sat back, swiveled the chair lightly, his eyes intent on Kasper. Kasper met his gaze and wondered what Ossian thought about all this, why he'd involved himself at all. Steps approached and Kasper saw Malte return with a glass of water in one hand. He put it on the coffee table and sat down, scratched his neck.

"How much do you remember from our last meeting?" he said.

The shock was practically electric. Kasper had had his suspicions, of course, but it was a different thing entirely to hear Malte confirm them.

"Nothing," he replied. "But I saw you at the gig."

Malte nodded.

"Ossian approached me last summer when it was decided that he would give voice to Grim's words. He wanted to get an overall picture of him. Just like you."

So Ossian was the one who'd dragged Malte into this. Kasper couldn't look at him. He was too repulsed.

"It turned out that we had had some shared experiences," Malte went on. "We had dreamed almost identical dreams about Grim." He made a sweeping gesture with his hand. "One could say that this is the third time we've been seated together, the three of us. The first time was at the table with Grim, when he invited us to drink from the cup."

Kasper pressed himself into the chair, arms wrapped around himself. The wind made the windows rattle.

Malte had also dreamed of Grim.

He claimed to have, anyway.

He could have said it after Ossian had told Malte about his dreams.

Or did this power call out to all three of them?

A ringtone cut through the room. Malte picked up his phone from his pocket, checked the screen, then muted the signal and put it back.

Kasper tried to steel himself before asking the question.

"What happened at the party?"

"We spoke," Malte replied, sounding almost bored. "You told me everything."

Everything. Kasper was trying to get a grip on what that could mean. In a worst-case scenario, it was really everything. The dreams, the things he found in the box, what his mom had said about them. The mirror in his room and the wound on his palm. The conversation with Tony. The horror he had felt when he hid with Santiago, the opening in the Hall of Mirrors.

"It must have been difficult to bear it all alone," Malte said.

Sympathy didn't suit his voice. It felt like Malte was trying to ingratiate himself with Kasper, but what would be the point of that?

"You have shouldered the burden well, though, I have to say," Malte continued. "To be near such a force for so long. Not many people could withstand it. But you've been searching for the truth and your journey brought you to me. That is how it was meant to be. Have you dreamed of him again?"

Kasper was thinking of the dark corridors. He thought about what had happened during the conversation with Ernesto, what he had found on the inside of the sleeve. Malte didn't know everything.

"No," he said.

"You have a strong bond with him," Malte said, and Kasper thought it sounded like a somewhat reluctant admission. "Your birthday. Your name. Your blood on the knife that he cut himself with as part of the ritual. I was actually surprised that Håkan had saved it and the record. But those objects have a holiness to them that even he must feel."

"Why did Grim bring the record?" said Kasper.

"It was also part of the ritual," Malte said, licking his lips absently. "To sacrifice something you have created, the thing you value the most. The old man said children were sometimes used in the past, but for Grim, of course, it was *Ancient Bloodlust*."

"And the phone number?"

If Malte didn't know about it before, he had to after questioning Kasper at the party.

"The phone number," Malte repeated.

Ossian regarded him with interest. Kasper got the feeling that, somehow, he viewed all this as entertainment.

"The note he had in his pocket," Kasper said. "My dad's number was on it."

"Yes, that's right." Malte's expression unchanging. "But it's immaterial."

He coughed, reached for the water. The phone number didn't fit into his story, and Kasper wondered if he had provoked Malte by bringing it up. If so, he might have to make everything worse: "What does the message inside the record sleeve mean?"

Malte stared at him. Kasper's pulse hammered.

It's the first time he's heard about this, he thought. He didn't know.

And then he understood. Grim had left the message there for the same reason he put the phone number in his pocket:

In case something went wrong.

444

In case things got so bad that he couldn't finish the ritual.

And it was obvious to whom it was addressed. The person he trusted the most in the world. It wasn't Malte.

"A message?" said Malte.

Did Grim really think that Kasper's dad would understand what he meant by just a drawing of a labyrinth and those words? Did that mean his dad knew something about what Grim was going to do? Or was the message as vague and desperate as it seemed? A barely coherent cry for help. The ambivalence he had carried with him to the very end. Kasper himself had experienced it, the deep remorse and profound horror, in The House last summer. He understood those feelings now.

Kasper shivered. A whiff of a familiar, nauseating scent, and then it was gone again.

"Tell me," Malte said sharply. "What was the message?"

Kasper told him, and he saw Malte's face change. His eyes turned inward, as if he was looking at something else.

"That was the license to depart," Kasper said. "The end of the ritual. Wasn't it?"

"It was thirty years ago," Malte said, meeting his gaze again. "I don't recall."

"Grim destroyed everything that had been written down about the ritual," Ossian added. "He memorized and destroyed it."

That was the first thing he had said since Kasper got there.

Malte gave Ossian a cold look, but Ossian's face didn't change. Kasper wondered why Grim would have done that, but maybe the answer was right in front of him: Malte. Did Grim want to keep the ritual away from him? Or was it just wishful thinking on Kasper's part?

"Either way, it's immaterial," Malte went on. "We don't have to perform the ritual, because he left the door ajar. That is why we can walk through it. With your help, Kasper. You are the link."

Malte looked at him. His pupils were huge, and Kasper thought that look would devour him.

Malte wanted his help.

Malte thought he'd help him.

Why did he think so? Because Kasper had chosen to come here? Because Kasper wanted to talk to him?

He thinks I'm looking for the same thing as him, Kasper realized.

"Today is the thirtieth anniversary of his departure," Malte continued. "The time has come. The gate will be open and we can step through it."

We.

"Why would I want to do that?" Kasper said faintly.

"You're going to live a completely insignificant life," Malte said. "What have you got to lose?"

Kasper didn't say a word. It felt as if Malte was looking right through him, as if he held his self-contempt up to the light, looked at it and confirmed that all the worst things he thought about himself were true.

"People don't change," Malte continued. "You might think they do, but it's just like stretching out a rubber band and"—he snapped his fingers—"you're back where you started. The only way forward is to leave. Walk out."

His stare was intense. What he said was the exact opposite of what Kasper's psychologists had said, what Iris had said, his dad, his mom, Tony, Ernesto.

And for an icy, horrific moment, Kasper thought: *Maybe he's right.*

What if the opening that had appeared to him was a way out of all this? In his dreams, he had wandered the dark hallways, his only respite during an endless summer.

He was so tired.

The conscience. The pain. The weakness.

Kasper closed his eyes.

Maybe this is what Grim wanted. Maybe he wanted to offer Kasper a chance to do what he himself had not been able to do. Or who said he had not succeeded? Maybe he wasn't lost at all. Maybe he'd ascended, was speaking to Kasper from a higher plane?

Then he detected that nauseating smell again. It was stronger now, so strong that it couldn't be ignored.

Kasper opened his eyes.

Rotten apples.

Malte sniffled, throwing an agitated look at the door. Then he turned to Kasper, staring as if something was slowly dawning on him.

"Rotten apples," Kasper said quietly.

Malte turned sickly pale, looked ill. He closed his eyes. Swallowed.

"They were part of the ritual," he said, and Kasper heard something happening to his voice. "They were part of the protection. The circle of salt. Stinking herbs to burn."

Malte coughed and then pressed his hand against his chest. Gasped for air. Drops of sweat gleamed on his forehead. He seemed to be fighting to regain his composure.

"We're leaving now," he said, choking on nothing at all. "I've found out where he performed the ritual."

"You've known all along." Kasper was surprised to hear himself say the words, but not as surprised as Malte.

"What did you say?" His voice was barely audible.

"You were there," Kasper said.

That was the answer he had been searching for. Suddenly, it was so obvious. Not just because of what that Romanian musician had told Ernesto. Malte had said that he warned Grim that he was in over his head, but that went against absolutely everything Kasper had read and heard about Malte, everything Malte himself had said.

Malte had been supposed to hold the string during the ritual. It had been his mission to ensure Grim didn't get lost.

"You were there with him," Kasper said again.

Malte stared down at the living room table, his expression unreadable. The stink intensified around them: rotten fruit and damp stone. It was as if the light was growing dim, as if the darkness was seeping in. Ossian looked slowly from Malte to Kasper, an expression of genuine surprise on his face.

"You left him," Kasper said.

The words were deadly to speak out loud. But Kasper still did it. Was it courage or stupidity that made him say them? Or was it something else?

In the corner of his eye, he saw Ossian's fingers gripping the armrest. Malte was still staring at the table. Kasper heard his strained breathing. Like he had trouble getting air into his lungs.

Kasper softly said, "You left, but you didn't get help. You didn't tell anyone. You went home. You left him there in the dark. How long did you let him lie there? One day? Two days? I guess you're the only one who knows that."

Malte looked up.

If Kasper had forgotten who he was, he was reminded of it now. He saw it in Malte's eyes. Malte had crossed so many boundaries, so many, and now Kasper had offended him in the worst possible way. This was the secret he had been carrying with him for thirty years: his own cowardice. Laid bare.

It all happened in a few seconds.

Every alarm bell in Kasper's head rang. Ossian was nothing but a movement when he threw himself forward, holding on to Malte, who was heading straight for Kasper. His eyes were black as pitch. Mad with it. He screamed something Kasper couldn't catch. The light had grown dim, the corners of the room darkening, closing in around them. A creaking, cracking sound, as if something huge was being pried loose, mutating, and the droning noise grew stronger, a vibration that seemed to come out of the floor and walls, close and incredibly far away. It was coming: a presence that made reality tremble. The stench was unbearable, stinging, animalistic: fresh blood and carcasses. It came through the passageways, it came through the door that had been left ajar, it moved through the house, since there is something of a labyrinth in every house. Cottage, mall, palace. Vaults and hallways open up to the force that wants through.

Kasper watched Malte's expression become one of rapture and recognition. Thirty years ago, he fled the horror of this moment, and now he was faced with it again, what he had feared and yearned for.

The sound grew impossibly strong, making Kasper's ears pop. The pain was so overwhelming that it felt as if his eardrums were going to explode. He crouched, pressed his hands to his head. He looked toward Ossian, who had collapsed on the couch with his face hidden in his hands. Malte remained standing, completely caught up in what was finally coming for him. A stream of tears down his face, a streak of blood from his nose. A dark spot spread gradually across the front of his black jeans. Kasper could sense the buzzing of flies. And just at that moment, he saw utter terror light up Malte's eyes.

It feels good to ally oneself with that which humanity had always feared: darkness, and death, and malice. But fragility remains.

There was a flash, and Kasper closed his eyes, hard. Red across black. Somebody screamed, but Kasper couldn't tell who.

The sudden silence that followed made his ears ring, a lingering tinnitus-like sound.

Kasper opened his eyes.

Ossian was sitting on the couch with wide eyes, his face gray. He didn't seem aware of Kasper's presence. Where Malte had stood, there was only a puddle of urine. The vase with its dried flowers was in shards, the record spinning silently, crackling. Kasper rose on unsteady legs and almost lost his balance, as if he had just disembarked from a ship after a long journey. He used the armchair as support, looked around. Took a few stumbling steps toward the hallway.

The front door was wide open, the stairwell dark. A light switch shone in that darkness like a red eye.

Did Malte run out?

Where was he? What happened?

Kasper heard Ossian get to his feet and turned around.

The two of them looked at each other.

"Where is he?" Kasper said.

Ossian opened his mouth but only managed to make a gesture, and Kasper understood that he didn't know, either. He had also closed his eyes in that final, terrible moment.

What was Ossian's real purpose in bringing Kasper and Malte together? Had he just wanted to see what would happen? Had he imagined that they would go into the underworld together, charmed by the idea of becoming a demigod?

Whatever it was, he had given up on it now. Kasper could see it in his eyes. Ossian was hungry and ruthless, in many ways, but he had a sense of self-preservation. And in the end, that was what ruled him.

Kasper went toward the door, took his jacket and put it on. Shoved his feet into the wet shoes. Then he looked toward the stairwell. What if Malte was out there, waiting? Either way, Kasper couldn't stay here. He was in a hurry. He went out and turned the light on, the old fluorescent lamps clinking a little. The door behind him closed so suddenly that he jerked. The lock clicked shut. And Kasper knew that Ossian's door would never open for him again. They were done with each other.

Kasper picked up his phone. The recording had been completed, meaning he must have somehow touched the screen. He saved it and went down the stairs with his phone in his hand, ready to call 911, but reached the street unmolested. The door was ajar. Kasper left it that way, in case he had to make a quick retreat.

The wind had died away. The cars raced across the wet asphalt, tearing up the puddles. Kasper saw a bus coming and ran for it. He didn't care where it went, ran as fast as he could, got on completely breathless. The doors closed behind him. He went to the back of the bus, sat down at a window, looked at Ossian's house until it disappeared from view. Where was Malte?

Kasper felt drained, as if he had been running for a long time without rest or water. He didn't have much energy left, but he couldn't stop now. He had learned what Grim had been trying to do. It was up to Kasper to finish it. He was the link.

And it was probably like Iris said, that he was too weak. He would never manage it. The river was rising and he stood there like a fool, hoping he could hold his breath until it ebbed again.

He leaned his head against the cool glass of the bus window. Drops of rain went sideways with the speed. He shouldn't be doing this alone, but how could he ask anyone for help?

He thought about Iris, when she came to him on the docks and they talked. When she told him he could do the job as a UC. When she made him promise to be careful. When she picked him up from the party and then slept over. When she asked him to stop digging into Grim's fate because she was worried about what it was doing to him. He thought about this entire long summer, when he must have disappointed her time and time again. It should have been the best summer ever, the two of them as UCs in The House, but he had ruined everything. He couldn't ask her for more.

In a few hours, she'd close The House. He'd go there, tell her to go home earlier, let him do the final round.

He closed his eyes and felt the vibrations of the bus against his head. A couple of older women talked animatedly about a TV show. Around him, the world continued as usual. Despite what Kasper had just experienced at Ossian's, reality remained intact. But he wasn't a part of it anymore.

His ears rang.

Tomorrow, he would turn twenty.

THE END

Grim has been dead for a few days when they get together in the rehearsal space. Malte was the one who insisted they meet up: he, Håkan, and Tony. Dark Cruelty consists of just three people now.

At first, Håkan slept for twenty-four hours. The following night, nightmares kept him awake. Now he's a shell of a boy, a body that simply exists. Empty on the inside. He walks around the room, can't sit still, pokes and prods at everything he comes across.

Malte, seated on the amplifier, blows his nose. He uses a proper handkerchief, which he then puts in his pocket.

"What did you want to talk about?" Tony asks him.

For once, he isn't sitting behind the drumkit, but leaning against the door. He's hollow-eyed and pale, his voice weary. Håkan can't look him in the eyes. Using his foot, he sweeps fine woodchips, splinters from drumsticks, into a little pile.

"We have to talk about the situation," Malte says.

His gaze moves rapidly between Tony and Håkan, who rests his fingertips against a cymbal. The cold metal. The feel of Grim's skin against his fingers. He removes his hand.

When the paramedics got to Grim, he was still alive, but only barely. Once his heart stopped, there was no saving him. That's what one of the cops had said, the one who talked, probably more than he should have. Tears had streamed down his mom's face. Håkan was sitting next to her, staring at his hands. How could Grim be dead?

The cops had asked for a photo of Grim and his mom's name. It was up to the local police to inform her about the death after the identification was finished. But it didn't stop there. They wanted to talk to Håkan and had thousands of questions for him.

He was the one who'd found Grim and alerted the woman in the ticket booth? *Yeah.* How did he know that Grim was in the tunnel? *Lucky guess.* Had the two of them been there before? *Once.* Did Grim have any known illnesses? *Don't know.* Addiction? *He didn't even take snuff.* Why did Håkan run from the station?

"Don't know," Håkan repeated.

Speaking was difficult; he was trembling as if with cold. His mom held his hand.

"You do understand he was frightened?" she demanded of the cops. Håkan wasn't used to seeing her defend him like this; not questioning authority was something she'd been raised with. "Why do you have to question him right now? He's in shock. He's a child."

"When a young person is found dead in this way, we have to start a preliminary investigation," the chatty cop said. "We can't rule out homicide. Naturally, we have to question the person who found the deceased. Then it's up to the prosecutor if an arrest is made."

Håkan should be afraid, but he felt nothing. Maybe it was just as well that they arrested him. Maybe he was guilty, in some way.

"You don't touch him," his mom said, gripping his hand more tightly. "He just found his best friend . . ." A sob escaped her. "Håkan wouldn't hurt a fly. Just because these boys dress differently and listen to that music, it doesn't mean—"

"Let's calm down, shall we?" the quiet cop interrupted, in a way that seemed to be directed at his colleague as much as to Håkan's mom.

"Håkan?"

Malte's voice.

Håkan looks up. Malte is holding a newspaper, one of the tabloids. Half the page consists of a grainy picture of a tunnel. *DEVIL WORSHIPPER FOUND DEAD IN SUBWAY TUNNEL.* Håkan walks up to Malte and rips the paper from his hands. He reads. A twenty-year-old man was found dead in the Stockholm subway system. *He was only nineteen.* According to paramedics, he was dressed like a metalhead and wearing a necklace depicting a Satanic symbol. *The pentagram.* Shocking discoveries were made at the scene. *Rotting apples. Salt and ash. The string. What else? Was there more?* We cannot rule out that there was foul play involved and are opening a preliminary investigation regarding homicide. Håkan stares at the words, trying to comprehend them. So far, he hasn't asked himself what happened to Grim. If he were to do that, he'd have to admit that Grim is dead.

"Have you heard anything else?" Malte is asking. "From the police?"

He is looking at the paper as if he wants it back. Håkan throws it aside.

"Why would they want to talk to me?" he demands.

"But your mom must have talked to Grim's mom, right?" Malte says, getting up from the amp to pick up his paper and smooth out a page that's slightly bent. "She'll know things, won't she? Grim's mom, I mean."

"I haven't heard anything else," Håkan says. "But the cops came to Stasse's last night and searched his apartment."

Stasse had phoned him to tell him about the search, said that they were obviously looking for drugs. One of the cops confidently stated to his colleague that "the kid died of a bad batch." According to Stasse, they left his apartment, despondent, with just a few bags of dried herbs to show for it.

Neither Stasse, Tony, nor Malte know that Håkan was the one who found Grim. He can't tell them about it, and he's begged his mom not to say anything to Grim's mom. The idea of her finding out how he'd failed to save Grim is unbearable. And Håkan can imagine how it would spread in their circle, how the others would hold on to their questions until they came pouring out after a few pints. The looks he'd get: pity, curiosity, contempt. Or worse: admiration, thinking he'd been brave, when his cowardice had been what killed Grim. If the Lake hadn't frightened him so much, he would have gone sooner, arrived before it was too late.

"So they're still investigating," Malte says.

Something about his tone strikes Håkan as off. Suddenly, he wonders if Malte knows something.

"The police came to you, too?"

"Yes," Malte says. "They came by. I didn't say a word, naturally."

He looks proud.

"A word about what?" Håkan asks, and in the corner of his eye, he can see Tony cross his arms over his chest.

"Well, about what Grim was doing down there," Malte says.

Håkan stares at him.

"What are you talking about?"

Malte looks so full of himself that Håkan could hit him. He really wants to hit him.

"You know that Grim was a practitioner of magic," Malte says.

Practitioner of magic. He sounds so fucking pretentious.

"You believe the shit that's in the paper then?" Tony's laugh is flat, humorless. "Devil worshipper?"

"The newspapers don't know anything, of course," Malte says, his cheeks going pink. "But I think Grim was there to perform a ritual."

"What kind of ritual?" Håkan asks.

"I don't know, exactly," Malte says, his eyes darting from side to side.

It suddenly hits Håkan that Malte probably is the last person to talk to Grim. And the worst of it is that Malte could be right. Håkan thinks of all those times Grim had talked excitedly about magic, the symbols on the drawings in his room.

Was that why Grim had that phone number in his pocket? In case something went wrong and he was found? But what could go wrong? Magic wasn't real, so a magic ritual couldn't kill a person.

Håkan is reminded of that book about the history of magic. It said that magicians often burned incense during their ceremonies, and that many of the herbs used caused hallucinations, or were downright toxic. Had Grim been burning lethal herbs? Had traces of it still been in the air? That would explain why Håkan thought he'd seen the string disappearing into the darkness. That deep, droning noise. The scents. The impossible shape. He's seen it all again in his nightmares.

"The important thing is," Malte says, pointing to DEVIL WORSHIPPER FOUND DEAD, "that we can use this."

At first, Håkan doesn't understand what he means. It's as if he's speaking a foreign language. And then it starts to sink in.

"What are you talking about?" Tony says.

He sounds genuinely confused. Håkan waits. He has to hear Malte say it.

"Think of what Grim said in his interviews," Malte pushes on. "That there were hidden messages in the songs and that he walked the left-hand path."

"And that a tame fucking wolverine followed him around!" Tony says, shaking his head. "Håkan and Grim made that all up together!"

Malte looks offended. For the first time, Håkan understands just how big an impact the things that he and Grim had written together had had on Malte, how Malte had mistaken it for some kind of truth. Not everything, but the core of it. Even after getting to know Grim, Malte had nurtured that image of him and fed it back to Grim. All because Malte wanted it to be true.

"It wasn't all made up!" Malte objects. "And that's the thing! What makes Dark Cruelty such a unique band!"

Håkan stares at Malte.

"Huh?" Tony says.

"Most people only *sing* about evil and the occult, and they're nothing but hypocrites." Malte babbles on, his speech more rapid than ever. "Like Alice Cooper and Ozzy, they're only devil worshippers and madmen on stage."

"So?" Tony says. "Do you think actors should kill each other for real, too? Are they worse at acting if they pretend to die and pretend to kill each other, or what?"

"It's not the same," Malte says without sounding wholly convinced. "Admit it. When you started listening to metal, you *wanted* the bands to be as dark and dangerous as you'd thought they were. Before you realized they were posers."

Håkan doesn't answer him. He knows exactly what Malte means. It's as if someone is holding up a fun house mirror in which everything Håkan and Grim discussed is reflected, but distorted, and horribly warped.

"I really don't give a shit about all that," Tony says, and Håkan knows he means it. "Music is music."

"But you and Grim had a vision for Dark Cruelty." Malte turns pleading eyes toward Håkan. "Don't you see what an opportunity this is? We can talk about how Grim died, the way he freely went into the darkness—"

"What was that?" Håkan interrupts him.

"He knew what he was doing," Malte says. "He understood the risk he was taking. We should honor him and spread his message in the scene."

"Oh, his message," Tony snorts. "What the hell was his message?"

"Ordinary morality is only for ordinary people," Malte says triumphantly. "So-called humanity is weighing us down. That's why we have to smash it, why we must pledge ourselves to destruction and darkness. To really go there. That's what Grim was doing, and we should be telling everyone, not sitting around and crying about it. He wouldn't want that."

Everything goes red. Håkan doesn't even notice what he's doing until he's grabbed Malte and is pushing him onto the floor, holding him down, yelling in his face.

"Shut up!"

Terror shines in Malte's eyes and he doesn't even try to tear himself loose, doesn't try to hit back. The pentagram has slipped into the pit of his throat.

"You don't know anything about him!" Håkan screams, and Malte closes his eyes when spittle hits his face. "You disgusting little shit! He's dead!"

Then Tony appears, dragging away Håkan, who is still screaming. Malte climbs to his feet, brushes dust off his coat. His face is drained of color. This hadn't gone the way he had planned it, and Håkan suddenly sees that Malte doesn't understand why it went so wrong, that he genuinely can't comprehend why Håkan doesn't like his ideas. It shocks Håkan so deeply that he goes quiet.

Tony lets him go but keeps one hand on his shoulder. Håkan bats it away.

"It's over," he says. He looks straight at Malte when he says it. "I'm breaking up the band."

Malte pales impossibly.

"Without Grim, there is no Dark Cruelty," Håkan says, and he leaves the rehearsal space.

Appendix 13. The final note in Kasper Hansson Nordin's sketchbook. Not dated.

all
 labyrinths
lead
 here

KASPER

The lights and neon of the theme park glowed in the September dark, glittered in the puddles, as Kasper entered the alley. The sounds from the rides like thunder, the shrill cries made him flinch. There was a screeching and ringing in his ears. In the distance, he could see Iris head out of The House. She called his name, waved at him. She had come to meet him, since he didn't have his access card with him. Iris hugged him and made some comment about how soaked he was, told him someone had smuggled a pasta salad into The House and spilled it in the Snake Pit.

"I had the grand honor of stepping in it and I still stink of pesto."

Kasper laughed, the sound as empty and fake as it felt.

"I'm glad you came by," she said, opening the door. "Are you coming to Skeppsbar, or what?"

She looked at him with her brown eyes. Kasper swallowed.

"I don't know . . ." He looked away, suddenly finding it difficult to lie to her. "I was nearby and wanted to say hi. I can close up if you'd like to leave early."

They walked up the stairs. Iris didn't respond, and Kasper wondered if she had heard him.

"If you want me to," he added. "I'm not exactly busy."

"Okay," she said. "Thanks."

His stomach ached.

"I'll just handle the meeting," she told him.

The demons were gathered in the Lab. Kasper smiled and greeted everyone. Smiling felt absurd, but he had to do it; that was the role he had to play right now.

"Couldn't keep away, could you?" Jennifer said, smiling.

Kasper noticed Krill watching him quietly. Something about his eyes was reminiscent of Malte. Kasper looked away. He leaned against the iron fence in front of the table, its surface stacked with test tubes and grimoires. He held on to the bars.

Iris went through the events of the day with Selam present as TL. Selam was glued to her phone while Iris gave the demons praise for trying out new scares even though the season was coming to an end. Kasper could only catch the occasional word, distracted by the way his tattoo had begun to itch, by the ringing in his ears. He only had to bear it a little while longer.

"Any funny stories about the guests today?" Iris asked.

Kasper didn't listen to the answer that made everyone else laugh. He'd shut his eyes. A flicker of red and black. That scream. Had it been Malte's?

When he opened his eyes again, everyone was leaving the Lab, and Iris was talking to Selam by the emergency exit.

"Congratulations," Selam said.

It took Kasper a moment before he realized that she had directed this at him.

"Well, in advance," Selam added. "It's your birthday tomorrow, isn't it?"

"Oh, right, shit," Kasper said, his smile automatic. "Thanks."

"Twenty," Selam said. "It's a big deal."

Kasper's smile felt glued on. What he really wanted was to shout at Selam and Iris to leave.

"Bye, then!" Iris called on her way out through the exit with Selam.

"Have fun," Kasper said.

"Come by if you change your mind!" Selam said. "We can celebrate you at midnight!"

"Yeah," Kasper replied. "I might!"

As soon as the door clicked shut, he went to the staircase and sat down. In fifteen minutes or so, The House would be completely empty. He took out his phone and checked the words he had to say, even though he knew them by heart by now.

This I say unto thee: Thou opened the gate when I called and I hereby license thee to depart without doing injury to any living creature. This I say unto thee: Thou art free to go, withdraw in peace under the blessing of the Most High, and seal the door that thou for my sake hath opened. This I say unto thee: Let there be peace between thee and me. Amen.

Kasper looked at the hands that held the phone. His hands. They were red and chafed and somehow foreign. The ringing in his ears rose and fell. He put on his headphones and turned on the recording he'd done of Malte. His stomach heaved at the sound of his voice, but he had to be sure he hadn't missed anything relevant.

It was a particularly advanced ritual. Nothing you can do by yourself.

But I'm just finishing it, Kasper thought. That's not the same thing.

And there were no alternatives; he knew that. His loneliness was so absolute, so impossible to deny.

He thought of Grim in the darkness underground. Had he noticed when Malte abandoned him? And what had Malte been thinking when he let the hours pass by without saying anything, without even phoning in with an anonymous tip? Did he just stick his head in the sand? Did he make a choice and stick with it? Or did he stall and hesitate? Did he hope that Grim would survive? Did he wish that he would die?

Kasper switched off the recording and walked up the stairs, continued through the Snake Pit, the Spiderwebs, and took the shortcut to the Pyramid. Passed the Nursery, where he had experienced Grim's horror at dying. Down the stairs. Symbols on the wall. The devil's statue by the Possessed. Into the Hall of Mirrors.

He stopped there, in the middle of the floor. He had no circles of salt to protect him, but he had the words. He knew what he needed to finish. And if he was the link, if he was in contact with this power, then shouldn't that be enough?

And then . . .

What then? He had poured all of himself into this, and when it was done, who would he be?

He had always thought that Grim needed him.

Maybe he was the one who needed Grim.

He saw his image in the mirror reflected, multiplied. The pale face, the tangled, lank hair. He thought about the opening, thought about the dark pathways.

You'll live an insignificant life.

People don't change.

The conscience. The pain. The weakness.

How could he abide it? Life stretched out before him, an endless, dull gray day.

A creaking, cracking sound could be heard in the distance. Kasper listened. Something was about to happen. His scar pricked and pulled. His hands shook. It was time.

He went into the adjacent room and turned off the lights in The House, then returned to the Hall of Mirrors. He waited in the dark. A shiver ran through his body. His heart was pounding so hard. Very soon, the labyrinth would open.

And then . . .

"Kasper?"

Iris's voice. The beam from a flashlight blinded him. He hadn't even heard her coming. Her silhouette appeared in the doorway leading to the Possessed.

"What are you doing?" she said.

"Leave," Kasper said quietly, then added: "Please."

Iris said: "No."

"You can't be here," he said. "It's for your sake, I . . . There's no time to explain."

"Do you think I'm completely fucking stupid?"

He could tell by her voice that she was crying.

"You come out of nowhere, on the thirty-year anniversary of Grim's death, and act super weird. I realized something was up. And I started to think . . . I was so scared . . . Fuck."

She sank into a crouch. The flashlight pointed at the floor.

"I've been the worst friend to you," he heard her say.

"What?" Kasper said. "What are you talking about?"

"I noticed that you . . . You disappeared."

"I know I haven't handled work properly," he admitted.

"What are you talking about?" she sobbed. "Kasper, please, you've done your job. Sure, you've been a bit . . . distracted, but you've been working way too hard. I've tried to talk to you about it tons of times. Selam told you, too, don't you remember?"

Kasper thought back on the conversations this summer. All he remembered was the numbing feeling of being somehow deficient, that Iris and Selam had taken him aside because he hadn't been good enough. But what had they actually said?

"When you said you weren't working during Halloween . . ." Iris went on. "I thought it was me. That I'd done something wrong." She looked worried.

"What?" Kasper said. "No, you didn't do anything."

"I thought you were pulling away because I . . ." she said. "I thought you were sick of me. God, how incredibly self-centered."

Kasper shook his head, even though he knew she couldn't see him. It was as if, very slowly and gingerly, she was turning his entire world upside down.

"I got so fucking scared," she managed. "I thought that you . . . That maybe you'd . . ."

Just like that, he understood what she meant, how close to the edge he'd been. How bad things actually were, that they had been for a very long time.

"I'm sorry," he said, and he felt the tears come.

There was the beam from the flashlight again, as she came toward him. They hugged each other close.

"I'm the one who should apologize," Iris said. "I should have understood. I should have seen it. God, we've even talked about this . . . But I thought that . . . You said you were seeing a therapist, so I thought . . ."

"It's not your fault," Kasper said, letting her go.

There was that sound again, a heavy creaking noise. Iris jerked back.

"What was that?"

"You have to go," he said.

"Why do I have to go?"

"There's no time," Kasper told her. "But I have to end . . . all of this. You have to go, you really do."

Rotten apples.

"What is that smell?" Iris whispered.

"Please," Kasper said.

"I'm not leaving."

He felt her take his hand in her own.

"I'm staying," Iris said.

"You don't know," Kasper whispered. "You don't understand."

"I'm staying," Iris repeated.

He knew he couldn't convince her to go. He didn't want to convince her to go.

"Switch the flashlight off," Kasper whispered, gripping her hand hard. "Don't let go."

"Not you, either."

A soft breeze brushed against his face. She turned off the light.

*

Kasper knows that his body isn't moving.

And yet, he walks out and *inside*. Into the twisting, turning paths of the labyrinth. They are not unfamiliar to him. He's spent so many nights walking them, and days, too, even though he didn't understand it at the time.

In the distance, he can hear a dull, droning sound, smell fresh blood and rotting flesh. There is a grinding, a crushing noise.

But that is not where Kasper is going.

He sees them, the shadows of those who found their way here, and the ones who ended up here. Some of them wanted to be gods. Most of them couldn't bear being human.

He walks toward the shadow, and it faces him, like his own reflection.

The entire time, he can feel Iris's hand in his.

And he reaches for Grim.

THE SILENCE

Grim makes the journey home one final time.

Håkan is in his room, unable to stop thinking of Grim's body being carted from Stockholm to Timrå. How do you transport a dead person? Grim would definitely have wanted to know, or he'd known already. Do you lay the body in a coffin and drive it in a hearse? A joke Grim once made pops up in his head: *How much power does a hearse have? 1 corpsepower.*

He shoves the heels of his hands into his eyes until it hurts.

There's going to be a funeral, of course.

Håkan doesn't know when. How do you even find out? He can't exactly call Grim's mom and ask.

When he thinks about her and Grim's sister, it's as if a huge, dark pit opens up inside of him. His shame outweighs his grief. And then he gets angry. Why should he be ashamed? Was Grim his responsibility?

I tried, he tells himself, but he can't quite remember when or how. The moments when he let things go, when he assumed that Grim knew what he was doing, when he didn't ask—those moments are painfully clear.

His mom cries in the evenings. She's sort of sprung a leak. She sits in front of the TV, and whatever's on, her eyes brim over.

"That boy," she says. "That boy."

Lillemor comes by with sponge cake and they talk for hours at the kitchen table, keeping their voices low. Lillemor knows a lot about loss, and in a year's time, when her son falls to his death from a scaffold during a break-in, she'll learn all about it. After that, she throws herself into volunteering for the church's provisions for the needy. She works in soup kitchens and in shelters, with his mom as occasional company.

"I can see him in the other boys," Lillemor tells his mom.

His mom understands. She tells Håkan that she'll come across someone sometimes who reminds her of Grim.

"Grim wasn't a junkie," Håkan will mutter when she does.

"That wasn't what I meant," his mom says, thinking that she thought he was lost, too, but she can't explain *what* she meant. Her confidence often abandons her when she tries to put things into words, and her thoughts and feelings remain unuttered, mute.

But that all comes later. Right now, Håkan is on his bed, surrounded by things that used to make him happy. The records. The tapes. The books. The letters.

Everything reminds him of Grim, and his limbs feel as heavy as lead.

There's a knock on the door.

His mom hardly ever knocks on the door. She only does it to announce that dinner is ready, if there's a call waiting for Håkan, or if he's overslept. But they've only just eaten and the phone hasn't rung.

"Come in," Håkan tells her.

His mom enters the room. She lingers in the doorway in the bluish-green apron she wears when she's cleaning, one hand clasping the other. Håkan feels bad. He knows he should be helping her with the cleaning, at least by vacuuming. Grim would have. Instead, he's just lying around, useless, totally incapable of action.

"I found out the date of the funeral," she says.

"What?"

His mom grips her elbows, as if hugging herself.

"It's on Wednesday," she says.

"Okay," Håkan says.

He stares at the ceiling.

"I thought you might want to know," she goes on. "If you want to go."

"I can't; I'm working," Håkan says, voice perfectly flat.

His mom sighs. Håkan knows exactly what's going to happen next: she's going to leave the room, closing the door behind her and leaving him alone with his guilty conscience. But she just stands there.

"They'll give you a day off if you ask for it."

Håkan says, "I can't."

"You're going."

Håkan turns his head to stare at her. Her neck and face have gone blotchy.

"*I* get to decide that, don't I?" Håkan shoots back.

"You're only seventeen," his mom says. "I am your mother and I am telling you to go."

"You can't make me go to a funeral!"

"No," his mom says. "I can't make you do anything. But I'm telling you to. Or you'll regret it for the rest of your life."

She is breathing rapidly. Håkan hasn't seen her this upset since the years after his dad left.

"But what if she doesn't want me to come? Did you think of that?" he says, his voice breaking.

There they are: tears. He turns away from his mom, crying into his pillow. He can feel the weight of her next to him, the warmth of her hand as she strokes his back.

"She does want you there, Håkan. I spoke to her."

Stasse has a driver's license and has borrowed a tiny car. Tony is in the front and three people have squeezed into the back: Håkan, Anja, and Dagge, who came up from Gothenburg. Ernesto said he couldn't get time off, and then there was something about Ossian, but Håkan suspects he just found it too difficult.

"I better not sit in the middle," Dagge tells them. "I get carsick."

Håkan offers to take the spot, a gentlemanly gesture he soon regrets. Sitting between Dagge, who isn't the scrawny boy he used to be, and Anja is uncomfortable. He tries to inch away, but despite her trying to move as close to the window as possible, their hips press together.

"Sorry for crushing you," she says, her smile faint.

"Likewise," Håkan mumbles.

There is a white rose on Anja's lap, the cut wrapped in soaked tissue protected by a plastic bag. None of the others thought of bringing flowers. Anja and Dagge are the only ones whose clothes look proper enough for a funeral, Anja in the black dress she wore when her granddad died, Dagge in an ill-fitting suit he borrowed from his big brother. Håkan wonders if Grim's mom will think he's being disrespectful, showing up in black jeans, sneakers, and a leather jacket, but he doesn't own a suit. Neither do Stasse and Tony. At least they're all wearing their least satanic shirts.

Stasse is a nervous driver with little experience, so the ride is somewhat jerky. Dagge does get carsick, and they have to pull over twice so he can throw up. Håkan doesn't know what scares him the most: that Stasse will crash the car, that they'll be late for the funeral, or that they'll get lost along the way. But Anja keeps an eye on the map. They make it.

The church is white, with a roof made of oxidized copper, and a tower where columns hold up a dome crowned by a gold cross. In the distance is the pulp mill's silhouette, its chimneys, which belch out smoke, reaching toward the sky. The highway rumbles in the background.

Dagge is still faintly green, taking careful sips of the juice Anja brought along in a thermos. They're standing away from the entrance, shivering. It's far colder than Stockholm. Stasse puts his arm around Anja.

"I've never been this far north before," Dagge says.

"We're right in the middle of Sweden," Håkan says automatically.

I send word from the very center of Sweden.

The wind changes direction and the smell of sulfur grows stronger.

The fart-smelling fumes of the pulp mill.

"What the fuck is that smell?" Tony mutters.

Smells like money.

From the corner of his eye, Håkan sees a man enter the church, and for a second, he imagines Malte suddenly appearing. He pictures leaping at him, punching him right in the face, grabbing his hair and smashing his face against the church. A red smear against that white wall.

His rage is so overwhelming it leaves him dizzy.

And then it dissolves.

He shoves his hand into the pocket of his jeans, touches the plectrum he brought. It belonged to Grim, was left behind when he moved, and Håkan took it on his way out this morning, not quite knowing why.

"Maybe we should go inside now," Anja says.

It smells like churches usually do: candles, wood, stone. The air is thick with silence. The churchwarden hands them each a pamphlet, and in silent agreement, they seat themselves at the back of the church.

Black spots disturb Håkan's vision when he sidles into the bench between Anja and Tony. He's sure he's forgotten something, maybe to breathe. He looks at his hands, which grip the pamphlet, its cover sporting a simple drawing of a dove. Håkan thinks of the dead rook dissolving in Grim's hands, wonders if his mom has seen that picture, doubts it. Kasper Arthur Johansson, born and then deceased. They know the precise time he died, but no one knows for how long he'd been down there. "At least twenty-four hours," Kasper's mom had told Håkan when he asked. She had heard it all from Grim's mom. "He was unconscious the whole time," his mom said. "They could tell by his body that he'd been lying perfectly still. He didn't suffer, Håkan." At that, he had to ask her to stop.

"It'll feel better afterward," Tony whispers in his ear.

Afterward, Håkan only remembers fragments of the funeral service. The psalms not one of them knows, the priest's feeble voice: *when a young person dies.* Coughs and cleared throats echoing through the hall, maybe a few sobs. In the middle of the service, Anja takes one of Håkan's hands and Tony the other. Three people trying to get through something unimaginable. A thought hits Håkan like a bolt of lightning: *I will attend the funeral of every friend I have unless I die before them.*

Suddenly, Tony gets up. It's time to approach the coffin and say farewell. Håkan follows automatically, staring at the floor, his long hair hiding his face.

When they stop in front of the altar, Tony starts to weep. His big body shakes and he sniffles when he touches the head of the casket. Håkan is next, eyes fixed on the white wood, the flowers decorating the lid. He looks up by accident and sees Grim's mom seated at the very front with a little girl by her side. They look straight at Håkan and he shivers as if with a sudden fever, averts his eyes again. He takes the plectrum out of his pocket and lays it on the casket. He presses the palm of his hand to the lid. His eyes sting and then it's over.

Afterward, they stumble into the daylight. The sun is out, a warm, autumnal sun that illuminates the yellowing canopies.

Håkan lights a cigarette and passes it around. Dagge looks frightened, as if he's experienced something he can't put into words. Stasse puts his arm around Anja and she leans against him. Her eyes are bloodshot; Tony's, too. It isn't until they're standing outside the church that Håkan realizes how few were inside it. Apart from Grim's mom, he spots a man who looks a bit like Grim's sister. Is that Grim's stepdad? A couple of twins, who could be Grim's cousins, are there with their parents. Three older people, faces full of wrinkles. A short, fat woman whose hair has been dyed with henna. That's it.

"Now what?" Dagge says hoarsely.

"Probably some form of memorial service," Anja replies.

"Do we go to that, too?" Tony mumbles.

"We should say hi to Grim's mom, at least," Anja says. "We don't have to stay long."

Håkan wants to throw himself back into the car but realizes that Anja is right. They can't just take off. His mom has spoken to Grim's mom and she saw him in the church.

"We'll say hi and then go," he says.

"God, I hope there's food," Stasse sighs.

Anja shoves him.

"I'm sorry, but I'm starving," Stasse mutters. "And I'm driving us home."

They all greet Grim's mom in the parish hall. One by one, they shake her hand, mumbling the only phrase they know, *my condolences*, the words awkward and old-fashioned coming from them.

"Thank you," Inger mumbles. "Thank you."

Håkan can't meet her eyes. What if she can tell, somehow, that he let her son down, that he was too late?

He catches a glimpse of the man who must be the little sister's father, sitting with the girl on his knee and nodding quietly at the long-haired strangers.

"We'll eat and then go," Stasse whispers to Håkan, glancing at the table, on which there really is food.

Looking at it makes Håkan feel sick. He goes to the bathroom, washes his face, and stares at himself in the mirror. He feels incredibly old and incredibly tired. Instead of joining the others, he sneaks out. You're not allowed to smoke inside the parish hall, so he has an excuse, should he need one. He lights the cigarette while crossing the lawn and positions himself so he can't be seen from the entrance. He takes a drag on the cigarette, then blows on his hands to keep them warm. Grim, who never got cold.

Gravel crunches behind him. Håkan hadn't noticed anyone standing there, but it turns out to be the short woman with the dyed hair. She looks kind. You can tell by her eyes that she likes to laugh. You can even see it now, although she's clearly been crying.

"Are you Håkan?" she says.

He nods.

"I thought so," she says. "You looked the most like a Håkan out of everyone in your gang."

What does a Håkan look like? Håkan wonders.

She walks up to him, stretches out a chubby hand.

"Berit," she says.

"Hi," Håkan says, thinking she looks a lot like a Berit.

"I just came out for some air," Berit says. "But can I have a cigarette? If I'm going to smoke, today's the day."

Håkan offers her a cigarette and lights it.

"Grim didn't smoke," Håkan tells her.

Berit shoots him a questioning look.

"So we shouldn't be smoking," Håkan explains.

"Grim," Berit repeats pensively.

"Kasper, I mean," Håkan says.

"But you knew him as Grim," Berit says, and adds, "I was his librarian."

She laughs at Håkan's surprise.

"He practically lived in the library, ever since he was a child. We spoke a lot. He showed me his magazine, and when he met you down in Stockholm, well, it was as though someone had lit a fire under him. He was graduating in a few months, and I tried to tell him to wait a little, but he wouldn't listen." She takes another drag on the cigarette, smiles. "A few months is an eternity in a young person's life, isn't it? And he'd already been waiting for so long. Waited and longed for a way out. Or a way in, I should say. He was so terribly lonely here."

Håkan's throat goes tight. Grim spoke so rarely about what he had left behind. His silence had been a wall.

"I know a teacher of his from junior high," Berit goes on. "She said he was remarkably intelligent, but only dedicated himself to whatever interested him. Didn't care for the rest of it. He probably had to put up with a lot in school. Around here, boys are supposed to be interested in hockey, things like that. So it must have been difficult for him. But oh, the way he talked about you when he visited me at the library."

Håkan tries to understand. Did she mean when Grim went to Timrå over Christmas?

But he must have gone back more often than that, Håkan realizes. The homemade cinnamon buns. He must have hitchhiked up north regularly. How could he not have noticed? How stupid could he have been?

"I don't know anything about him," he says out loud.

Berit looks at him.

"I mean, his life here. He never talked about it and I don't know . . . I can hardly ask . . ."

He gestures toward the parish hall. Berit nods. The sunlight sparkles in her rings when she raises the cigarette to her mouth.

"So he never told you anything?" she says, blowing out smoke.

"No."

Berit's sigh is heavy.

"Poor kid." Håkan is unsure whether she's talking about him or Grim. "It can't hurt . . ." She glances at the hall. "Let's go over here."

They cross the road, stopping at the fence that surrounds the graveyard. Berit leans against a whitewashed post and starts to speak.

"Inger's sister and I were friends, growing up, so I've known Inger since she was a child. Full of energy. Wouldn't stay put, and we were always chasing after her. After junior high, she ended up as a cashier in a grocery store, which was a bad fit. She hated her job. I remember her saying that she was withering away up here, that she wanted to see the world. Inger wanted a lot of things, but she had no direction, no goals. She had a lovely voice, so her sister and I convinced her to compete in a talent show. She won, of course, and the prize was a trip to Stockholm and the chance to record a single. Well, nothing came of that. The label wasn't serious. But she did go to Stockholm and then she stayed there. Met some hippie and followed him to Lund and then Copenhagen. That's where she met Kasper's dad. His biological dad, that is."

"Who was he?" Håkan asks her.

Berit smiles, shaking ash off the cigarette.

"Called himself Cary, after Cary Grant, because people said they looked alike. He played the guitar and Inger sang and, well, you get the picture, I suppose. She wrote to her sister and told her that she was madly in love. Head over heels. She didn't even know when or where he was born. People said a few different things, Algeria, Morocco, Tunisia . . . He'd just laugh and say the world was his home. There was a lot of flower power going on in their circles, you know. But he'd left something awful behind. He had scars all over his body, Inger said. Maybe from torture. He didn't want to talk about it, but he slept badly. Terrible nightmares. And one day he was just gone. He'd left her a letter saying he'd left for Amsterdam, that she was welcome to join him, but that they had to be free. That's when she discovered she was pregnant."

"Did she come back home?" Håkan drops his cigarette, steps on it.

"Oh, no." Berit follows his example. "She went back to Skåne. Lived in a commune for a while. When she got back, Kasper was two, maybe three. She started working as a lunch lady. Lennart was the janitor. He'd always liked her, so . . . And then they started a family."

"But what happened to Grim's dad?" Håkan says.

"Who knows?" Berit says, sighing. "It probably didn't end well. Afterward, Inger realized he'd probably been an addict, that she'd been too naive to see it at the time. But Grim had plenty of theories about his father, of course. Inger had told him the little she knew and that fueled his imagination. He'd talk a lot about it when he was twelve, thirteen. But then his sister died."

Håkan doesn't get it. Wasn't the girl at the funeral Grim's sister?

"The middle child," Berit, who must have noted his confusion, says. "Malin. She died of leukemia."

"When did this happen?"

"Kasper was fourteen or so. Malin was sick for a while and that's when Lennart decided to leave. That he has the gall to show up to-day . . . He left Inger when their child was dying. And Inger, she col-lapsed, went on sick leave. In hindsight, I've realized that Kasper handled everything back then. Cleaned, did the laundry, the cook-ing . . . Didn't say a word to anyone about how bad it had become back home. Not even to me. I just thought he was busy with school, that that was why he wasn't coming around as often anymore."

Håkan can feel his jaw tremble. He thinks he might cry.

"Music saved him, you know," Berit says softly. "Music and litera-ture. And then, when he found you . . . You were his first real friends."

Håkan squeezes his eyes shut, but the tears still well up. He wants to scream, because he can't tell what he's feeling. Gratitude for the explanation, rage and grief over Grim not telling him. Guilt for not being a better friend. He couldn't have been a good friend, or Grim wouldn't have died.

"We weren't as close at the end," Håkan manages, his voice thick. "Sometimes, I just think . . . If I'd just . . ."

He chokes. Berit puts her hand on his arm.

"Don't think that way, Håkan. 'That way madness lies.'"

Anja is standing in Grim's room and looking at his things. She doesn't know where to start; so far, Stasse has just let it all be. He couldn't make himself touch anything. It felt wrong. These are Grim's things. But when they came home from the funeral, Anja stayed the night, and Stasse said he had to empty it out. Grim's mom will want his things and Stasse can't afford the rent by himself, he said. Someone else has to move in.

Anja has said that she'll get started while Stasse is at work. She's brought out some empty moving boxes, but how to begin? What about Grim's clothes? Should she wash them or does his mom want them the way they are, so she can press her face into his shirt and smell him again? All that's left of him. Anja starts crying again when she thinks about it.

She looks at the piles of letters, the ones Grim never opened, and the ones that kept coming even after he died. She picks up some novels and notices that they're from the library. He probably has a huge debt.

Suddenly, the doorbell rings. Håkan is standing outside. He's so pale he's almost translucent, and Anja wonders if he's slept at all since the funeral.

"Hey," he says. "I just . . . I was nearby, so . . . I went to the restaurant and Stasse said you were packing up."

Anja lets him in. The coatrack is full, so he lays his leather jacket on the floor, removes his shoes.

"I haven't got very far," she says.

"Tell me where to start."

He sounds pained but determined.

"Maybe you could do his clothes," she suggests.

Håkan starts to fold the shirts that Grim has left on the floor, placing them in one of the boxes. Anja takes the books belonging to Grim, then moves onto the cassette tapes. So many cassette tapes. Their plastic covers click against one another when she lines them up in the box.

They pack up, side by side. The tension between them is gone. Håkan suddenly laughs and Anja looks up. It's one of Grim's drawings, a caricature of a muscular man straddling a tiny fighter plane on wheels.

"Who is it?" Anja asks.

"Just some jerk from the sorting center."

He puts the drawing on a pile and then starts removing things from the walls. Labyrinths and arcane symbols. He uses a pocketknife to gently scrape off the tape so that the wallpaper doesn't tear, so that there are no traces of glue left behind. He's so careful. Anja would never have the patience.

When Stasse gets home, he smells like a restaurant kitchen and is completely exhausted. Anja and Håkan tell him to go to bed, and they keep working into the night, even though both of them need to get up early. They have to finish.

Then there are only the bags from the police left, the ones Grim's mom doesn't want. Anja has seen that Grim's clothes are in one of them. She hasn't touched the other. Håkan sits down on the dusty floor and removes the objects from the bag, one by one. Grim's pentagram. *Ancient Bloodlust* and the knife from the band photo. A roll of string. Håkan removes the record from the sleeve. The vinyl is ruined, scratched up, and Anja can sense Håkan's despair. Did Grim do this? It's like having seen him harm himself.

Håkan puts the items back into the bag along with Grim's leather jacket.

"I'll get rid of the rest of it," Anja tells him.

Håkan nods mutely.

"Thanks for helping out," she says.

They embrace in Grim's empty room.

On his way home, Håkan leaves the pentagram in the graveyard by St. John's Church.

In three weeks, Ture in Exenterate leaves the band, and Håkan is asked to be their bassist. The following year, their first full-length album is released, and the entire scene changes. Anja wins a competition for young photographers with a picture of a dead fox. The prize is a scholarship and a trip to the United States. She stays there for a few years. Håkan will travel the world, meet his heroes. Then she'll come home again. She shows up for his twenty-fifth birthday. They see each other the way they did the very first time.

And then he comes.

Kasper.

OUTRO

It took me a long time to understand what had happened to Kasper and myself in The House, and I probably still don't. But it's the stuff of my nightmares.

He never let go of my hand. Not until he collapsed and the smell disappeared, the breeze died down, everything went quiet. Even though I didn't know as much then as I do now, I understood that he'd succeeded.

But he was on the floor, unmoving.

He didn't respond to me.

The ambulance sped away with him in it.

I told them we'd been talking when Kasper suddenly collapsed. What else could I say? I told that story to the paramedics, to my bosses, to Kasper's parents when they phoned.

Lying to his parents felt awful. The worst of it was that they were so kind, so grateful that I'd been there. *Who knows how it could have ended?* they said.

The first week was the worst one, when he was suspended between life and death, unconscious, without the doctors understanding why. I tried to focus on my studies and work. My bosses found it strange that Kasper and I had lingered in The House until late, the ambulance arriving at midnight, but we'd always been professional, and besides, what happened to Kasper was a tragedy. Håkan sent me short updates. One day he wrote: *We can take him home now.* After that there were a few days of silence. The moment I opened YouTube, I was faced with Dark Cruelty. Exenterate. Malodor. Vile Prophets. Nox Irredux. I cleared my profile and my search history. I deleted all of my playlists. (I regretted it later.)

Then Leah got in touch.

Kasper was awake, but the doctors said he showed signs of a deep depression. Had I noticed anything? I stammered out my answer. He was getting treatment, Leah said. He'd get better. He had managed so well last time.

I tried to write to Kasper after that, but he didn't even open my messages. Håkan was the one who contacted me. He asked me to come over.

We sat in the living room, Håkan and I. Kasper was asleep. He usually is, Håkan said. They think it's an extreme form of exhaustion, on top of untreated depression, he went on. He looked at me and I noticed that his hands were shaking when he held out Kasper's old sketchbook. *I found this,* he said. *There are some drawings of Grim in it. Do you know anything about them?*

I knew which ones he meant, of course. And I knew I had to try to explain. But when I began, I realized that he already knew. I could see it in his eyes and I went quiet. *I had the same dreams,* he said. Then asked, *What actually happened?* I told him, to the best of my ability. And then I got to hear his story, the one he'd hardly told a living soul.

During the months that followed, we tried to piece everything together. Kasper was awake sometimes, but he had trouble recalling what had happened to him. He'd tell Håkan or myself fragments of it, like finding the labyrinth, the words on the inside of the sleeve. *I can't believe I haven't seen it during all these years*, Håkan told me afterward. Kasper couldn't stay awake for longer than a few hours, and then he had to rest for an entire day. Serious diagnoses were discussed, but there was always something that didn't quite fit.

At first, Kasper had nightmares all the time. He worried that Malte would show up. *He knows that I know*, he said. I tried to calm him by saying that Malte had disappeared. It had caused a great stir when he suddenly couldn't be reached, not even by his own record label. A series of Nox Irredux shows were canceled. No one had seen him since that evening in September.

Naturally, the mythmaking is in full swing. The album he managed to finish would probably do well. I brought Caligari over to Kasper and he told me he slept better with the cat around.

I talked to Kasper's parents often, especially Håkan. Together, we tried to fill in the gaps. Not least because Kasper kept asking what actually happened. I wished I could give him an answer. I told Håkan that once. *Write*, he said, and he looked

at me. *Kasper told me you write.* I said, *I try.
It's not going very well.* Håkan said, *Try again.*

He spoke frequently about his friendship with
Grim, what it had felt like to share everything
with someone, someone who thought the way you did,
or who you assumed thought the way you did, until
you realized that person, too, contained hundreds
of secret sets and compartments.

The dead boy and the living one.

When everything closed down, we spoke on the
phone instead, Håkan and I. He told me Kasper
was getting a bit better. He said it might turn
around, and I could hear the hope in his voice,
how brittle it was. He remembers more and more, he
told me. But he still gets exhausted and confused.

Kasper and I spoke briefly after that. Suddenly,
he looked into the camera and said, *I dream I'm
still there. Sometimes I wonder if I am still there.*

He's looking for the way out.

That's when the idea started to take shape.

How do you find your way out of a labyrinth?

You go back the same way you entered. You follow
the thread through the twists and turns. There's
not much I can do, but I can do this.

I've written this as if it is a story, as if to
a stranger, because that's how it had to be. That
was the only way I could make sense of what happened.

But Kasper, this is all for you.

You freed him and I'm going to free you.

I am Daedalus and I am Ariadne. I've re-created
the forking paths and I am leading you out.

The magic is in the pattern, the pattern is in the story, and every word I've written is an invocation. A prayer that's kindled every time it's gazed at, the rhythm of a drum, barely audible, like a heartbeat.

I hope you can hear me now, my friend.

I know you can hear me.

I reach out my hand.

Come home. Come home. Come home.

ACKNOWLEDGMENTS

Writing this novel has been a long and winding journey, and it took me to many new places, both in inner and outer worlds, that I couldn't have imagined when I started. The assistance I got on the way has been indispensable, and there are many I would like to thank. First of all, I would like to stress that any errors, flaws, and bothersome elements are there because of me, and not my sources.

My previous novel, *Norra Latin*, takes place in the same alternative Stockholm as *Grim*. It contains characters that are famous actors in the book's universe. After the book came out, I was often asked: "Who is Jack Helander *really*?" The answer is: He is Jack Helander, a character in a book. It's only natural that readers "search" like this when you're writing about fictive celebrities. But knowing that many do so has haunted me during my work with *Grim*.

The Swedish film and theater world is huge in comparison to the Swedish death metal scene in the late eighties, which was as small (and its members as young!) as it's portrayed in the book. I would therefore like to emphasize that there is no *really* here. The events and characters of the novel *Grim* belong to fiction. I have been inspired by the currents in and behaviors of the real-world Nordic metal scene, and during the eighties, there were a number of young Swedish bands who explored similar concepts and ideas as Dark Cruelty. But Dark Cruelty is Dark Cruelty and the characters are none other than themselves.

My research has been extensive, but then I have gone on to build my own world. It got a lot richer because of the conversations I had with people from the real death metal scene. Thanks to them, I learned about those everyday details that would have been impossible to find elsewhere. Orvar Säfström, Ulf Cederlund, Jörgen Thullberg, Tomas Lindberg, Nina Kärki, and Chelsea Larsson Ness—you've each showed me such generosity and I am forever grateful.

Hail Ika Johannesson and Jon Jefferson Klingberg (*Blood Fire Death: The Swedish Metal Story*) and Daniel Ekeroth (*Swedish Death Metal*) who have mapped out, and expanded the image of, the Swedish metal scene in their books. A special thanks to Ika and Daniel for answering further questions.

Thank you to the employees at Gröna Lund, who helped me through different phases of my research. A special thanks to the "nightmares" I encountered in the House of Nightmares (I can strongly recommend a visit). Thank you to the staff at Fredrika Bremer high school.

So many fantastic individuals have contributed with their knowledge, enlightening conversations, and test reads.

Abysmal thanks to my guides Yosefin Buohler, Felicia Lantz, Jenna Lindborg, Susan Nygren (Bläck Tattoo Parlor), Mats "Vergil" Nylund, Anders Ohlin, Kristina Schön, Petra Skoglund, and Anton Vitus Westerlund.

Heavy thanks to Sofia Bergström, Gabrielle de Bourg, Martin Csatlós, Anders Dahlgren, Per Faxneld, Ingemar Isaksson, Maya Kärki, Felix Nordqvist, Henrik Palm, Linnea Risinger Nathanson, Marie Siegel, Olivia Skoglund, and Edward Summanen.

Brutal thanks to Liam Alvarez, Alva Andersson Taghioff, Alexander Astinder, Anton Bonnier, Henke Brannerydh, Hélène Dahl, Anna Drvnik, Gitte Ekdahl, Måns Elenius, Karin Hesselmark, Siska Humlesjö, Ronja Jonasson, Donia Krook, Emil Larsson, Jamal

Lazar, Nene Ormes, Megan Robinson, Johanna Strömqvist, Lovisa Söderberg, and Viggo Zingmark Lien.

Thundering thanks go to Liza Hermeline Andersson, Maria L. Bovin, Farzad Farzaneh, Helena Dahlgren, Kaly Halkawt, Odin Helgheim, Christian Jensen Haverling, Eli Jäderland, Johan Jönsson, Effie Karabuda, Satoko Matsushita Dahlström, Johan Maxén, Peter Neidestam, Aurora Percovich Gutierrez, Alexander Rönnberg, Hannes Salo, Tonje Tornes, Annika Troselius, Jessica Vasquez Sepulveda, Sophie Vuković, Tina Åhman Billing, Magnus Ödling, and the staff at Handen library, Akademibokhandeln in Haninge Centrum, and Sound Pollution.

Many thanks to my anonymous sources, and all the kind souls who offered to help, but couldn't due to time and the pandemic. Thank you to all my friends, acquaintances, colleagues, and strangers who talked about metal and Grönan with me and put up with my obsessed state of mind.

To my publisher, Ylva Blomqvist—thanks for unfailing support and for listening to my tirades throughout the process. To my editor, Sofia Hannar—thank you for your accuracy and enthusiasm. Thanks to Anna Dahlgren and Agneta Orrevall for proofreading. Thank you to everyone at Rabén & Sjögren who has worked with the book in different ways.

Thanks to Lena Stjernström, for valuable conversations, and the whole gang at the Grand Agency for your work.

Thank you, Lina Neidestam, for the unbelievably evil cover and your infernal patience.

Judith Kiros, Emil Maxén, Maria Fröhlich, Levan Akin, Mathilda Elfgren Schwartz, Margareta Elfgren, and Mikael Sveding: Thank you for being there when I got lost and when I found my place, and for yanking the string when necessary.

Adam Andersson, Claes Bergmark, Anton Bonnier, Johan Egerkrans, Minna Frydén Bonnier, Nahal Ghanbari, Erik Hansson,

Soraya Hashim, Jacob von Heland, Sofia Hertz, Karl Johnsson, Elin Lawless, Niklas "Webster" Natt och Dag, Ordmördarna, Johanna Paues Darlington, Mattias J. Skoglund, Mats Strandberg, and Elin Ajlin Tizihssane. Hordes of thanks to you, my invaluable ones.

Thank you, Elizabeth Hand.

Hail Lord Lemläst! Häxsvett rules!

Thank you to my beloved family. H, H, and E, you can read it when you get older. To Micke—thank you for your friendship, your love, your honesty, and your support. I'd always want to play in your band.

Grim was largely written while gigs were canceled and many artists and bands struggled. At Bandcamp.com, for example, you can support the bands and artists you like, and by going to your local record store and venues, of course.

The Blake quotes were taken from the poem "Auguries of Innocence." From Penelope Reed Doobs's *The Idea of the Labyrinth: From Classical Antiquity through the Middle Ages*, I borrowed some thoughts about labyrinths.

At 988lifeline.org there is help available for those who need someone to talk to. A portion of this novel's proceeds will be donated to organizations that provide support and work with suicide prevention.

This book is dedicated to those who struggle with their demons, and to those who are with them in that struggle.

About the Author
Sara B. Elfgren is an acclaimed Swedish writer, screenwriter, and playwright. She made her debut with the YA novel *The Circle* (2011), which she cowrote with Mats Strandberg. Together they penned the best-selling and critically acclaimed Engelsfors trilogy. *The Circle* has been translated into twenty-five languages and was made into a movie by Levan Akin. She has been nominated for or won a host of literary awards.

About the Translator
Judith Kiros is a literary critic, poet, and translator, whose debut poetry collection *O* was nominated for three literary awards. She has translated Mats Strandberg's novel *Slutet (The End)* and Warsan Shire's poetry collection *Bless the Daughter Raised by a Voice in Her Head (Välsigna dottern)*.

Discover more gripping YA titles from Arctis Books USA

"The masterful worldbuilding and viviid Nordic setting...are well served by the stirring prose. An immersive, darkly exhilarating read."— *Kirkus Reviews* STARRED REVIEW

Iron Wolf (Vardari Book 1)
ISBN 978-1-64690-015-2

"A stellar work of fiction that will cling to readers' minds and take hold of their hearts."— *School Library Journal* STARRED REVIEW

The End
ISBN 978-1-64690-800-4

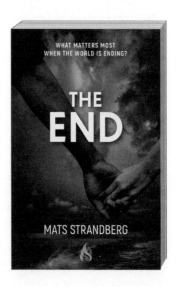

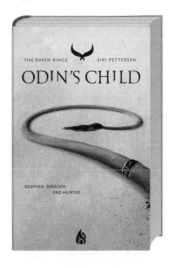

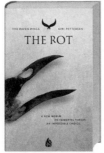